About the Author

Pamela Sargent received her B.A. and M.A. in philosophy from the State University of New York at Binghamton (Harpur College). She is the author of more than twenty stories which have appeared in **Fantasy & Science Fiction, Universe, New Worlds, Eros in Orbit, Wandering Stars, Two Views of Wonder, Fellowship of the Stars,** and other magazines and anthologies. She is also the editor of the anthologies **Women of Wonder, Bio-Futures,** and **More Women of Wonder** (all from Vintage Press). She is presently writing a second novel for Gold Medal. She lives in upstate New York.

CLONED LIVES

Pamela Sargent

A FAWCETT GOLD MEDAL BOOK

Fawcett Publications, Inc., Greenwich, Connecticut

Portions of this novel appeared, in substantially different form, in the following publications:

"Father," copyright © 1973 by Ultimate Publishing Co., Inc. Appeared in *AMAZING*, February, 1974.

"Clone Sister," copyright © 1973 by Joseph Elder. Appeared in *EROS IN ORBIT* (Trident Press).

"A Sense of Difference," copyright © 1972 by Pamela Sargent. Appeared in *AND WALK NOW GENTLY THROUGH THE FIRE* (Chilton Book Company).

CLONED LIVES

Printed in the United States of America

First printing: June 1976

1 2 3 4 5 6 7 8 9 10

Contents

1. Paul: 2000 **12**
2. Edward: 2016 **80**
3. James: 2020 **112**
4. Michael: 2025 **154**
5. Kira: 2028 **184**
6. Albert: 2036 **236**
7: Interface: 2037 **274**

For my parents

pared himself as well as he would have liked. A friend
at the Kenarov Observatory on the moon had sent him

That father without mother may beget, we have
Present, as proof, the daughter of Olympian Zeus:
One never nursed in the dark cradle of the womb;
Yet such a being no god will beget again.

—AESCHYLUS
The Eumenides

"The chemical or physical inventor is always a Prometheus. There is no great invention, from fire to flying, which has not been hailed as an insult to some god. But if every physical and chemical invention is a blasphemy, every biological invention is a perversion."

—J. B. S. Haldane
DAEDALUS OR SCIENCE AND THE FUTURE

"Good reasons in general for cloning are that it avoids genetic diseases, bypasses sterility, predetermines an individual's gender, and preserves family likenesses. It wastes time to argue over whether we should do it or not; the real moral question is when and why."

—Joseph Fletcher
THE ETHICS OF GENETIC CONTROL:
Ending Reproductive Roulette

"In view of the likelihood of such disagreements on standards for what changes in man are desirable, the simplest solution might seem to be a laissez-faire system in which society took no position on this at all. For several reasons, I believe this would be a very dangerous course to take. It would almost certainly lead to an immense proliferation of types of man, differing in much more substantial ways than the present races do . . . If we wish to avoid the interference involved, it may be necessary to renounce the modification of man through biological engineering altogether, which does not seem a likely development to me."

—Gerald Feinberg
THE PROMETHEUS PROJECT

11

1. Paul: 2000

AS the jet approached the Dallas–Fort Worth Regional Airport, Paul Swenson saw the nearest of the circular loops which made up the huge, monotonously efficient structure. There were thirteen circles, although Paul could not see them all from his seat, each of them more than a mile in circumference, each containing six subterminals, stretched in a row across the Texas plain. The circular loops were connected by a spine running through their centers, a row of roads connecting the airport with Dallas and Fort Worth.

The airport had been designed for ease, with decentralized terminals and underground trains linking the loops. It had one purpose—to move passengers in and out as quickly as possible. Paul remembered the brown concrete and unending repetition of the structure, the same no matter where one turned, and he wondered who would care to linger. The architect had made no aesthetic concessions. Yet from the air it was still an awesome sight, giant hieroglyphics carved out of the brown dusty land.

"I still think I'm right, Paul," Morris Chang muttered. Paul glanced at his young companion. Chang slouched in his seat, running a hand through red hair that contrasted sharply with his dark almond-shaped eyes. "I just gave my paper too soon. I may not have all the evidence I need but I *feel* as though I'm close to the truth." He stared ahead glumly.

Paul had been listening to these comments, with slight variations, ever since their sub-orbital flight from Brussels. When they had transferred to the local jet at the Kennedy Space Center, Chang had lapsed into silence, then began ordering double scotches from the stewardess a few minutes after takeoff. Paul had finally persuaded his friend to have some coffee. Chang's sober depression was a contrast to the alcoholic gaiety he had displayed throughout most of their flight, a gaiety cut short by a husky steward about an hour ago.

The jet began to circle over one of the loops below. "I think Irina Rostova was the one who actually finished me," Chang said. "I just couldn't handle her questions. After that I was too demoralized to answer anyone else's."

"Look, Morris, this was your first time, giving a paper before a group like this. Rostova's been going to these conferences for years. She knows how to find the holes in anyone's work. A valuable function, I suppose, but I have yet to see her present anything of her own that isn't trivial. She never risks the kind of treatment she hands out to other astrophysicists."

"I don't know," Chang said sadly. Paul sighed. He had encouraged the young man to present his paper. Chang was working out a theory of stellar evolution that would account for and include pulsars, quasi-stellar objects, "black holes," and other such phenomena.

"Look," Paul said, trying to cheer his friend up, "you're working out something pretty important and difficult. You'll patch up the holes, I have no doubt about that. I told you how excited Marcus was. He'll be writing to you about some of the problems, he thinks he can help. You know perfectly well you were ready to present the outline of your theory. You're just upset because you're not used to giving papers yet."

"You're probably right." Chang looked a little happier.

Paul remembered a similar conference twenty years ago. He had been twenty-nine, Chang's age, ready to present his first important paper to an international gathering of scientists. His paper had also been greeted with some skepticism. He had started to succumb to his nervousness and fear, regaining his confidence only when Eviane began to defend him strenuously, buzzing furiously at the others in the room.

The thought of Eviane draped a shroud of sadness over Paul. She had been dead for almost six years and he still could not accept that fact. Even now he would find himself turning in his seat, expecting to find her next to him. He would begin to speak to her and then remember that she was gone.

He had met Eviane when they were both twenty-eight. He was working at Mount Palomar and had just arrived at the observatory, anxious to use every minute of his alloted time. There was no one in the observatory except a tiny blonde who looked about sixteen years old. He wondered what had happened to his assistant.

The blonde girl was pacing in front of a desk, chewing on her nails. She stopped and looked at Paul speculatively. *Her eyes should be blue*, he thought. Instead they were as black as the nighttime skies.

"I wish they allowed smoking in here," she said loudly. "I'm having a fit. Are you Swenson?"

"Yes, I'm waiting for my assistant. I was told someone would be here to help with my observations."

"I know. I'm the assistant."

Paul tried not to look surprised.

"All right, Swenson," she went on, "I know you didn't expect a ball of blond fluff here but that's what you've got. I have a degree in mathematics, I have a doctorate in astrophysics, I've published a couple of papers. Maybe you read them. I'm Eviane Fosserier." She glared at him defensively. "I knew a guy once who said he couldn't take people under five feet, two inches seriously, they were just too damned small. I hope you're not like him."

He was feeling a bit ashamed of his six-foot height. "I didn't say anything," he said.

"You were thinking it, Swenson. Let's get to work. We're wasting time."

He had married her three months later. They had always worked together, combining their abilities. They had criticized and advised each other even when working on separate projects. There had been no room for children in their life, and Paul never regretted it until Eviane died. Now he had nothing of her except her papers and his memories.

She was a small bird, fluttering nervously through the rooms of their house, obsessive in her desire to organize her nest, always coming to rest in his arms. Don't ever fly from me, Eviane. But she had at last, stricken by a peculiar disease that would not allow her to absorb the nutrients her small body needed. She had grown thinner and weaker, unable to sustain herself. She had weighed only forty-eight pounds at her death.

Time, Paul thought, *is supposed to make these things easier to bear, soothe the pain.* Time had not worked for him, just as it had never eroded his feelings for Eviane during her lifetime.

The jet approached its runway and began to land, a giant metal eagle shrieking for its prey.

"So what are your plans for the immediate future?" Chang asked.

"I thought that I'd just take the train to Dallas and get a hotel room. I think I can use some rest before I head home."

"Rest!" Chang chuckled. "You must be suffering from time lag. Don't you know what tonight is?"

"No, at least I don't think. . . ." Paul paused. "Wait a minute, it's New Year's Eve, isn't it?"

"New Year's Eve, 1999," Chang said. "I just want to head home and lock my doors. I sure wouldn't want to be in Dallas."

"I don't know how I could have forgotten." Paul looked at the other man. "Do you really think it'll be that bad? I mean, I know New Year's Eve isn't exactly quiet, but I figured I could lock myself in and ignore it."

"Well, Paul, I don't know how it is in your Midwest, but Dallas has been close to hysteria recently. It was like that when I left after Christmas. After all, this isn't just New Year's. This is a new millenium."

"Properly speaking, the new millenium doesn't start until next year."

"Try telling that to the Apocalyptics, or the ones who expect to see Christ reappear." Morris Chang sighed. "I'd better put you up at my place. We can ride the local train through Dallas and you can catch your train tomorrow."

"I don't want to put you to any trouble."

"It's no trouble. Joanne would love to meet you."

"All right. I suppose you know what you're talking about." Chang lived outside Dallas in a security-conscious suburb. Armed guards patrolled the community and no one could enter without a resident or guest pass. Paul had never felt at ease in such places, knowing that their very existence was an admission of social failure. Many potential disrupters were shut out, but the citizens were also shut in. He had seen them glancing fearfully at every strange face that passed through their streets. Such carefully guarded suburbs were luxurious garrison states.

The jet had landed. Paul unfastened his seat belt and straightened his suit. Chang's talk about the Apocalyptics had reminded him of his discussion with Hidehiko Takamura before leaving for Brussels. Hidey Takamura had been insistent. He would have to make a decision soon.

For now he put Hidey out of his mind and prepared to leave the jet.

Ideally, there should have been no waiting at the Dallas–Fort Worth Regional Airport. One had only to walk about a hundred feet from the plane to the terminal, pick up one's luggage, and walk another hundred feet to an underground magneto-train station.

In fact, Paul and Morris had to wait an hour before even getting their luggage. The detachable baggage compartment of the jet was malfunctioning and at last a repair crew had managed to wheel it over to the terminal. Plane travel was becoming less comfortable and efficient. The airlines were now competing with magnetically suspended high-speed trains. Once the technical problems involved in their development had been solved, and the government had begun to subsidize the railroads heavily, the airlines had started to lose passengers. Air transport companies were now concentrating on sub-orbital flight, uncomfortable but fast, and space vehicles. For travel over land, the trains were as rapid as jets, and more pleasant.

When Paul and Morris finally boarded their train, it was crowded and Paul was beginning to feel hunger pangs. They found seats and placed their suitcases in an overhead rack.

"What time is it, Morris?"

"Almost eight. I was hoping we'd be enjoying supper by now, but. . . ." Chang shrugged.

Paul settled back in his seat and relaxed. The train hurtled soundlessly through its tunnel, levitated magnetically over the tracks.

He found himself thinking again about Hidey Takamura's proposed project. Hidey, a geneticist, had long been chafing under the restrictions of the moratorium on genetic engineering. Hidey's field was not the only one affected; the twenty-year moratorium on certain types of scientific research, put into effect by committees of scientists working with the United Nations, applied to other fields as well. But the biological scientists had been the focus of most of the hysteria and fear people felt, so they were under more stringent regulations. By 1980, there was a moratorium on almost all genetic research.

Paul remembered the arguments made by those who had desired the moratorium. An analogy had been drawn between the biological sciences and nuclear physics and a question posed: why wait until the biological equivalent of an atomic bomb was developed before doing something? Why not prevent its occurrence? Biology presented a threat to human society and evolution far greater than that of atomic weapons. It might enslave people or alter them beyond recognition. If used foolishly, biological engineering might set humanity on an evolutionary path leading it to extinction.

More moderate voices had argued for the continued use of techniques already discovered before the moratorium. The committees had agreed that there was no sense in outlawing such developments. One of those allowed was an ectogenetic chamber, an "artificial womb" which could nourish a fetus until birth. It was used only in cases of grave need, for women who could not survive a normal pregnancy or who bore premature children. Artificial insemination was still practiced, but limited now to very few people so as to prevent overpopulation. Synthetic viruses, injected into fetuses carrying hemophilia, diabetes, sickle-cell anemia or certain other genetic ailments, could alter the genetic messages carried by such embryos. They would no longer develop the disease or pass it on to future generations. These techniques, and some others, were acceptable. They treated already existing conditions. That was all right. It was the prospect of intervention at the start, the possibility of deciding what kind of people to produce, that was frightening. None of these discoveries had been pushed any further in the past twenty years. No new discoveries had been made. Experimentation with humans and in some countries fetuses had been banned.

Many biologists had argued against the restrictions in vain. Others, who had already decided not to pursue certain experiments on their own, remained silent. Governments, Paul knew, had been meticulous in supporting the restrictions. As long as one country did not experiment, others would not feel pressured to do the same. No government wanted to risk losing the hard-won gains of the past several years, not when the world had achieved an uneasy peace and a more even distribution of wealth. No government wanted society vastly altered. Everyone, it seemed, wanted more time at least to consider the issues.

The moratorium, however, had done more than simply halt experimentation. It had deprived the world of thousands of talented biologists. Funds for research dried up. Talented scientists who wanted to push beyond the present boundaries of human knowledge went into other fields where restrictions were either less severe or nonexistent. Almost the only biologists left were medical technicians and physicians, who used the allowed techniques, teachers, who often lost their most promising students to other disciplines, and laboratory workers.

And Paul could only guess at how many millions of unfortunate or diseased individuals existed whose suffering might have been prevented had research been allowed.

But with the beginning of the new year and the new millenium, the moratorium would expire, at least temporarily. Hidey had been preparing for this for quite a while. If Paul would cooperate, Hidey would make his move.

Hidey Takamura was familiar with embryology as well as genetics and specialized in cloning. He had cloned several types of animals, allowed under the moratorium, helping in the restoration of a few endangered species.

But Hidey wanted to clone a human being. The moratorium was running out. He had to move fast, in case the ban was reimposed. He needed a donor of genetic material.

Paul considered Hidey's motives. There was no doubt that his old friend meant what he had said, that he must find out if he could accomplish the task and what the results would be. It was a matter of advancing scientific knowledge. Yet Paul knew Hidey also wanted to be first, to become a scientific immortal.

"Why me?" Paul had asked when the project had first been suggested to him. "There are plenty of people who would be more valuable, who have more to offer than I do."

"That's one reason right there," Hidey said. "Because you ask that question. I don't want an egomaniac, and I'm afraid that's what many gifted people are. You're a brilliant and compassionate man. You're aware of your faults as well as your gifts. I've known you for more than thirty years and I've seen how you act in different situations. You are also, unlike others, capable in many fields. Your popular texts on biology and chemistry are better than anything I've seen, even ones written by specialists. You have a natural talent for music which you don't have time to explore fully. I've even seen those poems you hide from almost everyone else. People like you are limited only by the fact that they have one lifetime. Imagine what five or six Paul Swensons could do."

"I think you're wrong there," Paul replied. "If you have a group of Paul Swensons, I don't see why they wouldn't do what I've done. The fact that they're exactly alike might also affect them badly. They might have my temperament, and you know how moody and depressed I can get."

"You're thoughtful," Hidey said. "Any thoughtful person is liable to feel depressed, even suicidal at times. And I grant you that if we were cloning a narrow talent, we might wind up with people who would needlessly duplicate each other's efforts. But with a person of diverse talents, such as yourself, we might wind up with people who could put each talent to its maximum use."

"Still, there's a reason why I chose the field I did. I felt that's where my best abilities lay. A clone would feel the same."

"Well, let's see. We won't know unless we try. Genetic inheritance is like clay. You're limited by it, but there's also a lot you can do with it. Your environment influences you. You make choices. I've seen artists make things I didn't think could be made with clay and I've seen people do things that seemed far beyond the abilities nature gave them. Your clone would at least start out with some damned good clay. You're proven material."

Paul still felt dubious about the project. Maybe he was not as immune to the hysteria around him as he believed. *Why me,* he thought again.

"I don't want unnecessary flak," Hidey continued. "I know I'm going to get some grief. I can minimize it using you. You're the man who laid the theoretical groundwork for a star drive and there are more than a few whose only knowledge of science came from your books. You're a symbol of hope to many, you're admired. If I'm going to clone anybody, it might as well be you. Maybe those clones will continue your work and get us to other stars."

Why me?

"Cheer up. Things aren't that bad," Morris Chang said, startling Paul.

He grinned at the younger man. "Well, I'm glad to see you're feeling better, Morris. For a while there, I thought astrophysics would lose you to a whiskey bottle."

"Now that I'm away from that conference, all I want to do is get back to work."

"You'd better. My star-drive hypothesis would fit very nicely under your theory's umbrella, and I'd rather have it there than out in the rain with all the other anomalies."

Morris chuckled.

Suddenly the train hummed to a halt.

"What's this?" Paul asked, looking at Chang. "I thought this train didn't stop until we got to Dallas."

"It doesn't."

"Please remain seated," a trembling voice said over the train's speaker system. "There will be a temporary delay. Please remain seated."

"This isn't my day," Paul said. "First the jet and now this." He sighed. There was no sense in being impatient. He could do nothing about the delay. He began to look around at his fellow passengers.

Someone nudged him from behind. He turned in his seat and found himself staring at a bony, intense-looking young man.

"It's started already," the young man said. His moist brown eyes flickered, then settled into a steady gaze. "We may sit down here forever, buried from the sight of God."

"What do you mean?" Chang asked as he turned around also.

"Everything is running down," the man whispered. "By midnight it will have stopped. The dead will be resurrected. What a sight! I don't want to sit down here, I'll miss it all. By the time we're called to judgment, we'll have missed the whole thing."

The train hummed softly for an instant and crept forward slowly. "Well," Paul said, trying to smile, "it hasn't quite stopped yet."

"It will," the young man said. "You had better prepare your soul for judgment." He stared at Paul intently.

Paul was not certain whether the young man was an Apocalyptic or one of those who expected Christ to reappear, but it was hardly a crucial distinction. He was uneasy in any case.

"This train's moving pretty damned slowly," Chang muttered. "At this rate, we'll be lucky if we get to my house before ten or so. I'd better call Joanne at the Dallas station."

"I think we'd be better off staying on the train," Paul replied. "The one behind us is probably moving just as slowly."

"You'd both be better off if you started praying," said the young man behind them.

The train was approaching one of the stations on the outskirts of Dallas. Normally it would have passed this station, but it began to slow down once again.

Paul looked out the window at the platform outside. A group of soldiers holding stun guns was standing near the train. A small crowd milled around behind them.

"Clear the tracks," someone shouted through a loudspeaker. "Clear the tracks, or you'll be placed under arrest. Clear the tracks."

"They're holding up the train," a young girl across the aisle from Paul shouted. "Let's go see." The girl and two boys hurried into the next car, running toward the front of the train.

"Clear the tracks," the loudspeaker shouted again.

"Jesus Christ is coming," a female voice cried out over another loudspeaker. "Pray for your souls, brothers and sisters, the Lord is coming!" Paul looked around the train and saw the young man behind him and a woman in the back of the car on their knees. When he looked back out the window, he saw the soldiers dragging a few people along the platform.

Apparently the track had been cleared, because the train began to move once more. The platform disappeared and Paul again saw the dark tunnels around the train. "It looks," he said to Chang, "as though things are getting an early start."

Chang did not reply. The train was moving rapidly now, although not at the one-hundred-and-fifty-mile-an-hour speed that had brought it to the city.

It seemed only a few minutes later as the train pulled into the main Dallas station. There were a large number of soldiers on the platform outside. Several people got up from their seats.

"Attention, all passengers," a voice said over the speaker system. "Attention. If you're leaving Dallas, you must transfer to the elevated train in station D, two floors above. Other passengers must use the locals at stations M and N. Do not go to the station E monorail, the station E monorail is out of service. Underground trains won't leave Dallas for another two hours. Our apologies for the delay. Thank you."

"Come on, Paul," Chang said as he stood up. Both men followed other passengers outside. They pushed through the crowd over to the side of one soldier, a husky young man with a handlebar moustache. "Excuse me," Chang shouted at the soldier, "but can you tell me what's going on?"

"Goddamn Apocs. They're in the tunnels, holdin' up trains." Chang turned and Paul followed his friend through the crowd. They hurried up a flight of stairs to a large lobby. In the middle of the room, Paul saw a small group of people on their knees.

"I don't want to die," a voice near Paul cried. He twisted around and found a stocky dark-haired woman clutching at his arm. "I don't want to die." Her brown eyes were wide with hysteria.

"You're not going to die," he said to her. He felt helpless, wondering what he could do.

"Come on," Chang shouted. He grabbed Paul and pulled him away from the woman.

Paul followed him through the lobby to another flight of stairs. They climbed them as rapidly as the mob of passengers would allow. As they reached the top, Paul could see people pushing their way into the elevated train. He and Chang managed to board it just as the doors were closing.

They were standing in the first car of the train. It was packed with people, standing and sitting. Paul knew that he would not find a seat in any other car. He put down his suitcase and leaned against one of the seats. He and Morris were close to the front of the car and Paul watched as the engineer climbed into his cab. Although the train was run automatically, an engineer was always on board in case of an emergency, a practice Paul usually regarded as needless featherbedding. But he was glad to have the man on board tonight.

He looked around and noticed that some soldiers had boarded the train. One of the soldiers, a tall slender woman in a white helmet, remained in the front car while the others dispersed. She spoke to the conductor, then started to push her way to the engineer's cab. As she shoved past Paul, her leg jostled his suitcase. Her blue eyes glared at him.

"Get this thing out of the aisle. There's room up by the cab." Paul picked up the suitcase and followed her, with Morris right behind him. The train began to move forward. Paul rested against the cab and glanced out the front window at the tracks. Then he turned to Morris.

"What'll we do when they start collecting tickets?"

"Don't worry," Chang replied. "I have a commuter pass book, but I don't think they'd throw us off in any case." Paul looked around for the conductor and saw him standing near one of the doors. He did not seem interested in ticket collecting at the moment.

"Attention, all passengers." The soldier was speaking into a microphone attached to the cab. "Please don't be alarmed by the soldiers on this train. We're here to insure your safety, so please cooperate with us. Thank you."

"The whole damn world's gone crazy," said a fat man in the seat next to Paul. The man was sitting with an astonishingly beautiful redheaded woman dressed in a long green gown.

"We should of taken the earlier train, Joe," the woman muttered. "Now we'll miss most of the party." She looked up at Paul. "They say the world's going to end."

"I doubt it," he replied.

"If it is," she went on, "they're sure helpin' it along.

I'm glad I'm out of the Service, my whole night would of been ruined."

The fat man was looking out his window. "Oh, my God," he mumbled. "Oh, my God." Paul peered out the front window and noticed that the sky was lighter than it should be. Then he saw flames shooting toward the sky. The fire could be no more than a few blocks from the train tracks.

"I'm scared, Joe," the redhead moaned. The train passed the burning area and Paul saw more flames, farther away, burning near a large latticework arcology. The huge hexagonal structure looked vulnerable in the fiery light and its metal supports shone brightly, reflecting the fire. Groups of Apocalyptics had been claiming for weeks that civilization would have to die in preparation for a new age. Most were willing to let God handle the job, but a few were apparently trying to make their prophecies come true.

Paul turned away, sickened and saddened by the sight. "We don't have too far to go, Paul," Chang said. "It'll probably be safer outside the city." Morris sounded as though he was trying to console them both.

The train began to slow down as it approached a station. "Here's where we get off," fat Joe said.

"Do you think it's safe?" Paul asked. The fat man peered out the window.

"Looks like it," he replied. The station at which the train stopped did appear quiet. The doors opened and a few passengers rose from their seats.

And then Paul saw them. They ran into the station suddenly, screaming at the train, and he could tell that they were not those who were content to pray passively while waiting for the world to end. The train doors closed and Paul realized that the engineer must have decided to pull out of the station. But before the train could move, several people appeared on the tracks. The train could not move without running them down.

Faces, garishly painted, stared in at them through the windows. Then Paul heard the sound of metal grinding against metal. Two men were standing near the door of the front car, trying to pry it open from the outside. Paul could not imagine how the small group of soldiers with them could handle the mob.

The tall slender soldier was pounding on the cab door. "Move this train!" she shouted. "Move this train right now!" She pulled the door open.

"I can't," said the engineer. "I'll have to run them down."

"Move!" the soldier cried. "I'll take the responsibility. That mob is out for blood. You're endangering the passengers. Move!"

"Just let them try to get on this train," the redheaded woman said. She was kneeling in her seat. Her lovely face was contorted with rage. The mob outside was chanting, but Paul could hear only an undifferentiated roar.

"I can't," the engineer said. A passenger near the door screamed, then another near the back of the car. An old man was trying to calm a sobbing boy. Paul could see the edge of a crowbar between the doors of the car. It could not hold much longer.

"Damn it," the soldier shouted, "get out of that cab before I haul you out." She held the engineer by the collar. The man stumbled out and she climbed in quickly.

The train suddenly lurched forward. The brightly painted faces disappeared. Muffled thumps sounded against the train, shaking it slightly. Then they were on clear magnetic track, moving again. The engineer had collapsed on the floor next to Paul, holding his face in his hands.

Paul looked away from the windows, feeling nauseous. All the illnesses of the past century seemed to have reached their fruition. He thought of the flame-filled sky of Dallas and wondered if they would burn themselves out at last. He so often felt like an observer of the world around him, marveling sometimes at the irrationality of humanity as one might wonder at strange customs or superstitions. At other times he was in the grip of a feeling close to despair, worrying about humanity's aberrations and seeing the seeds of the disease in his own mind as well. But now he felt fear, a blind unreasoning fear of the others of his own kind. He had never felt that way about people before. He thought about his own work, his dreams of seeing humanity on other worlds, and wondered if he had only been aiding the spread of a cancer throughout the galaxy.

"Paul," Chang was saying, "Paul, are you all right?" The words seemed to float to him through a fog. He managed to shake off the feeling and nodded. Then he squatted next to the engineer, hoping to console the man.

"My God, my God," the engineer moaned.

"Served the bastards right," the redheaded woman muttered.

The train hurtled on through the night.

Paul was relieved to be back in the Midwest, to be home again. He had spent three days in Dallas with Morris Chang, trying to aid some of those who had fled the city. He had led medics to the injured, brought coffee to those waiting for word about their homes and families, and reunited a father with his missing son. When he left Dallas, after things were calmer, his friend Morris had decided temporarily to house a family whose home had been destroyed. He had wondered if he should leave, but Morris had persuaded him that the family needed the guest bedroom more than Paul's presence.

Paul stood in the small train station, inhaling the crisp winter air. He had almost expected to see ruin here too, but everything appeared unchanged. A white blanket of snow covered the ground in front of him and the city across the river from the station had a silvery glitter in the sunshine.

At last he saw the stocky form of Jonathan Aschen-bach trudging toward him. "Am I glad to see you," he said as Jon approached. "I feel as though I've been away for years."

"You don't know how relieved I was when you called," Jon said. "After what I heard, I didn't know if we'd ever see you again." Paul picked up his suitcase and they walked toward Jon's car.

"I heard it was worse in other areas," Paul said. "I expected to find nothing here when I got back."

"Well, there were wild parties, and some naked folk running around in the snow, but I guess we're basically stodgy. Only two cases of arson in the whole city." They stopped next to the car, a small dingy beige model that had seen a lot of wear. Jon opened the door and Paul hoisted his suitcase into the back seat.

"Thanks for picking me up, Jon."

"Don't mention it."

"Thank God Morris Chang lives where he does." Paul climbed into the car. "He keeps most of his notes at home. A whole general theory of cosmology could have gone up in smoke."

Jon drove the car out of the station's parking lot toward the new stretch of automated highway. As they approached the highway, Jon punched out his destination and the car moved along the access ramp, shooting out automatically into the stream of traffic.

"You can relax now," Paul said. Jon was still watching the highway attentively, holding the steering wheel with his hands.

"I still don't trust these highways," Jon said. "I'd rather stay prepared for an emergency. It's hard for me just to let go of the wheel and let the highway take over."

Paul had no difficulty in trusting the highway, feeling safer on it than on roads where cars were operated manually. The automated highways were a relatively new development and he doubted that they would soon replace local roads, but they were useful for traveling long distances. Although trains were popular, and necessary for traveling to cities where cars were not allowed, many people were too used to private transportation to give it up. The cars, with their nonpolluting engines, hydrogen fuel, and safety equipment, lacked some speed and maneuverability when driven manually. But on the automated highways, run by remote control electronically, they could travel at speeds up to one hundred miles an hour. All things considered, Paul regarded the cars as an improvement over the ones he had driven in his youth.

"I think Hidey wants to talk to you," Jon went on. "He asked me to tell you to get hold of him right away, as soon as he found out I was picking you up."

"Well, I feel like relaxing today, and I have some lecture notes to work on. I'll call him later on this week."

"He said it was pretty important." Jon seemed to be forcing the words out.

"You still don't approve of the whole thing, do you." Jon did not have to reply. Paul and Hidey had talked with him about cloning, partly because Hidey wanted to hear another point of view on the project and partly because of friendship. They had been friends ever since college. Hidey had eventually gone into genetics; both Paul and Jon had been students of astrophysics. Jon had shown great promise in the field and acquired his doctorate before making a decision to which Paul was not even now fully reconciled. Jon had decided to become a minister, after years in which he had flaunted his atheism. He was now the minister at a Protestant chapel near the university where Paul taught. Although he occasionally helped Paul with some of his papers, Jon's energies were taken up most of the time by his clerical duties.

Jon, as many clergymen were now, was closer to being a mystic than the sort of minister Paul remembered from his childhood. It was the universe itself and the principles behind it that Jon worshipped rather than a patriarchal God. He spoke of Jesus as an example rather than as the Son of God. The traditional concept of a deity was as dead for Jon as for Paul. Jon would have no difficulty in finding his ideas compatible with other religions or even with Paul's agnosticism. Jon had rejected further work in astrophysics not because it conflicted with his beliefs, but because it would take time away from tending to those who might need his aid and advice.

Paul might mourn the loss of Jon's scientific abilities, but he could not logically object to the choice his friend had made. He and Hidey had started college in high spirits, being inquisitive and often reckless. Jon, an older student whom Paul had met as a sophomore, had been scarred and embittered by his Army service in Vietnam. His needs and motivations were different from those of Paul and Hidey. Paul had never fully seen into the heart of the stocky, gray-eyed young veteran. Even now, the silver-haired minister would not talk of what he had experienced during war.

Jon had been startled when Paul and Hidey revealed the clone project to him. Paul knew that Jon would not raise objections based on purely theological grounds. Those objections were in a sense unverifiable. But Jon did have ethical objections.

"You must realize," Jon had said as the three sat in Paul's living room, "that you are violating a rather basic principle here. We've always assumed that any kind of experimentation with human beings requires the informed consent of those concerned. You must have their permission and their decision has to be based on knowledge of the possible consequences, they have to be aware of the dangers involved. I assume you two are aware of any dangers as far as you're concerned, but what about the clones you produce? You can't get their permission for the experiment as they do not yet exist. Yet their lives may be filled with problems you can't even predict. I'm not just talking about the way people treat them. You don't really know what they'll be like. They may not be able to function except as a group. They may be almost morbidly close to one another."

"That's a silly supposition," Hidey replied. "You can do better than that, Jon. We have the experience of identical twins to go by here. The bonds between twins may be strong ones, but they certainly don't function only as one entity. And as for the rest of your argument, well, we might as well tell people not to have children, since the children can't give their permission before they're born."

"Come on, that's not the same at all. In fact, don't we all believe that parents do have some responsibility for their unborn children, that they shouldn't bear them capriciously or without some concern for their welfare? People with diabetes or Tay-Sachs disease aren't even allowed to have children unless they agree to have the embryo treated for these ailments."

"This reminds me of what I used to say to my parents," Paul said, trying to lighten the discussion. "Whenever they wouldn't give me something I wanted, I'd tell them I didn't ask to be born, that they were responsible for me. It was an irrefutable fact."

"You're evading my argument," Jon continued, ignoring Paul's comment. "You still have to violate a principle that I regard as basic as far as experimentation is concerned, and which is one of the reasons I've been opposed to most biological experimentation of whatever sort. And even if we leave that aside, consider the implications of cloning itself. If it works, and you haven't given me any reason to think that it won't, every narcissist alive will be trying to use it. You'll be interfering with the course of human evolution with no conception of what the results might be. What would happen in the long run if even a sizable minority decided to reproduce in this way? You can't know."

"*Abusus non tollit usum*," Paul answered. "We can't refuse to use something simply because it may be misused. You ought to know that. We might as well have banned the use of fire because an arsonist could use it to burn down a home. The wedge cuts both ways, Jon, you know that. On those grounds we could ban anything for the first time."

"Speaking more pragmatically," Hidey said, "we're assuming that there will be some kind of control over this. The moratorium will expire, but I think it's unlikely that we'll move from such a rigid restriction to no restrictions at all."

"But you don't know," Jon said vehemently. "Scientists, as you well know, or should by now, don't have everything to say about how their discoveries will be used. You seem to be doing this for only one reason, simply to see if it can be accomplished. That's not good enough, not with anything as potentially volatile as this."

"But wouldn't you rather have us do it than some other group?" Hidey asked. "At least we're aware of these problems. Someone else might not care. And

there are some very humane reasons for wanting to clone
somebody. Parents who lose a child, say, and can't have
another, might want to have a clone of the child they
lost."

"Besides," Paul said, "this isn't a terribly radical proposal. Look at Hoyt's experiments in brain chemistry. If
he could work with people, he could theoretically drive
a sane man to murder. Consider Lubaaya's work on
genetic manipulation. He's got a gorilla in his office
working as a file clerk. Or think about Simon and her
miniaturized electrodes. They were feared once, but now
they help thousands of epileptics live normal lives. Things
like that would have far more radical consequences than
anything Hidey's doing."

"That's no argument," Jon responded," and you know
it. You're talking about the lesser of two evils."

"Damn it, Jon," Hidey said, "the option of cloning
should be made available to people. You of all people
shouldn't have such contempt for ordinary human beings
that you think they'll automatically misuse anything that
comes along. We can't afford to lose valuable abilities
simply because the person who possesses them has only
one life in which to accomplish anything. And there
may be other applications of the technique that we're
unaware of now, but which could be crucially important
later on. By using cloned organs, for example, we might
greatly extend the human life span. We could clone
people who carry certain recessive traits, traits which,
with the wrong parental partner, might become dominant
and adversely affect their offspring. Such people could
have cloned children until we can find a way of altering
such genes."

Hidey paused before going on. "I want to move on
this project, and I have to do it now. I think the restrictions might be back with us before long, I'd bet on it. If
we can accomplish something in the interim, and show
people that something constructive can come out of such
work, maybe they won't be so frightened of it in the
future. It's ultimately self-defeating to restrict research
out of fear. We have to use our knowledge constructively

and you don't do that by hiding from it and suppressing it."

Hidey seemed weary after making that statement, and Paul noticed that Jon too was affected by it. The stocky minister fell silent, running his hands through his short gray hair and staring at the floor. At last Jon looked up again.

"Maybe I was wrong about some of your reasons," Jon said. "But I still think, Hidey, that you also want to make a name for yourself in your field. You haven't been able to do much under the moratorium and this may be your only chance. And maybe you," he went on, turning to Paul, "need someone to at least partially relieve your loneliness since Eviane died. The clones will be your only children."

"A name for this is worth making," Hidey muttered.

"Is there something wrong with my wanting children?" Paul asked almost simultaneously.

"You're both practical people," Jon said softly, "especially you, Hidey, at least where your work is concerned. So consider something else. This project of yours may accomplish just the opposite of what you want. You'd like to see biological research open up after the moratorium expires, but your project might be the catalyst that would produce a reaction against what you want. It may be just the sort of thing that would bring about more restrictions."

The car rushed along the highway. Paul glanced at Jon and wondered if he might have been right. What were his own motives anyway? He wasn't really sure. Perhaps he was not really considering this business as carefully as he should but was simply letting himself be pushed into it. He had not even thought about how people might react to the project. He remembered the hysteria of New Year's Eve and shuddered. Perhaps that should be his biggest worry.

"I still haven't made up my mind, you know," he said to Jon. In a way this was true, yet Paul felt as though he had already assented to the experiment and the rest was simply a matter of details. He knew that he would go through with it eventually and had in fact already started planning for it. "I've been thinking about what you said, Jon."

"I doubt that it'll have much effect on you. If you agreed with me, you would have already dropped any idea of participating in this business." Jon looked away from the road and directly at him.

There was nothing to say in reply. "I imagine," Jon went on, "that you'll probably go ahead. Well, I'm still your friend and Hidey's too. I have a feeling you may need all the friends you've got pretty soon."

Paul thought of the Dallas mobs. There was no telling what public reaction would be and how much of it would focus on himself. Although Hidey and his people would be conducting the experiment, it was Paul whom they would clone and Paul who would be granted, in people's minds, the semblance of immortality. What would they think of a man who had been duplicated several times?

Paul wondered if his cloned children would live to curse his name. He had decided to raise them himself. Hidey did not think this was necessary, but Paul did. He would be their social father, yet more than a father. They would literally be physical reflections of him. There was no way he could avoid this responsibility. He had almost welcomed it. Was it then a need to alleviate his loneliness?

"I don't really *feel* that I'm doing anything wrong," he said to Jon. "I know that's not the most reliable indicator, but it's served me well enough in the past."

Jon was silent. Paul knew that his friend was not about to provide him with any comforting rationalizations. The car was suddenly filled with a loud buzzing noise and a light on the dashboard began to flash. Jon resumed control of the vehicle. They turned off the highway and onto the road that led to Paul's house.

"We have to move fast," Hidey said. "There's no time to lose."

Hidey Takamura, at fifty, was still a youthful man. Paul often asked if he had been engaging in gerontological research. Hidey's hair was still black, his face unlined and his weight the same as when they were undergraduates. Hidey's office was already clouded by the smoke of his cigarettes, which he continued to use in defiance of what Paul considered good sense.

Paul was sitting with Emma Valois in front of Hidey's desk. Emma, a psychiatrist, was also involved in the project. She would not be working in the laboratory but would study the psychological development of the clones after their birth. She was a tall lanky woman in her thirties with prematurely graying brown hair and hazel eyes. She was also one of the few people Paul knew who displayed complete self-confidence and control of circumstances around her. She had been examining Paul since November, trying to uncover any psychological flaws that might affect the clones or indicate that Paul was a poor prospect.

"Emma's given you a clean bill of health anyway," Hidey said, waving his cigarette in the air.

"I won't say you're average, or even normal," Emma said. "You have a tendency to get extremely depressed, I notice, but probably for good reason, and it hasn't debilitated you yet, so I don't suppose it will. And your family history doesn't indicate anything that might be genetically rooted. I must confess I was wondering about that grandfather who committed suicide." Her handsome face watched him speculatively.

"Jesus, Emma," Hidey said, throwing his hands up, "don't turn him down now. Everyone else I know is completely crazy.

"I don't think," Paul said, "you should hold that against me. He was an old man at the time, and very sick. He didn't want to linger on as an invalid."

"Personally," Emma said, "I don't like to rationalize any suicide, but. . . ." She shrugged. "I guess you'll do. Damn it, Hidey, I wish you'd give me more time. Those damn machines and tests can't tell me everything."

"Sorry," Hidey said. "I can't give you the one or two years I know you want. We've got to start, and by next week if possible."

They had decided earlier that they would create six clones. Hidey wanted to be sure that there would be

enough for a proper study. It would be interesting to
see whether an identical group of that size would diverge
or remain similar in their pursuits. Hidey also wanted to
allow for any error. It was conceivable that not all the
clones would survive, even in ectogenetic chambers.
It was known that one-fourth of normal pregnancies
were terminated by natural causes. Paul pushed that
thought out of his mind.

"How are you going to care for them?" Emma asked.

"I'm trying to find a reliable couple around here."

"Just don't tell them anything," Hidey said, "and for
God's sake make sure it's somebody who won't be scared
off when they find out. And when you've narrowed it
down to two or three couples, make sure you send them
to Emma right away."

"I'm having enough trouble trying to find one couple."

"You've got a good nine months for that." Hidey
leaned back in his chair. "The ectogenetic chamber has
never been used immediately after the moment of conception except with animals, but it should work with
humans. We have the best ones we could get and we've
added some refinements of our own. Frankly, we would
have had trouble lining up six women as hosts, and that
would introduce some variables I'd just as soon avoid."
He paused for a moment. "I was thinking, it might be
interesting to have two female clones in the group."

"Why two girls?" Paul asked, and was rewarded with
a glare from Emma.

"Look," Hidey answered, "we're dealing with a group
that's genetically identical, right? The *only* difference
among them will be the gender. I want to see if that makes
any difference in their personalities and development."

"Oh, honestly, Hidey," Emma said, "I can't believe
that you think it will."

"We don't really know, do we?" Hidey went on. "This
is a unique opportunity to investigate. It may not matter
but we might as well check it out." He put out his
cigarette and promptly lit another. "It'll be tricky, we'll
have to hook on an X chromosome and remove the Y,
which could be a problem. We should at least test the

technique on humans, though."

"But won't the girls be sterile?" Paul asked. "Isn't that just creating another problem?"

"I don't know," Emma said. "Sterility doesn't bother people as much as it used to, and of course the daughters could have cloned children of their own. Who knows, by the time they're adults, it might not matter at all. An ovarian transplant was tried before the moratorium, and it might work in the future."

"Do you mind having a couple of daughters, Paul?" Hidey said. "Or sisters. Hell, it's hard to keep reminding oneself what relation they are to you."

"Socially, they'll be daughters, and of course I don't mind. But you may not prove much one way or the other. I'm almost fifty and kind of settled in my ways. I might treat my daughters differently from my sons and not even realize I'm doing it." *Daughters,* he had said. Already he was thinking of them as his children, worrying about them before they even existed.

"Well," Hidey said. The three looked at each other and then away. "We'll be ready to start in a couple of days. Frankly, I'm scared."

"I'm glad to hear it," Emma said. "It makes me think you're not so crazy after all."

Paul sat in the faculty lounge of the biological sciences building and wondered if his apprehensive feelings were the same as those of anyone about to become a parent. Probably worse, he thought. He had to sit there and look calm in case some inquisitive person should walk over and ask him what was the matter. He was not proficient at lying. He would be forced to ignore the person or be overtly rude, and he was not good at either. Outside of the people involved in the experiment and Jon Aschenbach, no one could know for another nine months at least.

Paul understood the cloning procedure. The nucleus would be removed from the unfertilized female egg cells. In the absence of this haploid maternal nucleus, diploid material obtained from Paul would be inserted into the ovum. The egg, having a full set of chromosomes instead of a half set, would begin to divide as though normally fertilized, becoming a blastocyst. The blastocyst, programmed entirely with Paul's genetic endowment, would be implanted in an ectogenetic chamber. It would then attach itself to the wall of the chamber, protected by a synthetic amniotic fluid and nourished by an artificial umbilical cord winding around the outside of the "womb." *At least they'll have navels,* Paul thought, almost chuckling aloud. The ectogenetic chamber could expand as necessary throughout the "pregnancy," in imitation of a natural womb. After nine months, the clones would be removed from their chambers, be spanked, Paul supposed, and cry like any other children.

Paul had not wanted to be in the lab while the process of conception was taking place, nor even in Hidey's office. He worried about this now, wondering what it might mean. It suddenly struck him as ludicrous not to be present at the conception of his own children and he almost laughed aloud. But then he grew pensive, thinking that the clones might hold it against him some day. He was not indifferent, he knew that. Perhaps he was simply afraid to see it occur in the lab; maybe it was a threat to him psychologically in some way he did not fully understand. Men whose wives conceived by artificial insemination were often told to make love to their wives during the same day. This allowed them to believe, if they needed to, that the child just might be the result of their own natural efforts. Paul could not protect himself in any similar fashion. Still, he thought, here he was making an effort, the only kind relevant to this task. *I want those children.* The desire seized him more fiercely than it ever had in the past. *I want those children.* Wasn't that really the important thing after all? Many children were only accidental byproducts of a careless night, the focus of an unfulfilled parental ambition, or conceived as pawns to be used in a loveless battle. Some, even now, were concessions to a society just beginning to realize that parenthood was not a goal to which everyone should aspire.

Paul had achieved most of his goals and was as satisfied with his life as he could be. For the first time in his life he felt ready for parenthood. Wasn't it at least possible that the conception of these clones was as great an act of love as any other conception? He hoped it was. If he had any goals at all for his children, they were that the clones would in some small way change others' lives for the better, that they would bring people to some sort of understanding about themselves that they would not have had otherwise. If he had a goal for himself, it was that he would be a good father. It might turn out to be his most important accomplishment.

He picked up a journal from the table in front of him and began to leaf through it aimlessly. Gradually he became aware of the fact that a man on the other side of the room was watching him. Paul looked over at the man, who was leaning against the yellow wall, and tried to remember if he had seen him before on any of his visits. He had, directly or in passing, met or seen most of the people who worked here. Hidey practically lived in the biological sciences building and Paul had spent a lot of time with his friend here before the project. He couldn't recall the man, but that meant little since he could be a new faculty member or a graduate student.

The fellow apparently noticed Paul's gaze and started to walk over. Paul felt apprehensive. He scolded himself silently: *What are you afraid of? This business is making you paranoid.* He forced himself to smile.

"Héllo," Paul said in what he hoped was a jolly voice.

"Hello," the man responded. He was a young, handsome, and hairy person with blond hair and a thick blond beard. "I hope you don't mind my asking, but aren't you Paul Swenson?"

"Yes, I am."

"I thought so, I recognized you from a photo on one of your books."

"That's pretty good. They always use the same one. I had brown hair, a moustache and was ten pounds thinner. I didn't think anyone could recognize me by that. You've disillusioned me. I thought my gray hair was a pretty good disguise."

"Your face is still the same." The man paused for a moment to light a cigar. "Isn't that something, though. I read this book you wrote, what was it called?"

"I've written fifteen."

"*Studies of the Universe*," the young man said. "Jesus, I liked that book. I even got that cassette of stellar photographs with your lecture. What little I know about stars, I got from you."

"Thank you," Paul said. He still felt slightly uneasy.

"I didn't expect to see you hanging around here." The man sat down in a chair across from Paul and crossed his legs.

"I have a couple of good friends in the department of genetics. I think I spend more time here than in my own office. Hidehiko Takamura and I have been friends since college." Paul suddenly felt as though he had said too much. Something about the man did not fit in with the setting. He did not seem to belong here. *An idiotic idea*, he told himself, *who am I to decide who belongs here and who doesn't*?

"You must be new around here," Paul said, going on the offensive. "I guess you just arrived in time for the next semester. What's your specialty?"

The blond man looked a bit annoyed. "Oh. I'm waiting for a friend," he said finally, after a long pause.

"Anybody I know?" I've met almost everybody around here."

"I don't think so. Well, I just wanted to tell you I enjoyed your book." The man stood up. He nodded at Paul, crossed the lounge and sat down next to the windows.

Paul realized that he had almost forgotten what was taking place in the lab. There was no sense sitting there worrying about it. He pulled some revised lecture notes out of his briefcase and tried to concentrate on them. He would have to lecture that afternoon and had not prepared himself as well as he would have liked. A friend at the Komarov Observatory on the moon had sent him some material he was sure would be of interest to the class.

He stared at the notes and wondered if he would ever regret not going to the moon, which was rapidly becoming the most interesting place to study astronomy and astrophysics as well as the most highly selective. He and Eviane had looked forward to going once. She had been invited by the radio astronomers there, and those working on the star drive had asked Paul to join them several times. But Eviane had become ill just as they were getting ready to leave. After her death, Paul hadn't had the heart to go.

He now contented himself by trying to keep in close contact with the Lunar scientists, sending them voluminous notes over the computer link-up and making expensive phone calls to them when necessary. But he would go some day, when the clones were adults and when the Lunar gravity would be a relief to his old bones.

"Paul?" a voice said. He looked up and recognized Hidey's young colleague, Elijah Jabbar. Jabbar, superficially an impulsive young man who wore gold earrings and affected African dress, was in reality a serious, hardworking biologist whose desire for perfection exhausted those who worked with him.

"Everything's fine," Jabbar said softly, his dark face breaking into a grin. "At least so far."

Paul sighed with relief. "Wonderful," he said, then remembered the blond man by the windows. He got up quickly and left the room with Jabbar.

He stopped outside the lounge and gestured toward the man inside. "Tell me," he said, "have you ever seen that man around here before?"

"I don't think so," Jabbar answered in a low voice. The young biologist pulled at the woolen robe he wore under his lab coat, trying to adjust it. "But you know, he looks familiar. I can't place him, though. I know I've seen him somewhere."

Paul felt somewhat relieved. *I have been getting paranoid*, he thought.

"Is something wrong?"

"I don't think so," Paul replied. "I'm just nervous."

"If it's that guy in there, he's making me a little nervous too, I don't know why." Both men began to walk down the hall. "I still can't place him, but I'd almost bet he's not connected with the university."

"We're past the worst already," Hidey said, "at least as far as the chamber is concerned. They've been in there a month and nothing's happened yet."

Paul stood in front of the ectogenetic chambers. He could barely see the tiny beings encased in the plastic-like material of the artificial wombs. They were still no more than tiny droplets suspended in fluid.

The chambers were attached to their own power source, a generator down the hall which was being watched twenty-four hours a day by maintenance people on eight-hour shifts. There was an auxiliary generator as well; they were taking no chances on a possible power failure. The maintenance people did not know why the generator was so crucial, having been told only that it was being used in an important experiment.

Pipes and wires trailed out of the wombs. They were attached to large metal oxygenators which piped in nourishment and removed wastes. The blood circulating through the chambers was Paul's, donated for two months prior to the experiment. Paul recalled how doubtful he had been at the time, not really believing, in spite of the blood being drawn from his veins, that the experiment would ever take place. The oxygenator made it possible to recirculate the blood almost indefinitely, and Paul could always supply fresh blood if needed.

In a corner of the room, next to the chambers, sat a computer. It was connected to each chamber and monitored the life functions of the tiny embryos. Elijah Jabbar sat on a stool in front of the computer, watching various gauges and leafing through the last print-out. "I'm a little worried about number six there, Hidey," he said. "Maybe it's too soon to be sure, but I don't think it's doing as well as the others."

"Why not?"

"It doesn't seem to be developing at the same rate as the others, from what our readings show. That could always change, I guess. The computer's already checking the equipment for any small imperfections it might need to repair."

Paul looked at Hidey, who had been momentarily distracted by one of the lab assistants, a tall heavy woman named Nancy Portland. "Here's the new clone-watch schedule," she said, handing a sheet of paper to Hidey, "and we'll be giving the males their androgen next Thursday." Even though the computer could probably take care of any unexpected problems, someone would always be in the lab.

Hidey nodded, then turned to Paul. "Don't worry. They're better off in there than they would be in a natural womb. There they would be at the mercy of whatever bad health habits the mother had developed, and plenty of other things besides. A womb can be pretty goddamned dangerous, in spite of what some people think. We're not even allowed to smoke in this room. He sighed. "Not even me. Let's go to someplace a bit more lax, like my office."

As the three men left the lab, Hidey turned toward Jabbar. "Has that story from China been confirmed?"

"Yes. They aren't even trying to make a secret out of it." The three entered Hidey's office and sat down.

"They're not cloning," Paul said.

"No," Jabbar said, "but they are using the ectogenetic chamber. They aren't using it on a wide scale yet, just in a few large cities. Their press releases claim that they want to free women from childbirth so they'll have more time to work for the people. Sounds logical."

"Yet when the moratorium was in effect," Hidey said, "they were quick to say that it was a wise move, since the use of certain techniques might weaken and ultimately threaten the well-being of humanity. I guess they can rationalize anything over there, or maybe it's just their way of being flexible and innovative." Hidey lit a cigarette. "As far as we know, they're not cloning, but we don't know. No one knows we are either.

"Do you think some others might be trying?" Paul asked.

"Frankly, I'm not sure," Hidey replied. "I suppose somebody could be. This might sound arrogant, but I don't think anyone else is. This laboratory is the most likely place, we have the most talented people in this specialty. We've been cloning animals for longer than any other group in the world. Others might be planning to clone, but I think it'll take them longer to prepare for and set up an actual experiment."

"What about China?" Paul said. "After all, the synthetic placenta was developed by Huang Tsu. Their meat production has been increased by cloning cattle and hogs."

"So has everyone's. I don't think they'd be as likely to clone a person," Jabbar said. "The Chinese have assumed up to now that it is environment that makes a person what he is. Their collective society is designed to form a certain kind of human being. They wouldn't be likely to practice certain types of genetic engineering."

"Who knows?" Hidey said. "They might, just to demonstrate their point, that it doesn't matter."

"Well," Paul said, "I'd better get going. I have an appointment to interview a young couple at my house. I'll be by tomorrow."

"Sure," Hidey said. "I'll see you."

Paul left the office and walked down the circular hall toward the lobby of the building. His house was close enough to the campus to walk. Paul enjoyed walking, listening to the snow crunch under his boots and breathing the cold clean air. As he stopped near the door to adjust his coat something caught his eye. He turned his head slightly.

The tall blond man, the same man Paul had met in the faculty lounge a month earlier, was standing near a display case. The man glanced at Paul and nodded. He nodded back, then hurried out the door.

Paul hung up the two coats in the closet near the stairs, then wandered back into the living room. The couple seated on his overstuffed blue sofa were a study in contrasts. The young woman was short and stocky with a broad friendly face and straight black hair. Her husband was a tall bony brown-haired fellow with pale gray eyes. He looked almost morose, but then Paul noticed the wrinkles around his eyes and the smile lines near his mouth.

Paul settled into an easy chair across the room from the couple. "I'm Bill Hathaway," the man said, "and this is my wife, Zuñi."

"Except I'm Apache, not Zuñi, unless you count my great-grandfather," the young woman said. "That's just what everyone calls me."

Paul had read their resumé the day before. It was almost faultless. Both Hathaways had worked in the child-care center in the Alasand arcology for almost five years after graduating from college. Recommendations from their co-workers and friends had stressed the couple's friendliness, love of children, and ability to work hard. They had apparently decided to return to school for degrees in linguistics and wanted to work nearer the campus. They would be studying during alternate semesters, so their studies would not interfere with their work.

So far, so good. Paul wasn't satisfied with the previous applicants he had interviewed. One couple had interest but no experience, another couple had experience but had looked dubious about caring for children whom Paul suggested might have "special problems." The third couple had been somewhat nervous, and the man had suggested he would be willing to let his wife handle most of the drudgery and be content with giving orders.

"You already know something about this job," Paul said. "You'll be caring for six infants for three or four years while living in this house. Of course, you'll get time off and a vacation each year, and I'll want the kids to spend time in the university day-care center to get used to other children. But most of the time you'll be full-time parents, along with me. You might get tired of it after a while."

"I doubt it," Bill said. "If we thought so, we wouldn't

be here. We like kids, and it'll take us about four years to finish our degrees anyway. We would have had our own by now, but I'm sterile and we've been turned down for artificial insemination, the waiting lists are too long." Bill said this quite openly and apparently without shame. The man did not shy away from unpleasant facts, and Paul liked that. The clones, if they were anything like Paul had been, would be inquisitive and would not take well to having their questions ignored or pushed aside. "Eventually, we'll adopt," Bill went on, "but you know how long that takes. Or we'll become professional parents. When we heard about your job offer, it sounded ideal."

"I won't be able to pay you as much as you're getting now," Paul said.

"We're not in it for the money," Zuñi said. "If we were interested in that, we would have gone into child care administration a long time ago. We happen to like working with kids."

"All sorts of kids, I trust," Paul said cautiously. "Even children who might have special problems?" He watched the faces of the couple in front of him carefully. Bill's gray eyes and Zuñi's black ones stared back at him steadily.

"Don't all children have special problems of some sort?" Bill replied. "We've cared for crippled kids, emotionally disturbed kids, retarded kids and kids that throw temper tantrums every five minutes."

"I expected you might want a couple to care for kids with 'special problems,' as you put it," Zuñi said. "I mean, six infants all at once, it is a little unusual." Paul realized that the pair were drawing some tentative conclusions about him at the same time as he was trying to judge them.

"What sort of problems," Paul said quickly, "did you think they might have?" The question was a shot in the dark, a way of finding out just what the Hathaways might be thinking.

"We don't know," Bill answered. "At one point I thought they might be the fruit of several affairs, believe it or not, or that you had somehow defied bureaucracy and managed to adopt some South African war orphans. Then Zuñi had an idea that seemed pretty wild at first, but began to seem more plausible after a while."

"What idea was that?"

"The moratorium on genetic research has run out," Zuñi said softly. Paul's muscles tensed and he could feel himself sweating. "I know you don't work in that area, but friends of ours at the university know people who do. They told us once, just in passing, that you had some close friends there. So I thought . . . it is a wild idea . . . I thought maybe you might have offered to help raise some experimental subjects."

Paul managed to restrain himself from gasping aloud. He was dealing with an intuitive and intelligent couple who had come uncomfortably close to the truth. He began to wonder how many others might have reached the same conclusions.

"But that was just a crazy idea," Zuñi went on. *I'd better say something*, Paul thought to himself. "We shouldn't be speculating about it when you can fill us in on the facts."

"We still want the job," Bill said, "but I don't think it's fair to you to say we'll definitely take it if you want us until we know more about what's involved. It's easy to say you're willing to do anything when you're in ignorance about what's going on. I doubt that we would turn it down in any case, but we should know more." Zuñi was nodding her head in agreement.

"I'll be as honest as I can," Paul said, deciding to take a calculated risk. "Zuñi's on the right track, but I can't tell you any more than that, at least not right now. First, I have to send you to a friend of mine for psychological testing. I hope you're not offended by that. To be honest, I get a good feeling from you two, but we can't afford to take chances. I need as much objective evidence as possible that you two are right for this job."

"You're being sensible," Bill said. "We were given a few tests before we took our present jobs. Personally, I don't think you'll find much wrong, but no one knows everything about himself."

We'll keep the results confidential, of course," Paul said, "and I trust you'll do the same with what I've told you. I promise to fill you in as soon as the psychological testing is over, assuming the results are favorable."

"You can trust us," Zuñi said, "but you must know there are others, not many but a few, who are drawing the same conclusions about what's going on in the biological laboratories."

Paul considered this, and felt even more worried than usual. How would people react when they knew? Again he started to fear for his unborn children.

Paul felt a twinge of guilt as he hurried through the spring rain to the lab. He had been gone almost a month, visiting his sister Sonia in New York and giving a couple of seminars at Columbia. The seminars went well, although Paul was a little unnerved by the sight of armed guards in the lecture halls and around the periphery of the campus. He had not been greatly calmed when he was told that things had been fairly quiet since the New Year. The scars of New Year's Eve were still apparent: partially burned buildings, broken windows, ruined offices and hallways.

Sonia at least looked well. She had divorced her second husband six months before, but it had been an amiable divorce and the two still worked together for a firm that specialized in providing book manuscripts and taped lectures to computer complexes all over the world. It had dismayed Sonia more when her teenaged son Jerry chose to exercise his legal rights and left with her husband. Jerry visited her frequently and usually spent his weekends at her apartment, but she had been hurt by his action.

Paul ducked into the doorway of the biological sciences building and strode through the lobby. He was glad to be back. Hidey had encouraged him to go on the trip to New York, thinking the change would do him good. Paul had worried about leaving while his offspring were still gestating but Hidey had pointed out, quite reasonably, that there was really nothing for him to do until they were born. "You'll be tied down then," Hidey had said. "Right now you're not, and you said your students have all those taped lectures by other professors to keep them busy for the time being. You'd better visit your sister while you've got the chance."

Paul was thinking now that he had overstayed his welcome at Sonia's. Things had been fine for the first two weeks, and then Sonia had begun to reminisce about her marriages.

"I tried twice," she said, "once when I was young and foolish and again when I was older and more stable, and I've never found what you had with Eviane."

Paul mumbled something about it not being too late, she still had a good chance, and so on. But privately he doubted it, and wondered now whether or not it would be a good thing if she did. He had felt like half a man for too long now, feeling that he should have kept part of himself from Eviane so that he could have survived her death with something whole. They had shared everything, their work, their free time, all of their feelings, and with her death he had lost part of all he had. The doubts about the cloning experiment returned now, the notion that he had agreed to take part in it for neurotic reasons of his own, to assuage the loneliness which was his constant companion.

"Did you get my message, Paul?" Emma Valois asked. She was standing in the doorway of Hidey's office, arms folded across her chest. "I taped it on your phone."

"No, I didn't." They entered the office and sat down. "I should have checked, but I was tired when I got in last night."

"Well, it looks good on the Hathaways, they're so well adjusted they make me feel unbalanced." Emma crossed her legs and tugged at her dark green slacks. "I don't know how many others you talked to, but I'd wager a year's salary on the Hathaways. I can't be specific about anything without violating their confidence, but I'd hire them in a minute to look after my kids, and they're a handful sometimes, believe me."

"Good, at least that's one less problem for me. I just

hope they take the job. Where's Hidey?"

"He just went to the lab to check on things. I've been trying to convince him he needs more for breakfast than coffee and a cigarette, maybe you can. . . ."

"Paul." Hidey was at the door, his face anxious. "Come to the lab, we've got trouble." Hidey disappeared down the hall. Paul rose from his seat and followed him, with Emma close behind.

As he entered the lab, he could see Nancy Portland and another assistant, Jake Keleshian, cowering near the wall by the door. On the other side of the room near the chambers, Elijah Jabbar was holding the shoulders of a small pale man. "I ought to punch your face in," Jabbar was shouting as he shook the man. "You stupid son of a bitch, I'll see you blacklisted at every lab in the country."

Hidey began to pull at Jabbar's arm. "Come on, Eli," he pleaded, "that's not going to help us now. Let him go."

"What happened?" Paul asked, hurrying to the three men.

Jabbar released the small man. "Tell him, Hidey." Hidey turned and looked up at Paul.

"It's one of the clones, Paul." Hidey seemed to be saying the words only with great difficulty. "The umbilical, well, it got clogged somehow, we're still not sure how. Johnson here was on night duty. He should have noticed it right away and taken emergency measures, spliced in a new section of tubing."

"The computer was flashing an emergency signal," Jake Keleshian muttered. He clutched at his curly dark hair. "It must have tried to handle it alone, then found that it couldn't." He looked over at the computer sadly. Jake had helped to program the machine and now seemed to be sympathizing with it.

"He was asleep," Jabbar said. "Nancy found him in her office when she came in this morning. The bastard was asleep."

"It was a mistake," the man named Johnson protested. "It could happen to anybody. Nancy told me I could use her coffee machine so I could keep near here. I felt kind of tired, I only dozed off for a couple of minutes, it seemed like, and then when Nancy came in, we hurried as fast as we could with a new tube. . . . "

"A couple of minutes," Jabbar shouted. "You must have slept half the fucking night away."

"Which one?" Paul asked. He felt stunned, as if someone had just hit him in the stomach. "Which one?"

"Number six," Hidey answered. "The female we were a little worried about." He pulled out his cigarettes and lit one, apparently oblivious to restrictions. No one stopped him.

"Is she all right? Is she going to be all right?"

Jabbar turned away from Johnson. "No," he said. "I checked. That fetus was deprived of oxygen for quite a while, it's been damaged. It's barely alive now."

"She's still alive then." Paul wiped his face with his sleeve. He wandered over to the side of the sixth chamber and stared at the tiny fetus. It seemed defenseless, curled up in its womb.

". . . with brain damage," Hidey was saying. "I think it's dying now, Paul, and even if it doesn't it won't be normal."

"At least she's alive."

"Paul, are you listening to me?" Hidey was at his side, holding his arm. "We have to make a decision. Do you want this fetus to survive in that state? Wouldn't it be more merciful not to allow it to? You're going to have plenty of problems as it is. I think we should abort."

"No."

"Paul, consider the child, what things will be like for her."

"No."

Johnson was wringing his hands. "I'm sorry, Dr. Swenson," he said. "It was an accident."

Paul turned away from the wombs and stared at the pale laboratory walls. He was acting unreasonably, he knew. This was still an experiment and he had known there would be risks and possibly mistakes. There were problems enough with natural children. It would be nothing more than an abortion, perhaps more like a miscarriage. Yet he felt a sense of loss.

"I'm sorry," Johnson muttered.

"It's settled," Jabbar suddenly said. His deep voice drummed at Paul's ears. "It's dead. No life functions."

Paul turned back to Hidey and could think of nothing to say.

"I'll take care of things here," Jabbar said. "Why don't you two go back to the office."

"Stay here, Johnson," Hidey said. "I'll talk to you later." Paul left with his friend, joining Emma at the doorway of the laboratory. She said nothing, quietly following them back to Hidey's office.

When they were seated, Hidey pulled a bottle from his desk. "Have some whiskey, Paul, you'll feel better."

"No thanks." Hidey poured some for himself and Emma. Paul looked away from his friend and around the small windowless office. A folded cot leaned against the wall on his left and several books rested on a makeshift bookcase on the wall to his right. Hidey's desk was covered with neatly stacked papers and journals, three empty coffee cups and two ashtrays, carved out of marblelike green and brown rocks. The ashtrays were filled with small mounds of cigarettes and some of the gray ashes had drifted across the desk top.

"I can't help feeling a little sad about the whole business," Paul said at last. "Number six. She didn't even have a name. I guess she'll just go down the chute with all the other failed experiments."

"Come on, Paul, you know we're not that callous. She'll go to the crematorium and we can bury her ashes somewhere if you like. I've been working with life for too long now not to feel a lot of respect for it, or sorrow when it dies, in whatever form." Hidey drummed on his desk top with his fingers. "God, how I hate death. This may be an important step in the battle against it. Someday maybe we'll beat death altogether, and I hope we're all around to see it. That fetus didn't die for nothing."

"I know," Paul said. "Considering the circumstances,

I guess it's just as well." He wondered how the other clones would feel when they learned about the death of their sister, as they were bound to some day.

"Now I've got another problem." Hidey dragged thoughtfully on his cigarette. "That idiot Johnson. If I can keep Eli from committing homicide, I have to keep Johnson around until we release this story. If we fire him now, he may start talking. I've got to convince him that we won't and give him something innocuous to do until I can bounce him out of here." Hidey sighed. "I just hope he buys it, that's all."

"And we've got to tell the Hathaways about the clones," Emma said. "I think we can trust them, though. We'd better do it soon, in case they have second thoughts about your offer, Paul."

"I'll tell them," he said.

"That's everything, up to this point," Paul said. He had invited the Hathaways to his house for dinner, but had eaten almost nothing himself while relating the story. Now he stared at his still full plate, hesitating to look at them. Finally he forced his head up. He had left out nothing, not even the fate of the sixth clone.

Zuñi was sipping her wine. She put the glass down. Raising her head, she looked across the round oak table at him. "It sounds," she said, "as though you want us to take care of identical quintuplets. It's about the same thing, isn't it?"

"And they'll be like you," Bill said.

"There's no doubt about that. I'm the only parent, after all."

"That doesn't sound so bad," Bill said. "You're a nice fellow, Paul. I imagine the kids will be asking questions all the time when they're not being quiet and thoughtful, and doing quadratic equations by the time they're four. And they'll be good cooks too. That was a great supper." He patted his stomach.

"And you'll want us to treat them as individuals, not just as a group," Zuñi said. She brushed a few crumbs across the white tablecloth into her napkin. "I had two friends once who were twins. In fact, that's what people called them, the O'Hara twins, never Mary and Molly. Their mother used to dress them in identical outfits, the whole business. They got to resent it after a while, but they were very dependent on each other too. It'll be a thousand times worse with your kids. They'll be just like you as well as each other, and people are bound to make comparisons. They won't even be mirror images of each other, the way twins are. They'll be completely identical." She smiled slightly. "You want to be sure that each one has a sense of being a person in his own right."

"You sound," Paul said carefully, "as if you've already taken the job."

"Of course," Bill replied. "We're looking forward to it, and to meeting the kids as well."

Paul felt relieved. Maybe things were not going to be as bad as he thought. Zuñi and Bill hadn't found anything to fear in the idea of clones. But how many people were like the Hathaways? He had been lucky to find them at all.

"By the way," Zuñi said, "when do we meet them?"

"In the middle of September," Paul answered, "if everything goes as planned."

"No reason to think it won't," Bill said. "An artificial womb isn't going to have labor pains in the middle of the night."

Paul stood on his front porch, surveying the lawn. His house stood on the top of a small hill and at the end of the road leading past his neighbors' houses. The small suburban neighborhood was beginning to look a bit run-down. Overgrown and untrimmed yards blossomed with weeds. The porch in front of one gray house had been propped up with stones. The white paint on a nearby Colonial home had begun to peel away, exposing the wood underneath; flakes of whiteness littered the garden around it.

Many people were moving into arcologies such as Alasand, where they could live in homes on the various levels and yet be within walking distance of whatever they needed. Some had moved back to the city, which was almost pleasant without cars roaring through the streets. But Paul had grown used to his house. It was surrounded on three sides by wooded land; since suburbs were becoming unprofitable, a lot of land that would have been developed was reverting to nature.

Bill and Zuñi had decided to move into Paul's house at the beginning of June. It would give them time to feel at home in the house and, more importantly, feel at home with him. The Hathaways still worked at Alasand on weekends but would quit their jobs there in August, take a vacation, and then begin their new job.

They had brought surprisingly little with them when they moved in. They owned few books. The Hathaways, as did many people, purchased microfiche copies of those they wanted to keep, obtaining copies of others through the computer linkups almost every home had. Paul had about three thousand books of his own in paperback and hard covers. He still found pleasure in holding a book in his hands and enjoyed the smell of paper and old print.

Zuñi and Bill had quickly settled in one of the upstairs bedrooms down the hall from Paul's room. Almost immediately, Zuñi had decided to paint the two rooms which would serve as nurseries. Luckily the house was big enough so that by the time the children started school, and the Hathaways moved out, each could have a separate bedroom. Eviane had insisted on a large house. She had lived in apartments all her life and had wanted room to sprawl.

The weather was warm and sunny. Gentle summer breezes ruffled Paul's hair as he stood on the porch. Billowy white clouds sailed across the clear blue sky. Zuñi was upstairs, busily painting walls, hoping to finish the rooms before the end of June, when the weather would become hot, humid, and "lazy-making," as she put it.

She had also managed to buy five used cribs from the Alasand child-care center. Paul had been ready to buy new ones but Zuñi had persuaded him that would be a waste of money. Instead, she got new mattresses for the cribs, painted each a different color, and made toys out of old beads and wooden objects that could be attached to the cribs. These, she explained, would help the children develop their perceptual abilities. She had also insisted on installing a sound system in each nursery, after telling Paul of the marvelous results they had achieved at Alasand when classical music was played for the children.

"We have to stimulate them," she told Paul. "We have to encourage them to explore with all their senses. We already know that music can work as an anti-depressant and we think it helps the children in understanding mathematical concepts. It might make them smarter, believe it or not." As it turned out, Paul had saved little money on the used cribs after purchasing the sound system.

Bill was puttering around on the hydrogen-powered lawn mower in the front yard. He turned slightly in his seat and waved at Paul. "Hey," he shouted, "how about joining me with a cold beer?"

"Okay," Paul shouted back.

"I'll be done in a couple of minutes."

Paul headed back inside and went through the living room and dining room to the kitchen. He rummaged in the refrigerator for the beer. He was surprised at how easily he had adjusted to having the couple in his home. There were no arguments about how to handle things around the house. They had quickly settled into a routine, each taking on different household tasks in turn. It was good to hear voices in the house again, voices that managed to take his mind off the spirit of Eviane that he often felt was lingering in the rooms.

Bill was already on the porch when he returned, seated in the wooden rocking chair he had appropriated since moving in. Paul handed Bill his beer and sat in the white plastic lounge chair next to him.

"That tastes good," Bill said, taking a swig. "I'd better relax while I can. Zuñi'll be ready for the second room soon and she needs me to paint the ceiling."

"You two are working pretty hard already. You're going to be worn out by the time the kids arrive."

"Don't worry. When we're done, you're welcome to polish the floors and move the cribs in while we relax." Bill swallowed more beer. "Paul," he went on, suddenly sounding serious, "I don't want to alarm you, but something's bothering me."

"What is it?"

"Maybe it's nothing. When Zuñi was visiting our friend Irene at Alasand yesterday, she ran into this fellow, well, she didn't run into him exactly. She thought for a while he was following her. Then she got annoyed, turned around, walked up to the guy, and asked him if he was looking for something. He gave her some story about looking for a friend and losing his way. But then he started to pump her, began to ask a lot of questions. It seemed innocuous at first, she thought maybe he was trying to pick her up or something, but then he mentioned you."

Paul was startled. "What did he say?"

"Not much at first. He said he heard we were working for you and he wondered why, since he knew we were working at the child care center. He turned out to know a lot about us. He gave her a lot of talk about what a great fellow you were, how he read one of your books once and so on. She was ready to tell him off, but she controlled herself and said you'd hired us for some editorial work. It's a clumsy story, I guess, but our friends bought it. She said this guy looked like he knew it was a lie."

"Look, Bill, he could just be a nosy guy."

"That's what I thought at first, but then Zuñi described him to me. I know this sounds weird, but I could swear he was a man I saw in the biological sciences building the day Zuñi and I went to meet Dr. Takamura and Dr. Jabbar. I wouldn't have remembered him except that I could swear I saw him driving around this neighborhood the same damn day."

"Couldn't Zuñi tell you if it was the same man?"

"No. She didn't see him the day we went to the lab. Dr. Takamura's coffee machine wasn't working and I went to the lounge to get some. I saw the guy lurking at the end of the hall."

"What did he look like?" Paul asked, suspecting he already knew the answer.

"A tall blond man, good-looking, with a lot of hair and a thick beard."

"I've seen him," Paul said, "intermittently. I thought maybe he was seeing one of the women students or something. I always had the feeling he was nosing around."

"Maybe he is, but if he knew anything, you probably would have heard about it by now. It could just be chance."

"Maybe."

"How are the clones coming along?"

"Great. Eli says they should be very healthy kids."

"Good." Bill was silent for a few seconds, then went on. "Maybe I shouldn't tell you this, but I think I can be frank with you. I've been thinking a lot about cloning lately, and suddenly I realized that if it works, if the kids turn out to be normal, it means I could have my own kids."

"You're assuming," Paul said, "that there won't be any restrictions, that anybody would be allowed to clone and that facilities would be available."

"That's not the point. Let me see if I can explain it. I've known I was sterile ever since my teens. Frankly, it didn't really bother me much. It didn't affect my virility, I knew that, and I grew up in a family where my brother and sister were adopted. I adjusted to the fact that I would never have a child that was physically mine, whether we had artificial insemination or adopted or did both. But now. . . . " Bill paused for a moment and brushed back his thinning brown hair from his high forehead. "Now I know that theoretically at least I could have my own child. I don't know how to explain it, but it started to matter to me. I honestly never thought it would. I know logically that it's extremely doubtful I would ever be cloned, but emotionally. . . ." Bill stopped.

"Do you think it's going to bother you then, being in this house with clones?"

"If I thought it would, I wouldn't be here now, it wouldn't be fair to you. But I did go to see Dr. Valois about it. She told me pretty much the same thing you did, said she thought new restrictions would probably be put in effect by somebody. She told me that eventually I would accept the fact and realize it wasn't really possible for me to have a child, I had lived with it before and would again. It might just take a little while." Bill finished the beer and placed his bottle next to his chair. "She may be right. But I think I just might live long enough to see such limits lifted. The birthrate's falling and besides, people won't always be afraid of these techniques, at least I have a small hope now and that may be better than none at all. I don't resent you or anything, if that's what you're thinking. She asked me if I wanted to stay, I told her I did, and she said I should."

"I think you should too. And I'm glad you felt free enough to. . . ."

The phone was buzzing inside. Paul got up and hurried into the house. He picked up the receiver in the living room and saw Hidey's face on the small screen.

"We've got trouble," Hidey said before Paul could open his mouth. "I have a visitor here with me."

Paul's mind was racing ahead of him. *I know*, he thought wildly, *I know*. His mind was starting to add things up.

"Who is it, Hidey?"

"His name is Mort Jason and he's a big blond bruiser who works for the International Newsfax Service as a reporter and feature writer. He knows. I hope you can get here fast."

The tall blond man was the first person Paul noticed as he walked into Hidey's office. He had driven over as quickly as he could, not bothering to change. Now he felt suddenly ill at ease in his stained work slacks and denim shirt.

Emma and Elijah Jabbar were in the office too, seated on the cot over by the left wall. The office was gray with cigarette smoke, some of it the reporter's but most of it, Paul was sure, Hidey's. His friend looked worn and nervous. He glanced at Emma and Jabbar. Emma's eyes glittered and Jabbar's face was set like an obsidian sculpture.

Jason was apparently a pacer. He was not seated but was slowly wandering from one side of the room to the other, a model of good grooming in his sleeveless blue shirt and pale lace-covered slacks. Paul caught a whiff of a piney scent and felt even more conscious of his sweat-stained clothing. He closed the door and took the one remaining seat.

"Hello, Dr. Swenson," Jason said, "nice to see you again. I should tell you what I just told your friends. I found out about your little experiment. I know what's going on. I can't divulge my source, needless to say, but I filled Dr. Takamura in on what I found out so he knows I'm not bluffing."

"We know who the fucker was," Jabbar said suddenly. "He admitted it to me before I came in here. I hope you paid Johnson plenty. He'll never work in a bio lab again if I can help it." Emma put a hand on Jabbar's arm and his mouth clamped shut.

"Why are you talking to us then if you've got your story?" Paul said. Mort Jason stopped pacing and leaned against the door.

"I pride myself on *some* sense of responsibility," the reporter replied. "Now I could go and do a scary Faust story on Paul Swenson, the Nobel laureate who is so obsessed with his own greatness that he wants to give the world copies of himself, and all the mad scientists here who are tampering with the laws of nature and who don't believe every person born should be a unique individual, and about fetuses dying in the lab, that sort of thing. But I don't like that kind of trash. They had it thirty years ago and we wound up with a moratorium." Jason leaned toward Hidey's desk and put out his cigarette, then walked back to the door. He folded his arms and began to rock back and forth on his heels. "I like to inform people, not scare the shit out of them. I want your cooperation, but I should tell you that whether or not I get it I'll do a story and right away. Others are sniffing around. A few of us thought something might be going on around here when the moratorium ran out. It seemed a likely spot, although I did check some others. I want this story, and I want to do it before any of my journalistic brethren get wise."

"Just what sort of story do you want?" Hidey asked.

Jason stopped rocking and smiled slightly. "What I'd like is an interview with you people, pointing out why you're doing this, what you hope to find out, what motivated you. You could tell me how you went about the experiment and I could try to simplify things for the general public. It could be a sympathetic piece, a nice feature story in addition to being headline news. Or you can refuse to talk to me and I might have to start speculating about what you're trying to hide."

"Sounds like blackmail to me," Jabbar said grimly.

"What *are* you trying to hide?" Jason said. "You knew you couldn't hide it forever. I'm willing to de-emphasize certain unpleasantries, such as that one fetus which died. Accidents can happen, and mothers miscarry all the time, no sense in playing it up."

Jabbar and Hidey both looked ready to speak at this point, but Paul motioned to them with his hand. "Listen," Paul said, "we're not trying to hide anything. We intended to announce this procedure as soon as we were ready and we were afraid, I'll admit, of announcing it prematurely. We might have been stopped if we had revealed our intentions before starting. Even if we had announced it after going ahead, we might have been forced to abort the experiment. It would have been no different from aborting a pregnancy."

"I'll grant you that," the reporter said, "but no one's going to do that now. They're too far along. With modern techniques they could survive outside those wombs if you removed them right now. And I don't think any sane person will want them executed."

"Please let me finish," Paul said. "There's more at issue here than that. Those children in there may eventually suffer from any premature publicity, surely you

realize that. Look at what's happened in the past to quintuplets, who are a natural if infrequent occurrence. What
kind of beginning will it be for them if they're exposed
to unrestricted publicity? They'll have problems enough."

"You certainly do sound like the outraged parent,"
Jason said smoothly. "You can't hide it forever, Dr.
Swenson. If I break the story now, some of the excitement will have worn off by the time you bring those kids
into the world. They might have less trouble then. And
to be honest, I think you might prefer dealing with me
rather than some of my professional colleagues. I've
always thought this moratorium business was like hiding
your head in the sand. I'm somewhat sympathetic to what
scientists are trying to do. I can't say the same for some
others." Jason paused to light another cigarette. "I don't
want to brag," he continued, "but my name has some
influence and I'm presently negotiating with my employers
for a daily column and a weekly program of interviews
and commentary on one of the networks. I could be an
influential friend. Or I could be a thorn in your side."

"You don't leave us much of a choice," Hidey muttered.
"I guess this was bound to happen." He leaned over his
desk and rested his chin on his arms. "Could you give
us an hour or two to discuss this?"

"Certainly," Jason replied. He turned and opened the
door. "I'll be back around three. And please don't call
any other reporters. It'll gain you nothing but a momentary revenge, and make me forget my principles about
responsible journalism." He left the office.

Emma looked around at the others. "How the hell,"
she said, "are we going to get ready for an interview in
that length of time?"

"You sound," Jabbar said, "as if we're going to talk to
the bastard."

"We have to, Eli," Hidey said. "We have to make
the best of this, not make matters worse. Unless one of
you can figure out a way to commit the perfect murder."

"I'll be happy to volunteer," Jabbar said, but he
sounded resigned as he said it.

"Look, it could be worse," Paul said. "We'll play up

the positive aspects, dwell on Hidey's motives, concentrate on his sense of responsibility and his hope that this is a positive accomplishment and not just a capricious scientific adventure."

"Maybe it is," Hidey said glumly. "Maybe I was just too impatient for fame after being restricted for so long. I'll be famous, all right, and for what? A number of others could have done it with little effort. The techniques were already there, I didn't invent them, just refined them a bit in my work with animals. I only took the next logical step, the one everyone else was afraid to make."

"Oh, Hidey," Emma said, hitting her thigh with a fist, "don't start with a Watson complex now. All we need is for Jason to think you're loaded with doubts yourself."

Hidey looked up and Paul could see that his friend was pulling himself together. "There's one thing I have to do now," the biologist said. "I'm going to call the Chancellor and ask for some campus security people around here."

"Do you really think that's necessary?" Paul asked.

"My friend, we'll be lucky if we don't have to call in state police and the Army. We're incubating monsters, you know. Dr. Frankenstein will be here on the next train."

The windows in the faculty lounge were shattered. The sultry July heat penetrated the building as the air cooling system, unable to contend with various broken windows, had finally broken down. As he entered the lounge, Paul felt grateful at least that the laboratory which held the clones had no windows. The greenhouse had suffered most from the disorders that had erupted around the building intermittently in the past three weeks, and the botanists were not quite as friendly to the geneticists as they once were.

Jon Aschenbach was sitting in the lounge, in a chair near the wall farthest from the windows. Jon had called him that afternoon, asking calmly if Paul was free for dinner. "I know a nice place out past Alasand," Jon had said, "with good home-style Italian cooking."

"I don't know, Jon. I've been a little worried about

going anywhere lately." Mort Jason had kept his word about his treatment of the story, but many of his colleagues had not been so merciful. Some of the news reports had been almost lurid, and the reporters had done an excellent job of locating other geneticists who were disturbed by Hidey's actions and willing to be quoted, usually out of context. A group of outraged citizens had called for the resignation of Hidey and all those involved in the project with him from the university. The maintenance people had staged a two-day walkout in protest, leaving the biologists alone to tend the equipment until they came back to work. One of the state's senators had flown in from Washington and announced that he would introduce a bill that would ban cloning and other biological experimentation with human germ plasm in the United States, a wise move for a senator who was running for re-election.

"Don't worry about it, Paul," Jon had gone on. "It's a small place with dim lighting and the proprietor is a friend of mine. We can go in my car."

Paul had finally agreed, grateful to Jon whose friendship, he felt, was being strained to the limit. Jon was still not reconciled to the project, and it could do him no good to be seen with one of its principals. Yet he had been one of the first to call on Hidey and Paul when the story broke, as well as doing nothing to interfere with the project when they had decided to go ahead.

Jon stood up as Paul entered the lounge. "You look tired," he said.

"You should see Hidey," Paul answered. "He's got his hands full, watching over the kids and trying to save his job at the same time."

"He told me the Chancellor would fight for him."

"The Chancellor can only do so much before they start going after his hide as well. He'll back down then. He's pretty mad at Hidey and Eli himself but he doesn't want to lose the whole genetics department, and that's what'll happen if he doesn't at least try to fight for them."

"You sound as though he doesn't have a chance, Paul."

"He has a small one. He talked to Jenny Berg today.

She's the head of the Sciences Division here and she's sympathetic." The two men walked out into the hall and ambled toward one of the side exits. "She's going to ask that Hidey and Eli be suspended for a couple of years for misuse of funds or some such administrative reason. The rest of the group would get off with notations on their records. I told Jenny I would resign too."

"There's no reason for you to do that."

"Yes, there is. They're my clones. I don't need the university's money anyway, my royalties and those investments Eviane made will see me through with a little management. Besides, I always thought I was better at writing than teaching."

"And you think your resignation might take some of the pressure off Hidey." Jon pushed open the door leading outside. "You're not fooling me. I know you enjoy teaching."

Two soldiers were standing near the door. They glanced at Paul and Jon briefly. Paul felt uncomfortable, partly because he was not used to having soldiers in such an unlikely place and partly because he could sense their hostility. They would do their job, but he had learned from overheard snatches of conversation among them that they were no happier with the cloning project than the general public. They had guarded his house as well until a week ago. The police still had the house under surveillance.

Paul had felt curiously vulnerable sitting in the house with guards stationed outside, trying to adjust to the fact that people might want to harm him. At least Zuñi and Bill had stayed. He had worried that they might want to protect themselves by leaving. The Hathaways were generally ignored in the news stories, at least so far, but Paul was sure they would be spotlighted when the reporters began to look for a new angle.

"I had to park under the anthropology building," Jon said, gesturing at the square glassy building next to the circular six-story ziggurat that housed the biologists. "They won't let a car near Hidey's lab." They entered the structure and took an elevator down to the underground parking lot. Jon had parked near the exit and they were soon driving up the ramp and outside.

There was an entrance to the automated highway on the edge of the campus past the athletic fields. Cars were already in line at the ramp and the highway was growing thick with rush hour traffic. There had been talk of extending train service to the areas near the university and plans were being drawn up for the route. The automated highway was becoming crowded with local traffic.

Jon punched out his destination and waited for the controls to guide him onto the highway. Paul leaned back in his seat and sighed. "It's unnerving to see the military on a campus," he said. "It takes me back to my undergraduate days, except then I was afraid they might shoot me. Now they have nonlethal weapons and they're protecting me." Paul turned toward his friend. "I don't mind about myself, or even about Hidey and Eli, but I can't accept the fact that someone might try to harm the kids."

"They don't view them as kids right now, just as something to fear. Some of the stories I've seen talk about mass minds, or mental telepathy among clones. One even said they might be condemned to doing the same things at the same time. Maybe when they're born, people will regard them differently."

"Will they? I'm not so sure."

The car was guided around the ramp, then shot forward onto the highway. Paul drummed absently on his safety belt, accidentally releasing it. The car buzzed angrily at him and he quickly fastened it again.

"Look at it this way," Jon said. "It could have been worse. Someone might have tried to burn the lab down or bomb it. All you really got were a few disorderly citizens and some rocks through the windows."

"And a few nasty phone calls. I had to change my number."

"And a few students who come by now and then with signs. Think about what could have happened. People still remember how violent New Year's was, a disorderly end to a disorderly century. Most people are quietly fearful now. They'll give you a hard time and I don't doubt they'll pass a law restricting such things in the future. Maybe they'll nail poor Hidey, although I hope not. But after all that, they'll console themselves with the thought that at least it won't happen again."

"You're probably right, Jon." Paul started to relax. "And I've been feeling a little too sorry for myself lately. Right now Hidey's the one who needs sympathy. On top of everything else he got a call from one of his old professors. The man was cursing at him, saying he'd ruined things for every other biologist. Apparently this man thinks that if Hidey had waited and just let the moratorium expire, people in biological research could have taken the time to educate the public, get them used to the idea of possible experiments. He wanted to get a public relations campaign going that would point out possible benefits of genetic research that was carefully controlled."

"The man might be right. You do have to consider the society around you. Science doesn't work in a vacuum, figuratively speaking. What did Hidey say?"

"He exploded. He said that if science had to wait for a consensus every time something new was tried, we'd still be living in trees and eating raw meat. He said a few other things too."

"I wouldn't have expected such an oversimplification from Hidey, Paul. Surely he realizes that a scientist could accomplish little without some support from the society around him. How much did Leonardo da Vinci really do with his ideas? Renaissance Italy wasn't ready for them. And the society has a lot to do with how science is used, as you've heard a thousand times."

"Funny you should say that," Paul said. "Hidey said pretty much the same thing once he was off the phone and calmed down. But he also said it's both the gift and the curse of the scientist that regardless of these considerations, he keeps trying new things and looking for new answers. He can't help it and sometimes it's almost a compulsion. You found another interest so you left science. Hidey and I are still looking. Knowledge can't be supplied before we can think of what to do to help ourselves."

Paul could see Alasand in the distance. The arcology was a large hexagonal latticework, narrow at the top and bottom and wide across its middle. It towered over the surrounding forests and parks. A million people lived in Alasand or owned businesses there. They had the advantages of city life while living near wilderness. As Alasand glittered in the sunlight it resembled a giant's abandoned toy. The traffic thinned out a little as cars were guided off the highway toward the arcology.

"Sometimes," Paul went on, "I think we're all born scientists. When we're children we always explore, asking a lot of questions and trying different things to see if they work. But we get it knocked out of us. It's our most natural impulse and so many grow up to hate it."

Suddenly the car began to slow down. It came to a stop quickly and Paul could feel his belt holding him as he moved forward, then fell back.

The cars around them had stopped too. Paul looked over at the part of the highway going in the opposite direction. The cars there had halted also.

"I think we're going to be late for dinner," Jon said. "I hope it doesn't take them too long to make repairs."

They could do nothing but wait in the car which could not be driven manually while still on the highway. It was dangerous to get out since traffic could start moving again at any time.

"This is the first time," Paul said, "I ever heard of the highway breaking down."

"Everything seems to, sooner or later," Jon muttered. "If it isn't the equipment, it's the computers or the technicians or a strike." The car's air cooling system had stopped functioning also. Paul leaned over and rolled down his window.

"Hey, mister." A burly bearded man in the car on Paul's right was leaning out his window. The man had aparently removed his belt and harness. "You know what the hell's happening?"

"Probably a computer failure, an overload maybe," Paul replied. "About all we can do is wait." He didn't tell the man it might take a while. Modern transportation systems rarely suffered breakdowns and were doubt-less more efficient than their predecessors. But if the repairs needed were complex, and they usually were, specialists would have to be rushed to the source of the problem and would take their time repairing it.

The people in the car on Paul's left began to honk their horn. Paul glanced at them and saw that the car had five teenagers in it. One of them opened a door and stepped out onto the highway. He was a tall boy dressed only in a pair of green shorts. He stumbled a bit as he came closer to Jon's car.

"Get back in your car," Jon shouted at the boy. "It's dangerous standing out there."

The boy peered into the car with expressionless gray eyes. "We're not going anywhere," he said softly. "I might as well get some air."

"These cars could start moving any minute," Jon went on. The boy watched him coldly. Then he turned away and motioned to his companions.

"Come on out," he yelled. The others stumbled onto the road. A small dark girl, giggling loudly, hurried to Paul's side of the car.

"Come on out, mister," she said, grinning. "You're kind of cute for an old man."

"Get back in your car," he said. "These cars might start moving."

"They'd warn us first, wouldn't they? Sure they would." She leaned in the window. Her hands, dancing on the car door, seemed to have a life of their own, disconnected from her body. Her black eyes were glazed.

She's on something, Paul thought. One of her friends, a tall lean black girl dressed in a loincloth and beads, was hollering at the burly man on his right. Paul had heard of the kids who cruised the automated highways, punching out distant destinations while they drugged themselves in their cars. There was little that anyone could do about the situation as long as the young people endangered no one else, which they were unlikely to do as long as they remained on the automated highways.

Someone pulled the dark-haired girl away from his win-

dow. Paul found himself gazing at a scholarly-looking
boy with glasses and freckles.

"Excuse me," the boy said. His tongue seemed to trip
over the words. "I feel kind of sick. You got any stomach
stuff?"

"I'm sorry but I don't."

"That's too bad. I think I'm going to vomit." The
boy's speech was slurred. He squinted at Paul. "I've
seen you," he said in sonorous tones. "I know who you
are, I know I do. I watch the news a lot." The boy sighed.
Paul could hear the black girl and the burly man exchanging remarks. "You're the guy with the clones,
Paul Swenson. You want to hear a good one? What's
two identical tornadoes? Bet you can't guess." The boy
paused. "Cyclones." Paul could feel the perspiration on
his face grow cold.

The discovery seemed to galvanize the boy. "Hey!"
he screamed at his companions. "It's Paul Swenson over
here in this car!"

"Who's he?" the small dark-eyed girl asked. The black
girl came to the window and glared at Paul.

"He's the man," she said slowly, "who thinks he's
so damn fine there should be more of him around."

"What the hell," the burly man said. He was leaning
far out of his window now, thick arms over the car door,
staring at Paul with astonishment. "You're some kind
of a pervert, Swenson, you know that? Why can't you
have kids like a normal dude instead of freaks? Haven't
you got balls?"

Paul felt a tap on his shoulder and turned. "Paul," Jon
said, "one of the kids passed out on the road." Jon
unfastened his belt. "We've got to get him back in the
car fast."

"Do you think his friends will let us?"

Jon did not answer. He was already opening his door.
Paul released his own belt.

The tall boy and the black girl had moved toward the
car on Paul's right. "You fat bastard," the boy shouted
at the burly bearded man. He opened the man's car door
suddenly and the man tumbled into the road. "I don't

like your looks and I don't like you calling Corinne a black savage." The man, on his knees now, was trying to stand up. The boy began to kick him in the stomach.

Paul was out of the car and beside the boy without thinking. He pulled him away from the man, then felt nails digging into his arm. The black girl was clawing at him. He thrust her away.

Frightened faces peered out of the nearest cars. He would get no help from anyone else, he knew that. No one would risk getting out into the road.

"Come on, Swenson," the tall boy said. He circled Paul, weaving uncertainly. "I can take you. I can take you and your clones all at once. Come on." The boy threw a punch. Paul stopped it with his left arm and managed almost accidentally to hit the boy in the stomach. The boy groaned, then leaned over and vomited into the road.

The two girls had disappeared. Paul helped the burly man to his feet. The man got inside his car and Paul helped him fasten his belt. "Are you all right?"

"I don't know," the man answered. "I think so."

"There's a hospital at Alasand. Punch out at the next exit and drive over to it just to be sure."

"Thanks, Swenson."

The tall boy had stopped vomiting and was leaning against the side of Jon's car. Paul grabbed him by the arm and propelled him toward the left side of the highway. As they approached the boy's car, he noticed that the freckled boy was already climbing inside. The two girls were in the back seat with the boy who had passed out. Paul pushed the tall boy into the car.

"Why should there be five of you?" the black girl shouted at him. The dark-eyed girl was giggling softly. Paul stood in the road trying to figure out what to do next. He was afraid to leave the young people alone in their car, hurtling to whatever destination they had. The freckled boy was moaning softly, holding his stomach.

"Paul!" Jon shouted. "Get inside, now!" Cars all around him buzzed furiously in warning. He dived for the driver's seat, barely slamming the door behind him before the car began to move forward on the highway.

The car was still buzzing. Paul fastened his belt. He was breathing heavily.

"That was close," Jon said, wiping his face.

"Those kids," Paul said. His hands were trembling slightly. He realized he was sweating profusely. He suddenly felt frightened, although he was now safe in the car. The highway looked the same as it usually did, streams of cars rushing to their destinations.

"Are you all right now?" Jon asked.

"I'm fine." Paul closed his eyes. *I must be getting old,* he thought to himself, *I can't handle things well any more, I'm either a passive observer or I do everything wrong.* What he should have done, he told himself now, was put two or three of the kids in Jon's car, gotten into the kids' car himself, and met Jon at the Alasand hospital with them. There was no telling what they had taken or what its effects might be. All they could do now was call the emergency center at the hospital and give them the car's license number and the direction in which it was traveling.

Paul overrode the previous destination and punched out the next exit on the dashboard controls. Then he clenched his teeth angrily. *Why should I care about a bunch of idiotic kids who could have got themselves and me killed?* Perhaps the drug had only brought out a viciousness that was already present. The anger subsided, leaving a residue of shame. He was being unfair. They were not doing anything that different from what he had done at their age. He had once possessed the aggressiveness and impatience of the gray-eyed boy and the uncertainty of the freckled boy. He had gone to parties and taken whatever the others took. It had been fear of what might happen to him that made him stop, nothing more.

Still, he had been sheltered from the world's irrationality until recently, exploring his scholarly interests. He thought of his children-to-be. If left alone by the public, they would grow up in the same sheltered atmosphere and perhaps be unable to deal with others unlike themselves. If, on the other hand, they were overly exposed to the publicity and occasional cruelties they might encounter, they might retreat from the world, hurt and bitter.

But were his worries any different from those any parent might have? Becoming a parent for the first time should worry any sane person and his circumstances were more troublesome than most. Maybe he was, at almost fifty years of age, a little old to be embarking on parenthood for the first time. But he could make up for that. He had experienced more than many younger parents. He also knew more about what his kids would be like than most parents did. He almost chuckled at this. It would not be hard for him to put himself into the place of one of them when sympathy was needed.

The car turned off the highway and buzzed at him as it circled the ramp. Paul took control and drove along the road until he saw a pic-phone booth on the side. He pulled over.

Jon unbuckled his belt. "I'll make the call," he said, opening his door.

Paul hoped once again that the teenagers would be all right.

Paul was nervous. He stood next to Zuñi and Bill in the laboratory and wondered how he should feel. He would be a parent, probably before the hour was over if everything went as expected. He felt anticipation and anxiety displacing each other in rapid succession.

"If they *do* take after me," he said to Zuñi, "they should each weigh a little under eight pounds." She watched him, then placed a calming hand on his arm.

Mort Jason was standing to one side of the ectogenetic chambers, accompanied by a cameraman. A sound recorder was in a small pouch at Jason's waist; in his hand the reporter carried a slender silver wand no larger than a finger. They had given Jason the story as an exclusive in return for a sizable sum of money from his syndicate. Their decision had been motivated partly by fear of having the room overrun by reporters and partly by economic necessity. Paul would put his share in a fund for his children but Hidey and Eli would need theirs to sustain themselves during their two-year suspension. Hidey, never one to save money, was already deeply in debt. Emma, who had somehow hung on to her psychiatric practice in spite of adverse publicity, had refused her share.

The small laboratory next door was set aside as a temporary nursery. The clones would stay there for the next few days for observation and protection from infection. Then Paul would take his children home.

Hidey entered the room and closed the door behind him. He was the last to arrive. Outside in the hall, Paul heard the chatter of reporters milling around and waiting for pictures of the children after their "birth." Hidey walked over to Paul and grasped his hand.

"Did you bring a box of cigars with you?" he asked Paul.

"Nope."

"You should have." Hidey looked solemn then. "The Senate passed that bill last night. It'll be almost as strict as the moratorium. Now it goes to the House. It'll probably be law by October. It will allow the use of ectogenetic chambers from the time of conception and a bit more research on genetically inherited diseases and not much else."

"Did anyone vote against it?" Bill asked.

"Garson, Jimenez, and Langer. Langer didn't think it was strict enough. I took the liberty of sending Garson and Jimenez a telegram of thanks. They're finished politically."

Jabbar came up to them. "We're about ready," he said. Paul followed the two men over to the sink near the chambers and stood with them as they washed their hands in disinfectant. Nancy Portland was giving sterile face masks to all the people in the room. There were not many of them: Jason and his cameraman, two lab assistants, Zuñi and Bill, Emma Valois. Nancy handed Paul his mask.

"What are you doing with your money, Nancy?" he asked, trying to lose some of his nervousness in conversation.

"I may go to a health resort and try to lose weight,

believe it or not. Then I'll come back here and dazzle every man in sight." She rolled her brown eyes in mock flirtation. "Or else I'll travel and eat at the world's best restaurants. I haven't decided."

Paul began to fasten his mask. "Don't get too thin, Nancy, you'll be malnourished."

"You're a sweetheart, Swenson. No one ever accused me of being malnourished." The heavy woman grinned at him.

Emma, Zuñi, and Bill had retreated to the far side of the room. Paul stood awkwardly next to Hidey, feeling useless but wanting to be as close as possible to the chambers. He could see the clones, fully formed now, curled in their wombs. Next to him on one of the lab tables were five small beaded bracelets for the children, each with a name: Edward, Michael, Albert, James, and Kira. He had not given them unusual names, feeling that they would have enough problems, and naming one "Paul, Junior" seemed inappropriate under the circumstances. *I hope*, he thought, *I'll be able to tell the boys apart*. Jabbar tapped him on the shoulder and Paul put on the white coat held out to him. Nancy had disappeared into the next room.

"We're ready," Jabbar said. Paul suddenly felt panic. *Wait*, he saw himself shouting, *are you sure? Have you checked everything?* Instead, he waited silently. He remembered stories of fathers who had psychological labor pains. He had never met one of those fathers. His muscles tensed.

Jabbar moved over to the first chamber and pulled a small lever on the console beneath it. Paul watched as the flexible material containing the infant began to open at the side. Hidey reached in and gently removed the child. Jabbar cut the umbilical, then Hidey held the child by the legs as he patted its buttocks.

The infant, still covered partially by membrane, gave a lusty yell.

Paul trembled with relief. One of the assistants took the child into the next room to be bathed and placed in a bassinet. Then Jabbar moved to the next chamber and the second child, then the third. It all seemed so rapid to Paul, the birth, the cry, the baby cradled in the arms of an assistant. He was trying to record all the details of each birth in his mind. *Someday I'll have to tell them about it.*

The last one removed from her chamber was the little girl but she made up for it by giving the loudest cry. Hidey took her into the room next door himself. Paul followed with the small beaded bracelets.

The small room had been equipped with sinks, five bassinets, and a small stove for preparing formula. Heavy plate glass divided the room in half, separating the place where the children were from the part of the room next to the hall. Reporters could enter the room from the hallway and see them without risking contamination.

Paul handed the bracelets to Jabbar for sterilization, then peered into the bassinets. They seemed so tiny and frail, these identical infants. He was almost afraid to touch them. Then he noticed that each had a tiny mole on the right shoulder exactly like his own. Their eyes were bright blue as all newborns' were, but within six months he would see his green eyes in each face and brown hair on their presently bald heads. *This is what I looked like, exactly.*

"They're so small," he said at last. "Have they been weighed yet?"

Nancy Portland nodded. "Right after we brought them in here. The boys are eight pounds and two ounces each and the girl is eight pounds exactly." Nancy scribbled something on her note pad. "How much did you weigh, Paul?"

"A little under eight pounds."

Nancy raised her eyebrows. "Score one point for the chamber. Not only does it work, which we already knew, it's an improvement." She walked away and Paul looked back at his children. He hoped they would not grow up to believe they were only part of an experiment.

Jabbar was at his side, holding out a bracelet. "Would you like to put these on them, Paul?"

"I'd be all thumbs. You'd better do it for me." Jabbar

nodded. He attached Kira's first, then one around each boy's wrist.

The children were crying, not tearfully, but loudly nonetheless. Hidey came over to him and watched them. "They've got good lungs," he said, "and they definitely take after your side of the family."

"What other side is there?" Paul replied, smiling.

"Well, we've done our job. Now we just have to watch them grow up. What people do with these techniques may depend on what kind of people they become. That's a lot of responsibility to place on them, I know."

"It's a lot of responsibility for me as a parent, Hidey."

"You'll have plenty of assistance from Eli and me, we've got at least two years of spare time."

Paul leaned over Kira's bassinet. They were his children, yet closer to him than children. They were his twins, his brothers, and a sister too, separated from him only by age.

"Okay if we let in those reporters?" Hidey asked. "We gave them the word, no bright lights and keep the noise down."

"Fine," Paul said.

The reporters crowded together on the other side of the glass, cameras aimed, tape machines busy, a multi-legged, many-eyed, curious being. *They're just babies,* Paul wanted to shout, *not monsters or genetic freaks, just babies. Make sure your cameras catch that.*

Instead he reached over for Kira and picked her up, cradling her tiny diapered form in his arms. She pouted at him, puffing her cheeks. "You'll be all right," he said to her.

Then he held her out to the reporters and smiled defiantly. "My daughter," he said to them through the glass, and felt pride in the words.

Kira let out a loud cry.

"The nature of the bond between parents and their children, not to mention everyone's values about the individual's uniqueness, could be changed beyond recognition, and by a science which they never understood but which until recently appeared to provide more good than harm."

—James D. Watson
"Moving Toward the Clonal Man," in The Atlantic

"It is not mere sensationalism . . . to ask whether the members of human clones may feel particularly united, and be able to cooperate better, even if they are not in actual supersensory communication with one another."

—Gordon Rattray Taylor
THE BIOLOGICAL TIME BOMB

"Two like faces, neither of which makes us laugh when we see it alone, make us laugh when we see them together, because of their likeness."

—Blaise Pascal

2. Edward: 2016

EDWARD Swenson circled around the university campus, feet pounding against the hard surface of the road leading to his home. The house was about two miles away along this circuitous route. He paced his running almost automatically, moving his legs in a slow easy rhythm. His arms, bent at the elbows, kept time, alternating with his feet.

The autumn air had grown colder and sharper. Soon he would have to do his running at the indoor track his school shared with the university. He almost shuddered at the thought. He preferred to run by the road, alone. At the track he would see other people and could only hope that they would not recognize him or pay him little attention.

He left the campus behind him. The silvery towers surrounding a central courtyard, the glassy squares, rounded ziggurats, and stony gray rectangles which seemed to clutter the hollow below him, disappeared. He passed a coppery cylinder, a student dormitory, nestled among the almost denuded trees, and reached the most peaceful part of his journey. Ahead of him lay about half a mile of deserted road, bounded only by trees and shrubbery on both sides. He smelled dead leaves and heard them crackle under his feet. Parts of the road were strewn with them, bright red, orange and yellow shapes against the pavement. The wind rustled them and the trees sighed.

Ed had not joined any of the informally organized student groups that worked out on the outdoor track, nor had he tried out for the almost-professionalized school cross country team. He had rationalized his decision. He did not have time for the afternoon practices, the frequent trips to other cities for meets, he probably would not have made the team anyway, he preferred spending his time on extra math and music courses. Yet his brothers Al and Mike were on the soccer team and seemed to have plenty of time left over for more intellectual pursuits.

The truth is I don't want to be around anybody who thinks I'm a freak. It was better not to risk embarrassment and surreptitious remarks, to avoid any activity that might require camaraderie or close personal contact with others. In the winter he would be on the chess team, where nothing was asked of him except expertise and concentration. For enjoyment, he had his violin and music. For companionship, he had his sister and brothers. For advice, he had Paul, to whom he often felt closer than to the others.

He had left the road, turning into a side street. He began to pass houses in various states of repair, some with leaves neatly raked into piles along the road, others with toys carelessly thrown into the yards. His calf muscles were aching as he approached his own house, a rambling wooden two-floor structure set on a small hill at the end of one of the side roads. The suburban neighborhood was unpretentious, inhabited mainly by young couples, some students, and older people who could not afford to live in arcologies, new apartments or country houses. Several of the houses were owned by people who had pooled their government allotments and chose to pursue their own interests rather than working. Ed passed a split-level where one such group had started a business selling hand-made furniture and another that was actually a small restaurant. The police ignored these small businesses, which operated in violation of obsolete zoning laws. The successful businesses would probably, in time, move to new locations.

Ed had often thought about his father's reasons for staying in the run-down area. Paul had given several reasons for not moving: he enjoyed being near the university, where his work was; he doubted he could get used to an arcology; country houses were too isolated; he did not like cities; he had been nomadic enough in his youth and wanted to stay where he had roots.

But there were other reasons Paul had not mentioned. Ed and the others had pieced together the story of their first year of life from computer records. That year had been a time of turmoil for their father. Paul had gone to court to establish his right to bring up his children, defending that right against a move to declare the clones wards of the United States government. His lawyer had cited an early twentieth-century case in which a set of quintuplets had been declared wards of the Canadian government and the detrimental effect the action had on those children. Paul won the case, setting a precedent for the future. But it had cost him time and money. He had not regained his university teaching post until the clones were seven and he at last had acquired some financial stability. He could not have afforded to move before.

But Paul had emotional ties to the house as well. He rarely talked about Eviane but she was still present in the house. The books and papers she had written were on Paul's shelves and her photograph peered out inconspicuously from a corner of his desk. Her ashtrays, scattered throughout almost every room in the house, were never used except by visitors, yet Paul never put them away.

Ed slowed down as he reached the driveway leading up to his home and jogged slowly up to the front porch. Paul was probably still at the university and Kira was undoubtedly hanging around the biological sciences building pestering Dr. Takamura. She had persuaded him to give her a job during the summer and had been surprised, Ed knew, when she discovered that the job was nothing more than keeping track of equipment, cleaning out test tubes, and taking on any little jobs the regular staff did not feel like doing. But she had not complained, except to Ed and the rest of the family. She was now hoping to get more important work at the biological center. Kira had already decided she wanted to study biology and took courses at the university three days a week, showing up at the high school on the other two days. This wasn't unusual; many of the high school students had the same kind of arrangement. Ed himself studied calculus and topology two days a week at the university and he was sure Al and Mike would have made similar arrangements if they were not playing soccer. Jim, of course, went his own way.

Ed opened the door and walked toward the stairs. He needed a shower. "Hey," a voice called from the kitchen. Ed changed course and headed toward the voice.

Jim was seated at the kitchen table, chewing on the remains of a large sandwich. He looked up at Ed, brushing some of his long disorderly brown hair off his face with one arm.

"Hello," Jim said. "No one's here. Our athletic brethren have practice this afternoon." Jim grimaced at the words. "I don't know why they waste their time."

"You wasted plenty of time with them yourself last year," Ed replied.

His brother shrugged. "I didn't know any better. I think Coach Anders just wanted us on that damn track team so he could get publicity."

"He also wanted you because you were good runners," Ed said quietly.

"Then why the hell didn't you go out for the team? You're as good at the mile as we are. You can hardly help that."

"You know why not." But Ed also knew that the reason he refused to join a team was the same reason his brother Mike had for joining one. Mike was almost obsessed with being like other people. Al participated in sports because he enjoyed them, Mike because they helped make him more socially acceptable. From Mike's point of view, it was practical to get along with other people and try to be accepted as an individual. Yet at the same time Mike was able to hold himself apart from others, avoiding the danger of pain or rejection. He would go through the motions but retain his personal shield.

"Maybe Mike is right," Jim said suddenly, as if sensing what Ed was thinking. "But he won't change what we are. We're stuck. We may as well accept it." Jim gestured dramatically with his bread crust, then stuffed it into his mouth.

What difference does it make?, Ed thought. Mike went through the motions of sociability, Al treated everyone with the same friendly impartiality, Kira spent most of her time with biologists and other older people who at least tried to treat her fairly, Jim was openly obnoxious and antagonistic, and Ed kept to himself. They had all wound up in the same solitary place with only each other for company.

It seemed to Ed that they were constantly having to prove themselves to people now. When they had been younger, they had enjoyed playing tricks on those who could not tell them apart. Even Kira as a child, with her short hair and overalls, had been mistaken for one of the boys. When they were eight, they had played what seemed a masterful trick at the time.

Their elementary school classroom had not been unusual. It contained microfiche readers, simple machines designed to teach basic skills and several more specialized computer devices and learning machines. All of this was arranged in apparently random order about the cheerful yellow room with desks, tables, and chairs grouped in the center. Their teacher and her aide would normally supervise them on basic skills, oversee discussions, tests, language practice and music listening, then allow them time with the more specialized machines, testing them on what they had learned after that. They were supposed to alternate among the more specialized machines, spending only a certain amount of time at each so they would have practice in many areas.

Ed could not remember who first thought of the trick,

although he suspected it had probably been Al or Jim. Instead of alternating among the machines, they were to choose one machine each and remain there for the alloted time. Ed chose one of the math machines, leaving it for a few minutes at a time and then returning, becoming in turn Mike, Al, Jim, or Kira to the other children in that part of the room. Occasionally he would glance at Mike, who was busily constructing holographic models on the screen of a computer designed to teach mechanics and they would giggle, astonished at their cleverness.

It was then that Ed discovered his love for numbers. He became entranced by the math machine and fascinated by its geometrical models, which showed him an entirely new world of abstract beauty. The other clones had the same reactions to their own machines. Kira ran evolutionary projections on her computer and soon started to experiment with seeds and tadpoles at home. Jim spent his time on a reading machine, occasionally moving to one which taught history. Al and Mike began to set up experiments with pendulums and planed surfaces, and Al was soon spending afternoons struggling to read Paul's elementary texts on astrophysics.

Ed often wondered if that little prank was the beginning of their differing interests. They had chosen their machines for the trick completely by chance. At any rate, their teacher had discovered their prank when each of them began to fail tests on skills they had not learned. She had humiliated them in front of their classmates with a lecture, then called Paul on the phone, telling him the whole story. She told him that he would have to send the clones to school with name tags so she could tell them apart.

Ed recalled how Paul had struggled to restrain a chuckle when he conveyed the teacher's message to them. Yet he had complied with the request by sewing their names on their overalls; perhaps he suspected that they would switch their pinned-on tags.

Ed and the others had been embarrassed. Their classmates had resurrected old clone jokes for the occasion. Being a clone no longer seemed very funny. Their teacher

had not been sympathetic to them either. Ed realized
now that she had felt threatened by the computers. The
machines, with their programmed tests and attractive
components, seemed to be stealing her job, reducing her
to a supervisor. Parents had the right to allow their children to learn on computers at home, as long as the
children spent some time with others their own age in
child care centers or at hostels. Most were in schools only
because of custom or because their parents did not
care to supervise them at home. Their own teacher had
taken out her resentment on the clones because of their
trick. But at the time, Ed had thought her an old crank
who insulted and belittled the machines as she lectured
them on their behavior.

"Paul's going to the moon," Jim said. A shock ran
through Ed's body. He straightened involuntarily in his
chair.

"What are you talking about?"

"Dr. Aschenbach called before and asked if he had
decided about going. I guess some people there asked
him to come. I know he'll go, maybe he'll ask us first
if he should but. . . . " Jim did not finish the sentence.
He's always wanted to go, his eyes told Ed. *Don't tell
him to stay.*

Ed felt stranded and alone. *He can't.*

He will anyway. Jim leaned back in his chair, balancing
it precariously on two legs. "I'm going to the city this
weekend with Joey and Olive. Olive's uncle runs a hotel
and we can stay there for nothing. She said he'd let
us have a suite."

"What are you going to do?"

"I don't know. Throw a party. Get drunk. Joey has
some stuff from his older brother's plants he's bringing
along with him, and some mood-changers."

"Paul won't want you to go," Ed said.

"He can't stop me. I'm sixteen now, I have the right
to do anything I want that doesn't hurt others or isn't
physically, psychologically, or socially harmful or illegal."

"Getting drunk's illegal for you, taking moods is illegal
for anybody without a doctor's supervision, and hanging

around with Joey and Olive is what I'd call psychologically harmful."

Jim sighed. "You never miss a chance to insult my friends."

"I don't like them," Ed said, "and I don't know why you spend any time with them. I don't know anybody who likes them, they're so damn sophisticated, always acting as though they know more than anybody. All Olive cares about is parties and spending half the night with old guys in her car. I don't know how her parents can afford the rent on that car. And Joey's still on probation." Joey, technically gifted, had jammed the transmission in Olive's car, causing all the cars in his lane on the automated highway to come to a stop and nearly bringing about a serious accident. He had been saved from serious punishment only because of his age. "You don't like them any better than anyone else, Jim," Ed went on. "I know it."

"At least they don't treat me like a freak," Jim said angrily. He paused for a moment, as if realizing that he had not refuted Ed's statements. "Besides, Joey's an interesting person and Olive's one of the best artists at school. Jesus, if I'm going to be a writer I should have experience, meet different kinds of people."

"What a rationalization."

"It's the truth. I suppose you'll go to Paul now and tell him what we're going to do."

"You should know better than that. It's your decision, you'd go even if Paul said no. And it's none of my business anyway." Ed got up. "I have to take a shower."

He left the kitchen, annoyed with his brother. Jim always seemed to enjoy self-destructive situations and bizarre experiences. Ed had often heard his brother vomiting late at night in one of the bathrooms, sick from drugs or drinking. Paul had not forbidden Jim to see his friends but he had told him never to bring Olive and Joey to the house after Joey had stolen a bottle of scotch.

Ed climbed the stairs and walked down the hallway. He opened the door to his room. His bed, covered with an orange blanket, was against the wall on his right. His desk was in the corner to his left, separated from the bed

by a small night table under his window. He noticed that
he had left his barbells in the center of the room. Picking them up, Ed placed them inside the small closet
beside his door. Jim even kept a messy room, he thought
to himself, full of print-outs, piles of old books on the
floor and in almost every available space, a worn imitation Oriental rug in the center of the room, and various
useless artifacts Jim had bought in antique stores. Jim did
at least keep this mass of articles clean and seemed to
know where everything was, but the room had no sense
of order.

Ed pulled off his sweatshirt, then sat down in the
orange chair near his desk. As he untied his shoes he
tried to push these thoughts out of his mind. He would
take his shower, then try to clear his mind with some
meditation before dinner. He would avoid for the time
being the idea of Paul's prospective lunar journey and
ignore the apprehension that threatened to knot his
stomach and stiffen his spine.

They usually ate supper crowded around the kitchen
table. The dining room table, in the room between the
living room and the kitchen, was larger but they all preferred the informality of the kitchen during weekdays.

Paul, seated across the rectangular wood table from
Ed, seemed tired. Paul usually enjoyed cooking, feeling
that it relaxed him after work. They often helped him
prepare dinner, taking turns on different nights. But
tonight Paul had simply broiled some fish and steamed
some carrots and peas. Al had groaned when he came
to the table and saw the simple meal, subsiding when
Paul suggested that if he didn't like it he was free to
cook his own dinner.

Jim, seated on Ed's left, was struggling to drink a
cup of bitter black coffee with a straight face. Jim usually
refused the glass of milk the others drank and had
settled on the black coffee as a reasonably sophisticated
substitute. Kira, her short wavy brown hair held back
from her face by a white band, waved her fork as she
discussed her day at the biological center with Paul. Al

and Mike, seated on Ed's right, were commenting on what seemed to Ed some rather esoteric points about soccer, punctuating their conversation with raucous locker-room laughter. Both Al and Mike had grown impressive handle-bar moustaches in imitation of their coach and a few of the other athletes.

Paul lifted his wine glass and sipped. His green eyes met Ed's for an instant. *He's old*, Ed thought suddenly, and something within him panicked. He swallowed some milk quickly. *But sixty-six isn't old.* A reasonably healthy person could expect to reach a hundred with proper care and anti-aging shots. Of course Paul had only recently begun to take the shots; the government, still fearful of social consequences and uncertain about long-range effects, limited the shots to those already over sixty-five. Some people refused the shots, feeling perhaps that it was futile to prolong their later years. Even so, the shots had raised average life expectancy to over ninety and could postpone many old-age ailments until that time. Paul was still a healthy and youthful man capable of running a couple of miles a day or playing a vigorous set of tennis. His silver hair was thick and his face, aided by his high cheekbones, could have been that of a younger man. But there were lines etched around Paul's large eyes and sensitive mouth. His arms had grown thinner and his waist thicker with time. He was much older than the parents of Ed's classmates. Ed began to feel threatened in some indeterminate way by his father's age.

"You haven't said much tonight, Ed," Paul said. "Something wrong?"

"He *never* says much," Al replied. Ed glared at his brother.

"He speaks when he has something to say," Kira said, "unlike some people."

Paul's brow was slightly furrowed. "Maybe we can get out our violins later and play together, we haven't done that for a while."

"Okay," Ed mumbled.

"Dr. Aschenbach called you before," Jim said loudly. "He wants to know if you decided about going to the

moon yet." The others turned toward their father in
unison, heads tilted to one side.

"What?"

"When?"

"What trip is this?"

"I was going to discuss that with you tonight," Paul
said, returning Jim's belligerent gaze with a calm one.
"Since Jim brought it up, we may as well talk about it
now."

"There's nothing to talk about," Jim said. "If you
have the chance you should take it."

"Wait a minute," Paul went on, "I think you should
know what this will involve. I'll be gone all month, until
the beginning of December. The university's giving me
a small appropriation but the rest has to come out of my
own pocket. The lunar astronomical facilities are short
of funds right now. That means we'll have to cut down
on car rentals for a while and try to get along with the
one we own for the most part."

"We can get along," Jim said impatiently. "We can use
the trains."

"*You* can get along," Al said. "Not all of us have
friends with cars." He glared pointedly at Jim. Jim stared
back at his brother blandly.

Ed looked away from Al and back at his father. "I
also have to assume," Paul said, "that you're all responsible enough to look after things around here." His eyes
rested first on Jim, then on Al. "Jon is willing to look in
on you from time to time and I imagine Hidey will too
but you'll be on your own. Now I don't think I've been
too hard on you. I don't like to police everything you
do, but I won't be around to referee your battles or get
you out of trouble. And you won't be able to call me up
every time you want to talk about something without
bankrupting me." He looked at Ed.

Ed looked down at his plate. He talked to Paul more
often than the others. He would be the loneliest if Paul
left. *When* Paul left. He had already made up his mind,
Ed was sure, and was now simply settling the details.

"If you want, you could all stay at the hostel near the

school, at least for some of the time," Paul continued.

"No, we couldn't," Mike said bluntly. "We'd look ridiculous."

"Why? There are plenty of children who don't live with their parents or who stay there on occasion. They can do pretty much what they want to, the people living with them seem easygoing."

Ed glanced at Mike. "Paul, you don't understand," Mike replied, brushing a crumb from his moustache. "Those are younger children. When someone our age stays there, it looks silly if a parent still has custody. It looks as if your parents think you're a baby or don't trust you."

"Pardon me," Paul said, obviously trying to repress a smile. "I wasn't aware of the social restrictions."

Ed picked at his vegetables. He knew his father should go on his trip. The moon was becoming the real center of astrophysical research and Paul should have gone there before now. Space, in fact, was becoming the center of a lot of things. Many industries had orbiting factories and research facilities. Orbiting hospitals were used for certain types of operations. The United Nations and various governments maintained weather control stations, satellites that monitored earth resources and aided in the control of pollution, and communications satellites. The moon itself, once only a place for research, was becoming more populated and industrialized. Humanity, after spending time consolidating its gains, was once again looking outward and beginning to dream.

He knew the Lunar scientists might need Paul, even for a short time. Some of them were trying to realize Paul's dream of star flight. Two probes had already been sent out beyond the solar system. A few people were already lobbying for a human expedition to the stars if the probes reported anything worth investigating.

Paul could survey the work of the scientists, make suggestions, notice things that perhaps the scientists themselves, too close to the project, might not have noticed. At the very least, he would be stimulated and involved again instead of retiring to the sidelines. Paul should have

gone before and he would have if not for them. Yet Ed
wanted him to stay. He was fearful of being alone.

Don't go, please.

"I can't make my decision," Paul was saying, "without
knowing your feelings. So I'm asking you, and please be
frank. If for some reason you want me to postpone this
trip, tell me. You're all more important to me, you're my
first responsibility."

Ed's throat locked. He looked around the table. Al
and Jim were staring down at their plates. Mike was
looking at Paul.

"You should go," Mike said quietly. "We can certainly
take care of things for a month."

Kira nodded. "You should go," she echoed. "But we'll
miss you, especially at Thanksgiving." She blinked and
looked away.

"What the hell," Al said. "I wish I could go myself.
As long as you fill me in on everything it's all right with
me."

Jim had already expressed an opinion and remained
silent. Kira and Mike were watching Ed. Ed managed
to shrug. "Go ahead," he muttered, trying to smile.

Jim and Al got up and began to clear the table. "I
wanted to go over to the campus for a while," Kira was
saying to Paul. "Dr. Takamura's speaking to a group
tonight on bioethics and I think Mike wanted to go
to the physics building."

"Fine with me," Paul replied. Ed rose and started to
stack the remaining dishes. Anger simmered within him
for a moment. He found himself resenting Paul for wanting to leave and the others for so easily agreeing to his
plans. They had left him no choice but to go along
with them.

"We're staying home," Al shouted from the sink. "Jim
promised to help me with my English paper."

"Just make sure he doesn't write it for you," Paul
shouted back. The older man stood up. Kira and Mike
had left the room and Ed could hear them near the front
door, arguing loudly about something. "Ed," Paul said

more quietly, "how would you like to go for a little ride with me?"

"It's all right with me," Ed replied. *I haven't got anything else to do.*

They had gone to the small park many times in the past. The park was not far from home and only a few people made use of it now with so many other places within easy distance by train or highway. When they had been small, Paul had brought them here for picnics in the summertime. Once they had run into another family who recognized them and pestered them with questions. Paul had told them afterward that the father had commented to him about his own two children having to spend three months in an ectogenetic chamber: "They're twice-borns," the father had said. It had seemed irrelevant to Ed. Anything was more normal than being a clone.

Another time he and Jim had walked to the park with a bottle of bourbon Jim had managed to purchase at a nearby liquor store rarely curious about the age of the buyer. They had been too sick to finish the bottle and barely managed to stagger home for supper. Paul had been mad. After restricting them to the house for a week, he had driven them over to the liquor store, threatening prosecution if the owner ever sold them alcohol again until they were older. Ed had been embarrassed but Jim, the man of the world, had been humiliated.

Often each of them came to the park alone to think in solitude. Even though each of them had a room at home, Paul knew that in a house of six people there were times a person needed to get away. It was also a place where Paul could talk to each of them individually, where each could express feelings freely without feeling constricted by the nearness of the others. Often after these talks Paul would take Ed to a house nearby which doubled as a homemade ice cream parlor. They would have a sundae together and go home with some ice cream for the others. Each of them had had these talks with their father about their problems and Ed knew they usually felt much better about things afterward. Paul

was unlike some parents in that he did not wait for
problems to arise before talking to his children. Several
times a year, he made a point of taking each of them out
to dinner alone and Ed had known him to turn down
other invitations if they conflicted with one of these
planned occasions. Perhaps he realized, Ed thought, that
more than other children, they needed this individual
attention and reassurance.

But now, as Paul's car parked itself in the small lot
at the bottom of a hill, Ed began to feel nervous about
this particular talk. It had grown harder for him to talk
to his father and he no longer felt, as he had when he
was a child, that he could tell Paul everything he felt
and feared.

The two got out of the car and began to walk up the
path on the side of the hill. Paul did not speak until
they reached the top.

Here there was a small grassy area surrounded by
trees on three sides and marked off by a stone wall on
the fourth. The clouds of the autumn sky hid the stars.
Ed wandered over to the stone wall and looked down.
The lights of the automated highway one hundred feet
below glittered and he could hear the hum of passing
automobiles.

Paul joined him at the wall. The air was cool but comfortable in the absence of a wind. Ed could smell dead
leaves and pine trees. He waited silently for his father
to speak.

"You don't want me to go, do you, Ed?" Paul said
quietly. He didn't respond. "I imagine," Paul continued,
"that you don't want to say anything because you feel
pressured by the others, you don't want to be the only
one to say no. If I stayed, you feel it'll be because of
you, since the others already agreed. You might feel
that somehow you've prevented me from doing something
I want to do and you'll feel guilty about it."

Ed was silent.

"Isn't that true?"

Ed nodded.

Paul leaned against the wall and folded his arms across

his chest. "Look, son, I don't want you to feel guilty about anything. My first responsibility is to you kids. I took that on voluntarily and I don't regret it. I don't want to do anything that'll cause you unhappiness. I did most of my important work a long time ago, as far as astrophysics is concerned, and I think of this trip as a luxury. Sure, I'd like to go up there and poke around, but I've kept up on what's going on through the journals and by contacting people who have come back from the moon. It's extremely doubtful that my old mind is going to be of any help on Luna."

"But maybe it will," Ed said almost belligerently. "It's your theories they're working on and at the very least they might be inspired just by having you around, you don't know. And discovering a way to make a star drive work, maybe building a ship, is a lot more important than we are, you know it is. It'll change everything. You should have gone before, and not just for a month but for a year or two years."

"I don't happen to think you are less important than a star drive. Maybe I'm mistaken but I think in time your existence and the research that develops out of cloning and other applications of biological science may change the world as much as a star drive could. I don't think the bans on such research will last. You'll probably live to see other clones born and stranger things than that besides. Anyway, I happen to think my kids are pretty intelligent and my most important job is helping make it possible for you to develop into people who will contribute to the world. I've done my work. Pretty soon it'll be time for you to do yours." He paused. Ed glanced down at the highway and back at his father.

"You know, a lot of crap has been written about me," Paul went on. "Some people call me a great man. Even Hidey mouths those stupidities sometimes." He sighed. "It occurred to me that most so-called great people make the lousiest parents in the world, they're too involved in their work. When I was young, I used to tell my friends that every research scientist, creative artist, or scholar should be sterilized. I didn't want kids then, I was happy working with Eviane, it was my life. If she were still with me I would have been content." Ed was startled at the mention of Paul's dead wife. "But when Hidey decided to go ahead on his project and wanted me to help that life was over. You shouldn't feel that I was giving up anything for you kids. It was already gone. I was lucky to get the chance to begin something new, being a parent. A lot of people don't get that chance at my age. Young people often don't make good parents, they have too many other things to do. If biological science does nothing more than make it possible for more older and experienced people to become parents, I think the world might be a better place with happier children."

Paul smiled. "My God, I can't stop lecturing, can I? You'd think I had enough of it in my classes."

"It's all right," Ed replied. Paul had never been quite as frank with him before. He felt older, and more lonely. *He's asking me to make a decision.* His stomach tightened.

"Well, Ed?"

"I don't think it's fair to ask me to decide," Ed said almost angrily. "Besides, the majority already voted, didn't they? You can't stay just because of me."

"I want to know what you think."

Ed took a deep breath. "Go, Paul. I'm old enough to take care of myself. I wish you would stay, I don't know why, maybe it's just selfishness. I don't have anybody else to talk to, I don't have any friends and I can't really talk to the others the way I used to. They've got other things to do anyway. But I don't want you to stay just because of me."

Paul was silent.

"Besides," Ed continued, "it won't be that long." *I should be glad he thinks we're responsible enough to leave alone.* Instead he felt empty. Suddenly he wanted to throw himself into his father's arms as he had when he was small. He was ashamed of the feeling.

"I know how you feel," Paul said. "A lot of kids are lonely at your age and it can hurt more than it should. Everything is so much more intense when you're young. But if you can learn to deal with these feelings, overcome them somehow instead of giving in to them—I can't do that for you, Ed. I wish I could."

You have to go. I'd just feel worse if you stayed.

"You wouldn't like it if I stayed anyway, son. By the time I get back, you'll wonder why you were upset about it." Paul moved closer to Ed and threw a comradely arm across his shoulders. "Why don't we go to that new bakery and get fat on some pastries?"

"Sure," Ed said with little enthusiasm. *I have to stop being such a child.* They walked to the path leading back down the hill.

Ed sat in the corner of the Student Resources Center with Cindy Jennick and Harriet Blum, waiting for the two girls to finish the math problem he had given them. His eyes drifted over the shelves of tapes and microfiche books, past the tables surrounded by seated students, past the learning booths at the other end of the room. Inside the clear cubes of the booths sat students, earphones on their heads, listening to lectures or viewing required holographs.

He found himself looking out the large window next to him. Outside, the girls' cross-country team was doing laps. There was Mayli Chung, churning along behind the others, looking tiny in spite of the heavy gray sweatsuit she wore. Ed sighed. He had wanted to ask her out several times but kept putting it off. *Maybe she'll call me.* She never had. He contented himself with sitting next to her in the calculus class at the university, snickering when she passed him a caricature of the professor or one of their classmates.

"Well?" Harriet said. He turned and faced the girls seated across from him. Harriet seemed threatening in her long black dress and dangling gold earrings. She had sprinkled gold dust on her eyelids and cheekbones. She brushed back her long dark hair and pushed a paper toward him with gold-tipped fingers. Cindy was hunched over her paper, scrawling on it with one hand and twirling a strand of her oily blond hair with the other. Cindy's pimply cheeks were perpetually flushed, as if she were constantly feverish. She grunted and Ed caught a whiff of halitosis.

He looked down at Harriet's paper. "Your mistake," he said, "is right here, near the end. See if you can figure out what it is."

"Christ," Harriet said as he shoved the paper back. "I thought I had it this time. I can't do this shit."

Cindy handed him her paper. She watched Ed with her sad brown eyes. "Good, Cindy," he said mechanically. She flushed even more and folded her arms over her large breasts. "Try the next problem."

Harriet was still staring at him. "Why don't you tell me what the mistake is?" she asked.

"I want you to find it yourself this time." He could feel his cheeks reddening as he addressed the girl.

"But I looked at the way you did the last problem, I did mine the same way, I listened to everything you told us before. I just can't do it." For a moment Ed wanted to tell Harriet her mistake just to ward off her blue-eyed stare.

But then she looked down at her paper. "Oh," she said, "*oh*. There it is. Jesus, I'm dumb." She began to work on the next problem.

Ed wished he hadn't decided to tutor the two girls. Still, he hadn't had much choice. The school expected better students to help worse ones.

Cindy, already finished, was waiting for Harriet. The dark-haired girl completed her scrawlings and shoved the paper at Ed.

He looked down at the two papers, Cindy's neatly organized one and Harriet's messy one. "You both got it right," he said, relieved.

"Thank God," Harriet said, standing up. "I'll see you next week, Ed." She turned and strode from the room, her small buttocks bouncing under the shiny fabric of her black dress.

Cindy rose more slowly. Her plaid tunic made the big-boned girl look even larger than she was. She clutched her papers to her chest. "You going home, Ed? I can give you a ride if you want." Her face had grown almost beet-red. "I mean, my father said he'd send the car over, it'll be here any minute."

He looked away from her. "Uh, I have some stuff to do here," he lied.

"Okay," Cindy said. When he looked up she was retreating across the room, tugging at her tunic with one hand.

Paul would not be home. The realization hit him with the force of a fist. He had almost forgotten. They had all been busy for the past week, looking after the house and the meals while Paul taped lectures for his classes. Then they had gone with him to the train station that past weekend to see him off on the first leg of his journey.

Kira had been the first to hug him goodbye at the station, then Jim, then Al. Ed had stood apart with Mike, offering Paul only his hand, ashamed of his sadness and fear.

When he was sure Cindy was gone, Ed got up, pulled on his parka and left the Student Resources Center, striding out the door and down the curving hall past the empty classrooms. The clicks and thuds of his shoes against the tiled floor echoed in the corridor. He remembered lying on the living room floor as a child, struggling against sleepiness but unwilling to go to bed, listening to the comforting murmur of Paul's voice as he talked with his friends. He remembered the first New Year's Eve Paul had let them stay up until midnight and Jim had fallen asleep, aroused at last when the others pummeled him with pillows.

With a longing so strong that it stung him, Ed wished he was a child again. For an instant, he could believe that he would find Paul at home, waiting with a cup of hot chocolate and some conversation.

He came to the school's back exit and opened the door under the impersonal gaze of electronic cameras hidden in the wall. He had gone to school for years watched by the cameras, which were designed to monitor thefts and violence in the building. He and the other students were so used to it that he found it strange when he heard older

people comment about the insidiousness of such devices.
It was easy enough to outwit such things anyway if one
wanted to and no point in worrying about them.

He walked outside across the athletic fields. The school,
a three-tiered round layer cake made of metal and brick,
receded as he approached the road which circled the
university campus and led home. The weekend ahead,
without Paul's companionship, seemed as bleak as the
sky and as empty and cold as the air that whistled round
his head.

Saturday morning was cold and gray, with rain outside
that threatened to become snow. Ed lay in bed for as
long as he could stand it, wishing he could sleep through
the weekend.

He finally got up at ten and wandered down the hall
to one of the bathrooms, planning ways to fill his time.
He could view some lectures in one of the learning booths
downstairs, plan the meals for Sunday—it was his turn
to cook, read that Nabokov novel and discuss it with
Jim before doing his paper, look at the newsfax sheets
when Kira was through with them.

When he went downstairs, Jim was lying on the sofa
with a microfiche reader propped on his stomach. "You're
going to have a hell of a neckache," Ed commented.

Jim turned his head. "I already do." He sat up and
put his portable reader on the floor.

"I thought you were going out with Joey and Olive."

Jim shrugged. "I didn't feel like it."

"Paul isn't here to stop you."

Jim, apparently ignoring the sharpness in Ed's voice,
rubbed his neck with one hand. "I don't know. I guess
I'm kind of bored with them. That's a shitty thing to say
about my friends, but. . . . " His green eyes met Ed's. "I
don't know."

Ed became aware of the house's silence. "Where's
everybody else?"

"Al and Mike went over to Alasand to do some shop-
ping and Kira's over at the university pool, she's thinking of going out for the swimming team. Takamura'll give

her a couple of afternoons off. He doesn't need her hanging around all the time anyway. Besides, she should get out of that place more." Jim sneered. "Our birthplace. That goddamn lab gives me the creeps, God knows what they're up to."

"Not much, with the moratorium."

"I don't know how Kira can stand the place." Jim picked up his reader and settled back on the sofa.

Ed went into the kitchen and took some eggs out of the refrigerator. He began to make an omelet, adding some leftover ham-flavored soy protein. He poured himself a glass of milk and gulped it down while he waited for the eggs. At last he put the omelet on a plate and sat down at the kitchen table. The food seemed tasteless as he chewed and he wondered absently if he should have used more seasoning. In Paul's absence, the meals had gone downhill; none of the Swensons was as good a cook as he was. Ed sighed. He had plenty of time to plan something special for tomorrow. Maybe he would attempt veal and mushrooms in a white sauce. He had watched Paul prepare it often enough.

He heard the humming of a car in the driveway and wondered if Al and Mike were back. As he stood up and put his dishes in the sink, he heard loud knocking at the back door. Puzzled, he crossed the room and opened it.

Joey Melville and Olive Prescott stood there. Olive's hazel eyes flickered across him briefly. "Hello," he mumbled, holding the door open.

"Which one are you?" the girl asked.

"Ed," he answered.

"Peas in a pod," Joey said, chuckling, "peas in a pod." The two shoved past Ed. Their raincoats dripped along the floor, leaving a wet trail beside their footprints. "Where's that brother of yours? Hey, Jim!" Joey pulled off his coat and threw it toward the table. It landed on the floor. Olive's coat followed it. "Jim!" The two walked on through the dining room and Ed found himself picking up the coats and placing them on a chair in silent anger. *I'll have to wipe off the floor now.*

He followed them into the living room. "What the hell are you doing here?" Jim was saying.

Joey fell into a chair across from the sofa and put his hands behind his blond head. Joey was a tall, big-boned boy with large brown eyes set above broad cheekbones. Olive presented a contrast to him with her small-boned, almost fragile, build and dark hair. She perched on the arm of Joey's chair, folding her arms across the front of her red tunic. "You're not supposed to come here," Jim continued.

"What difference does it make? Your father's upstairs with the loonies, so who's to know?" Joey grinned. "Unless Eddie here calls him up long distance, and he wouldn't do that." Ed did not reply. He took a seat by one of the two computer booths in the corner of the room.

"We just wanted to see you, Jim," Olive said in her husky voice. "We haven't seen you for a while. I might almost think you don't like us any more." She stood up, lit a cigarette and dropped the match in one of Eviane's ashtrays.

"Am I dead!" Joey said. "We must have spent all night on the road. You missed a good car party, we must have had eight people inside, friends from the city. One guy was this great big wrestler. I thought he was after Olive, turned out he was after me." Joey snorted. "His mind got so mangled we had to shove him out at this exit a hundred miles away, I don't know how he got back home, probably went to sleep right there."

"I've been busy," Jim said.

"You got a whole damn house to yourself, you should have invited us," Joey said. Olive drifted around the living room, running her hands over the furniture, before settling in a seat next to Ed.

"Are you on the soccer team?" she asked softly.

"No, that's Al and Mike," Ed answered. He clasped his hands together. His arms and legs were suddenly heavy, obstacles to movement. He wanted to get up and flee from the room, retreat upstairs. He was locked to the chair and he could feel himself blushing.

"What do you do?" the girl asked. He found himself staring at her feet.

"I'm interested in math," he answered. "I play the violin and I'm taking some math at the university." *Sounds pretty boring, doesn't it?* He found himself grasping for something else to say. "I'm in the chess club," he added, and immediately felt that made things worse.

"You are?" she said tonelessly. He chanced a quick glance at her face. He met her eyes and quickly looked away again. "I like chess," she went on. Surprised, Ed looked back up. "I'm not very good at it though, so I didn't join the club."

"It doesn't matter," Ed said. "If you practice, you'll get better. That's mainly what the club is for."

"Olive's after Eddie," Joey said loudly. "She's moving on you, boy." He began to smack his lips.

"Shut up and stop acting like a turd," Olive shouted angrily. She turned back to Ed. "Don't pay any attention to him.

"I'm hungry," Joey announced. He got up and went with Jim to the kitchen. Ed waited for Olive to follow them so he could make his departure. Instead she remained seated, still watching him.

"I don't like to do things I'm not good at," Olive said. "I'd rather not do them at all. I'm not good at much so I don't do much." She blew some cigarette smoke toward him. "My mother says I'm incompetent. I think the only reason she had me was so she would have someone to show off in front of. She's a doctor in one of the orbiting sanatoriums so luckily I don't see her much."

Ed felt embarrassed. "If you work at something," he said, "you'll get better at it." The words seemed obvious and trite.

"You sound like Elise," Olive muttered. "She's my father's other partner, she's always telling me that. I have to listen to it every time I go home, so I live in the car most of the time."

"Isn't that expensive?"

"My father's a stormrider, he can afford it." She must not see her father often either, Ed thought. Stormriders spent most of their time in space, watching the weather, ready to harness severe hurricanes magnetically and steer them away from populated areas.

Ed felt warm and closed in by the walls. He prepared to leave the room, searching his mind for an excuse.

"What's it like, being a clone?" Olive asked. The question was a splash of cold water. "I asked Jim once, but he wouldn't say, he didn't want to talk about it. He really got upset."

"I don't know."

"Isn't it weird, I mean, being just like your father and the others?"

"I'm not just like them," he managed to say, swallowing his anger. "We all do different things, we have different interests."

"You're all alike physically."

"So are twins." We're just twins, that's all."

"That isn't the same at all."

He looked over at the girl and thought he detected a gleam in her eye. *She's not interested, it's just one more weird thing for her to do, hanging around with clones.* He could hear someone at the front door and he quickly jumped up, glad for an excuse to leave the room.

Kira entered the house, shaking moisture from her hair. "Hey, who's here? I got a ride home and we noticed a car when we pulled up. . . . " She took off her coat and looked past Ed at Olive. Ed made a face and Kira contorted her own in response before hanging up her coat.

Joey suddenly burst into the living room, clutching the remains of a sandwich. "Look who's here! Hello, sweetheart." He darted toward the hallway and circled around Kira, waving his velveteen-covered arms. He stuffed the rest of the sandwich into his mouth and managed to swat her on the ass before she pushed him away.

"Go to hell," Kira said.

"Joey, stop acting like a turd," Olive shouted. Ed glanced at Jim, who was standing silently in the doorway leading to the dining room. *Why doesn't he say something?* He waited for his brother to act but was already convinced he would do nothing. Jim was too much like

Ed, too intimidated by others, wanting them to accept him as a person like themselves but also convinced that the only people who would ever really know him were the clones.

"I'm going upstairs," Kira said, in effect throwing the situation to her brothers for solution. She turned and Ed listened to her tramp upstairs in heavy-footed, angry fashion. Joey wandered over to Olive and sat in the chair next to her. "What have we here?" he asked, fondling one of her breasts. "What have we here?"

The girl pushed his hand away. "You make me sick sometimes," she murmured to him. Ed, sensing the under-current of violence in her tone, almost shuddered. Olive turned her hazel eyes toward Jim. "And you and your brother give me the creeps," she went on. "Look at you, you're even standing the same way." Ed quickly altered his stance and then realized that Jim was doing the same thing. "You try so hard to be different, going to different classes, wearing different clothes, doing different things, trying to be like everybody else. Well, it won't work. You're still freaks. Your father must be the biggest ego-maniac that ever lived."

Ed noticed that Joey, his face flushed, had subsided into a shocked silence. Jim's face had grown pale. The veins in his neck seemed to bulge and his hands trembled slightly.

Ed moved toward Olive, his fears temporarily forgotten. *Get out of here.* He opened his mouth to say the words. Olive's eyes suddenly turned to him and the hatred flowing from them paralyzed his vocal chords.

"Jesus, Olive," Joey mumbled. The hatred drained from her face, leaving only a cold and empty mask. Ed began to speak once again, then heard his brother's voice.

"I think you'd better go, Olive," Jim was saying. "I know what you really hate. I've been around you long enough. Counting Elise, you have three parents and maybe we only have one, but he cares about us, he wanted us. You can't stand that, can you? And maybe we're physically alike, and we have our problems, I grant you, but we also have someone we can go to when things are bad." Jim paused for breath and leaned dramatically against the dining room entrance. Ed could tell that Jim, although angry, was savoring his words, trying to shape them into weapons that would tear at the girl. Ed knew that his brother, in his strange way, was also enjoying the scene. Jim wanted to strike back at Olive but he wanted the event to be aesthetically pleasing in some way.

"I feel sorry for you," Jim went on. "I can't even get that angry." Ed, watching the tightness of the skin across Jim's face, knew that to be a lie. "Someone cares about us and no one cares about you. Well, I could have cared. I could have been your friend but I won't now. Joey doesn't care, you're just entertaining to him."

Ed saw Olive look at Joey quickly, as if fearing the words were true. The tall blond boy turned away.

"You know something?" Jim said, smiling slightly. "You would have been better off being a clone, Olive. Then someone might have paid attention to you. You're the freak, not us. You're so bad off no one wants to be with you except a bored rich guy and a clone."

Olive choked. A few tears ran down her impassive face as she struggled to control them. Ed, watching her, felt sick.

"You'd better go," Jim said.

"I need a drink," Olive shouted, even now apparently trying to intimidate Ed and his brother into passivity. The picture-phone next to the wall began to buzz. Ed ignored it, waiting to see what else Jim would say.

"You know where the liquor is," Jim said, gesturing with his arm. "Joey, give her a drink and then get her out of here. I don't want to throw you out, but I will."

Ed turned from them and hurried to the buzzing phone. He picked up the receiver and saw the almost life-size face of Jonathan Aschenbach on the large flat screen. The minister's face seemed contorted somehow. His gray eyes stared ahead sadly.

"Hello, Dr. Aschenbach," Ed said. Behind him, he could hear Olive and Joey rummaging through the liquor cabinet in the dining room.

"I just found out, from the latest newsfax sheet," Dr. Aschenbach said. The older man spoke with difficulty. "If there's anything I can do . . . I was just on my way over." He paused and peered out at Ed from the screen. "Oh, dear God. You don't know yet, do you."

"Know what?" Ed clutched at the phone. A hammer seemed to hang over him, ready to smash.

"It's Paul." The minister's eyes filled with tears.

Ed froze. Background noises, the clanking of glasses in the dining room, Jim's muffled pacing on the living room carpet, a low humming sound upstairs, seemed suddenly sharper. "An accident, he was on his way to one of the Russian labs and his flittercraft crashed into a mountainside. There was a quake earlier, they think the driver might not have. . . . "

Ed opened his mouth. *Is he all right? Is he hurt?* The words were locked up and refused to come out.

"He's gone, the Russians got to him and the crew, there were only a few other passengers. They managed to get them all into cryonic storage, but. . . . " Dr. Aschenbach too was groping for words. "They were badly hurt, they can't do anything."

"No." Ed forced the word out. "No." He clamped his mouth shut, afraid a stream of words would flow from him.

"I've called a car, I'll be over there in a few minutes," Dr. Aschenbach continued.

Ed nodded and hung up the phone. The air seemed thick and his body was numb. He turned to Jim.

"Paul's dead," he managed to say, hurling the words at his brother. Then he walked into the dining room. Olive was sipping a pale brown liquid from one of his father's glasses.

"You better leave now," he said. He pulled the glass from Olive's fingers and smashed it against the floor. She retreated toward Joey. "Leave," he shouted.

"But. . . . " Olive murmured. She threw up her hands as if to ward him off.

"Get out, getoutgetoutgetout." The room spun past him. He suddenly found himself at the back door, slamming his fist against the wall. Olive and Joey were running through the yard in the rain, holding their coats.

"Ed," Jim was saying. Ed spun around and saw his own mirrored grief-stricken face.

"I should have told him not to go," he heard himself say. "I should have insisted. You should have insisted. You all let him go, you wanted him to."

"Ed."

He pushed past Jim and ran through the dining room, up the stairs, into his room, where he closed the door and stood silently against it. He searched for his sorrow and found only a dull ache. He could not accept it. Paul could not be gone. If he were truly dead, he would feel the pain lacerate him, would feel more than this numbness, dead at the center. He pressed against the door, waiting for the tears to come from his dry eyes, waiting for some way to release his grief, waiting.

They had left it to Mike to slam the door on reporters, to arrange some sort of memorial ceremony, to handle whatever friends came by to offer condolences. Mike was the practical one. He would grieve in his own way while taking care of whatever was necessary. The reporters had to content themselves with shots of the clones greeting Paul's friends at the door.

Ed, alone in his room, could hear Mike and Kira talking downstairs with Emma Valois and Hidehiko Takamura. Nearer to him, on the stairs, he heard Bill and Zuñi Hathaway murmuring to Al. Jim had hidden himself in his own room.

Paul had been dead for five days. Even now, Ed's mind sought a way out. He had picked up the phone when the Russian called. He could not remember his name, but he remembered the face; a thin, pointed face, not at all Slavic, and he remembered the broken phrases. The Russian's English had failed him finally and he had continued in Russian, unashamed of the tears flowing over his cheeks. All the Lunar scientists were grieving, mourning their departed colleague. The man had left unsaid what everyone knew; that the bodies in the cold Lunar crypts could contribute organs to those who might need them.

Ed had thanked the man for calling. The Russian had not been the only one to call from the moon. Others, ignoring the cost of calls, had spoken to them.

Or Paul was dead, and the Russians who stored him only sentimental fools who refused to accept it. He thought of them carrying Paul's lifeless body across the barren moonscape toward their cryonic chambers. Paul's frozen body was their monument to him, the ultimate expression of their feeling for him and their regard for his work.

Ed slumped over his desk and placed his head on his arms. He would have to accept Paul's death, deal with it somehow, then go on. He could not stand the limbo in which he had remained for the past days much longer. He would have to accept it and watch part of himself and the others die with that acceptance. He would be deluding himself with anything else.

He did not realize he was crying until he felt the moisture on his face and arms. He managed to wipe the tears away and reached over for his violin case. He removed the instrument, tuned it, and rubbed some resin on his bow. Then he lifted the violin to his shoulder.

He drew the bow over the strings, losing himself in the music, trying to become a part of it, retreating from the confusion around him to another world, a more precise, ordered one, a world of structured beauty where death, at least for a time, did not exist.

"Another source of irreversibility is the changes in the most fundamental aspects of human existence, such as man's biology, or his psychology, that the decisions may involve. As we shall see in some specific instances, such changes necessarily intensify certain aspects of human life at the expense of others. In the new situation that will then be created, some new possibilities will exist, but some old ones will vanish."

—Gerald Feinberg
THE PROMETHEUS PROJECT

"Each of us is someone's monster."

—**Paul Chauchard**

3. James: 2020

AS Jim Swenson left the brightly lit doorway and walked outside, the shadows embraced him, hiding him from the girl he knew was watching him. He looked back and saw her raise an arm. Her face was hidden. She was a black shape outlined by the lights behind her.

"Moira," a voice called from inside the dormitory, and she disappeared.

Jim walked toward the path leading through the wooded area around the dormitory, then stopped and looked back. The circular building was surrounded on three sides by trees and faced a large courtyard. Other cylindrical dormitories, several stories high, overlooked the courtyard. Beyond them, in the distance, Jim could see the tall towers that housed the library and various research facilities of the university.

His birthplace was among those towers.

Jim turned and walked on through the woods. The shadows beneath the trees shielded him from the moon, where scientists lived and labored in an attempt to carry on the work of his father, where Paul Swenson lay in a cryonic vault colder than that rocky and desolate surface.

They should have buried him here, in the earth, among trees and flowers, not left him in the sterility of that dead world. On the earth his spirit, if it existed, might roam its old haunts, warming itself in the sun. But perhaps Paul's spirit had outwitted its captors after all, returning to a sphere of souls around the world, watching over the children who were pieces of itself.

They had left the memorial service almost four years before, where Paul's friends had spoken a few simple words, Jim holding Kira's arm, his three brothers following closely behind. Looking up, Jim had seen them, as he knew he would, crowded in a herd a short distance away. The newspeople did not have to come close to record accurately the grief written on his face. Their equipment would memorize every detail of his sorrow and transmit it to a billion newsfax sheets and millions of holographic screens. The newspeople had huddled in the distance, ready to swoop.

He thought of Moira.

"A newsfax man came around," Moira had said, her black eyes smiling at Jim. "I guess someone told him we were seeing each other, and he wanted a personal story or something, what it's like to go with a guy who. . . ."

"What did you tell him?" Jim asked, grabbing her arm. Moira looked at him, her eyes wide.

"Why, nothing," she said. "I have better things to do than discuss my personal life with the press."

He clenched his fist. "Why can't they leave me alone?" Moira reached over and took his arm.

"I guess," she said, "it'll be a long time before a clone has a private life." She said it gently. He reacted angrily, slamming his fist against a small table in her room and knocking over a small sculpture of a cat. The sculpture crashed to the floor and his muscles tensed.

Moira's voice grew harsh. "You've broken it. You didn't have to do that." He knew her mother had sculpted the cat for her years ago.

"It was a lousy sculpture," he said. It was the wrong thing to say to Moira, who was already overly sensitive about her mother's second-rate abilities as an artist. Her black eyes narrowed and the skin across the high cheekbones grew taut.

"So," she hissed, "she's not a good sculptor. She tries. At least she isn't an egomaniac, convinced of her great

worth, her invaluable abilities, she never needed to see
five duplicates of herself around before she could feel
secure." She leaned over Jim, her black hair brushing his
face. He looked away and kept picking up the broken
pieces of the cat. "She wasn't like the great Paul Swenson."

Jim reached the end of the trail through the forest and
paused for a moment. He turned and walked along the
edge of the bicycle path near the road that wound past
the houses surrounding the campus.

Duplicates.

The warm wind breathed softly, rustling the leaves over
his head.

Duplicates of Paul Swenson. The wind hurried past
him and was gone, leaving behind grassy odors.

Egomaniac. No, the Paul he had known was a gentle
man, almost self-effacing. He had tried to communicate
what he knew to as many people as possible, yet was
embarrassed when he became regarded as an authority.
Paul had only wanted to help humanity by perpetuating,
in five new people, any abilities he had that could be
of service. He had wanted a family.

So Jim had always thought. Yet it was at least possible
that Paul might have been lured by dreams of a new
and unique kind of immortality, or by an inner convic-
tion that Paul Swenson was worthy of being reproduced
in exact detail and duplication, five times. The line between a sense of personal worth and megalomania might
be very thin. But that was a problem in any kind of
parenthood.

Paul Swenson had been admired and honored once.
But at the time of his death Jim had already sensed the
attitudes of fear and skepticism that colored the feelings
many people had about Paul. His father was no longer
present to contradict them and his absence seemed to
magnify the fears. The fact that the Russians had insisted
on preserving his body had not helped. Cryonic freezing
was sometimes used in emergencies, suspending a person's
life processes until specialists could reach him or a needed
blood type could be found; it had worked in a few cases.
But Paul's frozen body was a memorial monument. Once

again people near Paul had set him apart from other human beings. Jim had even heard rumors that Paul was not dead at all, that some part of him had taken possession of the clones.

He had thought that Moira, at least, knew better. But she had not known Paul and could only make judgments based on what she had heard or seen about him.

He sighed and moved closer to the edge of the path as two cyclists passed him. He thought of the others: Ed retreating from all social contact, residing in a tidy, ordered, mathematical world; Mike and his desire to leave them all and forget his origins; Al and his growing obsession with study, afraid that he would not be able to measure up to Paul's achievements. He thought of Kira as well, hovering over them, concerned with their problems. Perhaps not, Jim thought, maybe she only thinks she *should* worry and would rather retreat to her own world. Maybe Paul had gone through the same thing. Jim considered what he had heard about Paul's youth from his old friends, and dismissed it. People edit their pasts, he knew, and remember what fits their notions of themselves. There was no way of telling what Paul had really felt.

Jim left the bicycle path and turned down the road that led to his house. All five of them had remained there after Paul's death. It was practical, near the university, comfortable and roomy. But Jim sometimes felt it was haunted by Paul's ghost, watching them. He thought of Paul standing in the house observing them, perhaps with concern, perhaps laughing as he saw them play out his own youth, his own mistakes, seeing his own soul taking up residence in the five genetically identical bodies, as some thought it had. He shuddered at what else they might think.

The house was at the end of the road, its brown painted planks blending with the small grove of trees around it. Jim looked at the small hill on which the house stood and thought again of the contrast between the unpretentious dwelling and the somewhat grandiose view people had of Paul. He walked up to the front door, hesitated, then opened it slowly and entered the house.

He walked through the small alcove and stood in the living room, watching as the four turned to face him.

Al, thick brown hair to his shoulders.

Ed, clean-shaven with hair cropped to his skull.

Mike, pulling at his moustache.

Kira, with short wavy hair and the same face feminized.

They had all tried to differentiate themselves in the past couple of years, yet four sets of green eyes, copies of his own, looked at him and asked, *are you all right, Jim?*

"Jim?" Kira said. His brothers watched.

He turned and fled to his room.

Jim sat in front of Dr. Valois, feet propped on her desk, weaving images for her, speaking about portions of dreams, reaching into his pocket for a scrap of poetry he had jotted down to work on later. Emma Valois looked at him from her side of the desk, head nodding at intervals, hazel eyes gazing at him steadily. He continued to weave his verbal tapestry, trying to ignore the anxiety gnawing at him. The psychiatrist continued to nod.

Dr. Valois had observed their psychological development for as long as Jim could remember. When they were children she had seen them only infrequently, talking with them and allowing them to play with the machines in her office. When they had found it difficult to talk with her they would sit in Psyche, her computer booth. Psyche had listened to their problems and set up games for them to play. Jim had enjoyed the games; the construction of holograms, word association, scenarios in which he and the computer would take opposing sides.

After Paul's death, they had all, except for Mike, visited Dr. Valois more often. *I guess they thought we'd need a psychiatrist. They expected us to be freaks.* He read the poetry to Dr. Valois and continued to avoid speaking about the feeling of despair that had brought him to her office. He could not bring himself to express it. He put the paper back in his pocket. Dr. Valois nodded.

Jim removed his feet from the desk and stood up.

"I've got some work to do. In the library," he mumbled.

"You have nothing else to say?" She probably suspected him of concealing something.

"No."

"Something's bothering you, Jim."

"I'm all right, really. It's just a mood." He hurried from the office, slowed down in the hallway and moved toward the elevator. He stepped into it automatically, jostling a man who was standing in the corner.

He was in Moira's room. "I love you," he said to her, reaching for her hand. She turned from him. His brother Mike was standing at the door. Moira walked toward him and left Jim sitting at the desk.

As he hurtled along the road, Jim took manual control of the car. He accelerated until the surrounding scenery was a blur, then quickly turned off the road. He felt the car plunge into nothingness. He reached out to death and began to fall into a deep sleep.

He was walking across the campus, alone, as the news-fax man approached. "How about an interview? I'll make it worth your while." The reporter's facial features were a blur. "What's it like to be a clone? Do you feel funny with four people around just like you? Can your friends tell you apart?" Jim grabbed the recorder and smashed it over the man's head.

"Jim," Moira's voice said. He looked around, startled. "Jim." He was standing just outside the elevator.

Moira came toward him, her aqua sari fluttering at her ankles. He took her arm. They walked through the lobby and outside. The spring rain had stopped and the air smelled fresh.

"I must have said Jim five times," Moira murmured. "You looked like you were ready to kill somebody." They continued walking through the courtyard, surrounded on all sides by high silvery towers housing offices, research facilities and broadcasting studios. Few of the thousands of students were around. Most were either doing research or lab work or were in their rooms watching lectures. Some were probably in the library, preferring its quiet to the noise of the dormitories.

"Just thinking about things," Jim said. "I guess. . . . "
He paused, feeling uneasy, and looked around the courtyard. All he saw were small groups of students and faculty
going about their business. "I guess," he went on, "I
should go home and dial my Sci and Sym lectures. I'm
about three lectures behind."

Moira shrugged. "It's an easy course," she said. Jim
knew she did not think much of the Science and Sym-
bolism course. She had chosen to study literature that
either did not deal with science at all or only dealt with
it peripherally. She did not care for science and had never
progressed beyond the basic courses recommended to
all students. Jim glanced at Moira and thought he saw
contempt in her eyes. Contempt for him? Contempt for
Paul Swenson? Contempt for all the biologists who had
produced Jim?

"You can dial the lectures in my room," Moira said,
"if you want."

Jim did not want to dial them at all. Apathy settled
around him, and he saw himself continue through the
courtyard, past the buildings, through the wooded areas,
past the dormitories. . . .

Moira saw the group before he did. She pulled at
his arm and gestured at a group of five teenagers being
shown around the courtyard by a tall black man. She
waved at the man.

"Hey, Walt!" she shouted. The tall man waved back.
"That's Walt Merton, he's been seeing my roommate
Ilyasah. He's in chemistry." The corners of her mouth
turned down. "Look at those kids, they look so serious
and awestruck."

They began to walk toward the group. "Hi, Walt,"
Moira said as they approached. "This is Jim Swenson,
I don't think you've met." She grinned at the teenagers.

"Hi, Jim," Walt said.

"Jim Swenson the clone?" a small blond girl asked.
Jim forced himself to look at her. He felt beads of
sweat forming on his forehead and under his beard. "Are
you the one in astrophysics? That's what I want to study."

A wiry dark boy hooted, "How do the profs know

which one of you's taking a test?" Jim felt his body tense. He was immobilized. "My grandmother says you've got mental telepathy," the boy continued, "because you've got one mind."

Jim stared at the boy. Dr. Valois had refuted that story long ago, yet people still believed it. He wanted to tell the kids they were being rude. He thought of himself writing a book of etiquette for social relations with clones. "Never reveal to the clone that you do not know who he is." "Tell him how unlike the other clones he is." "Never seat clones on the same side of the dinner table." He restrained the hysterical laugh that almost escaped from his lips.

"I don't have telepathy," he managed to say.

"Of course he doesn't," the small blond girl said to the boy.

Jim turned from the group, aware that both Walt and Moira were looking at him strangely. Then he noticed a chubby man lurking around an oak tree near the center of the courtyard. The tiny camera in the man's hand was almost invisible, hidden by his fingers. Jim thought of newsfax pictures, he and Moira in the courtyard, captions: "A Clone in Love," and, in smaller letters, "Can She Tell Them Apart?" He stopped in front of the man, grabbed the camera from his hand and smashed it on the tree trunk.

Moira was behind him. "Jim, what the hell are you doing?" She grabbed his arm. The man's brown eyes reflected shock.

"I'll do that," Jim said, "every time I see one of you idiots with a camera." Moira was tugging at him.

The man sighed. "Young lady, tell this man it is not against the law to photograph buildings." He reached into his pocket and handed Jim a card. "I would appreciate it if you sent me twenty dollars for the camera, and consider yourself fortunate that I'm not billing you for my wasted time."

The man walked away. Jim looked at the card. Herman Steinfeld, Professor of Architecture.

"What's wrong with you?" Moira asked.

He stood there, holding the card, staring past her at the tree.

"I'll see you tomorrow, then," Moira said. Her image disappeared from the screen in front of Jim.

He got up and wandered into the kitchen. Kira sat at the table eating a sandwich. The room smelled like a delicatessen. She looked up.

Moira had not stayed on the phone very long. He remembered the impatience in her voice.

"Want a sandwich?" Kira asked, gesturing at the plate of cold cuts in front of her. He could tell that she was worried and trying to hide it. Kira, when upset, would eat almost compulsively.

"No." He sat down across the table from her.

"Was that Moira? I'd love to talk with her." Kira looked down at the table. "I wish I looked like Moira Buono. Too bad Paul didn't have dark hair. Too bad he wasn't smaller, too, I feel like an elephant next to people her size."

Please shut up, Kira, and let me sit here in peace. Stop pretending you're worried and trying to cheer me up.

"You should ask her over sometime," Kira said.

Jim shuddered. He thought of Moira meeting his brothers. Would she be bored by their scientific studies? Would she compare him to them? Perhaps they would all fall in love with her. It was logical to assume that they might. How much real difference was there between them? "It just might be," he said, trying to restrain his anger, "that I want Moira to see me as an individual, not part of an identical herd."

Kira changed the subject. "I saw Dr. Erman today," she said quickly. "He said you hadn't dialed his poetry discussion in a while, and he wondered. . . . "

"Can't you shut up?" Jim said. "You don't have to mind my business for me." His voice was loud. He looked around, hoping that the others had not heard him.

"I was just. . . . " Kira stopped. She put down her sandwich. The concern he saw on her face needed no words. She brushed some of her thick brown hair from her forehead.

Jim got up from the table suddenly and hurried out into the living room. Al was seated in one of the booths at the other side of the room, earphones over his head, eyes fixed on the screen. Al was retreating too, into his work rather than from it. As a student of astrophysics, he was in competition with the memory of Paul's work, suffering doubts about his ability to do as well. He had applied for a grant to work with the scientists on the moon. He did little else but study in the meantime, forsaking even the sports he enjoyed.

Jim turned away and began to climb the staircase to his own room. Al could not be bothered with his worries. He walked to his room and paused at the door. He could hear Ed and Mike talking in Ed's bedroom. They could not be bothered either. Mike was hoping to leave eventually for California, wanting to do advanced work in plasma physics there. Jim also knew that Mike wanted to get as far from the rest of them as he could.

Jim entered his room and closed the door. He flung himself across his bed, trying to hide from the house and the others in it. He lay on the bed, arms hanging uselessly over the side.

He heard the sound of Ed's violin. The music slipped under the door and crept around him, circling mournfully.

Jim thought of Ed, Al, Mike, and Kira. He saw Kira sitting in the kitchen, pretending concern. She was studying biology and ethics, the only one of them actively studying the issues and circumstances that had brought them into being. His mind recoiled at the thought. *Keep at it, Kira, and maybe someday you'll produce something even more monstrous than ourselves.*

He lay there and thought of the pieces of Paul in the house, fragments of the original man, each emphasizing a different facet of the original. *Are we each a whole?* he wondered. *If one died, would it matter?* He rejected the thought and tried to empty his mind.

He was alone.

Jim sat in Moira's room and stared at the wall. He could not understand what Moira and Ilyasah were saying. Their words were disconnected syllables that he heard but could not interpret.

Moira had seemed annoyed when he showed up at her room earlier that evening. Ilyasah Ahmal, a student of ancient Egypt, had been sitting in her booth taking part in a discussion. He had sat in the room quietly while Moira read and Ilyasah spoke to the faces on the screen in front of her, her words smothered by the clear sound-proofed cube around her.

Jim had wanted to get out of his house. He had been making notes for a story when Dr. Aschenbach arrived. He had taken one look at the minister's friendly face before deciding to leave quickly.

Why do you keep coming by? he had wanted to ask Jonathan Aschenbach. *Do you think you can recapture an old friendship with Paul by using us?* Instead, he had mumbled something about meeting Moira and had left, riding aimlessly around the campus in the car before deciding to stop at Moira's dormitory.

Jim felt like an intruder. But he had nowhere else to go. He couldn't talk to anyone he knew; others could not really understand him. He could not say anything to his brothers and sister. They understood only too well, and had retreated. Jim saw them as they must appear to others—identical, a closed group, undifferentiated, and inaccessible. *We're components, interchangeable parts,* he thought. Even their different pursuits were probably accidental.

He sat and heard the voices of Ilyasah and Moira, background noise that complemented his thoughts. Could Moira, the girl he loved, tell them apart? She had only met Kira. He had never introduced her to his brothers, had never dared. The faces of Ed, Mike, Al, and Kira merged in his mind, becoming the same face—that of Paul Swenson.

". . . if they had cloning then," Ilyasah was saying. Jim sat up with a start.

"What?" he said, then suddenly realized he had shouted the word. Ilyasah looked surprised and ran her hand over the hair that stood out around her head like a black cloud.

"I was only contemplating," the black girl said. Moira glared at Jim. "I was thinking about what an Egyptian Pharaoh might have done with cloning. Instead of marrying brothers to sisters, they could have. . . . " Ilyasah stopped. Jim, almost unaware of his actions, found himself standing over her, fists at his sides.

"It was a dumb idea," Ilyasah said softly. "I'm sorry, I didn't think. . . . "

He turned quickly and left the room, unable to speak. He moved through the curved hallways of the dormitory, unaware of his surroundings.

He suddenly found himself outside next to his car. His hands shook. He looked back at the dormitory and saw Moira standing in the doorway. She had followed him, and was undoubtedly ready to vent her anger.

Goodbye, Moira. He had lost her too. He was numb at the thought. It hardly seemed to matter.

The car hurtled along the automated highway at high speed. The headlights of cars moving on other lanes were bright blurs streaking past him.

Jim huddled in the car, his back against the door, arms around his knees. His safety belt and harness were tight around his body.

He was a child again, standing with Mike at the doorway of the bright yellow school building, watching the other children. Some older boys walked toward them. He looked around uncertainly.

"What comes in vanilla, vanilla, vanilla, and vanilla?" a large fat boy said. "Ice cream clones," his companions shouted in unison. Jim laughed hesitantly, not quite understanding why he was laughing, not quite sure of what the real joke was.

Clone jokes, old ones revived temporarily by some of Jim's classmates, had been popular at the school for a while. At last Mike and Kira had put a stop to it by beating up a couple of the offenders on the playground.

A buzzer sounded on the dashboard, signaling that his car was approaching the exit he had punched out earlier. The car turned off the highway, moved around the exit bypass, and stopped as it reached a narrow road perpendicular to the exit. It waited for Jim to give it further directions.

Impulsively he took manual control of the car and turned onto the narrow road. He accelerated recklessly until he could hear the sound of wind rushing past him. He had pushed the vehicle almost to its limit when his buzzer sounded again, signaling danger. The car slowed automatically.

Ahead he now saw the small park where he had often gone when he needed solitude. He drove around its parking lot and continued into the park along a narrow path. He kept driving, moving the car up a steep hill, until the road became bumpy and he was forced to stop in front of a clump of trees.

He got out and walked along the path on foot. The area seemed deserted. Student ecologists had recently finished the restoration of a large wilderness section farther out. Kira had assisted Dr. Takamura in creating cloned eagles for the wilderness, and had taken time off from her studies the year before to work for the park service. Jim shuddered, thinking of the identical eagles flying over reforested land. He preferred the small park to which few people now came.

He came to the clearing at the top of the hill. The stone wall he knew so well sat at the edge of the clearing, overlooking the automated highway. He walked toward the wall, stood by it and looked down at the highway one hundred feet below him.

He sat on the wall, dangling his feet over the side. *He was a child once more, sitting with the others counting cars on the highway.* He thought about his past. They had few friends as children and fewer now. He thought of Moira and felt pain. He had never grown as close to her as he had once been to the other clones and knew he never would. She was gone now, he was sure, annoyed by his moods and unable to understand what was torturing him.

His body was a prison, forcing him to live and struggle. He was too tired even to fight the feeling. *I should go to Dr. Valois and get some moods to tide me over.* But he would not dance on the strings of a chemical puppeteer, not now. He thought of the drugs he had once taken with Joey and Olive, wondering if they had forever damaged his mind.

He saw himself writing a report to Dr. Takamura and Dr. Valois. *The experiment with cloning has failed. One of the experimental subjects can no longer live with himself; the others are only four bitter people, denied even the small pleasure of feeling like unique individuals.* He knew they had wanted a team, a Paul Swenson multiplied by five, working together, synthesizing what they learned in different fields, minds so alike they could see connections where others might not.

Jim felt far away from the house where he had grown up, the house that even now was dominated by Paul Swenson's presence. He thought of his father with bitterness. *I'll at least rob you of part of your immortality,* he thought, looking down at the highway beneath him. And at last he admitted to himself what he had always known unconsciously; he had been almost relieved at Paul's death, saddened but relieved, freer to go his own way. But he hated himself for the feeling.

It made no difference. He had no real ties to anyone. He would leave only four young people lost in their own worlds, a puzzled psychiatrist and biologist who had taken part in an abortive experiment, and a minister trying to recapture an old friendship.

He pulled one leg up on the wall and prepared to leap.

"Jim," a familiar voice called from behind him. He turned and saw Kira standing near the trees, Dr. Aschenbach at her side.

He groaned. "Kira, leave me alone, please."

She began to walk toward him. He shifted forward on the wall, holding on with one hand. "Get back!" he screamed. Don't make me jump in front of you, give me that much."

"Wait, Jim," Kira said. She moved forward.

"Stop!" he cried. She halted. "Why are you here? Quite a coincidence, isn't it." He looked from her to Dr. Aschenbach. The stocky minister stood silently behind Kira. "And you," he said to the clergyman, "don't you have any other souls to save? You might better spend your time with people you know have them."

Al and Mike appeared behind Dr. Aschenbach. They stopped suddenly. Jim watched the four shadowed figures. Dr. Aschenbach held out his hands, pleading silently. The three clones stood in identical positions, hands clutched to their chests.

Jim found himself chuckling. "What is this, a jamboree?" he shouted. "I'm surprised you didn't bring a newsfax team, and I don't see Ed around." The four figures were quiet. "I guess he has other things to do." His voice was shaking. He felt tears trickling down his face, losing themselves in his beard. He tried to ignore them. "Well, where is he?" he shrieked. *Why should I care?*, he thought.

"He's home," Kira said, "waiting, in case you went back there." Her face, in the moonlight, seemed shinier than usual. He could see silvery streaks under her eyes.

"For God's sake, will you go!" he cried. Kira began to move toward him. He held up his free hand. Still clinging to the wall, he pulled up both legs, squatted, then stood up, wobbling precariously. He looked back at Kira. She seemed paralyzed. He began to walk along the wall, arms held out for balance.

"Don't do this to yourself," the minister said.

"Save your breath." Jim balanced on one leg. "I wonder why you came to see me die." He stood on two legs again. "Maybe you're just seeing Paul die again, I don't know. Don't worry, old man, you've still got four Pauls left." The tears continued down his face; he could not stop them.

He turned from the four people and looked down past his feet at the highway. There were fewer cars on it now.

He found himself wondering almost absently whether or not he would land on a car. He decided that his body would hit near the edge of the road.

He heard Kira's voice, although it sounded faint. "Jim, please come down." Mike was saying something too, but he could not hear the words.

He poised himself on the wall. *Please give me some peace*, his mind murmured, *let me rest*. He thought of the others. *Forget me*, he cried to them silently.

He felt his feet lift off the wall. Silence thundered in his ears. He strained, trying to hear voices, and heard only wind whistling past him. He was weightless, arched over a cushion of air, seeing the ground turn under him. . . .

Kira was next to him, one leg over the wall, hand clutching his. She straddled the wall, holding on to him. Her face was streaked with tears. She was shouting something at him, but he could not make out the words. He squatted, then sat on the wall. At last he heard her clearly.

"Jump, then," Kira said, softly this time. "Jump, but you'll have to take me with you." She continued to cling to his arm. "Go on." He tried to free himself but she would not let go.

He looked down at the highway. The spring wind was growing cooler and his beard felt cold and wet. Suddenly he found himself shaking with sobs. He clung to her. "I've lost Moira," he managed to say. "I know it. We shouldn't fall in love. How could anyone love us?" He stopped for breath. "And you, you're all strangers."

"No, Jim," she replied. She released his arm and held his hand gently. "Moira called tonight. She was worried and she said you were depressed. Why do you think we came here? I knew you'd be here, we always did come when we had to, and poor Ed, he would have come too, except he thought you might come home and need him." She grasped his hand more tightly. "Can't you see? We need you, Jim, come back with us."

Mike and Al had come over to the wall and were leaning against it, watching him. Dr. Aschenbach stood behind them.

"And why are you here?" he asked them. "I know what it's like, I look at you every day and see all my gestures, all my features, sometimes even the same thoughts going through our minds. Don't you think I know you feel the same? We're all trying to pretend the others don't exist."

"Maybe we've been wrong too," Mike said. "I know, it sounds funny coming from me. I haven't made a secret of how I feel." He paused. "Maybe I shouldn't try so hard. We *are* different. I'm doing physics. I suppose I have some imagination, but I can't look at a theory and express it in a poem the way you can, or even explain it to people. You can." Mike looked over at Al. "And Al thinks he's competing with Paul, but he isn't really. Paul did his work, now Al will do his."

"He's right," Al said. "After we study what we have to, there's no reason why we can't work together the way Paul wanted."

"Certainly," Jim said bitterly. "People expect that of clones. They think we have one mind as it is."

"Oh, Jim," Kira said, "don't you see? People have to work together. If you're apart from them, with no ties, you work only for yourself. People can't live like that. Are any of us so unusual? Don't people all have the same roots anyway? No one's an isolated self, we're all different really, but that doesn't mean we have to isolate ourselves."

He shivered. The night air had grown very cool. Kira was still watching him. She swung her legs over the wall and stood up. "I'm getting cold," she said almost apologetically. "I guess you have to make your own decision. You know how we feel, but we can't force you." She turned, then looked back. "Please come home. Give us a chance, give Moira a chance."

She began to walk toward the trees. Al and Mike looked at him uncertainly, then followed her.

Dr. Aschenbach remained. Jim glared at him. "I suppose Paul sat here once and thought of jumping."

The minister shook his head. "No," he said. "I won't say he never got morose, but there were people around who loved him and he cared about them too. He didn't want to hurt them."

"Didn't he hurt you when he decided to have us cloned?"

"I disagreed with him, but I never doubted that he only wanted to do what was right. He felt he was under an obligation to use his talents for humanity's benefit. And when he was offered a chance to perpetuate those talents, he took it."

Jim turned from the minister. Dr. Aschenbach had not lightened his burden, only increased it. He had reminded Jim of obligations he would abandon if he jumped. He turned back to the clergyman, but he had left, disappearing among the trees.

There was no one to prevent him from leaping off the wall now, nothing to stop his escape from the chains Dr. Aschenbach had tried to place on him. It would be quick, a few seconds of soaring over the earth, then oblivion, no chance for thinking or regret. They had left him alone after all. He stood up on the wall and looked down.

No, not alone. They have left me free. Or maybe they had known that he could not jump now and felt safe in leaving him there. He sighed.

The scent of pine reached him, wafted to him on the night air. He jumped off the wall and hurried toward the trees. "Kira!" he cried. "Al, Mike!" He shouted their names at the trees which stood silently, holding their leafy limbs toward him. He heard the rustle of underbrush, of running feet.

The four appeared. Kira was the first to reach him, then Al, then Mike and Dr. Aschenbach.

He stumbled toward them.

After they made love, Jim leaned back on his elbows and looked at Moira, gazing at her olive skin and large black eyes. Her nose was a bit too large for her delicate face. As she lay at his side, her small breasts seemed flattened almost to nonexistence. Her abdomen was a concavity between two sharp hipbones. Her legs contrasted with the slenderness of her torso; they were short, utilitarian, well-muscled appendages that carried her around efficiently and without much strain. She was beautiful.

She watched him with dark eyes. Her black hair lay carelessly around her head in the green grass and her face bore a calm and peaceful smile. She reached out for his hand and drew it to her belly. In the distance, he could hear Ilyasah Ahmal's high-pitched laugh and the deeper rumblings of Walt Merton. He traced the outline of shadows on Moira's body, shadows created by the summer sun's rays and the leafy branches of the trees overhead. A breeze stirred the branches; the shadows drifted and changed shape on Moira's body.

Jim took his hand away from her and got up. His penis felt cold and sticky. He pulled on his shorts and began to walk toward the clearing ahead. He knew Moira was watching him, probably puzzled, perhaps a little angry. He came to the clearing and walked toward the stone wall. The grass brushed against his feet, tickling his soles. Two grackels perched on the wall, cawing loudly at sparrows darting overhead. As he approached, the two black birds lifted, cawed at him from above, and were gone.

Jim leaned against the wall and looked down at the automated highway. The cars fled along the road in orderly rows. He watched them and thought of Moira. She had retreated from him again, hiding even at the moment he had entered her body. She had been an observer, looking on as he held her, sweating and moving to a lonely, sharp spurt of pleasure. She was an onlooker, smiling at him from a distance as he withdrew, her black eyes a shield between their minds.

They stood in a gray formlessness. "Moira," he said, and she looked at him, seeming to be perplexed, seeming to be impatient. She withdrew and clouds of grayness began to cover her, hiding her legs, then her face and shoulders.

His view of the highway was suddenly obstructed. "Are you trying to ruin today, too?" Moira's voice said. He pulled at the shirt she had draped over his head and put it on.

She sat on the wall to his right. Her skin looked sallow next to her yellow shorts and shirt. She stared past him at the trees.

"I'm sorry," he said, "it's just a mood." He wanted to take her hand or touch her hair. Instead, he went back to leaning against the wall. He looked up at her face. Her eyes were pieces of onyx, sharp and cold. Her skin was drawn tightly across her cheekbones.

"I'm sorry, it's just a mood," she said. "How many moods do you have? Must be half a million by now. And they're always ones you have to apologize for."

Jim turned and saw Ilyasah coming toward them. He forced himself to smile.

"You were right about this place," Ilyasah said. "Nice and quiet. Ever since they reclaimed that area up north, you can't go there without falling over bodies, I heard they might limit the number that go up there at one time. Something wrong, Moira?"

"No," Moira muttered.

"Give us half an hour," Ilyasah went on, "then we'll get the food out."

Jim took the hint. "Sure," he said. Ilyasah left and disappeared among the trees. The black girl had still not shaken off the remnants of her rigid Muslim upbringing and wanted to be certain no one observed her with Walt. Moira had returned to her dormitory room with Jim one evening a little too soon. They had calmly excused themselves and gone to one of the lounges instead, but Ilyasah had been embarrassed for days afterward. "I guess we'd better watch the path," he said to Moira. "I wouldn't want anyone else to embarrass your roommate." Moira shrugged and continued to sit on the wall.

He tried to fight the tightness in his stomach, the feeling of isolation that was once again wrapping itself around him. *Talk to me, Moira*, he thought, *don't make me stand here guessing and worrying*.

The dark eyes looked at him. "I'm leaving next week," she said quickly. "I'll probably come back in August, but my mother's fixing up her new studio and she needs some help." Her eyes challenged him to respond.

"Why?" he cried. "Why didn't you tell me this before," he said more quietly.

"I didn't know before."

"Oh, you knew it before, she's been after you for a month about it and you said she had enough help. Now all of a sudden you have to go home."

Moira hopped off the wall and paced in front of him. "I suppose," she said, "I have to go through a whole explanation."

"No," he said. *Of course you do.*

"All right," she went on, "I decided to go home a while ago, I would have told you before, but. . . . "

"Why not? Why didn't you tell me before?"

Moira smiled suddenly. "You really don't understand, do you? If I had told you before, you would have gotten upset and tried to talk me out of it, or acted as though I was planning something terribly wrong. So I tell you now, so you won't have time to talk me out of it. I thought you were feeling better about things lately, I thought you were over your depression. But of course you're going to act the same way anyway."

"I want to be with you. Is that so wrong?" Jim swallowed, worried that he had whined the words. "I don't like to be separated from you, that's all," he said in a lower tone.

"No, you'd rather be underfoot all the time. I can't read in the library without you, I can't visit any of my friends alone. I can't even meet your brothers. Every time I mention that I might like to talk with them, you evade the whole thing. Why?"

He was silent. He could feel sweat forming on his face and under his beard.

"I guess," she said, "you're jealous of your own family too."

He shrugged and tried to smile. "I guess it isn't so bad," he said. "You'll be back in August, and we can. . . . "

"No." She stopped pacing and stood in front of him, arms folded across her chest. "No, Jim. I don't know yet, I want to think about things. I don't want to make any promises now, I'll just have to see. Maybe that's hard on you, but. . . . "

She sighed, then walked over to the trees. She stood there, leaning against a trunk, her back to him.

"Moira."

No answer.

"Moira." She was gone again, having said what she had to say. He could stride over to her, grab her by the shoulders, shake the slender body while shouting at her, and she would only look at him with empty eyes.

Do I love you, Moira? Do I even know you? He stared at the girl's back, stiff and unyielding under the soft yellow shirt. Was he too possessive, too demanding? Did he fear rejection so much that he required a total and unconditional committment? Or was she simply telling him in her own way that she couldn't love him, that it might be as easy for her to love one of his brothers if she knew them?

Moira, look at me, try to understand, he wanted to shout. He walked over to her, afraid to touch her, afraid to reach out and hold her. She was lost in her own world and seemed unaware of his presence.

It was over this time. He was sure of that, in spite of Moira's comments about waiting until August.

She turned around and looked at him, black eyes expressionless. "The fact is," she said, "that you're trying to use me to prove something to yourself, to show everyone that you are an individual, that I only love you, that I'm completely yours. Well, I've got better things to do than build up your ego."

She still refused to speak. *You could at least say what you mean,* Jim thought as he looked at her back.

"Hey!" He turned and saw Walt Merton on the path leading into the woods. "Come on," Walt said, "we're getting the food out."

"Yeah," Jim replied. "We'll be along in a minute."

Walt looked from Jim to Moira. "Sure," he said. His slender moustached face showed concern. He looked doubtfully at Jim, then turned and went back down the path.

"Let's go," Moira said suddenly. "I'm starving." She smiled and took him by the hand. She was hiding behind cheerfulness now, *nothing's wrong, Jim, everything's settled.*

"Damn it," he said harshly, "can't we at least talk it over?"

She ignored his question. "Let's go," she said, still smiling, still holding his hand.

The rain had started as a summer shower but was now coming down steadily, forming puddles on the lawn. Jim sat on his front porch. The evening air was cooler and fresher than it had been for several days.

Farther down the narrow road before him, in front of a Spanish-style stucco house, a group of naked children danced in the rain. On the lawn, his brothers Al and Mike were throwing a football. Mike had dragged Al outside almost as soon as the rain began to fall.

Al's thick brown hair was plastered against the back of his neck and shoulders and Mike's moustache drooped on both sides of his mouth. "Whup," Mike yelled as he drew his arm back and made a forward pass. As the ball left his arm, he slipped on the grass and landed on his buttocks, bare muddy feet poking high into the air. Al hooted and caught the ball. He began to run with it, laughing as Mike got up, with mud and wet grass on his shorts.

Jim watched his brothers. They had not insisted that he join them, understanding almost instinctively that he needed some solitude. He had gone to the university early that morning to ride with Moira to the train that would take her home.

The night before, he had tried once again to talk her out of leaving. "I can't believe your mother needs your help with all those others around," he had said. Moira's mother lived with five other women. Moira herself had been raised communally by the group with three other children. She saw her father rarely. He had retreated to Nepal years before, emerging only occasionally to face a world that frightened him.

Moira shrugged. "She can still use some extra help."

"Come *on*," he shouted. "Stop being so evasive. At least be honest about why you're really going."

She was silent as she continued to pack her things. He had finally left her dormitory room, angrily telling her she could rent a car or take the shuttle from the university to the train station.

He had relented, of course, punching out his destination, riding onto the automated highway, leaning back in his seat as the highway took control. Then he had reached for Moira. She had watched him, her black eyes seemingly veiled.

She unfastened her blue sari and draped it over the back of the seat. Then she unzipped his shorts and crawled onto him, holding his penis firmly with one hand. He was suddenly inside her, clutching her, gazing up at her face. Her eyes were closed. The car buzzed softly, protesting Moira's abandonment of her safety harness.

"Moira," he whispered to her. "Moira." He came quickly. She withdrew from him and moved back to her side of the seat.

He shivered in the air-conditioned car. As he zipped up his shorts he looked over at the dark-haired girl. She was fastening her sari while staring out the window at the blurred scenery. *What was it, Moira, a formality because you're leaving? A way of saying you still care? A way of saying goodbye, Jim, it's the last time?* She gave him no answer, not even a clue. Once again she had remained unresponsive, giving him no sign that she had taken pleasure in the act.

He grabbed her, pulling her sari from her, and pushed her against the seat. Her face was hidden from him. Her buttocks pointed up at his face. He crawled on top of her, pushing inside roughly. He pounded against her, waiting to hear her moans, waiting to see her abandon herself to him at last.

He continued to sit behind the wheel, still watching

her. She had finished fastening her sari. She turned toward him, a tentative smile on her face. *I've never reached you, Moira.* At last he pulled her to him. She sat there, head on his shoulder, her body stiff, her muscles tight. He was alone once again.

Al stumbled onto the porch, picked up his towel from the chair next to Jim, and massaged his head and shoulders vigorously. "Am I out of shape," Al said. "I'm going over to the gym tomorrow, I have to do some lab work anyway, so I might as well work out."

"Yeah," Jim said.

"Want to come along, we can play some handball."

"No." Jim looked up at his brother. "I don't think so." He looked away. Al was probably thinking: *is it that girl, Jim? You're been sitting around for months, no interest in much else, you haven't even written for a while.*

"Well, if you change your mind," Al said. He turned and went inside the house, towel draped over his shoulders.

"Catch," Mike shouted. He threw the football to Jim as he followed Al through the front door.

Jim tucked the football under his chair and continued to watch the rain. The thought of Moira suddenly saddened him all over again. He had been numb for most of the day. *I would have been with her now, we would have been running through the rain together.* He felt purposeless, empty, and alone.

A car was approaching along the road, a small green Lear model. It stopped in front of the house and he saw his sister and the short stocky figure of Hidehiko Takamura get out. The two raced through the downpour to the porch. Kira was laughing as she shook the water from her hair.

Jim wanted to disappear, but he sat there and nodded to Dr. Takamura.

"What a downpour!" Kira said. "Can I get you something, a beer maybe?"

"Better make it tea," Dr. Takamura replied. "And I think I'll sit out here, I've been inside all day."

Kira looked at Jim. "I'll have some too," he said. She hurried into the house.

Jim looked over at Dr. Takamura as the older man seated himself. The man was still here at the university, still working at the same research center that had produced them. Jim shuddered. Of course the man did not have the authority he had once held; it was a wonder that the university had taken him back at all. Takamura had won the fame he probably thought his project would bring to him, but it was a fame of notoriety. Some thought he had made a serious error in judgment; others thought he was a criminal. The old man's problems, however, had not diminished his air of decisiveness. Jim often felt intimidated by him.

"How's everything, Jim?" The man still retained a youthful appearance and was active, in spite of his being almost seventy years old. His straight, collar-length black hair was only lightly sprinkled with gray. "I haven't seen you for a while."

"I haven't been around the house much."

"I *have* seen you from a distance, wandering around the campus with a very attractive young woman."

"Oh, Moira." Jim hesitated, thinking he should say more. "Moira Buono. I met her last winter. I was at home here, tuned in to a lit discussion, and we got into a debate. Then after the discussion was over we stayed on, just talking, so finally I asked her where she lived and went over to her dormitory. She's gone home until August," he finished lamely.

Kira returned and sat down next to Dr. Takamura. "Ed'll bring the tea out." She looked over at Jim, eyes inquisitive, *everything all right?* He tried to smile back at her.

"We were just discussing the young woman I've seen Jim with." Kira appeared startled. She brushed some of the hair off her face and leaned forward. "You know," Dr. Takamura went on, "she resembles a girl Paul was seeing when he was about your age when we were both at Chicago, Julia something, her name was, she left for Israel a couple of years later. He was very serious about her for a while."

Jim began to feel uneasy. Kira sensed his mood. "It

sure is raining," she said. "Must be about two inches by now."

Jim leaned toward Dr. Takamura. "What was she like?" he asked. His hands felt sweaty. Kira was still watching him.

"I didn't really know her that well," the older man replied. "She seemed, well, distant somehow. She was always friendly, sometimes very talkative, but she always seemed to be holding something back somehow, never really telling you anything about herself. Paul was always with her. He practically lived at her apartment and they were thinking of getting one of their own."

The weather seemed to be colder. Kira coughed softly. "Certainly took me back," Takamura said. "I haven't thought about that whole business in years."

"What happened," Jim mumbled. "What happened," he said more clearly.

Dr. Takamura was gazing out at the lawn. "She broke it off, I don't think she ever told him why. Paul was pretty damned depressed for a while, apathetic about everything, but he pulled together. Jon Aschenbach and I managed to get him through his finals."

Jim shivered. "That was a long time ago," Dr. Takamura said.

Ed came out on the porch, carrying a tray with three mugs of tea. Jim took one of the mugs as his brother exchanged greetings with the biologist. Ed looked austere with his clean-shaven face and short hair, a monk who loved mathematics and music more than people.

Jim heard their voices but not their words. He saw Paul and Julia on the Chicago streets, Paul and Moira . . . he had thought Moira could not bring herself to accept him because he was a clone. Perhaps it was not that at all, but something else. *That would change the way I feel*, he thought.

No.

This was worse.

I'm living Paul's life. He felt paralyzed. He saw himself as a puppet, walking through an ever-repeating cycle. *I'll go through it again*, his mind murmured, *I'll go on feeling the way I do, acting the way I do, and I won't have any choice. It's all happened before and I have no way of changing it.*

Moira was gone. He knew it. Moira was gone forever. Julia had not come back to Paul. Paul had eventually forgotten Julia and Jim supposed he would forget Moira too. The thought, instead of cheering him, simply sat there in his mind, cold and damp, with no power to move him at all.

The early July weather was hot. The grass was beginning to look scorched; the flowers were wilting. The sun glared down at the earth, only occasionally disappearing behind a cloud and then emerging once again to mock the stifled world below.

Jim sat on his heels, removing weeds that threatened the bushes alongside the house. His hair was tied back on his head. He had debated with himself about shaving his beard and decided against it, knowing he would regret it when winter returned. There was another reason for not shaving it, he knew. It was his way of differentiating himself from his brothers.

He put down his trowel, sat back and looked over at Kira. She was seated under one of the trees, reading a book. She held the small flat microfiche projector in her lap with one hand, turned a small knob on the projector with the other. Jim still preferred the feel of a book in his hands. He enjoyed turning the pages and liked the smell of print and old paper. He had insisted on keeping the books in Paul's library, even though they took up more space than the tiny bits of tape he could have purchased to replace them.

He was like Paul in his attachment to old things. Paul had remained in this slightly run-down house. He had raised them in the peaceful, almost timeless atmosphere of the university, feeling that this would be best for them. He had wanted them to have a quiet place where they could discover themselves and gain intellectual tools. The university had been, in a sense, a retreat for them. Now Jim wondered if they might have become too easily adjusted to it and afraid to look beyond.

"Why don't you go inside?" he asked Kira. "It's a lot cooler there."

"It's too cool," she replied. "I don't think the regulator's working, I shiver all the time and I had to put blankets on my bed last night. Mike said he'd check it later."

Jim wiped sweat off his forehead with the back of his arm. He continued to watch Kira as she resumed reading. She was letting her hair grow longer and had pinned it up. She wore a sleeveless blue-green tunic that barely covered the tops of her thighs. She suggested a woodland sprite who at any moment might disappear among the trees.

In spite of the heat and some painful blisters on his hands, he felt content, more at peace than he had been for a long time. He and Kira had been busy since the day Moira had gone home, making repairs on the house, painting the kitchen, putting some new shingles on the roof. They had done most of the work themselves. Al was working at the university's child care center, Ed had voluntarily taken over daily chores such as cooking and cleaning, and Mike was busy with his studies, trying to get his degree as quickly as possible. Jim had buried himself in physical work, tiring himself so he could sleep soundly, hoping to keep the thought of Moira at a distance. Kira too had time on her hands. Takamura had gone to Kenya to advise its scientists, who wished to clone needed animals for wildlife preserves.

He and Kira had worked together, laughing and joking most of the time, exhausting themselves. One day Jim had realized that his sorrow had receded a little, returning in force only during the night, just before his fatigue pushed him into deep sleep.

Yesterday had been different. They had been sitting with Ed on the front porch, talking about one of Jim's poems, listening to Ed play the violin, discussing some of the work Kira had done with Dr. Takamura. They talked for a long time, their minds drawing together, communicating ideas, disagreements, and feelings with perfect understanding. Then Al and Mike had joined them. They sat there until very late, drinking beer, finally giving in reluctantly to sleepiness; and Jim realized, as he lay in bed, that he had not thought of Moira all day.

"Hey," he said to Kira, "how about going up to the lake for a swim? It's too hot to do anything else."

She looked up from her projector. "I'd love to, but you know there'll be a mob there." She put the projector down at her side. "I went up with Jonis Ettinger last month, you could hardly find a place to put a towel down. So we went over to the nude beach and it was worse there. And there were picnickers all over the woods, and empty containers just thrown all around." Kira sighed and pulled up her legs, wrapping her arms around them. "They think the containers'll just disappear, they don't stop to think it takes whole months for them to dissolve completely, and they forget to put their glass bottles in the bins. Jonis said she heard that guys go up and take pot shots at the eagles and the other birds. They don't care. After all, we can always clone more. It makes me so damned mad I sometimes wish they'd kept it closed after reclamation."

We can always clone more. He suddenly felt sorry for the cloned birds. "We could drive to the park, it's always pretty empty," he said. "It'll be cooler there than here, and we could take some supper along for later."

"Great," she said. "At least we'll get away from the house for a while." She stood up, brushed some grass from her tunic, picked up her projector and walked toward the house, tanned arms swinging loosely at her sides.

Jim watched her until she disappeared around the corner of the house. Then he picked up his trowel and followed her inside.

The night air was still warm, but pleasantly so. Jim and Kira had jogged around the perimeter of the park until the heat had subdued them. Then they had climbed the hill to the stone wall where they sat with legs dangling over the side as they drank beer and finished the remnants of supper.

It had been a pleasant afternoon. He was silent as the sun set, sitting quietly, ignoring the highway below and watching the moon rise, remembering Paul. He tried to ignore the tendrils of thought brushing at the edges of his consciousness. A warm breeze stirred the trees behind him.

He sat with Moira on the wall, holding her hand lightly. He gestured toward the moon as he told her of his father's hopes, trying to communicate the reasons behind Paul's dreams. He looked at Moira as she sat listening quietly, seemingly interested, then heard her soft sigh of impatience.

He looked at Kira. She too was watching the moon. He wondered what Moira was doing now. He had managed to keep from calling her since she had left, afraid that she would misinterpret his motives. He should not have come to the park. It had only deepened his pain, bringing it to the surface once again. Kira turned slightly and her eyes met his.

"I never," he said, "really told you much about Moira, did I, not even that time. . . . " He looked away in embarrassment. He saw himself standing on the stone wall again, ready to leap to the highway. "Very melodramatic performance," he mumbled, and felt her hand on his arm.

"Don't degrade your pain," she said softly.

"She didn't just go home for the summer, you know. I don't think she wants to see me when she returns."

"I know, I could tell. You don't have to talk about it."

"I don't know what's wrong with me," he went on. "It's funny I should care so much about Moira when, if I were honest about it, I'd have to admit I never really knew her. I know she didn't understand me. She just withdrew if it was too much for her." He looked at Kira. "That sounds so cold. The whole thing, it's like a fever or a drug maybe. You keep doing things that make it worse, destructive things, you don't care about anything else. And you don't really want to shake it off either, even when it hurts the most, you know you're alive, that you can feel, and occasionally something happens that makes you so happy it's worth all the grief. It's as if you're the only two people in the world."

"Don't dwell on it, Jim. You can't analyze a thing like that, and you'll just feel worse if you try." She swung her legs over the wall and stood up. "Want to take a walk? My legs feel a little stiff."

"Sure." He picked up the small picnic basket and followed her.

They walked along the narrow path that wound through the woods. The path was lighted by the moon. The trees on either side of them were a dark and impenetrable forest. There was a smell of pine and wildflowers. Above him, Jim could hear the movement of a small creature along the limbs of a tree. An owl hooted and was answered by crickets.

Moira stopped, leaned against one of the trees, and smiled at him. He moved to her side, put his arms around her slender waist, and she rested her head contentedly on his shoulder.

Jim halted to rest against a tree. His stomach was a closed fist; his face was hot, his mouth dry. He struggled to restrain a moan. The picnic basket slipped from his fingers and hit the ground with a dull thud. The handles clattered loudly against the sides of the basket.

"Jim." Kira stood in front of him, clutching his shoulders. "Jim." She released his shoulders and embraced him, cradling his head with one hand. "I know," she said softly.

He was a child again, curled on Paul's lap. "I know," Paul whispered, stroking his hair. "Let it out, Jim, don't ever be ashamed to cry." He squeezed his eyelids together, but the tears would not come. She brushed his hair from his forehead.

She seemed to understand his pain. He rested against her and felt some of the loneliness subside. "I guess," he said finally, "this place must have brought it all back." The tightness in his stomach began to ease.

He stood up straight, arms still around her, and looked into her green eyes level with his own. She was a dryad, a part of the forest in her tunic and sandaled feet; and it seemed that she might suddenly release him and vanish. He held her more tightly.

He felt his penis stiffen. He let go of Kira and stood awkwardly in front of her, arms dangling at his sides. She did not move away but continued to stand with her arms around his shoulders. Her face was pale in the moonlight. She tilted her head to one side. *Don't move away*, her eyes seemed to say, *don't retreat*. She moved closer to him and kissed his lips gently.

The park had grown silent. He was paralyzed, rooted to the ground as surely as the tree against his back. He strained to hear the sounds of the forest, but there was only a thundering in his ears.

She released him and they faced each other, silent and still. He tried to raise his arms. They trembled slightly as he reached out to her.

She unfastened the sash around her waist and let it flutter to the ground. She grasped her tunic with both hands and pulled it over her head. Then she slipped off her pants, balancing first on one leg, then the other. She moved slowly and as precisely as a dancer. She stood naked in front of him at last, and met his eyes again.

He saw apprehension and fear on her face as well as love and concern. He moved toward her, taking one step, then a second—and he was in her arms, holding her tightly, afraid to speak. Kira was trembling. He stroked her hair.

He loosened his shorts with one hand and dropped them on top of Kira's rumpled tunic. He ran his hands along her smooth back to her buttocks, only slightly wider and rounder than his own. She was no longer trembling.

They knelt, then lay on the ground together. He reached out and held her breasts gently as she watched him. Her face resembled Ed's in the moonlight, ascetic and austere. Then suddenly she smiled, reminding him of Al in one of his playful moods. She touched his penis, running her thumb lightly over its tip, then grasping it firmly.

His fear faded. She thrust her hips up and pulled him

to her. He thought of the uncertainty he had always felt with Moira, the lonely climaxes. There was no uncertainty with Kira. She was his female self, reaching for him now with the same urgency and impatience. Her hand held him and guided him inside her.

She drew up her knees and they lay on their sides, facing each other. Still gazing into the green eyes, he thrust with his hips, ran his hand along her thigh. Her lips parted and he heard a soft sigh. He continued to move and was conscious of her response; she was moaning now, clutching his shoulders tightly. He saw himself as a woman, receiving a man, opening to the hardness that plunged inside her, and knew that she was seeing herself as a man. They moved together, grinding their hips in perfect rhythm, and he felt the core of his excitement increasing, threatening at any moment to hurl him outside himself for a few timeless seconds.

This has never happened before. He suddenly realized that as he moved inside her, sighing his responses to her moans. *Never before. He saw generation after generation evolve, becoming more differentiated, genetic structures changing and mutating. He saw millions of men and women seeking mates, trying to find those who would complete them, make them whole again, yet always separated from them by the differences passed on to them by eons of change. He saw Kira and himself, reflections of each other, able to move along their individual paths and yet meet in perfect communication. She was no longer his sister, but his other self, closer to him than a sister could have been, merging with him so completely and perfectly that they were one being.*

He moved with her, breathed with her, sensitive to every movement of her hands on his body. Then he stopped, held his body absolutely still, prepared himself for the final thrust. She was still also, waiting, watching him with wide eyes. Her lips were parted and swollen. The warmth inside her body had grown even more intense.

At last, unable to bear it any longer, he thrust again and she moved to meet him, gasping quietly at first, then crying out, shattering the night silence. He spurted inside her. He trembled, moving with her, suspended in a pocket of timelessness. He was adrift with her in a universe contained by the skin of their bodies, and he called out as his pleasure compressed itself in his groin, then erupted throughout his body. He cried out again, no longer caring which cries were his and which were Kira's.

Then it was over and he realized with a tinge of sadness how short a time it had actually been. He withdrew from her slowly but remained beside her, resting his head in her arms. He became aware of the sweat which covered their bodies. Now he kept his eyes from meeting hers.

Kira held him more closely. "Don't, Jim," she whispered. "Don't feel ashamed. I love you, I've known it for a while. How could I help it?" She was right, of course; the old codes and ancient prohibitions could not apply to them, had not even allowed for their existence.

He looked at her face. She lay at his side, stroking his hair. It was Paul's face that watched him, smiling, gently reassuring him, protecting him with love. He curled up next to her.

The thunderstorm had passed by morning, leaving behind it cool air and large fluffy clouds. The sun, previously a malevolent eye peering balefully at the earth, was now a friendly presence, occasionally hiding behind one of the white clouds as if ashamed of its former fit of temper. Jim had carried the light plastic chairs off the porch and placed them on top of old newsfax sheets and computer print-outs in the front yard. Aiming his spray can at one, he began to cover it with a surface of gray paint.

He glanced at Ed and Kira. They had moved the old beige car out into the road and were washing it down with the hose. Their shorts and shirts were plastered against their bodies. Kira hooted as she aimed the hose at Ed, drenching him completely. He grabbed the hose from her and began to spray her with water. Kira danced on her toes, laughing loudly.

Jim moved to spray the next chair. He had been trying to accept and understand his new link with Kira. He turned it over in his mind, trying to view it objectively: it wasn't harming them, it affected no one else, it gave them pleasure. Yet it seemed cold and somehow negative to think of it that way.

"Is it so strange, Jim?" Kira had asked. They had been sitting on her bed, legs folded in front of them, elbows on knees, heads in hands, perfectly matched. "Wouldn't it be stranger if we didn't feel this way, weren't drawn to each other?"

He continued to spray the chairs. *How do I feel about it?* he asked himself. *I'm able to reach someone else, able to love and communicate without rejection.* He thought of Moira. His love for her had been nervous and feverish, an uneasiness that was always with him, occupying his entire mind, refusing to let go. With Kira he was at peace, except for the occasional guilty doubts that nudged him from time to time, then retreated under the onslaught of his rationalizations. With Kira, he could work at his writing or talk, easily sharing his thoughts and feelings and understanding hers as well. Then he wondered if he were simply using Kira to mend his wounds, and refusing to admit it consciously.

Kira and Ed were walking toward the house, leaving the hose on the lawn. They seemed to be discussing something. Ed gestured with his right arm as they climbed the steps to the front porch and disappeared into the house. Jim finished spraying the last chair and glared at the hose. He was annoyed that Ed and Kira had not rewound it and put it away; it was not like them.

The chairs would have to dry before he moved them back to the porch. He ambled to the front door, depositing the can on the porch, and went inside.

The house was silent. Al was on the day shift at the university child care center and Mike had gone to do some lab work. Jim wandered through the living room and into the kitchen.

The kitchen was empty. Jim was surprised, having assumed Kira and Ed had come in for a sandwich. He left the kitchen, went back through the living room and up the stairs, deciding he would ask them if they wanted help with the hose, or if they wanted to have some lunch with him. The door to Ed's room was open and there was no one inside. He went past Mike's room, then his own, and stopped at Kira's door.

It was closed. He knocked, heard the sound of someone moving in the room. "Kira?" he said. He knocked again, then opened the door.

Kira and Ed were sprawled on the bed. Both were naked. Ed turned and looked at Jim. Kira seemed calm. "Oh, no," Jim said. He clenched his hands into fists. He felt himself shaking. The twin faces on the bed were watching him.

He wanted to pound his fist into the wall. He wanted to hurl one of his sister's potted plants through her window. He turned and fled down the hall to his own room. He stood there trying to sort out the thoughts that tumbled through his mind.

He heard soft footsteps coming down the hall. They stopped at his door. "Jim." He did not move. "Jim." He turned and saw Kira standing in the door, a long red robe draped over her shoulders.

He gestured at the robe. "Your one concession to modesty," he said bitterly. She came into the room and closed the door.

"Why are you so angry, Jim?"

He turned from her and sat on the chair at his desk. "There's no reason to be angry," he muttered. "I found out that we're interchangeable to you too, that's all."

"No, Jim," she said softly, leaning against the door. "That's not what you found out. Do you think for one moment I confuse Ed with you? Forget about yourself for one minute and think about him. He's just about given up trying to reach out to anyone, including us. He's so quiet about his problems, it's easy to pretend he's just shy or not that interested in people. You know how you felt, how lonely you were, but at least you kept trying with Moira, and you could reach me. Ed gave up trying, and about all you've accomplished today is to reinforce the way he feels. Now he's sitting in my room feeling guilty and ashamed."

Jim looked over at Kira. She was looking at the floor, folding her arms across her chest. "Oh, I don't know, maybe I have my own problems too. Don't I have a right to solve them, or at least try? Am I supposed to limit myself to you, and ignore Ed? Has this business really changed anything you might have found out through me?" She sighed. "Maybe it'll be harder for us, Jim. We have to find our own answers in our own way, and we don't even have the rough guidelines everybody else has. Some people would look at us and talk about incest taboos, and others would probably find it strange if we loved anyone else but the other clones. The point is, we have to try, and maybe we'll make mistakes, but. . . . "

She turned and opened the door. "I still love you, Jim, just as much as I did before. Maybe none of us will ever feel the same way about anyone else, maybe we really can't. Ed needs me too."

She left his room, but did not close the door. He sat at the desk, trying to sort out his thoughts. He considered himself and the others, turning over their problems and relationships in his mind, wondering what he should do now.

Jim lifted the suitcase and put it in the back seat of the rented car. Al was leaning against the open car door. "We'll miss you," he said.

"I won't be gone long," he replied. He turned to Kira. Her forehead was wrinkled with worry. He reached over to her and grasped her shoulders. "Come on, cheer up," he said. "I'll be back in a month or so, I'm not running away. I know what I'm doing, and I know why." He wondered if the others sensed his uncertainty.

"I think you'll be gone longer than that," Kira said. "I have a feeling. . . . " She smiled at him tentatively and he kissed her lightly on the forehead. Then he climbed into the car, waving his arm at the porch where Ed and Mike sat.

He had explained himself to them as best he could

and was satisfied that they understood him as well as could be expected. He would drive up to Moira's home first. He would not make demands of her, would not force himself on her. He would not give up if she drew away from him. He would leave and go to a poetry workshop in Minnesota he had heard about, meet people there, work, be like anyone else. The plans ran through his head like a litany; he clung to them.

Kira had come to his room the night before. They had lain on his bed, arms and legs entwined, as he told her about his hopes and his plans.

It would be easier to stay with Kira, easier to give up on other people. He would not let himself do it yet, not until he had tried and failed many times.

He started the car and drove away from the house slowly. When he got to the end of the narrow road, he turned his head and looked back. Kira and Al were walking to the front porch. Suddenly he felt doubtful about his resolve, wondered if he should leave, asked himself if he really wanted to go.

He drove on until the house was out of sight and he was on the road leading to the automated highway. He put the car into automatic. He thought of Kira again, saw her head resting on his shoulder, and wondered if he were making a mistake. *Will anyone love me the way you do? Will I love anyone else in the same way?* The image of Kira faded from his mind. She had given him as many questions as answers.

The world out there was just as worthy of his attention as his own personal problems. It was a world very different from the sheltered enclave of the university, a world of neatly organized cities inside pyramids and under domes; and disorganized, dirty cities that sprawled across the landscape. It was a world of people who looked beyond earth to the stars, and people who sought to preserve old customs and ancient ways. It was a world with shiny glass surfaces capturing the energy of the sun and mud huts next to wood fires. It was a world of abundance for many and starvation for some, of green and fertile reclaimed wildernesses and eroded deserts. It was time that he tried to understand his own place in this world.

The car rode onto the bypass. He punched out his destination and leaned back as control took over, guided his car around the curved bypass and shot him forward into the stream of cars on the highway.

"The suppression of knowledge appears to me unthinkable, not only on ideological but on merely logical grounds. How can the ignorant know what they should not know?"

—Joshua Lederberg
"Orthobiosis, the Perfection of Man

4. Michael: 2025

WHEN Michael Swenson was small, too young for school and still attending the pre-school child care center, Paul had been a giant, striding through the rooms and hallways of the house as if it were a palace. He remembered big hands reaching down for him, a laugh that thundered around him as he was swooped up and the room spun in a bright swirl of colors. The floor was suddenly miles away and he would clutch his father's arms, terrified but unwilling to make a sound. Then he would be on the floor again; knowing he was safe, he would shriek in delight.

"Do it again, Paul!"

But by then Paul would have picked up Kira or Ed. Paul had always been as impartial as possible, even in moments of spontaneity. Even now, Mike did not know if Paul once had a favorite among them. He bore no resentment toward his father for this perhaps forced impartiality. It had been the best way to handle what was at best a difficult situation. Besides, resenting the dead for their actions was a pointless exercise.

Zuñi and Bill had been impartial too, but in a different way. Zuñi in particular had thought nothing of spending a lot of time with only one or two of them. She had seemed supremely confident that everything would balance out eventually, and it usually did.

Once, in a fit of childish perversity, the others had gone off to play an elaborate game in the back yard, refusing to let him join them. Zuñi had found Mike alone in his room, brooding.

"Why aren't you outside with the others?"

"They don't want me. They say I don't know how to play the game." Mike had already forgotten that last week Al was the one who did not know how to play. Al had not seemed to mind. When they rejoined him, Al was in the kitchen with Bill, eating cookies and milk and looking as though he had put one over on them.

"The hell with them, then," Zuñi said. "We'll just have to walk down the street all by ourselves and get a fruit bar at the health food restaurant."

So they had gone by themselves and Zuñi had told him stories about the clouds and the shadows cast by the trees. Of course the stories were completely fanciful, but they served their purpose. Mike forgot all about the game he could not play.

Mike rarely thought about his youth now. It was pointless to reminisce unless there was some purpose in so doing. Sometimes after work at his company's research laboratory, he would go with a few of his fellow workers to a bar near the lab. Mike drank only enough to feel pleasant and relaxed; he had been drunk only once in his life and hated the loss of control over himself. He had stumbled around, babbling meaninglessly, unable to focus or to direct his body with any degree of accuracy. He had been sick the next day. He had never allowed himself to fall into that state again. He would sit in the bar with his co-workers, listening to them recount their lives, watching as they gradually became more incoherent.

Joe Lahani, a huge muscular Hawaiian, would usually start the reminiscences, bellowing stories about his exploits at Punahou High and his youthful golden days as an undergraduate. "Why the hell did I leave the islands?" Joe would invariably end. "Why the hell did I come here to a God-forsaken sinkhole like L.A.? I'm getting out of here at the end of the month, I'll go home and live on the beach with the friendliest wahine I can find."

By then the others would have started on the stories of their lives, talking at or through each other, unwilling to listen to each other's tales but enjoying the shared drunken companionship.

Mike usually attended these drinking sessions in the company of Esther Pressman, an engineer, whom he liked for her serene attitude and businesslike demeanor. Esther was a small, slender woman whose brown hair and dark eyes gave her a quietly pretty appearance. She would usually nod gravely at Mike while the biographies were being told and shake her head disapprovingly. Oddly enough, she usually drank as much as everyone else but she never betrayed it, becoming only more solemn and unusually articulate.

The morning after, Mike would hear the comments of his fellow workers:

"Never again."

"Jesus, what a head! I'm killing myself."

"I could drink twice as much ten years ago and never feel a thing."

"Why do you keep doing it, then?" Mike would ask. The only reply he ever received was a shrug or a cryptic remark.

Mike went with his friends to the bar for one reason. He believed in having friendly relations with co-workers. People who got along worked better together. They did not waste time and money in personal gripes, usually disguised as procedural disagreements or bureaucratic disputes, at work. His tasks would be easier and more productive if the others liked him.

Yet he loathed the way they would wallow in their former lives while drinking. *Open a bottle*, he thought, *and you wind up with a time machine plus pointless aggressiveness and silly ideas*. His friends, normally intelligent and rational, became transformed. He could not understand why intelligent people would want to do such a thing. At times, he thought with a shudder, they reminded him of his brother Jim, self-indulgent, giving in to every mood and whimsy that passed through his mind.

He looked up from his desk at his sparsely populated bookshelf and remembered guiltily that he still had not read Jim's novel. It had been published the year before under a pseudonym. Jim had not wanted to be associated with Paul or cloning, hoping that the novel would be judged on its own merits.

The paperback book sat on the shelf above Mike, silently rebuking him. Jim had been disappointed with the critical reaction. Only a few people had noticed the book, although those few had complimented him on his style and said he showed promise. He had been criticized for choosing an undemanding subject.

"They all want those goddamn cosmic visions now," Jim had said to him over the holophone. "They said I was too twentieth-century American, too narrow, Nabokov *cum* Hemingway. What's wrong with that? They expect a writer to integrate all knowledge every time he sets down a sentence. I'm doing something different, that's what it comes to."

Well, what did he expect with a first novel?, Mike thought. He looked away from his brother's book. He enjoyed reading, but it took up time better spent in keeping up with the latest applications of fusion power. He had to be selective about the few books he read outside his field. As far as he knew, Jim had not written anything since the book came out, and the novel had not been picked up by a microfiche publisher. Jim was probably living on what Paul had left, small as it was.

Mike leaned back in his chair and closed his eyes to rest them. He found himself remembering something else from his childhood, one of the few incidents upon which he cared to dwell.

He was eight years old again, walking home from school across the playground. Jim and Al were being kept after school for programming obscene holograms into one of the computers. Kira and Ed were at the university swimming pool.

Three older boys were lounging next to the swings. Mike recognized only one, a big redheaded boy named Bucky. This was reason enough to avoid the group. He began to walk away from them toward the nearby road.

"Hey!" someone shouted. Mike kept walking. "Hey, clone!" The older boys left the swings and quickly surrounded him. They were all bigger than he was. The two with Bucky were a mean-looking blond boy and a black kid with straight dark hair.

"He's one of the clone kids," Bucky said. "They grew him in a machine, guess his father don't like fucking." The other two giggled. "Well, does he?" Bucky continued, shoving Mike in the shoulder. "Does he like to do it? Maybe he likes machines more." The redheaded boy shoved him again and he fell over on his side in the grass.

Mike, feeling frightened now, refused to answer. The blond boy grabbed his books.

"Wat here don't think you need books," Bucky said. "Do you, Wat."

"Nope," the blonde said. "I mean, he can get the same ones from the other clones. Besides, they're the same, him and them, he knows what they know." Wat threw the books down and began to stomp on them, crushing the tiny microfiche container and Mike's reading machine.

Mike clenched his fists to keep his hands from trembling. His face flushed with anger. He wanted to punch Wat as hard as he could, but then the others would gang up on him. He said nothing.

"Quiet little bastard," the black kid said.

"He won't be quiet for long," Bucky said. "Come on." He and Wat began to drag Mike with them, pulling him first one way, then another. His arms hurt and it seemed they would come right out of their sockets. Mike bit his lip and kept silent.

They stopped. "See that hill?" Bucky shouted.

Mike looked down the small but rocky and steep hill at the edge of the playground. "You're gonna roll down it as fast as you can go," Bucky went on.

"No."

"You're gonna if I have to throw you down it." He felt himself being lifted and then he was in the air. The ground rushed up to meet him and he rolled, tearing his overalls on some rocks as he hurtled to the bottom of the hill.

He got up. He had a cut on one knee and some bruises for sure, but luckily he had landed on a soft piece of ground. He stumbled back up the hill, forcing back tears.

"Roll!" And he was tumbling down the hill again, ripping his clothes and bumping his head against a rock when he reached bottom. He climbed up while his stomach burned and tightened inside him.

"Well, cloney, you're just going right down again." Down he rolled. Hours seemed to pass. He would be trapped here forever with the mad trio, rolling over and over. He was dizzy and wanted to vomit, but he managed to control himself. He wanted to cry but he would not let the boys see his tears.

Mike did not know how long they forced him to roll down the hill. But at last, as he stumbled up for what seemed the hundredth time, trying to ignore the pain of a twisted ankle, he noticed that the boys had stopped laughing. He stared at them steadily, as if daring them to do more.

"He didn't cry once," Wat said. "Jesus."

"Not bad, cloney," Bucky said. He sounded a little worried. "You must be crazy." He said it as though it was a compliment. Then the three were gone, probably afraid a teacher might come outside and catch them.

Mike had been a mass of dirt, scratches, bruises, and torn clothing when he got home. Paul had been angry. Mike knew he did not believe him when he said he had tripped and fallen by accident. But Paul seemed to understand his need for keeping silent and stopped questioning him after a while. After that, Mike had not taken the obvious actions. He did not tell his teacher about the three boys. He did not ask the other clones to help him beat up the group, though they probably could not have beaten the older boys anyway. But Bucky and his friends never bothered him or the others again.

Mike was still, irrationally, proud of this distant exploit. It had proven something to him that he had attempted to follow ever since. He would not allow himself to give in to useless emotional responses. He would deal with things as they came along, doing what he could and expecting nothing from others except perhaps respect. Once he had been hurt by cruel remarks about himself and the others. He soon learned he could spend a lifetime in self-pity, a useless and unproductive enterprise. After a long time, he could listen to jokes about cloning and feel nothing except a mild boredom. He did whatever he had to do efficiently and as well as he knew how, wasting little time in worrying about it afterward.

When Paul died, he had grieved, and then locked up his grief in a small private chamber in his mind. He greeted the people who called or came by to offer condolences. He arranged for the small memorial service that Paul would have liked, inviting Paul's close friends to give short reminiscences about him. Paul had never been one for prayers, religiosity or inordinate praise. Mike was relieved when his father's friends spoke simply without mumbling words of an afterlife or calling Paul one of the great men of science.

Mike returned to school the day after the service. Jim and Ed, who were busy shuffling around the house feeling depressed, called him heartless. Al and Kira said nothing, but he could read what they felt in their eyes.

All he had said was, "Crying won't bring him back. He would have wanted us to go on." Eventually, of course, they realized he was right and returned to their own studies. Naturally, they had let him discuss the details of the estate with Paul's lawyer. Between them, they had managed to set aside enough money to live on for some time in spite of the high inheritance tax, and there were Paul's royalties plus the trust funds. Mike had organized all of it with the lawyer, even noting a couple of items the attorney missed. But the others had not been particularly grateful. In fact, they had not been interested in hearing about it. He wondered if they would have preferred getting by on the minimum income and student grants.

He had only slipped once. During a visit to Dr. Valois, he had told her about his attitude in greater detail than usual, expecting at least some understanding from her. He had not cried a tear for Paul and was proud of his forbearance.

But Dr. Valois had become concerned.

"Mike, I don't want to tell you how to feel or behave. I'm certainly not recommending that you give way every time you feel depressed or unhappy about something. But emotions shouldn't be repressed, to use an old term. There's a time for joy and a time for sorrow."

"And a time to live and a time to die," he said mockingly.

"You can utilize your feelings, let them out in constructive ways. You're just sitting on yours."

"I don't care to give in to them."

"In other words, it's a defense. You won't get hurt."

"I can't feel certain things, that's all." He had said it calmly, vaguely disappointed in Emma Valois.

"You're not letting yourself, you mean. Why, Mike?"

"What difference does it make, whether I can't or I'm not letting myself? It's the same thing. I'm not a sadist, I don't go out of my way to hurt others. I get along. People who give in to such things make themselves and others miserable."

It had been his last visit to Dr. Valois. There was obviously nothing more she could do for him. He had been tiring of the visits anyway. Occasionally she had called the house and spoken to him for a few moments. He had always been pleasant, cheerful, and noncommittal. He had written her a kind note when he left for California. He did not want her to think he did not care.

Mike heard the door of his apartment open and got up. His brother Ed passed his office, leaned in, and mumbled a greeting.

When Mike came out to California, Ed had come along. Mike had decided, a bit reluctantly, to share an apartment with his brother. Although he had looked forward to being on his own, it had been more practical to live with Ed. They had both been studying at the same university. They had shared their rented car and their home computer hook-up.

Kira had remained in Paul's old house, continuing her studies with Takamura and his people. Al was on the moon and Jim was God knew where. Mike had received two calls from him in the past ~year, one from Toronto and another from Zimbabwe. Why Jim had gone to Zimbabwe, formerly Rhodesia, Mike did not know. Its citizens were still not overly enthusiastic about white visitors, but were starting to give in to the financial benefits of tourism.

Mike had finished his doctorate two years after coming to Los Angeles. Rather than staying on at the university for a post-doctoral degree, he had gone to work right away, anxious to apply what he had learned. He was now a member of a research group working on new applications of fusion power and ways to utilize it more efficiently. It was important work. The world had grown greedy for power. Poorer nations wanted their share of the wealth. Threats, unspoken and implicit, had existed beneath their requests for aid: *Help us, or we shall not be responsible for the consequences. Some of our more impatient citizens may take matters into their own hands.* It would have been easy to smuggle an atomic weapon into a large western city. Any country with a city destroyed in this manner would have had impossible alternatives. They could acquiesce in the destruction, taking no action; they could go to war using ground forces and some tactical nuclear weapons; or they could decimate the offending country with atomic bombs, killing thousands of innocent people. The unspoken threat had been sidestepped. It was easier and more sensible for wealthier nations to volunteer their help.

It's possible, Mike thought as he watched his brother in the doorway, *that I may be heading to some place more distant than Zimbabwe to help technicians there.* His company, one of many supra-national, multi-tentacled organizations, often sent its people to aid poorer nations. It was its way of doing good, gaining more power, and acquiring more wealth at the same time. He couldn't very well drag Ed along with him. Yet he had grown used to his brother's quiet presence. At times he felt he would be sorry to see Ed leave, though he usually tried to ignore such feelings.

"You got another letter from Arthur Gordon," Mike said in response to his brother's greeting. "I put it in your room on your desk."

"Thanks," Ed replied, turning to leave.

"Wait a minute. I assume it's another offer. I don't know why you're still farting around here if you have a chance to study with a man like that."

"There are good people here," Ed said quietly. "I'm satisfied. Besides, with the computer booth, I can always tune in his lectures or discussions if I want to, and the print-outs keep me up to date on all the important papers. I might go East and wind up seeing Arthur Gordon twice a year. You know how it is, studying with people of his reputation."

"I suppose that's why he wrote you a personal letter with the formal offer. And you know goddamn well that a computer booth is no substitute for actually being at a school and being able to associate with certain people, though it's probably good enough if you have no other choice. You mathematicians don't have any practical sense sometimes."

"Math isn't like physics." Mike sensed a note of scorn in Ed's voice. Ed seemed to feel that the pure truths of mathematics were superior to more practical, and ambiguous, knowledge. "And a computer could have written that letter."

"Assume it did. Gordon still had to go through finding out all those details on your work, he or somebody had to go do the programming. And I doubt that a computer would have put in all those personal touches."

"I didn't know you were in the habit of reading my mail." Ed's tone of voice was still the same, but his face tensed slightly. Mike realized that his brother was very annoyed.

"I'm in the habit of reading anything that's lying around on the kitchen table when I'm drinking my morning coffee. You should have put it inside your desk."

Ed shrugged and left the room. Mike heard his footsteps and then the closing of Ed's bedroom door. Ed was
going to spend another solitary evening with his books
or violin, as he almost always did. He was unhappy with
his life, Mike could sense that, yet he did little to change
it.

Ed was overly sensitive, just like the others, although
at least he did not overwhelm Mike in emotional turmoil
the way the other clones often had. He could at least
talk to Ed and be more open with him than with out-
siders. His brother's presence was often comforting. Kira
and Jim, with what Mike considered to be a rash and
emotional act, had simply made life at their old home
unbearable to him. Mike had seized the opportunity to
escape. And Ed certainly had not gained anything by
those sexual transactions; he too had willingly left. And
Al was puttering around on the moon, confusing his work
with Paul's, wanting to be near their father's grave while
trying to surpass him. When he bothered to think about
it at all, Mike wondered how he could be so closely
related to people who were so often capable of monu-
mentally foolish acts.

He glanced at his watch. He had already spent too much
time on these ruminations. He began again to read the
papers on his desk.

Esther Pressman lived in the same arcology as Mike,
in a small house near the top level. She shared her home
with two other young women. Mike often stopped by
after work to discuss things with her. Esther was gifted
with a practical turn of mind and an analytical intelli-
gence. She rarely wasted time in excessive chatter.

Sometimes he had dinner with Esther, who was fond
of serving plain, simple dishes without undue ceremony.
She, like him, did not care to clutter up her digestive
system with difficult-to-digest foods that inhibited clear
thinking. Once in a while they would treat themselves to
something more elaborate at a nearby restaurant.

He had stayed overnight with Esther a few times.

These occasions were the only ones in which she had abandoned her normal reserve. Mike had been fearful the first time, afraid that Esther might drag him into an emotional morass. It had happened to him before with one of his fellow students at school. But he had underestimated Esther. She gave no sign of caring for him as anything other than a friend.

Mike stepped off the elevator and walked along the roadway leading to Esther's house. Most of the people on this arcology level lived in square stucco bungalows. Several had managed to grow flowers in front of their homes.

If he walked to the end of the road, some one hundred feet from Esther's house, he could see much of Los Angeles, ribbons of automated highways and trains, a few silvery towers, thousands of tiny houses with tiny blue puddles surrounded by green shrubs, and three arcology latticeworks. The arcology he lived in had been built after the rubble left behind by a severe earthquake had been cleared away. It could supposedly withstand strong quakes; its structure was designed for it. But Mike knew that many of its residents had not taken the extra trouble to anchor their houses or apartment buildings firmly. He envisioned them sliding off the open arcology shelves, tumbling through the barriers around the edges, smashing against the highways below.

Esther was standing in the doorway of her house, dressed in a loose, worn pair of green shorts and a black shirt. She twirled an ice-filled glass in her left hand. As he approached, she lifted the glass in greeting.

"Just getting some air," she said with artificial brightness. As he passed her, she touched his arm lightly and whispered," Joe Lahani's inside. Good news."

Mike walked into the living room. Three dancers swirled around him, trailing ribbons of brightly colored cloth. He walked through one of the twirling figures. The three dancers disappeared as Joe Lahani turned off the holovision.

"Hey, Mike," Joe rumbled in his low voice, "I tried to call you after work and your brother said you'd be over here. So I thought I'd come over and tell you."

Joe sat on the couch with Polly Anton, one of Esther's roommates. Polly was a tall, slow-moving young woman who worked on satellite repair and was rarely home. She was probably on a month's leave.

"Tell me what," Mike said.

"I'll go and change, Joe," Polly said. She got up slowly, stretching and running her hands through her short red hair. "Joe's going to take me down to the gym for some handball," she said to Mike. "God, I get so out of shape up there, it's so hard to force yourself to work out." She patted the large hips under her brown dress. "I always feel so tired when I first get back." She looked past Mike at Esther, who had re-entered the room. "You should have brought Joe around before, Esther. We both like handball and swimming and sailing. He's a nice guy."

Esther shrugged.

"You're a nice guy," Polly said to Joe. She blew him a kiss and then padded out of the room on bare feet.

"Polly tends to be effusive," Esther said. She settled into an egg-shaped red chair, tucking her feet under her. Mike seated himself on the couch with Joe.

"The news," Mike said.

Joe waved his bottle of beer. "Morel was talking to me today, he was fishing around, you know, trying to find out something and not saying what it was. So I finally said to him, okay, brother, what do you want to know, and he sort of. . . . "

"Joe, please get to the point," Esther said.

"He and the company need someone to go to Bihar in India, set up a power station near Patna. They want to do what we knew they'd have to do sooner or later, put the power station in space and beam the power to Patna using microwaves."

At last, Mike thought. There were few stations generating fusion power on the earth's surface, but the demand for them was increasing, in spite of the other sources of power that existed. Energy was needed for industry, for recycling, for lighting, heating, or cooling homes. No matter how much geothermal plants, wind-

mills, the use of solar power and the utilization of hydrogen produced, the need for energy kept growing. Fusion,
unlike the other sources of power, produced energy that
had previously not existed on the earth in any form; Mike
knew that the heat generated by too many fusion stations on the earth's surface could alter its climate. He
was relieved to hear that his company was not waiting
until it was too late before considering this problem.

"Anyway," Joe went on, "Morel said he had his eye
on me and Janey Elton, Janey for the supervisory and
business side of things and me for setting up a research
team, filling them in on possible projects, especially after
the thing's done. We sorta go as consultants, you know,
iron out problems and get the thing finished. The Indians
there are trained, of course, we're just going to help with
details, for about a year or two. Actually. . . . "

"*Joe,*" Esther said.

"Well, Morel talked to Janey and she agreed with
him that you were just the man to go, brother. Naturally
I said you were too. Think of it, we get more pay, a promotion and a chance to do something besides sit on our
asses in L.A. trying to find refinements and applications
for power stations that the engineers could run by themselves."

Esther grimaced.

"Hell, the computers could run them," Joe continued,
looking at Esther. "They just keep you people around
so they can have someone official-looking in a white
coat to take the public through the lab or over to the
station on tours."

Esther chuckled. "They just keep you around because
one out of a million of your bright ideas might be worth
being put into practice by us engineers."

"I hate to admit it, but they're even sending a couple
of your people with us. Of course, they'll be out in
space half the time, puttering around."

Mike looked down at his feet. "I didn't know they
were thinking of sending me," he muttered.

"Why shouldn't they, brother? You're one of the best."

Mike suddenly felt uncertain. The feeling was distasteful to him, breaking in on his stability. He was annoyed with himself.

"You don't look so happy," the big man said. "I tell you we're going to India, getting a real chance to help somebody and do ourselves good besides, and you look like they assigned you to recycling."

"I don't know," Mike said. "I don't know if I can go to India."

Esther was watching him. He could imagine what she must be thinking.

"You can always say no," Joe said. "And you won't get another chance too soon, not unless you've got a damn good reason."

Mike watched his sandaled feet curl on Esther's grassy rug. What could he say? He would not feel right about leaving Ed alone in Los Angeles. *But it's not just an emotional thing,* he thought to himself, *Ed needs me here now, it's an obligation.* It would not be right to leave the insecure Ed by himself.

"If you aren't interested in your own welfare, better think of mine and Janey's, brother," Joe said belligerently. "How do you think we're going to look for recommending you so highly?"

Leave it to Joe to drag in something like that, Mike said to himself. "Don't be ridiculous," he said aloud. "Morel picked me, he'd have to blame himself and the personnel computer, not you and Janey." Mike could hear Esther move in her chair. "It's just that I'll have to arrange some things, that's all. I don't have to decide right away, they'll give me a couple of weeks."

"Oh," Joe mumbled. "Oh," he said again, as if suddenly discovering something. "You and Esther. I didn't think. But if you tell Morel, he'll fix it so you can have a few weekends now and then and you'll have your vacations together. He'll understand that."

Esther sighed.

"Come on, Joe," Polly's voice said from the doorway. Joe got up and lumbered across the room.

"You think about it, Mike," Joe muttered as he left. "Morel'll probably call on you tomorrow."

He was alone with Esther. "Why didn't you tell him?" she said as she rose and went to the small cabinet in the corner to pour herself another drink. She waved the bottle at him and he shook his head. "Why didn't you tell Joe it has nothing to do with me?"

"Couldn't it?" he tried to say lightly.

"I don't fool myself," she said, settling next to him on the couch. "I like undemanding friendships. I'll miss you a little, but I can live without you. I don't like being tied down any more than you do. So what's the problem?"

"It's not really any of your business, Esther."

She smiled, seemingly unannoyed. "You're right, it isn't. And I'm not particularly worried about you, you can usually take care of yourself. But I'm afraid if you make the wrong decision now, you might hurt yourself. Oh, you'll hurt the company a little, but they can get someone else, there are plenty of good people around. But after a while, you might regret your decision and then you won't function as well. It'll affect your work."

"I don't regret things. It's a waste of time."

"You might, and then whatever or whoever held you back will suffer your resentment. No one will gain anything. You have to consider yourself first, or you won't be much good to anyone else." She paused. "It's your brother, isn't it."

"It doesn't matter."

"It is. You're being very foolish. Ed isn't a child."

He was suddenly angry with Esther. His anger seemed to grab him by the throat and he was unable to pull away from it. "Shut up," he said quickly, "it's none of your business and I don't need your advice. Just keep out of it!" He was shouting. Startled, he grabbed her arm and realized his own was shaking. He was frightened now, shocked at the forceful demonstration of his feelings. The wave of anger receded, leaving a residue of shame.

"Relax," she said calmly. He could not read her face. She was a hard, brittle thing, her eyes were dark pools with nothing behind them. He did not want to be with her, or anywhere around her.

He fled from the house, but not before hearing her quiet last words.

"Call me if you feel better, and don't slam the door."

Mike managed to keep from committing himself when Peter Morel came to his office. But his own voice had sounded hollow in his ears as he reassured the small reticent man that he was delighted at the opportunity to go to Bihar, but needed the weekend to think things over.

"Of course," Morel said as he opened the office door to leave. "You think it over. Don't take too long. We want to start you people on hypno-training in Bihari. You'll still need some time after that with the language computers if you're to be fluent. You'll need it even if most of your co-workers do speak English, which I'm sure they do." Mike realized that Morel already assumed he was going. *Why shouldn't he? Only a fool would turn it down.*

"I'll be seeing you," Morel said, still lurking by the entrance. Mike nodded his head in dismissal and Morel, twitching nervously, almost lunged through the doorway, slamming the door behind him.

Morel was definitely the wrong person for his job, Mike thought. When he had to give a person word of a promotion, he was as excited as if getting it himself; when he had to let someone go, one could almost feel Morel's ulcer twitch in sympathy. When faced with uncertainty, the poor man grew nervous with fear. He found Morel irritating, but maybe his empathic traits endeared him to some who received his messages. Still, an average working day must be an emotional morass for a person of his kind.

The thought of Morel disturbed him. He turned his attention to the papers on his desk. He would have to type another research progress report into the computer soon. He sighed softly and made a note to do that tomorrow. There were some technical papers to be read. He wrote down the titles of the ones he would read that night, dialing them at home and billing the company afterward.

There was a meeting of physicists in Berkeley tomorrow morning that he had promised to attend; he would tune it in on his holo at home and come to the research center in the afternoon.

He was ready to leave. Ed had an evening class and had taken the car with him, so Mike would have to catch a train.

He walked out of his office and past closed office doors. He nodded to Lonnie Samuelson as he passed him in the hall. Samuelson, a tall, cool, blue-eyed man, approved research projects and checked on their progress. He would read Mike's progress report and would undoubtedly, as he nearly always did, stop by Mike's office to discuss the report with him. Mike supposed that Samuelson's job was necessary, yet he was often annoyed by the man's constant checking, his visits to the laboratory, and his insistence that each project have a clearly defined goal at its inception. *He should realize*, Mike thought, *that in research you often don't know what your result will be until you get to it*. But then Samuelson and his people were probably not intelligent enough, even though trained scientifically, to do research. Mike sometimes felt sorry for them.

He passed an open laboratory door and heard the voices of children. The company, which ran a child care facility at the research center for the sons and daughters of workers, encouraged the children occasionally to watch their parents at work. It also welcomed young people who might wish to have a scientific career. Mike had, on a few occasions, explained his work to groups of students. He would direct his remarks to those who were obviously interested rather than to those who betrayed their boredom by restlessness.

In his imagination, Mike could almost hear the hum of the generators in the plant several miles from the research center as they fed the hungry city. It was the generators that were most impressive to the schoolchildren and citizens who sometimes toured that facility. They were often disappointed by the sight of the fusion process itself. It was so apparently simple, the small pellet of fuel in a vacuum chamber, met by a laser beam which compressed the pellet and heated it to over one million degrees. Its energy would be carried from the chamber by a stream of liquid lithium which, by heating water into steam, the large generators that supplied electrical power. The generators got the applause of the crowd, yet to Mike the laser fusion process itself was infinitely more impressive. It could in time, using orbiting power stations, give people as much power as they could use.

Of course, people would still use solar power too, much of it beamed to the earth from orbiting solar panels. They would also make use of geothermal power, of hydrogen, of windmills in some cases. It was good that people had a choice, he thought, different areas had differing needs and differing levels of technical expertise. Yet in time one form of energy production, that which could provide the most energy at the lowest cost, might win out.

Mike hoped he would live to see the day when the world was no longer divided into poor and wealthy, with the wealthy hoarding their riches and defending them with weapons that themselves took much of the wealth. He did not feel altruistic. He simply found it wasteful and unproductive to conceive of a world in which human minds were wasted and the more fortunate had to worry about others. Better to give everyone a chance and then let a person make his own choices and decisions.

He came to the nearest exit and soon found his way to the moving sidewalk that would take him to the train station. He looked back at the research center. It was far from beautiful, a square, four-story block of gray surrounded on three sides by a grassy park area with benches under palm trees. Beneath the park was an underground parking lot. Beyond the park he could see the basin of Los Angeles, covered with the vines of automated highways and municipal train tracks. The fusion process had become available none too soon for this city, providing the power from the automated highways and trains that had kept it from becoming an uninhabitable, smog-filled valley. Los Angeles had, with the aid of new technologies, preserved its freeways and its decentralized life style. Its arcologies, small cities in themselves of half a million people each, provided a less isolated existence for those who preferred to have friends, stores, and businesses within walking distance.

His work was important, perhaps the most important work being done on the earth. He thought of his current research project, still in a very early stage. If he and his colleagues could perfect their matter-scanning techniques, have an image of every atom's place within an object, they could, with the energy released by fusion, duplicate almost anything. Every person on earth might eventually have access to any material goods he desired or needed. Rare metals and other resources could be created as needed. No one would spend time any more in trying to acquire food and shelter, and human minds could turn to other problems. They would find intellectual or aesthetic challenges, and a world now starting to grow more comfortable and bored might become revitalized.

It was important for him to go to Bihar, to India, and work there to give others the same chances he already had. Innovations and technology were the only things that the United States had left to sell, the only things that gave it any influence at all in world affairs. Even in those fields, they had been hard put to be as creative as many other nations. The day was not far off when all the powers of the world would be equalized, when their greed and material comfort, cemented by a humane technology, might let them at last trust each other and work together on the next set of problems that would confront humanity.

He would have to decide what to do about Ed, who was suddenly an obstacle not only to him but to the well-being of those in Bihar. He chuckled to himself. No, someone else could always go to Bihar, it was just that he wanted to do the work himself, wanted to know that he was carrying out his self-assigned obligations. The thought of leaving Ed, when he dwelled upon it, seemed unaccountably to make him afraid. Thoughts chased each other through his head, disorienting him.

"Are you feeling any better today?" a quiet voice asked. He turned and saw Esther walking along the moving surface to catch up with him. He nodded, She stood at his side and smiled briefly. "It wasn't like you to lose your temper."

He looked past her, over her head. "I didn't feel like discussing my private affairs."

"Are you busy tonight, or do you want to stop somewhere for dinner?"

"I don't know. I was just going to go home and read some papers, maybe talk to Ed later." Mike felt as if he was saying too much.

"Aren't you going to meet everyone later for a few drinks?" They stepped off the moving walk and hurried toward the train stop, a small building which housed a computerized newsfax and magazine stand. Several men and women stood outside the building, waiting for the train to arrive. The municipal train service was not as good as it could be since most people still used cars or commuted on the long-distance rapid trains to places outside the city.

"I can't," Mike mumbled. "I have to tune in a conference tomorrow morning and I promised myself I'd go to my office and get a progress report done. I'd rather do that tomorrow than have to do it first thing Tuesday morning."

"Did Morel see you today?"

He nodded. Somehow his self-control was slipping away from him. He felt incapable of standing up to Esther, of telling her to stop bothering him.

"Well, you'll have to decide pretty soon," she said. "Look, why don't I come home with you, we can make some supper and talk about it. I won't stay long."

"All right." Easier to hand everything over to Esther for the time being. He was suddenly weary, feeling as if he could fall asleep on one of the nearby benches, just go to sleep and let someone else decide for him.

Somehow Mike had managed to put a meal together out of odds and ends; some leftover meat-flavored soybean and nut loaf, fish-flavored protein meal patties, and fresh asparagus spears. He ate it, along with a salad Esther had made, without tasting it, shoveling the food into his mouth and chewing it perfunctorily. It seemed dry and he found himself drinking more wine than usual. He could not even enjoy the asparagus and fresh salad vegetables, which Ed had purchased while in an extravagant mood.

He gazed absently out his kitchen window at the courtyard below. His apartment building, a set of cube-shaped modules stacked together like a child's set of blocks, was on the fifth level of the arcology. People wandered through the well-lit courtyard past the shallow pools reserved for children. A few people sat on benches near the flower beds; others, more active, were playing on the tennis courts.

As Esther stacked dishes in the sink and shoved napkins down the recycler, Mike hurried out of the kitchen. He stopped in front of Ed's bedroom door. He paused only for a moment before entering the room.

He was an intruder, a burglar. He had not entered the room of one of the others without being asked to since childhood. Paul had insisted on a respect for privacy, perhaps to an extreme because of their unusual circumstances. Even now he felt like a criminal.

He stood by Ed's desk. On top of a pile of data sheets sat a letter with Arthur Gordon's name on the envelope. Ed's name and address had been written by hand.

The letter must have arrived that day. Gordon had apparently gone to the trouble and expense of having an actual letter delivered instead of simply typing it into a computer and having it punched out here. Mike hesitated, then grabbed the letter, pulling it out of the envelope before he could think about what he was doing. The letter was also hand-written, signed by Gordon.

He scanned it quickly: Gordon still wanted Ed to study with him, could not offer a fellowship since they were now taken but could find him a teaching job in the fall and get him a fellowship for the following year. The remainder of the letter was a short comment on one of Ed's papers, much of it in the form of equations.

Mike knew little about mathematicians, that group of impractical drifters through airy abstract heights, who seemed to talk only of truth, beauty, and clarity. He was interested only in math that aided him in more practical tasks. But even he had heard of Arthur Gordon. He knew enough to know that Ed would be turning down a great opportunity if he refused Gordon's offer.

He put the letter back in the envelope and placed it on the desk where he had found it. He was suddenly frightened, cast adrift. Ed might have replied to Gordon already. Perhaps he had decided to leave. Why this possibility frightened him, he did not know.

Esther was standing in the doorway. "Do you always come into your brother's room when he isn't home?"

He pushed past her and retreated into the living room. Somehow he had lost control. He sat down on the small beige couch in one corner of the room and buried his head in his hands. He had drunk too much at dinner. He was not used to it, that was all. He had slipped temporarily. "I'd like some coffee," he said to the walls.

"I'm making some. You'll have it in a minute," Esther said. Her green skirt swirled around her ankles as she left the room.

Mike clenched his fists, then sat up. This simply would not do. He would not allow himself to wallow in this way, to shame himself. By the time Esther returned with the coffee, he was sitting up, trying to smile.

"You'll have to excuse me," he said quietly. "I'm not used to having that much wine." She handed him his coffee and sat next to him.

"You know what I think?" she said. "You're afraid of having Ed leave."

His body tensed. "Not at all. He's a pretty solitary sort, you know, I dont know how he would handle himself if he were alone. He changed after our father died. He was kind of shy before that, but afterwards. . . . "

"I've seen Ed. He doesn't really seem to mind being alone. He has his math and his music. I don't think he's really that unhappy."

"You don't understand, Esther. I've known Ed a lot longer than you have. He's pretty morose sometimes and I'm the only one around he can talk to unless he's going to spend a fortune calling Al on the moon. I have a responsibility to him." *I can't just go off and leave him the way Paul left us.* He was startled at the ripple of resentment that washed over him at the thought of his father. *Going off and getting himself killed in a stupid accident.* He tried to concentrate on Esther.

"You're more solitary than he is," she was saying. "He's probably changed, and you're seeing him the way he was. You may need him as much as he needs you."

He sank back into the couch. He longed to sweep Esther out of the room, out of the building. He opened his mouth to reply and could find nothing to say.

"Ed's probably the only person you confide in at all, if you confide to anyone. You don't really interact with anyone else, you know. And at least he's an audience when you're alone here. You probably feel better just knowing he's around."

He had obviously misunderstood Esther, thinking she had more sense. She was starting to meddle with his mind, trying to confuse him.

Instead of replying he sipped at his coffee, avoiding her dark eyes. A door slammed and he heard footsteps. "Hi, Ed," he heard Esther say.

He looked up and saw his brother enter the living room.

"You're home early," Mike said.

Ed shrugged. "Short discussion." Ed was pale. His white face had rarely been exposed to the sun and his short hair was still dark brown unlike Mike's sun-streaked hair. He sat down in a low dark-blue chair across from Mike and Esther. "I should have dialed the discussion here, but I wanted to talk to some people afterward."

"Did Mike tell you about his offer?" Esther asked. Mike straightened and tried to signal her with his eyes. She was staring at his brother and did not notice. "He was approached by Peter Morel today, the company wants him to go to India and help set up an orbiting fusion power plant."

"Are you going?" Ed said.

"I haven't decided yet."

"I didn't think they'd give you something like that this soon. It must be quite an honor."

"I haven't decided. I'd rather continue the project I'm working on now."

"Gordon wrote to me again. His letter just got here today. He's getting insistent." Ed turned to Esther. "Arthur Gordon wants me to study with him. Maybe you've heard of him. I'm surprised that he even noticed my papers."

"I know his work," Esther said. "I took a lot of math before I decided on engineering. Sounds like quite an opportunity for you. You should take it. I've been trying to talk some sense into your brother here, he actually doesn't know whether he should go to India. If he doesn't, he might be stuck where he is, you know, the company will wonder why he turned it down and they might not be as inclined to listen to some of his ideas later on. You know what people are like. They draw all kinds of ridiculous conclusions from people's actions. They might think. . . . "

"Esther, you can leave now," Mike said.

"What's wrong?" Her innocent gaze and injured tone did not fool him.

"You can leave," he said again. He put his coffee cup down on the small end table next to him. "I'd like to talk to Ed alone."

"All right." Esther stood up. "Maybe you can talk some sense into him," she said to Ed. She left the room and Mike heard the door slam behind her.

"You were pretty rude," Ed said. "I thought Esther was your friend."

"Sometimes she gets on my nerves."

"That's no excuse. Well, is it true, this business about India?"

"Yes."

"Will it help you with the company, or is it just another job?"

Mike had to be honest. Ed could easily detect a lie. He pulled nervously on his moustache before answering. "It's a fairly important project. It'll show them how I can handle that much responsibility. They might put me in charge of a whole research section when I get back instead of just a small lab group. I'd get more freedom to push the project I'm working on now, get more funds and workers for it."

"You should probably go then."

"I don't know, I have to think about it. Morel gave me the weekend to decide. I have three days to consider it; I don't have to decide right now."

"I think you should go. I don't want to push you or anything, but if you did, I could go east and study with Gordon."

"What do you mean?"

"Well, I've been worried about you, Mike. I don't want to leave you here alone if it'll make you unhappy. I've been worried about that. I have a responsibility." Ed's words seemed to echo in his brain, reminding him of similar words spoken by Paul to all of them long ago. "If you need me, I'll stay."

"What are you talking about?"

"You can't fool me, you should know that by now. I'll admit, I didn't want to be alone at first, you were the only one besides the others that I could talk to. But I think I'm ready to go off now. I think I can handle things by myself. I just didn't know about you, I didn't want to leave if. . . . "

"Go," Mike said. "Go, I don't care. I've been worried about you. I don't know how the hell we can know each other for so long and still be this thick. Go."

"Are you all right?"

"Go." Mike fled from the room and stumbled toward

his study, his mind in a turmoil. He was suddenly afraid of being alone and deeply ashamed of that fear.

Mike sat in Esther's kitchen, trying to swallow the orange juice she had placed in front of him. He tried not to think of his brother who was home busily packing his things. He would forget the past week, his attempts at being lighthearted while Ed prepared to leave. He would ignore the fact that by tomorrow, he would be alone in his apartment. *After all, I always wanted to get away from the others finally.*

He would get to know Joe Lahani better in India. He would arrange with Morel to get some weekends off with Esther. He would be more open with her than he had been. She might even stay with him in his apartment until he left.

He was beginning to feel a bit better. He looked over at Esther as she sat down across the table from him.

"I was right, then," she said. "Well, now you can go to Bihar and get some sense into your brain and Ed can do what he wanted to do."

"All right, all right."

"You'll be better off, you know."

He finished his juice. "I have to ask you something, Esther. Why did you do it, telling Ed all of that business about Bihar? I wasn't going to, I didn't want to make him feel guilty about standing in my way."

"I figured it was best for you if I did. I think I was right."

"That's not the only reason. I don't know why, but I feel as if there's another reason."

"You're right, there is." She got up and circled near him, brushing against his shoulder with her bare arm. "I want you to go to Bihar, I don't want you around here any more. I might start falling in love with you, I feel as though I have been for a while. I don't like it, it makes me feel dependent and foolish. I'd rather look after myself, you know. Besides, I know enough to know you won't ever feel that way about me, and there are all those damned clones competing for your attention. If you leave, I'll have enough time to forget you."

He forced himself to look up at her. Her brown eyes seemed to shine. "Esther," he started to say. He took her hand. "It doesn't have to be that way. I think I. . . . "

She pulled away. "Don't you understand?" she cried. *I don't want to be like this.* "I was going to put in for a transfer if you didn't go. I don't *want* to feel this way."

"Esther. . . . "

"We'll both be better off this way. I'm not substituting for Ed."

Mike left the kitchen and soon found himself outside her house. He hurried toward the elevator. The houses on either side of the road seemed to swirl around him. He bumped into an older man and shoved him aside angrily. He pushed his way onto the elevator and heard it humming around him as he moved down past the levels of houses and office buildings.

". . . efforts to control biological modification of man will have to be carefully thought out in advance, not only in their technical aspects, but, more significantly, in their ethical aspects, and many of the biologists involved in the research that will lead to biological engineering have called for just such thought."

"The fact that 'the nature of man' is plastic under a variety of forces, including biological engineering, psychological conditioning, etc., urgently raises the question of what forms of man are to be preferred and condoned."

—Gerald Feinberg
THE PROMETHEUS PROJECT

5. Kira: 2028

THE eagles soared, flying out over the wooded land below the barren hill. Kira Swenson watched them as they separated from each other and flew on, each searching for its own path. The Indians who comprised the Park Service here had been concerned; not enough eagles, too many smaller birds and rodents. Some of the birds had been shot at by tourists and left to die in underbrush.

The number of people allowed in the park at any one time was already limited. But several younger Indians had spoken of barring white people from the park altogether, where the Indians lived in an attempt to combine old ways and new knowledge.

The eagles would fly out now and feed on the smaller birds and animals, bringing the reforested park into balance. *We all live on blood and death*, Kira thought, *we kill to stay alive and die to make room for others. We stand on the blood of a billion ancestors, the descendants of those who were strong enough to save themselves by murdering others. We have blood on our hands, and so few of us do anything to make all those deaths worthwhile.*

She was bringing more death to this park. Unsuspecting sparrows and mice would be seized by talons today, carried off to the nests of the eagles. Perhaps they would have starved otherwise, perhaps not. Kira often found peace in the park and in places like it, removed from the noise of people and their machines. At other times she was depressed and disturbed by the wilderness, suddenly aware of the constant warfare among species. Ants were dying by the thousands around her, birds searched for food, deer guarded their young, rabbits fled from larger creatures, and people found beauty and peace.

She thought of her brother Al on the moon and understood how he and others had come to love its austere surface, where nothing died and only humans lived. Yet even there life was precarious; a punctured dome, a defective spacesuit, a flittercraft accident, a malfunction in life-support systems, and death would arrive there also.

A wren alighted on a tree below and warbled. Kira smiled slightly. At least for now, the bird was happy, at home in the park. Time enough for food-gathering later, or for fleeing from a dark shape overhead.

"You're not worrying again," Jonis Ettinger said. Kira turned to the slender blond woman beside her. Jonis was already growing pink in the sunshine; she rarely went outside, preferring to spend her time in study or experimentation. Her pale gray eyes flickered over Kira.

"What do you mean, worrying again? I don't worry that much."

"I do," Jonis replied. "I worry about whether we're going to get any money for some real work someday, or whether Hidey is going to drop dead with all his cigarettes, or whether I'm going to lose my job or whether the moratorium repeal is going to pass. Right now I'm worrying about what this goddamn sun is doing to my skin." Jonis picked up one of the cages they had brought and motioned to Kira. "We could have let one of the students who trained the birds bring them out here."

Kira picked up the other cages and began to follow Jonis down the hill. "It's good for you to come out here," she said. "You need some exercise anyway. Besides, I like to bring the birds and animals here, it makes me feel a little more responsible for them, more . . . I don't know."

"I guess you feel you have something in common with them." Kira was not offended by the remark. She was used to Jonis after being friends with her for so long. Anyway, Jonis was probably right.

They reached the bottom of the hill and headed along a path to the small truck they had parked near the edge of the woods. They passed a group of well-constructed Indian homes almost hidden among the trees. The wooden houses, with their rounded sides and pointed tops, suggested tepees. But these tepees were heated by solar power, not campfires. The people who lived in them were now spending the summer looking after the park while pursuing old crafts. In the winter, when they returned to their homes, their children would study on their computers and holos. Many would leave for high school and college and many would remain to work in the outside world. But others would return here to apply what they had learned and to train their own children to hunt, track, and fish.

"Hidey's been looking tired lately," Jonis muttered as they put the crates into the truck. "Has he been working too hard or have you been keeping him up nights?"

"I haven't seen him, except at work," Kira said. Her throat grew dry. She had said nothing to Hidey during the past few weeks that did not concern laboratory work, and Hidey had gone back to living in his office, with occasional trips to his apartment.

Kira was not sure how it had all started or what had precipitated it. Hidey had stopped at her house several weeks ago, as he often did, probably out of habit more than anything else. They talked, mostly about the growing movements to repeal the legal restrictions on experimentation which had culminated in a bill being brought to the floor of the Senate. Hidey spoke about some of the projects he might want to pursue if the bill passed the House. She offered him some tea.

Suddenly she was more aware of him than she had ever been. She began to grow conscious of his eyes, of the gray hairs sprinkled across his head, of his stocky body. She felt awkward and knocked over one of the empty tea cups with her hand. She reached for him at the same time as he reached for her.

Hidey stayed with her that night. He remained with her as they both traveled from the house to the university. She had pushed her doubts aside, trying to forget Hidey's age, his relationship to Paul, his responsibility for her own existence. Everything around her grew more intense, things seemed to happen more rapidly; her life seemed bounded by Hidey both at the lab and in her home. Eventually the feelings she had for him, she knew, would change. The longing and desperation would become a peaceful contentment with sparks of warmth and passion from time to time. Or the feelings of love would die completely and she and Hidey would be left with friendship and some memories. Or the relationship would grow sour, they would grow away from each other, perhaps with bitterness and anger, and never feel at ease together again. These were the alternatives she saw in her mind; her feelings were ruled by the present reality. She could not bring herself to believe that she would ever feel differently about Hidey, although it was probable that in time she would.

He had remained with her for two weeks, migrating to the biological research center with her. But he had not been able to put aside his own doubts. He began to feel foolish; a man in his late seventies having an affair with a young woman. She noticed that he became uncomfortable with her in public, worried about what people might think, afraid that they would guess their relationship. He expressed doubts about the wisdom of allowing their love to develop when she would inevitably survive him and spend most of her life without him.

At last Hidey was unable to make love to her one night. He worried about that too. The anti-aging shots could not preserve him forever, in spite of the fact that he had been unusually vigorous and youthful for his age when he began receiving the treatment more than ten years ago.

She tried to put his mind at rest. He worried too much. He was just feeling tired. If she had to live without him eventually, she would at least have memories of him and would not regret the years spent with him.

She discovered that his doubts went deeper than she had suspected. She was Paul's clone. He had brought her into the world. He too was her father in some sense. And he had been one of Paul's closest friends.

Finally he had come home with her and refused to stay. "I have to think a while, by myself," he said. In the light by the front door, he looked older than she had ever seen him look before.

"I think you should stay," she said desperately. "If you brood over things, they usually just look worse than they are. I love you, Hidey. All that other stuff doesn't matter, not to me."

"I can't help it. I'm an old man, it's not easy for me to forget things, to dismiss a past I have to lug around on my shoulders wherever I go, that constantly produces certain associations in my mind. I was Paul's friend, I keep thinking of him when I see you. I've got about fifty more years to haul around than you do, and it makes a difference."

"It doesn't have to."

"It does anyway."

She had wanted to cry, to scream at him, somehow force him to see things her way. Instead she simply kissed him goodbye, leaning slightly over the shorter man as she did so, and watched him drive away.

"You scare me sometimes," Jonis said as they got into the truck. "I get to thinking you're more sensible than I am, that you know what you're doing, and then you go into such a gloomy mood that it even scares me."

"I'm sorry, I've got a lot on my mind."

"Sometimes you think too much. You look too closely at things and it just gets you depressed. Let's go somewhere for a drink this evening and get our minds as close to a blank as possible."

Kira was tired when she returned home. *I ought to move*, she told herself as she walked through the house, *get out of here, move to Alasand or a campus apartment if there's an opening or maybe to the city for a change of pace*. She was beginning to grow tired of being keeper of the hearth, ready in case one of her brothers should return for a few days. She was still tied to the past of her family both through the house and through her work as well. *I should close the house and sell it.* But then she would have to pack the books, find a place to store some of the furniture, decide what should be given away or sold, and she did not have the time nor the stomach for that.

She began to climb the stairs to her room, then stopped and went back downstairs. Hidey might have called and left a message. She tried not to hope too much. She went to the phone in the living room and pushed the message button.

Mike's moustachioed face appeared on the screen. "I'm calling from L.A.," the face said. "I'll try to call back later." The life-sized image, slightly fuzzy around the edges, faded.

The voice had sounded weary. She decided not to wait for the call. She pressed the numbered buttons below the screen, seating herself as she did so.

She heard a click, then saw Mike's face again. As usual, the image was slightly blurry; getting a good connection had been almost impossible lately. "Mike?"

"How's everything, Kira?"

"All right. I was out having a drink with Jonis Ettinger. What's bothering you? You look upset about something."

"Just tired. I've been working late. I'm responsible for our whole research section now. We've been constructing a model scanner and we'll be testing it soon. I have high hopes for it."

"When are you coming to visit? Take a few days off and bring Sita, I'd like to meet her."

"Sita's gone." His voice was cold. "She wasn't at home here. She went back to Patna. I can't blame her, she's needed more there."

"Oh, Mike, I'm sorry." The words seemed an empty formality.

"There's no need to be. We had a good few months. It just didn't work out. I might have gone with her, but

I have too much to do here. We did the only practical thing."

She was sure Mike was more hurt than he cared to show. She remembered his call from Bihar when he had been married. He had looked happy and carefree for the first time in his life as he brought the small dark woman with him over to the phone screen. He had at last dropped the cold facade that had shielded him from everyone, including his family.

Now his reserve was back. He might never open up to others again. She suddenly saw her brother slump in his chair, covering his forehead with his hand.

"Maybe I should have tried to stop her," he muttered, "maybe if I had tried, we could have worked something out, I don't know. She's gone." He straightened up and his face hardened. "I talked to Jim the other day."

"Is he still visiting Ed?" Kira asked, hoping to distract him from his troubles.

"He's with Aunt Sonia in New York, she got him some sort of editorial position with a microfiche publisher. I don't know how long that'll last. He sounded bored. Sonia said he could have her apartment, she's retiring and moving out of the city; she wants to be a senior in a child care center. But I don't think he'll stay there. He never sticks to anything. He asked me if there was anything going on in L.A., but I'll be damned if I'll have him out here, catering to his delicate creative constitution, and I told him so. I have too much to do. He might try finishing another book just once."

"He's had problems, Mike."

"Most of them are self-imposed. You'd think no one else had any worries. He ought to settle down somewhere and get to work instead of leading that gypsy existence." Mike sighed. "How's everything with you?"

"All right." There was no point in discussing Hidey with him or with the others for that matter. She had not even told them about it while it lasted.

"Maybe you should pull up your roots, Kira, get out of that house."

"I don't mind it. My work is here, I don't have the

time to move around. I should think you'd understand that."

"I guess you're right. But I couldn't stand it myself, staying there. I'd better get off now. I've still got some reading to do."

"Mike," she said impulsively, "try to be a little more sympathetic to Jim. He doesn't need to have somebody picking on him."

"That's exactly what he does need. He gets enough sympathy from everyone else. I'll try to call you again when I get a chance."

"Good night." She pressed a button and disconnected. She continued to sit by the phone, staring into the darkened living room. She felt a stab of guilt. *There I was, asking Mike to be more sympathetic to Jim.* It was Mike who needed some understanding now.

Soon Al would come downstairs and they would make plans to do some viewing through his telescope if the sky was clear. Paul was calling them to dinner.

At last she got up and walked through the empty house, then up the stairs.

"Drop your weapons, everybody," Bert Ramsey shouted from the laboratory door. "We're having a party in the lounge down the hall. The anti-moratorium bill just passed the House."

Kira, in the middle of making some notes for a report, heard the others in the lab give a few quiet cheers. Chairs and stools squeaked across the floor as people began to file out of the lab and down the hall.

She got up slowly and turned toward the door. "Coming?" Bert asked.

"I'll be down in a minute," she said slowly.

"You must be even happier than the rest of us, you probably feel vindicated." The short, slightly overweight man leaned against the door. "This may mean more funds, more lab assistants. I bet Hidey'll have us pretty busy applying for grants."

"It doesn't mean we'll get any. There may not be that

much money, and most of it's already tied up. The medical people will get more."

"Maybe, maybe not." Bert straightened up. "I'll see you in the lounge."

Kira sighed as Bert disappeared. The passing of the bill was a mixed blessing for her. As a scientist, she welcomed it, but she was sure that even now some reporter was looking for her. She and her brothers would get some more unwanted publicity, more stupid questions, and she was not ready for that. They had avoided it for so long now. And when the press realized that she was herself a biologist . . . she shuddered. She could tell them she had nothing to say but then they would voice their suspicions about what she, a clone, might be up to. No, she would have to rehearse a few harmless and innocuous statements for them: *We are still considering possible projects. Of course, anything we do would have to be approved by the university administration, and whatever it is will, we hope, be of value to everyone.*

The President could veto the bill, but this was unlikely. Kira did not follow politics closely, but she was sure that the President would still sign the bill. The world was well on the way to being a more peaceful, quiet, middle-class place, but there were a lot of younger people who thought it was time to be more adventurous and a lot of old people, lives lengthened by anti-aging shots, who could remember more exciting, if more dangerous, times. And the middle-aged, who might be expected to wish that things would remain quiet, were starting to look at their older relatives and wish that they might themselves be able to stay around longer and enjoy more of the things they were at last able to have. People were basically greedy. There were still many who would make noise about the bill's passage, but more who believed they had a good chance of living long enough to reap some of the benefits of new research. Greed would win out, as it usually did. It was probably the only thing that cemented people together in the end.

Of course a fuss would be raised in the United Nations.

But no one would pay attention, since other countries were already passing their own bills or, in the case of dictatorships, setting up their own projects. *But we'll have to be careful*, Kira thought, *we've messed things up before and if we do it now it may set us back permanently*.

She left the lab and walked down the hall toward the lounge. The gathering there was getting fairly noisy. As she entered the room, a strong smell of tobacco and marijuana reached her nostrils. The room was already blue with smoke. A man shoved past her with a plastic bag of ice.

"Kira!" Jonis shouted. Kira pushed her way through the crowd over to her friend's side. "What do you know, real work for a change. Hidey's almost rolling on the floor with glee." Jonis waved her glass, managing to spill some of its contents on Kira's lab coat. "That is, if we can get any money. And if we can decide what we want to do and if we can get some time off from teaching to get the work done, which is doubtful unless we can hire more people. We'll probably have to work on our own time. I guess the bill doesn't mean much after all. Well, it was a nice dream while it lasted."

"You always find the dark side."

"I'm a realist. That's usually the only side there is. Well, not entirely. We get the rest of the afternoon off so we can get stewed."

"You do. I have a class to teach in an hour."

"What did I tell you? There's always a dark side."

"Excuse me, Jonis." Kira moved through the room, managing to shout hello to Emma Valois as she went.

Hidey was standing in a corner with Moshe Spatz, who had wandered over from the chemistry department. "You tell me," the bald chemist was saying as he gestured with his bony hands. "Everybody in my department is starting to come to me with his own pet project now, not even waiting for the news to sink in. I am going to have my hands full keeping them from flying at each other. I should not be chairman at such a time. I am a teacher. My talent is organizing teaching schedules and advising students." He glanced at Kira. "Hello, Ms.

Swenson, you are looking charming today as always."

Kira smiled as Moshe turned back to Hidey. "You will decide what your people will do and they will do it, however they might feel. You command a personal loyalty. I haven't that talent."

"You're flattering me," Hidey mumbled, lighting a cigarette.

"I am stating a fact."

Hidey looked uneasily at Kira. "Moshe's right," she said to him, then suddenly realized that Hidey might misunderstand her remark. "I mean, we all feel that way." She felt as though she was floundering, searching for the right words.

"Larry," Moshe said, turning to speak to another man. Kira was left facing Hidey. She felt awkward and embarrassed. "Have you thought about anything we might work on?" she asked, trying to fill the silent void between them.

"I'll be calling a meeting sometime this week," he answered. "I do have something in mind. I've been thinking of it for years."

She pulled at a button on her lab coat. "Well, I'd better go get ready for my class," she said, looking away from him. She turned and almost collided with Emma Valois.

"Hello, Kira," the psychiatrist said.

"Hello," Kira replied, feeling trapped. "I wish I could stay and talk, but I have a class soon. I'd better get going." She found herself wondering if Emma knew about Hidey.

She moved through the room and into the hallway, sighing with relief as she headed for her office.

Kira left her office late. The students in her comparative anatomy class had been livelier than usual. She often felt that the summer students, many of them older workers making use of their three-month vacations, were more interesting than the younger students she taught during the rest of the year. Two of them had followed her back to her office, one needing advice on which courses he should take, the other, a bad student, needing help on getting through this one.

She was thinking about the bad student as she walked through the hallway. He should never have taken the course in the first place, but it was a little late to drop it. The end of the summer term would be upon them soon. The student had, as usual, waited until now before panicking and it had quickly become obvious that he was under parental pressure; his parents were medical researchers and expected him to do the same. The old story. People never seemed to change. There was at least one of these unfortunates in class every semester.

She saw that Hidey's office door, up ahead on the curving corridor, was open. She halted, suddenly afraid to walk past it. *You're being ridiculous.* She took one step forward, hesitated, then started to turn around.

The door to Hidey's office moved and she found herself facing him. She gestured with a hand in greeting.

"Kira. Do you have a moment?"

"Sure," she replied, shrugging in what she hoped was a nonchalant fashion. She followed him into the office and sat down as he closed the door.

"I guess," she said, "you want to talk about what kind of research we might do. Jonis mentioned something to me about organ regeneration, she's been pretty interested in O'Connor's papers on the subject. Of course it's pretty theoretical, but she thinks O'Connor's laid the groundwork. If we can find the mechanism that would trigger regeneration, we could put the organ banks out of business. We could certainly get a grant from the military for the work, if you don't mind going to that particular source of funds." She was stating the obvious, running off at the mouth.

Hidey, instead of seating himself in a chair, had paced toward the wall, then perched on the edge of his desk. "I'm afraid I've been very foolish," he muttered, looking at the floor.

She opened her mouth to speak, then closed it again. "I've become disappointed in myself," he went on. "I like to think I'm free of the prejudices that other people have, I always thought I was. But I wasn't, and pretty soon I realized how easy it is to make problems where there aren't any."

She did not know what to say. She waited, curling her hands in her lap. "You were cloned from the best friend I ever had and ever will have, and it made a difference to me. I thought there was something wrong about what I felt. I couldn't see you as an individual, as a separate person. It would have been more surprising if I hadn't felt the way I do. I thought I was turning into an old senile fool, cavorting with a young woman, but I was only doing what I've been too busy to do for most of my life."

"Hidey," she said at last. "You don't have to make excuses to me."

"Certainly I do. I haven't been too considerate of your feelings. I have some bad habits, I'm used to women who ask nothing of me and are there when I have time to fit them into my schedule, or when they have time to fit me into theirs. I noticed how you've been acting around me, at first it bothered me, I didn't know why you couldn't just forget the whole thing, and then I realized it might be for the same reason I couldn't."

He was silent. She wanted to walk across the room to him, say something, but she seemed locked to the chair. She forced herself to look at him. He was watching her with his brown eyes.

"I want to get out of this office for a while and just have a quiet dinner with you somewhere, try to make up for lost time, you might say, if it's all right with you."

At last she was able to stand. "Come on, then," she said, and felt herself smiling. "I'm starving." He reached for her hand and she grasped his. "Sometimes you're an awful dope, Hidey."

"I know."

She was nudged awake early. She could smell coffee being waved in front of her nose. Groaning, she pulled the covers over her head.

"Come on, it's eight-thirty." Kira opened her eyes and

saw Hidey, already dressed, sitting on the edge of the bed with a mug in his hand. He put the coffee down on an end table next to her.

"Damn it, Hidey, this is the only day I can sleep late, I haven't got a class until eleven."

"I forgot. Wake up anyway, we can go have breakfast somewhere and talk about possible projects. Or I'll cook some here with that crap everyone nowadays thinks tastes like bacon and eggs."

She put her arms around his neck. "There's only one thing I'm going to wake up for."

He leaned over and kissed her. "I'd better head over to my office then, even though I'd rather stay here. I've got a desk full of work crying out to me."

"Let it."

"I can't. I'm an old man, Kira, I can't change my habits overnight."

"I don't want to hear that 'old man' stuff. You're up and ready to go to work while I'm exhausted and ready to sleep all day. You did all right last night for an old man."

"I promise I'll leave early tonight." He kissed her on the forehead. "All right?"

"All right." She heard him get up and leave the room as she closed her eyes.

But she could not go back to sleep. She thought of the night before, the few hours of sleep snatched between sessions of lovemaking. Images flashed through her mind, some so vivid that she could feel as well as see them: Hidey's hands on her hips, his body under hers as she knelt above him, his arms around her as he slept.

She threw off the covers and got up, putting on a robe as she walked toward the bathroom across the hall. She showered quickly and then remembered the coffee next to her bed. She wandered back to her room, the blue robe over her arm. The coffee was already cold and she would have to make more. She was combing her hair, thinking of Hidey again, when she heard the front doorbell.

She put the robe on again and hurried downstairs,

curious about who would be there at this hour. Maybe Hidey had decided to come back after all. She would have to give him a key. She moved toward the door, smoothing her shoulder-length hair with her hands.

She opened the door slightly and peered out through the crack, then flung it open.

Her brother Jim stood there, holding a battered suitcase. Two young women, one a tall brunette and the other a slender redhead, stood behind him.

"I would have just come in, but I thought you might be home, so I rang." Jim drifted into the living room, the two women following him.

"I thought you were with Sonia in New York," she managed to say. The women sat on the sofa while Jim sprawled in a chair. "Mike said something about you being an editor."

"You could go crazy in New York," he said. "I couldn't take it. I didn't have any time for writing anyway."

Jim had grown thinner. His shaggy beard needed a trim. He stretched his legs, clothed in shabby brown slacks, in front of him. He looked slightly flabby as well, as if he had gotten no exercise for a while.

He gestured at his companions. "This is Carole Elashvili," he said, waving his arm at the brunette, "and Ellie Clayton." He motioned toward the redhead. "I met Carole in New York," he went on. "She and Ellie wanted to see the country and I wanted some company on the trip."

Kira looked at the women more closely. Carole seemed oddly remote. She resembled an ancient Egyptian with large brown eyes and heavy black hair that hung to her shoulders. Her perfect lips curved in a small smile. Ellie grinned awkwardly, running her hand through the unruly red curls on her head.

"I hope you don't mind them staying for a while," Jim said.

"Of course not, we have the room." Kira smiled at the women. Carole, clothed in a long white sleeveless dress, hardly moved. Only her eyes darted restlessly around the room.

"Jim's helping me with my writing," Ellie said. Kira tried to place the woman's accent; Tennessee perhaps, or West Virginia. "I shouldn't even call myself a writer, why, I haven't published a word, unless you want to count some brochures I did for a cassette company." Ellie pulled at the waistband of her green shorts. "I just had to leave the city for a while, that town was grinding me down. I may take a look at what's doing at the university here, maybe if I knew more, I'd have more to write about."

"Are you a writer, too?" Kira asked Carole.

Carole was gazing over Kira's head. "I was working in a bank." She said nothing more.

"Can I get you some coffee?" Kira asked, beginning to feel at loose ends.

"I think we're going to retire, if you don't mind," Ellie replied. "We didn't get much sleep last night. Don't you let us bother you, just keep doing what you were doing before we got here." The two young women stood up. Jim led them out of the room and upstairs.

Kira wandered into the kitchen and put on more coffee. She felt disconcerted by her brother's visit. She did not know if she was ready to deal with Jim's moods now. He was obviously "between things" again, as he seemed to have been for most of his life.

She thought of Hidey again and was suddenly afraid of what Jim would think. *It's none of his business.* She sat down at the table as Jim came into the kitchen.

He looked at the coffee pot, then sat down across from her. "How do you like Mike?" he said quickly. "Ed called me before I left and told me about him and his wife. I couldn't believe it. Competent Mike who could handle anything. I guess he's just like everybody else after all." He smiled bitterly.

"Have some sympathy for him."

"Sympathy! He sure showed me a lot, with all his sanctimonious shit about how I should do this and do that. He refused to get me anything with the p.r. people in his company, you know. He said I wasn't reliable. Why should I care about his fuck-ups?"

"Jim. . . ."

"Just let him try to lecture me about my life once more." Jim looked at her more closely. "How's everything with you?"

"All right."

"Are you and your biologist friends getting ready to cook up some more horrors now that the ban's off?"

"Don't start that again." She got up, poured two cups of coffee, and slammed Jim's down on the table. A little coffee spilled over the sides of his mug. "Just don't start criticizing my work. I would think you'd know better by now."

"Maybe Takamura'll start cloning more people. That would be interesting. We wouldn't be the only ones any more. He should clone himself and see what it's like, having a bunch of identical little Takamuras running around."

"Shut up, Jim." She was angry now. She sipped at her coffee quickly and burned her lip slightly.

"What do you think of Carole and Ellie?" he asked, changing the subject.

"What can I think of them? I only saw them for about five minutes. Ellie seems nice."

"Carole's very shy, that's why she didn't say much. It just takes a while to get to know her. She's only eighteen, she was in New York for only a few months. She's trying to decide what she wants to do. Ellie's a little older. I met them at a party."

"Maybe you should decide what you're going to do," Kira said acidly, "before you start advising everyone else."

"You sound just like Mike."

"He does say something sensible once in a while." She drank some more coffee, then got up and put the cup in the sink. *I shouldn't start bickering with him*, she thought, feeling slightly guilty. "I'd like to sit around and talk," she said gently, "but I have to teach a class this morning. I'd better get ready."

"Now you're trying to make me feel guilty."

She was irritated. "I'm just saying that some of us have work to do."

"Christ!" Jim slammed his palm on the table. "I can't believe I came out here to listen to this. I've been working pretty hard. A microfiche publisher bought my novel, you know."

"It's about time."

"So I figured as long as I had some money, and Mike wasn't going to help me, I'd come here and try to get a book finished. You seem to think that just because someone doesn't go to a place of employment every day, he's not doing anything."

"All right, Jim, I'm sorry." She sighed wearily. "I have to start getting ready."

She left him in the kitchen and went back upstairs. As she entered her room, she saw her rumpled bedding and wondered if Jim had noticed it when he passed in the hallway. *It doesn't matter, he couldn't know about Hidey.*

She made the bed quickly.

They gathered in one of the conference rooms in the late afternoon. Hidey, sitting next to a large ashtray, smiled at Kira as she entered the room with Jonis and sat down at the round table.

Bert Ramsey was next to Hidey. Next to Bert was Ike Jefferson, a lean black man who had arrived the year before from a southern school. Cesar Gomez, puffing on a large aromatic cigar, was discussing something with Kurt Schultz.

Apparently none of the instructors or laboratory assistants had been called to the meeting. Bert looked around the room quickly and then back at Hidey.

"Shouldn't there be more of us?" Bert asked.

"I didn't call the people who are only interested in teaching," Hidey replied, "and I left out others who have their own projects to do, although we'll consult with them later."

"Why don't you give us your ideas first, Hidey," Bert said. "You've probably got more to say about a possible project than the rest of us anyway."

Everyone seemed agreeable to this. Hidey leaned forward. "I should say a few preliminary things first. Whatever kind of project we undertake is just going to mean more work for everybody here, at least for a while. We all have pretty full schedules right now and even if we can get a grant, we'll still be overworked. I don't mind that myself, I'm used to sleeping in my office and working on weekends, but some of you may feel like having more time to yourselves." He paused to light a cigarette. "I know," he went on, "that none of you here are used to working on any kind of crucial research project. All you've done is improved on what was done thirty years ago, refined some techniques; that's all the moratorium has let us do. We always know in advance what we'll come up with. Now there's no reason why we have to do anything else. The university would be just as happy to let us go our own way and the park service will keep giving us grants to clone endangered species at least until they finish setting up their own facilities. If any of you want to keep on with what you're doing, just say so, and we can all go home."

Cesar Gomez gestured with his cigar. "I'm just speaking for myself," the small dark man said, "but I was trained to do research and so was everyone else here. We haven't been able to do a damn thing with our training. I enjoy teaching, but I'd enjoy it a lot more if I was training students to do something more than develop what we already know. Everybody knows what a disaster that moratorium was, even if they don't want to admit it. We've lost a lot of the best students over the years. They knew they wouldn't be able to achieve anything, that they would be little more than technicians. The rest of us have just been hanging on like damn fools, waiting for the day when we might really be able to work again, and wondering if it would ever come. We haven't even been able to teach, really, we've just been indoctrinating students in a static field. It's going to be years before we can get some of those minds we lost replaced as it is. I say we go ahead."

"Same here," Ike Jefferson drawled. "I'm mighty tired of arousing the curiosity of students and then having to tell them they can't try to answer certain questions. It violates the spirit of free inquiry and everything else we should stand for." The others nodded.

Hidey smiled and seemed to relax. "There's another problem that might be easier to resolve, a political one. You all know how a lot of people, even now, feel about me. I was accused of grandstanding in the past." Kira saw Kurt Schultz's blue eyes drift in her direction. "No matter what we undertake, a lot of people are going to be watching me. You may make your work easier if you let me retire. I've got my pension and I could probably find something to do. The only reason I've been here this long is by threatening to take the university to court if they force me to retire, and every old person around, even the ones that hate me, would be on my side there. No one wants forced retirement established again."

"No," Kurt said, running his hand over his short silvery blond hair. "You stay. If you go, Kira will have to go also. We would get just as much interference from those who might wonder what kind of project a clone might work on, considering that she was the result of one of the last projects before this moratorium. We cannot concern ourselves with such matters. Besides, I doubt that we could think up a reason for getting rid of Kira. We would be obligated to help find her a new position and then we would have to find two replacements for you both. That would not be easy, given the lack of talent in the field at the moment."

"Let me get to the point," Jonis said. "Without Hidey, I doubt that any of us could agree on anything. He's the only one who's kept us from getting into time-wasting feuds. I don't want us to be like the chemistry department or anthropology. I don't think those people could agree on what model coffee machine to get." The blond woman stared across the table at Kurt. Kira knew Jonis had never particularly liked him. Kurt stared back coldly.

"I am forced to agree with you on that, Ms. Ettinger," he muttered at last.

"I don't believe what I just heard," Bert said, chuckling and glancing from Jonis to Kurt. "There's hope for you two yet."

"All right," Hidey said, and Kira watched as everyone turned back to him. Hidey had somehow mastered the art of inspiring loyalty among his associates. It might have been that talent that had made her own existence possible in the end. Several people, she knew, had wondered how he had persuaded others to go along with the then-dangerous project of cloning Paul Swenson. Even after the project's conclusion, when many of those involved had to face several problems, she had never heard of any of them turning against Hidey.

Yet Hidey seemed genuinely surprised whenever anyone pointed this out. Maybe that was part of the talent.

"I have an idea for something we might work on," Hidey continued. "I don't know how much I want to say about it right now. Maybe I've been too close to it for too long. It's something I've been thinking about for thirty years, in a way it's something I was working for back when I cloned Kira and her brothers from my friend."

Kira waited. Hidey had said little to her about his ideas. "The reason I cloned Paul Swenson," he said, "was that I felt one human lifetime was too short for him to make full use of his talents. The same thing is probably true of any person. However, I don't think cloning everybody is really the answer here. I have something else in mind, although it would utilize the techniques of cloning."

No wonder he didn't mention anything to me, Kira thought. *He probably didn't know how I'd react.* She tried to give him a reassuring look.

"We've already extended the human life span with anti-aging shots," Hidey continued. "Because of social reasons, administration of these shots is delayed, but I have no doubt that if they were given at an earlier age we could hope for an even greater life span."

"There's talk about doing that already in Washington," said Ike, the only one of them who seemed to keep up with politics. "They might lower the age for receiving them to fifty-five."

"That's really beside the point anyway," Hidey said. "It'll still be a half-measure, even if you could get shots at thirty. I'm sure there are people doing that in spite of the penalties and the chance of getting caught. So you might live, say, to one hundred and fifty, maybe two hundred. But you wouldn't be able to replace lost brain cells, lost nerve cells, you would just be clearing out old ones."

"Still, you could double our life span," Cesar said. "I'd settle for that."

"Oh, we'll have it one of these days," Ike said. "Not in our lifetime, maybe. It'll be a gradual kind of thing, getting people psychologically prepared, adjusting our institutions, a continuation of the process that's already taking place."

Hidey, Kira noticed, was growing impatient with this meandering. "What about an indefinite life span?" he asked. There was silence as those around the table looked at each other, then back at him.

"It is theoretically possible," Kurt murmured. "Even with the little we now know as a result of the moratorium."

"Who would want to live that long?" Jonis asked irrelevantly.

"Surely you people can be a little more adventurous," Hidey said. "I believe we could develop a method within the next few years."

"An application of cloning," Kurt said, leaning back in his chair. "Yes, I think I see where you are leading us."

"We have the technology for producing clones," Hidey continued. "We also have available to us a means of clearing out the collagens and wastes acquired in the body through aging and the cross-linkage of proteins, namely the anti-aging shots. What if we were to clone a person, then, when the fetus reached a certain point of development, make serum from the different organs and inject it into the person? The various cloned cells would presumably migrate to the different parts of the body, replacing old cells that had been removed by anti-aging shots. The body would be renewed. Aging would be halted, perhaps turned back. The person might be completely rejuvenated. If the process were repeated at intervals, there's no reason why the subject couldn't live indefinitely."

Perhaps forever, Kira thought. The word Hidey was refusing to say was *immortal*. Suddenly she had an image of herself and her brothers cut up and injected into Paul. She managed to repress a shudder. *I can't look at it that way.* Besides, the use of fetuses in such a project would, she was sure, be temporary. The process could be refined; eventually only certain portions of the body, certain organs, would be cloned, rather than the entire person.

"We couldn't get a grant for that," Bert said. "No way in the world."

"Sure we could," Jonis replied. "You just have to word the application in a certain way. We could probably get some kind of grant for medical research, repair of damaged organs, something like that."

"I can't believe it," Ike said, slamming his palm down on the table. "No one here seems to realize what Hidey's saying. You're all talking as if it's just another project. He's talking about something that would change us forever, that would dislocate our entire society. This won't be so easy for people to brush aside or suppress. If people get the idea that they might be able to live indefinitely, if it works, how is it going to be handled? Will everybody get a chance and if not, who's going to choose? We've just started to stabilize our population, what's this going to do to that? Do you really think people are ready for it?"

"What do you want us to do, Ike?" Hidey said quietly. "Forget about trying and condemn everyone to a certain death? Or do the work and then try to handle it some-how?"

"I'm saying," the lean man replied, "that you have

to consider things in a context, as part of a system. You can't go off in a hit-or-miss fashion. We must ask questions, I admit, but we must coordinate our findings. We have to give more thought to educating people about alternatives. We especially have to avoid imposing our own personal ideas about what's right for everybody in the world. We won't be able to control how our findings are used and I don't suppose that we should, but we must give some thought to whether or not they'll be truly beneficial in the end."

"I guess everybody here's been living with the moratorium too long," Kira said. "We're afraid. As long as we were under imposed limitations, we didn't have to think about these issues."

"It may not work," Hidey said. "Not everything does, you know. You're all used to having everything turn out as you expect it to. Replacing brain cells, for instance, may erase memories. We might end up with what Jonis would have us write down on an application, a treatment for diseased organs."

"I doubt that any of us can decide anything," Kurt said, "until we familiarize ourselves more with the literature on the subject. We must decide whether or not the project you propose is feasible, either in terms of the goal you propose or in terms of knowledge to be gained. If it is, we must then decide if we are willing to work on it. That is the time to consider our various objections. Personally, I feel that a consideration of societal consequences of any project before undertaking it will gain us nothing. We should then be doing for ourselves what the moratorium has been doing for us."

"All right," Bert said. "We'll start reading."

"I was going to suggest it anyway," Hidey said. He reached for the folder in front of him and began to pass out a list. "We'll meet again a week from now and see what we've come up with in the meantime."

The men picked up their lists and started to drift out of the room. Jonis stood up and grimaced at Hidey. "You know how to pick them, don't you?" she said. "Nothing small or simple. Try for the jackpot." She picked up her list and walked out.

"Jonis doesn't sound too happy about it," Hidey said.

"If we all decide to go ahead, she'll go along," Kira responded. "That's the way she is."

"What do you think?"

"I don't know yet." She looked down at the list. She felt unaccountably depressed suddenly and could not shake the feeling.

He took her hand. "We've got time. Why don't you forget it for now? We can go to your house and have a quiet supper, relax a bit."

"Are you going to be the subject of this experiment?" she heard herself ask savagely, and wished almost immediately that she had said nothing.

"Of course not." He looked concerned. "Is that what you thought, that I simply wanted to benefit myself? Surely you know me better than that."

"I'm sure such a desire has something to do with it," she went on, and wondered why she could not let go. "No, I'm sorry," she forced herself to say. "I didn't mean it."

"How can any of us be sure of our motives, Kira? We just have to do the best we can." He released her hand and stood up. "Why don't we go, you're probably tired anyway."

"I'll meet you in your office in about ten minutes," she said quickly. "I've just got a few things to do." She tried to smile and then kissed him quickly as if attempting to make amends.

She hurried down the hall and then realized she could not go to her house with Hidey, not with Jim there. What could she say to Jim, and why hadn't she told Hidey her brother was visiting?

She should go home alone, tell Hidey that Jim was visiting and that she wanted to talk to him his first night there. But she did not want to talk to Jim yet. She wanted to be with Hidey, wanted to lose herself for at least a while in lovemaking.

Why does everything seem to happen at once, she

thought angrily as she entered her office. She put the list of readings under a metal paperweight decorated with a symbol of a double helix and contemplated the phone. They could go to Hidey's place. She would call Jim and tell him she would not be home.

She sat down and punched out the number. The phone rang several times before Jim picked it up.

"Hello, how are you doing?"

"Are you going to be doing anything tonight, Jim?"

He yawned, stretching an arm over his head. "I'm going to be writing. I just got up. Carole wanted to know when you'd be home. She's making supper tonight. I think she kind of wanted to do something special."

"I just wondered. I don't know if I'm going to be home tonight."

"Carole'll be disappointed. Maybe tomorrow would be better, though. She's still tired from the trip."

"Tomorrow's fine," Kira said. She had committed herself now. *I hope I'll be up to it.* "It'll be better, I don't want to put Carole to any trouble if she's still tired." Kira was hoping she did not sound as guilty as she felt.

"Where're you going?"

"Out with Jonis," she lied. Jim shook his head. She should have learned by now it was difficult to keep a secret from the others.

"Come on, Kira, you don't have to fool me. You're probably seeing a guy. I don't expect you to be celibate, you know. Carole and Ellie keep me pretty busy."

She did not care for the offhand way he talked about the two young women, the hint of contempt. *What do you expect? He doesn't think that much of himself, not really.* "I'll see you tomorrow," she said.

"Have a good time."

They hurtled along the automated highway toward the city, Kira's head on Hidey's shoulder. "Where to?" Hidey asked. "Enzio's, that barnlike place with real home cooking, or do you want to take a chance on my culinary expertise, or lack of it?"

"Anyplace," she responded. She did not feel particularly hungry in spite of the fact that her stomach seemed to be flooding itself with acid.

"I feel like indulging myself, frankly," he said. "I feel like a big antipasto and a bowl of spaghetti with hot sausage, even if the sausage is mostly soybeans. You know, old Enzio would have never used soy protein and he made his own pasta, but what can you do? No one knows how food tastes any more. I suspect young Enzio buys the sauces already made, his *spaghetti caprice* isn't anything like his father's was."

Kira said nothing.

"Thinking about the meeting?"

"Jim's back," she said, finding her voice at last.

"Well, why didn't you say so? Maybe you should have gone home, you probably want to talk with him."

"I called him from my office, he said he would be busy. Anyway, I saw him this morning before I went to my class." She was growing more nervous. What would Hidey say if he knew about her one-time relationship with Jim?

"You don't sound particularly happy."

"It isn't that. You know how Jim feels about my work, about science in general. It's hard to talk to him, I feel more like an adversary sometimes than a sister." She stopped, feeling vaguely disloyal.

"I can understand that, in a way. He still isn't reconciled to himself and he resents the processes that brought him into being. He's extended the attitude to all sciences. Besides, his attitude is one thing that distinguishes him from the rest of you, so in a way it's useful." He paused to light a cigarette. "A lot of people resent being born, they unconsciously think of their parents as irresponsible or capricious, dragging them into existence without their consent. Sometimes that can result in sexual problems, but that could hardly be the case with Jim. He instead resents the science that. . . ."

"I know all that," Kira said with some irritation. Hidey was sounding as though he understood Jim better than she did. "I'll see Jim tomorrow, I promised that. Maybe he. . . ." She could not finish the unworded thought.

She would try to put Jim out of her mind at least for the night.

"How's the book coming along?"

"I got a couple of pages done. I don't know. It's not going the way I thought it would." Jim poured himself another glass of wine. "Maybe I just have to get used to new surroundings."

Kira glanced across the table at Carole and caught her with an anxious look on her face which changed quickly into remoteness. "The food was delicious," Kira said to her and was rewarded with a relieved smile. "Maybe," she said, turning back to her brother, "you should be writing something else."

"You haven't even seen my manuscript."

"I just thought there are a lot of things you could write about, that you have a unique perspective on."

"What the hell's that supposed to mean?" Jim set down his glass. Carole and Ellie seemed to shrink slightly in their chairs, looking uneasily from Jim to Kira. She looked at the two empty wine bottles on the table and realized Jim had been drinking more than she had noticed.

Ellie leaned over and placed a hand on Jim's arm. He shook it off. "You and my brothers, trying to act as though it doesn't make any difference. You think it's just something you can accept, like being born with green eyes, but it isn't the same."

"Fortunately most people don't seem to share your attitude," Kira said angrily. "If they did, I doubt the moratorium would have been repealed." She suddenly wanted to hurt him. "Face it, Jim, you're in a very small minority. Your attitudes are the ones people find foolish, not mine, not any more."

"The only reason that business was repealed was because people want to get something out of it, they're selfish and think they'll gain something, they're bored. They'll see where it gets them." He reached for one of the wine bottles and saw that it was empty.

"Jim," Ellie murmured. Carole began to clear dishes

off the table. Her face had become an expressionless mask.

"I have a theory, Kira. You want to hear it?" He picked up the third wine bottle and refilled his glass.

"Go ahead."

"I think something went wrong when they put us together. I think they made a mistake, I think they left something out of me."

"You're insane."

"Or maybe they messed up Mike too, he's mad enough in his own way. It's possible."

"Damn it, it isn't," she said loudly. "Don't you think they would have noticed if something went wrong? They were monitoring things all the time; they found out right away about the one who died." She realized that the incident of the sixth clone was hardly something she should mention at this time and hurried on quickly. "And even if something had gone wrong, they would have found out about it. A computer was monitoring us. They would have had a record of any mistake on the print-out. They would have found out about it then."

"How do you know they didn't?"

"What are you talking about?"

"How do you know they didn't?" he repeated. Carole returned and quickly retreated again with more dishes. "Why should they tell us? It would only make things harder. Better to shut up and let us think we're at least partly normal."

The idea was ridiculous, but he made it sound plausible. *No*, she thought, trying to shake off doubts that were starting to dig in and take root. "No," she said out loud.

"Do you think Takamura would have admitted a mistake after the mess he was already in? He would have shoved our dead sister down the incinerator and hidden that if he could, believe it."

"Do you know what you're doing?" she heard herself shout. "You're trying to evade any responsibility for what you are and what you've done. You'd rather blame anything else, because it's easier than thinking about how you feel and what you believe. If you examined it at all, you might see how stupid it all is and then you'd have to do something about it. You might even have to change your mind about certain things. You might have to do something hard, like thinking instead of just following your impulses."

"You don't understand me at all, do you?"

"I'm not finished." She was slouched over the table now. Carole hovered in the door to the kitchen. "I think I understand you pretty well. How different are we, really?" She ignored his grimace. "How different are we?" she repeated, as if to rub it in. "I could have been like you, any of us could have. So could Paul, for that matter. Maybe the only difference is that, confronted with you, the rest of us were forced to be a little more rational, we couldn't give in to ourselves the way you do. You're still acting like an adolescent. I could understand it once, but I can't now."

"Stop it, Kira."

"No." She was upset now, unable to stop the flow of words. "I am sick of it, Jim, and I imagine the others are too. I'm sick of your self-indulgence and willful ignorance, I'm sick of getting calls every few months or so when you're bored or feel like committing suicide. I'm sick of nursing your delicate soul through every little emotional crisis. You can't get along with yourself and you take it out on us because we remind you of yourself. And now you're trying to shift the blame to Hidey and everyone else because it's easier than doing anything yourself."

Jim was motionless. Ellie looked distressed. Carole had disappeared again.

"You act," Jim said finally, "as if I *enjoy* being the way I am. Don't you think I'd be happier some other way? This is just how I am."

He was trying for a reconciliation. His green eyes pleaded with her. *Throw him a bone*, she thought bitterly, *and forget it, open another bottle and get drunk and talk about old times, the good ones*. "You can do something about what you are," she said. "I think you *do* enjoy what you are in some strange way. I don't think you're really

interested in changing. I think something in you enjoys
being tormented, even if you have to invent a whole
mental construct of superstition to do it and believe
things that appeal to you aesthetically in some weird way
instead of trying to find out if they're true."

Jim buried his head in his arms as she stood up. "Don't,
Kira," Ellie said. "Be fair, please."

"So he's got your sympathy," Kira said harshly. "You'll
learn." She walked out of the room. She could not stay
here, not now. She could go to her office, try to do some
reading, call Hidey later. She could stay with him for
the weekend, calm down. She opened the front door.

The sultry night air seemed to seep through the open
door past her. The road and the houses on either side
were misty, blurred by a humid haze.

"That's right, walk away," said a voice behind her.
She turned and saw Jim standing in the living room doorway. "We're always doing that, aren't we. We just throw
our punches and walk away, not even examining the
casualties."

"I need some time by myself."

"Where are you going?"

"None of your goddamn business." She hurried outside.

"What are you hiding, Kira?" he shouted after her.
"There's something you're not telling me, isn't there?
You think you can see through me, well, let me tell you,
I can see right through you. You're not telling me some-
thing, but I'll ferret it out, I promise."

She kept going toward the car, afraid to turn around.

As she was driving away, she saw Ellie pulling at Jim's
arm. Then the door closed, hiding them both.

There were more graffiti on the side of the biological
sciences building, replacing the words that the maintenance people had removed the week before. A picture
by an anonymous campus artist had also appeared on
the building; a cheerful-looking Frankensteinian monster
held a beaker in one hand and pointed to the entrance
with the other. Next to his head, in yellow paint, were

the words *BACK TO WORK!*

Kira smiled in spite of herself. She was still tired. Her muscles ached and her back seemed jarred permanently out of line. Hidey's apartment was more of a way-station than a home, almost bare of furniture, with a small, out-of-order holo projector, an old computer booth and a narrow bed. She had tried sleeping on the bed with Hidey, but at last had been forced to retreat to the sofa, which turned out to be a little too short.

She had not mentioned her problems with Jim to Hidey and had been afraid to call her brother from Hidey's place, afraid he would see where she had gone. At last on Sunday she had gone out, down the city streets to a phone on the corner. Jim had not been home, or was refusing to answer.

Hidey had driven in early, awake and alert as usual. She had followed an hour later. She suppressed a yawn. Entering the building, she went down to the lounge in search of a cup of coffee. A group of lab assistants and students were playing cards at a table in a corner; they looked up as she came into the room and went back to their cards.

She punched out some coffee and sat down, wondering if she should try to call Jim again, then remembered that he usually liked to sleep late. *I can't keep hiding from him.*

"Why in hell didn't you bid spades?" one of the young men in the corner said loudly.

"Good morning, Kira." She looked up and saw Kurt Schultz getting some coffee. He sat down next to her. "Have you read the material Hidey gave us yet?"

"Some of it," she said.

"I'm not criticizing his project," Kurt went on, "but I think he may be deluding himself about the results. He is assuming that aging is the result of random metabolic errors. We can prolong life with the use of anti-aging shots, but I wonder if it could be prolonged very much more even if the shots were given earlier. There is as much reason, given the state of our research now, to assume that aging is genetically programmed into us."

"That's a pre-moratorium theory. Besides, wouldn't our project have some good results anyway?"

"Indeed it would, the medical benefits Jonis mentioned. That is all. The cells of the immune system appear to become less efficient with age, the DNA polymerases make more mistakes as the cells divide. The process eventually breaks down."

"But what if there's a replacement of those cells?"

"You might have some prolongation. But it is my opinion that any work Hidey wants to undertake that would accomplish his particular goal would have to be done simultaneously with basic genetic research. If the DNA in a system could somehow be programmed not to make errors of this kind, particularly involving the breakdown in amino acid structures, then both projects might achieve results similar to what Hidey wants. I doubt that his project alone can produce what he is looking for."

"Excuse me for saying this," she said, "but you sound as if something else is bothering you about this proposal besides what you've just outlined. Hidey's read the literature, I'm sure he knows about the difficulties."

"I shall confess that I have my doubts about his motives."

"Come on, Kurt, you don't believe that Hidey just wants to make a name for himself."

"He's an old man. He does not want to die, none of us do. But death is a little closer to him than to the rest of us. I think he might be deluding himself about how much he can do. Consider how he presented the project, how he announced it. No conservative estimates of goals, just the words indefinite life, immortality if you will. And he had us believing it because he so obviously did. What is he going to do when he finds out that it may not work?"

"I think he's mature enough to handle it," she said coldly.

"I shall admit that you know him better than I do," Kurt continued. "I've only been here for three years and you have known him all your life." He sipped at his coffee. "Hidey has been a guest in my home on several occasions, however, and recently I have noticed an attitude of his that very much disturbs me."

"What's that?" Kira mumbled into her cup.

"I can see two hearts," a young man shouted from the corner table, "but why in hell did you bid three?" Kurt's attention seemed to wander to the bridge players.

"Go on," she said.

Kurt's pale eyes focused on her again. "Excuse me, I am a compulsive kibitzer when anyone is playing bridge." He finished his coffee in one gulp. "My wife very much enjoys Hidey's company in our home. She is a paramedic and likes to discuss things with my colleagues. One evening recently we began discussing death, a gloomy subject to be sure, but then we had all had a fair amount of wine. I tend to be somewhat fatalistic about death, believing that we can forestall it only for so long. I accept it as a part of life, and expressed this opinion to Hidey. He became perturbed. Death, he claimed, is an aberration and an insufferable one. He said that everything he had ever done in his work was ultimately designed to fight it. He called it an adversary, and one which he would, he hoped, defeat one day."

"And you find that strange?"

"Indeed I did. Does that surprise you? We must all die some day to make room for those who will be better adapted than we are. That is the way evolution proceeds. No amount of genetic manipulation will produce unforeseen and spontaneous mutations possessing qualities humanity may need in the future. Any mature person accepts death. Only the very young believe that they might live forever. The rest of us are all too aware of our mortality."

"And why can't we improve ourselves?" she asked. "Why can't we change and stay on instead of waiting for death?"

"What I am trying to say is that Hidey may be deluding himself about this entire project. I can ignore his attitudes, strange as I find them, unless they threaten to affect our work here. But with his attitude he may affect this project, if it should be undertaken. He may rush things, or take foolish chances. He has a grandiose vision that may interfere with how he views reality."

"You're wrong." She finished her coffee and put the cup down on a nearby table. "Don't you think he was personally involved when he cloned me? Paul was his best friend. It didn't interfere with his work then."

"Perhaps it did. If I were to clone anyone at that time, if I had been around then, I might have cloned the child of parents, for example, who had lost their child and could not have another. That is, if cells had been available. That would have proved whether or not the process was a possibility at that time. Cloning five copies of a friend was somewhat extravagant. His feelings must have had a great deal to do with his decision."

"There were things he wanted to find out that he couldn't have if he had done what you suggest."

"Perhaps, perhaps not. I am still worried about this project."

"You seem to be worrying a great deal," she said, "about problems you said at the meeting shouldn't concern us."

"The issues presented themselves as I considered the proposal. I could not ignore them."

"You don't think it's worthwhile at all, then."

"You persist in misunderstanding me, Kira. I believe the project might be worthwhile and the results interesting and perhaps beneficial. I have doubts about whether it will achieve the end Hidey so ardently desires. I would be delighted to pursue this research unless I think Hidey's wishes might interfere with our work in some way." Kurt stood up. "Perhaps you too are personally involved in what should be a scientific enterprise."

"My feelings for Hidey have nothing to do with this," she said defensively.

"I was not referring to your personal relationship. You are a sensible person who, I am sure, can keep such things in perspective. I meant that you are the outcome of one of Hidey's former projects and thus might have a personal interest in this one that, through no fault of your own, you are unable or unwilling to acknowledge."

Kurt's silvery blond hair seemed to glitter almost metalli-
cally under the lounge lights.

"Forgive me, Kurt, but I can't help feeling that you're
patronizing me."

"That was not my intention."

"What will you decide at the meeting this week?"

"I do not yet know." He gave her an almost formal
nod and wandered over to the bridge players.

Kira got up slowly and began to walk toward her
office. This was not going to be a good day, she was
certain of that. She nodded to some students absently
as she ambled through the hall and managed to smile as
she saw Hidey approaching her.

"Good morning!" he said brightly, then looked more
closely at her. "If you looked any happier, I'd call a
psychiatrist. Anything wrong?"

"Just tired," she said. There was no point in mention-
ing Kurt, she could tell him later.

"I can't be getting too old if I can tire you out." He
took her hand and gave it an affectionate squeeze. "How
about lunch in my office later? We can dial a couple
of those indigestible sandwiches from the lounge and I
think my office machine might be persuaded to come
up with some soup."

"Sure."

"Got to run, I'm going to check out on grants at the
science division offices and I want to beat the mob." He
gave her hand another squeeze and took off.

He's already planning the project. She worried about
what he would do if others beside Kurt began expressing
their doubts, then dismissed the thought. She did not
have to worry about Hidey. He was probably aware of
Kurt's attitude anyway and could take care of himself.

Kira unlocked her office door and entered the room.
Again she thought of her brother. *One thing at a time,
damn it.* She had a class in an hour, a lab group in the
afternoon, a seminar for people in the community, via
computer screen, just before dinner. She did not feel
like doing any of it and began to toy with the idea of
saying she was sick and going home. She could crawl

into bed with a good book and forget about everything
for a while.

And contend with Jim when he wakes up. Well, she
could not have gone home anyway, guilt about her
neglected tasks would pursue her even through sleep.
She wished she was a little less responsible.

At last she picked up the phone and dialed. Emma
Valois appeared on the screen. "Hello, Kira," she said
cheerfully. "What can I do for you?"

"Do you have any free time today?"

"I've got about an hour after lunch, one to two."

"I need to talk to you. It's not a social call."

"The time's yours."

Jim was seated in front of her office when she returned
from the seminar, his back against her door. Startled,
Kira paused for a moment, then walked to his side.

"I didn't expect to see you here," she said, trying to
sound lighthearted. He stood up and she unlocked the
door. "I thought you'd be eating supper by now." They
went inside and he sat down in one of the chairs, slouched
over, legs extended in front of him.

"I didn't exactly relish the thought of coming over,"
he said, "but I was here talking to one of my old professors in the English department so I thought I'd come
over here. I was beginning to wonder if I'd ever see you
again."

She felt irritated for a moment, then realized he was
only kidding her. "I did sort of disappear."

"I tried calling you here but you weren't in. Ellie and
Carole wanted to go out to dinner and drive around a
bit, so I told them I'd look for you."

"Did you talk to Hidey at all?" her voice sounded
too tense. "Or Jonis?" she added quickly.

"I think they're doing some lab work. I didn't want to
bother them."

She put away her seminar notes and sat down behind
the desk. "I did try to call this weekend, but you weren't
home. I hope you weren't worried."

"Why should I be? You can take care of yourself."

"I just didn't want you to stay mad."

"Kira, I'm not really that upset, except for one thing. What are you hiding?"

"Nothing."

"I'm not a policeman or anything. You're acting as if you have to guard me from something. I guess I resent it a little, I thought we were past the point where we had to hide our feelings. I suppose you have your reasons." He smiled crookedly and she felt herself mirroring his expression. "It's not so easy talking to the others either. The last time I talked to Al I got a lecture on space ships. The three-second delay didn't help."

I should say something. Emma had listened to her but had given no advice, only outlined the alternative courses of action. She was being foolish in letting this deception persist. Jim was her brother. She looked at him and wondered if she knew him at all.

Hidey will come through that door and Jim will know. A wave of panic washed over her. *Stop it. I have nothing to hide. He'll find out sooner or later anyway.*

"Well, I am seeing somebody," she said quickly, plunging in before she had second thoughts. "I should have told you. After all, it's not anything clandestine. I'm seeing Hidey."

For a moment she thought she had gotten away with it. *Jim was chuckling. She smiled back. Well, I hope you're happy, Kira, that's all.*

He was silent for a few seconds. At last he said, "You can't be."

"I am." She said it harshly.

"I'm surprised he can still get it up."

"Don't insult him."

"I should have seen it coming. You've spent enough time with him. I knew he wanted to keep his friendship with Paul alive, but I really didn't think he'd go this far."

"Damn it, Jim, it has nothing to do with Paul."

"How do you know? That may be all it is, whether he chooses to admit it or not."

"I know it isn't. I'm closer to him than you are."

He was suddenly at the desk, hands planted on its

surface. "It makes me sick, just thinking about it. I keep seeing him in the lab, putting us together, observing us in those goddamn wombs. Don't tell me it's a normal love affair. He's really sucked you in, hasn't he? First he has you involved in all these projects of his and then. . . ."

"I don't have to listen to any more of this. And while you're thinking about Hidey, you might remember what we did a few years back and think what people would say about that."

He pulled away slightly as if she had slapped him. She stood up and glared across the desk at her brother. They faced each other, feet apart, fists clenched. The door opened and Jim spun around.

Hidey stood there, looking first at Jim, then at Kira. She tried to relax and saw Jim attempting a strained smile.

"Hello, Jim," Hidey said quietly. "I haven't seen you in quite a while. How's the writing?"

Jim seemed stunned for a moment. "He's working on another novel," she said quickly, and heard Jim echo her words: "I'm working on another novel."

Hidey took out a rumpled pack of cigarettes and lit one. "I really admire people who can write," he went on. "All I've ever managed are papers for the journals, reports, that kind of thing, and I usually have to rewrite them and then have my computer correct my spelling."

For an instant Kira thought that her brother was going to create a scene. She watched his jaw muscles tighten, then relax. Jim shrugged. "It's just a skill you have to learn, a craft," he said. "It comes easier to some people than others."

"What's the book about?"

"I can't explain it in a sentence."

"He hasn't even shown it to me," Kira interjected. Her voice sounded too high.

"I'd like to talk to you, Jim, come over sometime, I'm usually free during lunch. Right now I have to go tape a lecture. I'll call you later, Kira."

"Fine," she managed to say. Hidey left, closing the door.

They were alone again. Kira's knees felt weak and she sat down, slouching in her seat. Jim gazed absently at the door, then turned back.

"Does he know?" he asked as he sat down.

"Know what?" she muttered, already sure of what Jim meant.

"About us way back."

Her throat tightened. She was silent, answering him soundlessly with her eyes.

"I wonder what he'd say."

She stood up slowly. She moved around the desk until she was standing over him. He started to rise and she quickly reached out, shoving him back into the chair.

"If you say a word to him, just one word. . . ." She was hovering over him. "I'll find that book of yours and rip it to shreds, don't think I won't." She did not care what she said now, wanting to frighten him and somehow gain the upper hand.

He suddenly laughed. "Do you think I'd care? I've been thinking of tearing it up myself." He chuckled softly. "You'd be freeing me, you know that? I wouldn't have to sweat over it any more, I could start something else. A nice clean start, that's what I need. You'd be doing me a favor. Tell you what, you throw out my book and I'll have a little talk with Hidey and we'll both be better off."

She grabbed his shoulders, digging through his worn blue shirt with her nails. "You make me sick sometimes." He seized her wrists. She pulled away from him. "You accomplish nothing. You're a parasite, living on Paul's royalties, your share, and mine, and most of Al's too, if you must know. You'll probably get Ed's share when he gets promoted next year and the only reason you don't have Mike's as well is that he's too smart to get taken in by your bullshit." A look of surprise passed over Jim's face. "Oh, yes, and the only reason you weren't smart enough to figure it out is that you're too damn lazy to pay attention to little details like finances, you think it's an endless stream you've got coming to you. You probably didn't even think to ask the computer who was crediting the money to you." She paced across the room. "And you live off us in other ways too, suddenly showing up and needing a job, some companionship, a place to live after you've spent your money on car rentals and travel to improve your mind. And you have nothing to show for it but one book you finished after you left school, I don't know how. You've finished nothing, not school, not another book, nothing. And when the rest of us try to accomplish something, all you can do is come along and try to prevent us just because you want company in your misery. If Al weren't on the moon, you would have been pestering him by now, I wouldn't put it past you to scrape up the passage money and try."

She stopped and waited for his reply. He was gazing at the floor. At last he looked up and she forced herself to face him.

He seemed oddly calm. "What I'm doing takes a little longer than what you're doing. It's a different sort of thing."

"What a rationalization!"

"I won't fight you if you want to kick me out, I can find another place." She could not read his eyes, green pieces of glass flickering in the light. "None of you told me about the royalties, no one asked me if I minded taking the money. You sent it to me to buy me off, probably, or because it was easier than arguing about it. Don't you think I had a right to know?"

You're twisting things now, as if we're the ones at fault, not you.

"Maybe you're at fault," he went on, as if picking up her thoughts. "I might have worked harder if I'd known. I could have applied for a writer's grant."

"Oh, sure!" She began to laugh, and her laughter shattered against the walls, breaking into tiny sharp slivers. *Don't listen to him.* She slumped into another chair. "Oh, sure." The words trailed off.

Hunched over in their chairs, they watched each other. Kira realized her shoulders were shaking. She was crying.

Ashamed, yet unwilling to acknowledge the tears, she let them slide down her cheeks silently.

"Kira," Jim said. The word seemed a distant moan. "Let's go home." *I'm sorry*, he said without speaking.

"Let's go home," she repeated.

When they were small, things had been easier, in spite of the occasional torments of their classmates. There were Bill and Zuñi, arms to hold them, laps to crawl onto. There was Paul.

Why are we different, why weren't we made like other kids? I cried when Zuñi and Bill left, I thought they didn't love us any more, but Zuñi said that wasn't true, they loved us just as much but it was time to go, they had work to do and it was time for us to grow up. And I cried because I knew I wouldn't see them any more, and I didn't until Paul died.

She and her brothers had been closer as children, communicating easily, often soundlessly, able almost to hear the whispers of each other's thoughts. Paul had taught them chess, and they would often play with him to test their skill. It was more difficult playing with each other; often the games would end in stalemates unless one of them made an error. Team sports were better in some ways. After school, they would play basketball with some other children, anticipating each other's moves. They were quicker then, unencumbered by the baggage of maturity. It was a happier time.

The others resented us, forcing us together. We had no other friends. We sat together, wishing we were like other people.

Kira had once hoped that they would eventually grow closer when they were older, but that it would not be an unthinking, defensive type of relationship, as it had been when they were young, but a mature relationship, that of people who would work together as a team. Instead, they grew more distant every year. Oddly enough, their similarities seemed to aid in driving them apart, as if each resented the part of himself he saw reflected in the others. . . .

It had grown dark outside. Part of Kira's mind began to nag her as she sat on the porch in front of the house: *finish your reading, start preparing finals for the students, call Hidey.* The warm nighttime air was making her lethargic, unable to stir from the corner of the porch.

A dark shape emerged from the front door and moved toward her. She squinted and saw that it was Carole. The girl had pulled her hair back and was wearing an old shirt that reached to the middle of her thighs. She had transformed herself from an Egyptian statue into a small child; her slow graceful movements appeared to be a mask for the underlying shyness and awkwardness.

Carole sat down in a nearby chair and nodded at Kira. "Hello."

"You fought with Jim again," Carole said. It was a simple statement, not a challenge.

"I know," Kira said. "We apologized. I don't think it really settled anything."

"He had a bad day. Ellie was mad at him this afternoon, you know. They were fighting about his book, I didn't really understand all of it. Ellie said something about he was afraid to finish it, that he was worrying about what people would say, that he kept thinking about it while he wrote instead of concentrating. Then she said he was thinking he wouldn't have anything left to write after he finished, so he really didn't want to get it done. I don't know. He's trying as hard as he can."

"I haven't seen the book."

"I read part of it. It seemed really good, but I'm not one for reading a lot, I don't know that much about it. Ellie said he was indulging himself, whatever that means. I hope you're not still mad at him."

"No, I guess I'm not."

Carole turned toward Kira. Her face was hidden in the darkness. "Jim needs somebody that cares about what he does, someone that encourages him. I don't like to talk against anybody, but sometimes Ellie really makes him upset telling him things. He probably thinks you don't like what he's doing either. Ellie thinks he should stay here and work until he finishes the book, but I don't know how he can if he thinks everybody's upset with him."

"What do you think he should do?" Kira asked.

"I don't know. This may be a bad place for him, sometimes he just sits around and talks about stuff that happened when he was a kid. I don't know if it's good for him to do that, it makes him sad, and he's sad so much of the time. I wish I could do something about it."

"I hate to say this, Carole, but sometimes he makes himself sad. It's as if he doesn't want to be content, that he's supposed to be unhappy."

"Why should he do that? It doesn't make any sense."

"It does in a way. He doesn't write about what he knows, but what he feels. Read his first book and you'll see. It was a little different when we were younger, but now. . . ." Kira paused. Carole seemed puzzled. "I guess we're all a bit melancholy, call it a family trait. Why did you come here with him?"

"Why do you think? Because I love him. Ellie does too, in her own way, but maybe she pushes him around too much, maybe he isn't ready for that. I know you care about him too, but he's kind of afraid of you."

"No, he isn't."

"He is, in a way."

"Oh, Carole," Kira said in exasperation.

"He says he's afraid of what you're doing."

"Oh, my work. Well, we've been arguing about that for a while."

"Not just that. He's afraid of the way you feel about it."

Kira opened her mouth to explain something, then stopped. She did not know what she could say to Carole. It would probably be better not to argue with her at all.

"He's so unhappy," Carole said quietly. "I wish he weren't. I wish I could do something about it, but I guess I don't know enough. I try to cheer him up, but I don't really understand him sometimes." The young woman seemed to be struggling with her words. "And Ellie tries, but she thinks a person can get rid of feeling depressed if he just wants to badly enough. Maybe you're the only one that can really help him. You're more like him, for one thing."

No, I can't help him, we have nothing to say to each other now. He's a mystery to me, too. "You may be expecting too much of me," she said aloud, standing up. "Where's Jim now?"

"In his room."

Kira left the porch and went back inside. Ellie was in the living room reading a book. Kira climbed the stairs, walked down the hall and knocked on Jim's door.

"Come in."

She entered the room, and felt momentarily as if she had stepped into the past. *Jim was hunched over his desk, writing. In the background she could hear the sound of Ed's violin. Give me some help with this theme for Mr. Grey and I'll explain the carbon cycle to you.* Then Jim straightened at his desk and she was back to the present again. He was too thin, his clothes worn and rumpled. She thought she noticed some silvery hairs in his beard. For a second she saw how she must look to Jim; slightly thicker in the waist, her long brown hair confined in a bun on the back of her neck, her face more gaunt. *I still think of myself as sixteen.* She remembered a girl with short loose hair and good reflexes, clothed in a short tunic. The modestly dressed woman with tiny lines near the eyes from too much sunlight was a stranger.

She sat down on the edge of Jim's bed and tugged at her pale green slacks. "You came to see how my book was going, I suppose," he muttered. She looked at the rough draft piled on either side of his typewriter. He had corrected a few pages and put them through his compositor; the clean pages lay next to her on the bed. But he was obviously not satisfied with them; he had already marked them up, crossing out entire paragraphs.

"No," she replied, "I came to see how you were. I guess if you kept asking me how I was doing, whether I was getting anything done or not, I'd get mad too. Right now I should be preparing for the end of the term, as well as getting some reading done." She remembered the project and realized that was not anything to bring up at the moment. "Look, Jim, I won't bother you about the book or anything else. You can stay here and take the time you need."

"I made a mistake coming here," he said. "I should have thought about it. Too much has changed, and not enough has." He rested his head on his hands. "I think I still care more about you than Ellie or Carole. Isn't that ridiculous? An adolescent incident we'd both be better off forgetting." She stared at him. "They'll probably leave. Ellie's thinking of going back to New York anyway. You could help me, Kira, I know you could. Maybe we could do some traveling, you haven't really had a chance to see too much."

"I can't, Jim." She forced herself to speak more clearly. "I can't. I have work to do. I'm in love with Hidey. . . ."

"Him!"

"I am, I don't know how it'll turn out, but I'll stay here to see. You're trying to get me to make your decisions for you again. Don't ask me to do that, it's not fair."

He turned back to his typewriter. "Well, it was worth a try." He sounded resigned and passive. Something had been taken out of him, or worn down, a spark or a passion. She might be making a mistake, she could not tell. *Regrets, always regrets.* No matter what she did, something would be wrong, something would be unresolved.

"Don't do anything suddenly," she said, trying to be helpful. "Take some time to think things over. Carole and Ellie care a lot about you, don't be too quick to leave them out of things." Her words seemed empty formalities.

She got up and left the room quietly, leaving Jim alone with his ghosts.

She had driven off the automated highway and through the city streets to the apartment towers, parking the car underground and hurrying up to Hidey's apartment in the elevator. The words were flowing from her lips as soon as Hidey opened his door, tripping over each other as she spoke them.

They huddled together in his small bed as she finished what she had to say. He held her gently, smoothing back her hair.

"Oh, Hidey, he's so unhappy."

"I know."

"You aren't disgusted by what we did once?"

"I was a little startled, I have to admit, but there is a kind of logic to it. I can't be disgusted by your actions, though, knowing the reasons for them. Jim needed you then, obviously."

"He says he needs me now." She turned over on her back. "I came here because I want you to tell me what to do, just like Jim wanted me to decide things for him. And you can't do that, I know. It would be easier if you just told me to go, or told me you loved me too much to let me go."

"I can't do that, Kira. Look, you needed to talk and now you probably need to sleep."

She closed her eyes, trying to calm her mind. "He may," she heard Hidey whisper, "make his own decision. It's entirely possible, he has before. I can't tell you what to do, or Jim either."

Kira sighed. Things could never be settled, never resolved, it seemed. *Where are the victories,* she wondered, *where are the moments that make it all worthwhile?* She drifted, her mind was floating, not quite conscious yet unable to rest. She lay suspended in that state, dimly aware of Hidey at her side.

Kira began to catch up on her work, avoiding the house for the next two days. Occasionally she would call, prompted by guilt, but Jim was never home, or refusing to answer. She left messages, *call the office, call Hidey's apartment.*

Jim did not call.

She had not devoted much time to Hidey's proposed project, and quickly remedied that situation. There was little doubt in her mind that the others would go along with it, in spite of their objections to certain details. She had sensed the atmosphere in the department, had overheard snatches of conversations in the halls, the lounge, and the laboratories. Hidey, in the minds of the others, was in a sense the department. People such as Ike Jefferson and Cesar Gomez had come to work here because of Hidey. They would allow Kurt to voice objections, perhaps agreeing with some of them, but in the end they would go along with Hidey. The meeting would become a formality.

Kira shuffled the pages on her desk and considered the project. They would begin tests with animals, of course; if everything proceeded smoothly, they would then work with a human subject. She began to wonder if she would falter at that point. She would not be able to regard the cloned fetus with quite the same attitude as the others; she might see herself in the ectogenetic chamber, being readied for injection into Paul. It could have happened that way, given different circumstances; she and her brothers might never have existed except as serum in Paul's veins.

She shook her head. She was behaving like Jim, being fanciful. It was not the same thing at all. *It's not the same at all.* And people now alive might never have existed if their parents had not made love at a particular time. She could not involve herself in such *ex post facto* considerations.

She would have to go to the meeting in a few minutes. She doubted she would have much to say. She would wait for the others to speak before offering anything. Hidey had not spoken with her about the project; at first she had not wondered at that. But now she found herself worrying about it. Did Hidey have his own doubts? Or was he so obsessed that he was afraid to speak to her about it, afraid she would see that and join with Kurt against him? If that happened, Jonis would go along with her and probably Bert Ramsey as well. *But Hidey isn't like that.* She would wait.

"Kira?"

Surprised, she looked up. Jim was standing in the doorway. She motioned to him and he entered, seating himself on the edge of her desk.

"What is it, Jim?" The approaching meeting prodded at the edge of her mind. *Damn it, I don't care, I can at least give Jim some of my time.*

"Ellie went back to New York, I took her to the train this morning."

"You don't seem too upset."

"Why should I be? She'll be happier doing that anyway. Ellie had to work hard all her life, that was one of the problems. She decided she didn't want to give up her job after all, and she was starting to resent me and my book. Maybe she was right about some things, I don't know. She wasn't mad when she left, she told me to keep in touch."

"What are you going to do now?" Jim had obviously decided something, she could tell that. He seemed calmer, more in control of himself.

"I'll be leaving." He smiled slightly, then shrugged. "Not right away. I'll finish the book, or at least figure out where it's going, then leave. I'll be gone by the end of the month. I'll look for a quiet place where I can work for a while."

How long that feeling would last, she did not know. But she could at least encourage him until he was gone, and hope that he would persist.

"Carole said she'd come with me. I didn't expect her to, but she will."

"You'll do fine," Kira said. "I shouldn't have worried." She should have been pleased. Instead, she felt vaguely let down. She had not really helped Jim that much; it was easier to evade the situation. She would be a spectator of her brother's life and something inside her was objecting to that, saying *it's not right, things should be different.* But Jim did have to lead his own life. *We have our own lives, that's what we all say, and the ones who can't make it alone fall by the wayside.*

"I think we've played this scene before," he said.

"Yes, we have." She had cried then. Now she extended

a hand and managed to smile. He took her hand and pressed it.

"I'll see you at home." He paused before going on. "Maybe you can bring Hidey along. Carole would probably like him."

The words had cost him a lot to say, how much she was not sure.

"Maybe, Jim. I know he'd like to talk to both of you."

He released her hand. Suddenly she felt as though she were inside him, slipping over the edge of a precipice, unable to get a foothold, sliding downward. *Something's lost, something's gone forever.* Jim could not find what he wanted in the present or the future. He would always be looking behind him, trying to weld bits of the past into a coherent and pleasing life. Her mind seemed to grasp his, pulling him up from the abyss, at least for a moment.

His eyes held hers and he smiled briefly, then retreated from her again. "I'll see you later, Kira."

He left the office, fumbling for a moment with the door, then vanished into the hallway. She heard his footsteps echo on the floor.

Kira was late to the meeting. She entered the room quickly, nodding a silent apology while noting the expressions on the faces around the table.

Kurt was speaking. She sat down and waited for him to finish.

"You've heard my objections," Kurt said. "I do not think we can accomplish what Hidey so fervently desires." He paused. "In spite of that, I would be interested in pursuing the matter, as long as we keep our goals within reasonable limits."

Jonis glanced at Kira, apparently as surprised as she was. Bert leaned forward and squinted at Kurt skeptically.

Hidey was smiling. "I realize that those who give grants have the foolish idea that we can always predict our results," he said, "but those of us who have done research before, as few of us as there are left now, learned a long time ago that you don't always come up with exactly what you expect." He put out his cigarette and immediately lit another. "Well, we'll satisfy the grant-givers, we'll make some notation about medical benefits." He leaned back in the chair. "We'd better discuss the mundane details of how to approach this now. I have a feeling we might be engaging in quite an adventure."

An adventure. Kira found her mind wandering back to her brother. He might live to benefit from whatever they discovered, but she wondered if it would make any difference to him. He seemed to be seeking death as ardently as Hidey sought life by looking through death, retreating from the world which was already starting to change before his eyes. And it would get worse for him. Kira wondered if people, used to a somewhat static world for a while now, might be frightened again when they began to realize what might happen. There was no way to tell. She could only hope that the rewards would be more alluring than the fears.

Jonis was speaking now. Kira forced her attention back to the present.

". . . exploration of space beyond the planetary system is a dead-end occupation."

—Dennis Gabor
INNOVATIONS
Scientific, Technological, and Social

"Where there is no vision the people perish."
—Proverbs 29:18

6. Albert: 2036

ALBERT Swenson was at peace as he moved across the lunar landscape, lumbering a bit in his spacesuit as his feet pushed lightly against the dust. The deep black shadows at the foot of the mountains to his left were lengthening as the two-week-long lunar day drew to its close. Behind him, three large, concave metal disks captured the last of the sunlight. The underground lunar settlement, housing about fifty thousand people, was run primarily by solar power. Another fifty thousand lived in a settlement to the south of this one and two thousand miners spent most of their time in a camp two hundred miles away. Yet few of them came here intending to settle permanently; most still returned to Earth after one or two years. No children had yet been born here. That was too final a step; the children, raised in lunar gravity, would never be able to go to Earth. Their lighter bones and slimmer bodies would make them perpetual exiles.

But there was a growing number of people who, like himself, had grown accustomed to the austerity of the life here. Many of them regarded the moon as their real home. It was only a matter of time before some of them chose to settle here with families permanently. What did it matter if their children could not live on Earth when there was all of space to explore? What did it matter when there were asteroids, brought into lunar orbit to be mined and now being transformed into hollowed-out living places? When there was Mars with its small but

236

growing settlements not unlike those here? When there would someday be spaceships attempting to travel the vast distances between stars?

Al looked up at the blue-green, cloudy roundness of Earth, hanging in its accustomed place overhead in the black sky. It was an ever-present sight, never moving from that spot, always beckoning to the people who had abandoned it. Yet the Moon-dwellers almost never saw it, living underground as they did, unless they chose to come to the surface to pay Earth their respects. And the radio astronomers, working at their lonely tasks on the other side of the moon, never saw Earth at all.

Al had gone home twice. He had visited Kira and Ed after their marriages six years ago; two years later, he had journeyed to some of the places on Earth he had never visited. These were the reasons he had given himself for the two trips; in fact, he had been almost forced to go by the administrators at the astronomical observatory where he worked. He had been on the moon too long, they had told him, and too long a stay might be disorienting, physically and mentally.

It had been the journey to Earth that was disorienting. The space station was bad enough, but the sensations that assaulted him when he reached Earth itself were dizzying. It was not the gravity that bothered him; he had kept himself fit and suffered only a sense of fatigue and weariness that left him after a few days. It was the sights: people moving through the terminal dressed in red, violet, orange, green, blue, yellow; the sounds: a cacaphony of voices shouting, whispering, chattering, booming from the intercom; the smells: sweat, hamburgers, perfume, tobacco, marijuana, coffee. The earth suddenly seemed overwhelmingly crowded; a peculiar loneliness had seized him. He could not shake it off, even by the end of his visits. He slept badly at first, feeling as though an unseen hand was pressing him into the bedclothes. He was also reluctant to leave the enclosed space of houses and hotel rooms for the open, almost unpredictable outdoors. Although he had recovered from the sleeplessness in time, he had been relieved to get back to the moon.

He would, he was sure, have to visit Earth again sometime soon. But at least he could look forward to acquainting himself with his niece and nephew, who had been little more than infants on his last trip. Isaac, his nephew, born to Ed and his wife Sheila a few months before their marriage, would be almost seven by now. Al had spoken with Isaac briefly over the holophone; the boy, bearing a marked resemblance to Ed, seemed a serious and introverted child.

Rina Takamura-Swenson was apparently quite different. Al had shamelessly spoiled his niece while on Earth and still indulged himself with frequent calls to her and her parents. The lively inquisitive little girl, he was sure, was one of the brightest kids he had ever seen. It was not long before Rina understood the reason for the three-second delay in talking to her uncle and began to make a game out of it. She was now, at the age of five, able to carry on what Al considered a fairly sophisticated dialogue for a child.

Kira, of course, had always been sterile, a byproduct of being the clone of a male. But she and Hidey had obtained permission to clone a child of their own. Rina had been produced by the same process that had produced the Swensons. The difference was that both Kira's and Hidey's germ plasm had been used. Rina had been born from an ectogenetic chamber; although still not common, the procedure was becoming more usual as a convenience for mothers. People who wanted only clones of themselves were still frowned upon, unless the circumstances were unusual. But there were other children like Rina; children of homosexual couples, of sterile couples, or of groups who raised children communally. Permission to use such processes was not as difficult to get now. In spite of Al's impressions, the earth was becoming less crowded. As more of its six billion people had become reasonably well off, the birth rate had dropped. Almost one-sixth of the world was too busy with other pursuits to bother having children at all. Young women were not pressured into fulfilling themselves through childbirth; among some young men, sterilization had become popular, a way of asserting their masculinity, of showing people that they were secure enough in their manhood not to require the perpetuation of their genes. A growing industry catered to childless people; among many others, having only one child was increasingly common.

Al knew that this pattern might change if the population declined too rapidly. But right now there were too many other things for people to do. Travel was common among young people undecided about their lives. Scholarly sorts could spend a lifetime in study without ever leaving their home computer complexes. Less scholarly types could find a variety of entertainments. Various groups were experimenting with different social structures, some of them based on older models, others entirely new. Those who looked outward could work in space, on the moon, or on Mars. Those who looked inward could care for the wilderness areas set aside for recreation. Those who wanted a change of scenery could live in space communities, underwater domes, towering cities, rural communes, or arcologies.

There were drawbacks, of course. If there were those who enjoyed exploring alternatives, there were also those whose lives were bounded by one pointless pursuit after another. If there were older people who were integrated into society, some of them beginning new careers in old age, there were others who felt isolated and banded together defensively. There were children who, although wanted by their parents, sometimes suffered the disdain of those among whom a dislike of children had become stylish. Although almost everyone could be assured of a place to live and food to eat, almost no one could ever hope to become wealthy; those who were worse off would still steal from those who were better off. Some people could get along with others different from themselves; others were overwhelmed by diversity. Computers and communication equipment, while linking the world and providing education and entertainment, had also, in spite of legal safeguards, robbed everyone of some personal privacy.

Ahead of him, on a barren plain, Al saw a small group of people in spacesuits. It was difficult to tell how far away they were; in spite of some time spent on the lunar surface, he was still not completely accustomed to its peculiar perspective. The horizon was not far enough away; there were few landmarks by which to gauge distance.

The suited people were lumbering fatly and clumsily about, aiming cameras at two people who stood at the center of the activity. Al approached, waving silently at a small bulky figure hovering near them. The figure raised one finger, indicating that he should maintain radio silence. Then it moved toward him, bouncing slightly, kicking up dust which began to settle slowly back on the plain.

The figure reached him and they touched helmets as Al checked to be sure his radio was off. "*Je t' aime*," he heard through the helmet, and then, after a pause, "What are you doing here, Al?"

"I missed you, Simone."

"I cannot believe that. I have been gone for two hours at the most."

"Well, I thought it was time to reacquaint myself with the surface."

"Oh, Al, I missed you too. This film has become even more ridiculous. Do you see the two people standing there? They are being pursued by a miner who has sworn to kill them for. . . . " Simone Tran lifted her head and waved her arms slowly. He motioned to her and they touched helmets again. "I have been trying to tell the director," she went on, "that the lovers would be dead by now for lack of air, but he refuses to listen."

"I don't know why you bother."

"There is money in it. When I get paid, I will have some good wine shipped up here and we shall celebrate."

The film crew, cameras lowered, began to stumble toward a small dome near the solar disks, a dome which housed one of the entrances to the underground lunar complex. They were filming their adventure story on location, an expensive process, but not nearly as costly as duplicating the moon believably with a set. Lunar adventures had become a popular form of entertainment, even more popular than the romanticized stories about twentieth-century truck drivers that Al remembered from his childhood. The films, however, portrayed lunar life as more violent and exciting than it actually was; their plots tended to resemble those of the trucker films, which in turn had been modeled on stories of the old American West. Simone had managed to get a small job as scientific advisor to the director; it paid a lot for very little work, since the director ignored most of Simone's advice anyway.

From the sublime to the ridiculous, Al thought. Humanity's ventures into the solar system were having an effect on the arts, opening up new themes and settings. The results were Nikita Rogov's "free-fall" ballets, Ramon Hernandez's "space-scapes" which suggested the distances between stars, Althea Rhadames's so-called "Martian poems," and adventurous yarns such as the one being filmed on the moon now.

Simone moved away and turned on her radio; he did the same. They followed the crew toward the settlement, bounding lightly over the ground. It was probably just as well that Simone did not spend much time with the film crew. Dmitri Grol and some of the others on the space flight project already resented the amount of time she was spending on the film. They had wanted her, like Al, to visit Earth. Simone had not seen Paris, or any other part of Earth, for almost three years. She too regarded the moon as her home.

They shuffled into the dome behind the film crew and descended into a small waiting-room-sized airlock below the surface. They closed the sliding panel above them, an extra precaution in case the dome was accidentally punctured, waited until air had cycled into the room, then proceeded into a vestibule, where they began to peel off their suits.

Simone lifted the helmet off her head and Al smiled at the familiar sight of her face; almond-shaped brown eyes, a wide mouth, framed by short, straight black hair.

She, like him, was dressed in a loose, short t-shirt and shorts. The film crew was, like most visitors, overdressed.

Al had decided, after working with Simone Tran for almost a year, that she was the woman with whom he would most like to spend the rest of his life. His love for her had grown gradually; the realization that he loved her had been sudden. Two years ago, while sitting in a dining room discussing his work with Simone, he had understood that he needed her and wanted her desperately. They had spent almost three months in a sexual daze before the passion had subsided enough to reveal to them both how deep their feelings really were.

Simone, almost forty-five, had divorced her husband before coming to the moon, unable to resist the opportunity to work with the scientists there. She was a Vietnamese, but her grandparents had emigrated to Paris and her parents had known no other home. She waved to the film crew as they left the room, then made a face at Al.

"Idiots," she muttered. "Fortunately, they will return to Earth soon. They will have my credit line in very small letters and perhaps I shall not have too much shame to bear. The public will forget their entertainment after they have seen it and no one will be the wiser."

They left the vestibule and walked through a corridor carved out of the lunar rock, moving through it in a peculiar stride that lifted them off the ground slightly with each step. At the end of the corridor, they emerged into a huge, cavernous courtyard. A few small trees and shrubs lined the center pathway, lit by lights set into the rock overhead. The plants, as well as providing some oxygen, were meant to give a less alien feeling to the lunar settlement. But it was the trees and shrubs themselves that seemed alien in this underground setting.

The center path was lined on both sides with small dome-like structures housing the hotels, restaurants, and other facilities used mostly by tourists and visitors. Some of the lunar residents also lived and worked here; most of them could be found in the mazes of rooms lining the corridors that led away from this cavernous place. Al and

Simone approached one of these corridors and bounded lightly through it. The hall was soundless; Al heard nothing but Simone's breathing and the muffled thud of their feet on the floor. They stopped before one door, opened it, and were met by a multilingual roar.

The large room they entered functioned as a recreation area, cafeteria, and meeting room. One group in a corner was eating; others were playing chess or sitting at tables piled high with computer runs. Al waved at Menachem Alon, a big Israeli who was explaining something in Arabic to Ahmed Maheib, a small slender engineer. Ahmed, in spite of his size, had a deep resonant voice which was solemnly overriding Menachem's comments.

One had to speak at least four languages in order to socialize among these people. Most of the scientific work was done in Russian or English and everybody knew at least one; most spoke both. It was useful to know Chinese as well; although the Chinese tended to keep to themselves, they did exchange information with the others. Socializing was done in any language the parties could agree on. The more languages a person knew, the more friends he was likely to make and the more chance insights he might acquire into his own work. Al, in addition to a good command of Russian and French, had undergone hypno-training in German, Japanese, Chinese and Swahili, all of which he spoke with widely varying degrees of fluency. The hypnotic techniques were useful, but there was no substitute for frequent practice. Al, like most of the Americans, was occasionally at a disadvantage compared to the other scientists. He wondered sometimes how Tom Abijah must feel; the man from New Guinea had found no one who spoke his tribal tongue and was in danger of forgetting it altogether.

He and Simone sat down next to Menachem and Ahmed, who politely switched to French. The two had been discussing the one thing that was uppermost in the minds of all those on the moon; the starships under construction in lunar orbit.

Three of the huge ships were being built. Work on them had begun only five years before; it had taken three

years of intensive negotiations before all the governments
and industries involved had come to an agreement. Luckily,
there had been little public resistance to the project.
Anyone who was not excited by it was apathetic, as
long as he did not have to suffer economically. Tradespeople and other workers saw the venture in more prag-
matic terms. There were jobs to be had, and higher pay
plus more vacation time for anyone who worked in orbit.
The workers, with these incentives before them, had
managed to arrive at agreements among those who were
members of established unions, those who had joined
newer unions in opposition to the old ones, and free-
lancers who belonged to neither group.

Some officials had wanted to wait until signals indicating
the presence of habitable planets were received from the
unmanned probes that had been sent out long before.
But they had been won over by a group of astronomers who had presented a lecture on stellar evolution
and the probabilities of habitable planets being within
twenty-two light-years of the solar system. In addition,
space travel, as opposed to local travel within the solar
system, held an appeal for the more adventurous.

Fortunately, by the time the star ship designs had been
ironed out and construction had begun, a signal was received from Epsilon Eridani, twelve light-years away, indicating the presence of a gas giant. Although this did not
mean a habitable planet was present, it did mean that the
system was worth a look. Other planets were undoubtedly
circling the star. The news had been greeted with enthusiasm and some relief, then quickly forgotten by those unin-
volved in the project. As it was now, Al thought, the
project was sustained by the tradespeople's desire for jobs
and the fact that so much had already been spent that no
one wanted to disband the project. It had at last acquired
its own momentum, held up at times only by engineering
problems and disputes among the workers about how many
nationals of each country would be hired to build the
ships. That debate had centered around whether or not
the tiny but growing number of people claiming alle-
giance to no state should be counted as citizens of their

birthplaces; it had been decided to consider them as a separate group. The most serious incident, which had resulted in a strike by technicians from India and the Soviet Union who wanted fewer Chinese on the project, had been overcome within a month.

Al forced his attention back to the conversation around him. Ahmed was expounding on a minor flaw, recently ironed out, in the engine of the starship design. The engines were nuclear-pulse models, fueled by frozen deuterium. The fuel itself would make up most of the body of the ship, being contained in a huge "snowball" about one thousand feet in diameter. The living quarters, attached to this large globe, would be inside a cylinder three hundred feet in diameter and one thousand feet long. At the end of this cylinder three smaller globes, each two hundred and fifty feet in diameter, would house engineering compartments; thrust units would be attached to these compartments.

The ships, Al thought, would resemble halves of barbells from a distance, with the large globular snowball reflecting images of stars from its metal surface. Each of the three ships would house at most three hundred passengers and it was expected that this population would increase to about two thousand during the journey.

For it would be a very long journey, perhaps a lifetime for many of those on board. The secret of faster-than-light travel still eluded them. Even though the ships could travel at thirty per cent of light speed, years might be spent in exploring Epsilon Eridani. After replacing the supply of deuterium, using the gas giant known to be there, the travelers might decide to go on rather than return. And those born on the ship might have no desire to come back to Earth, which would be for them only a name.

There would be so many possibilities on such a voyage, Al thought. While traveling at thirty per cent of light speed, subjective time aboard ship would pass more slowly than time on Earth. Even if they returned, it would not be to the earth they had known. Although anti-aging shots were now being given to those in their fifties and there was talk of lifting restrictions altogether, those alive now might not live to see the ships return. If one went on the trip, he would have to assume, barring any exceptional circumstance, that he was cutting all personal ties with those on Earth.

"One of your brothers is working on the engine, is he not?" Ahmed said in English to Al. Al felt slightly irritated; even after all this time some of the personnel, especially newer ones, took care to address most of their social remarks to Americans in English. Some justified this on the ground that it was difficult to discuss certain concepts in their own languages, and that fluency in English was almost a necessity here, but others no doubt thought of the Americans as backward children. Not surprisingly, this kept the Americans less fluent in other tongues, thus feeding the prejudice. The Japanese suffered from a similar prejudice; it was widely believed that the Japanese learned other languages only reluctantly. Some of Al's compatriots, annoyed with this state of affairs, had taken to speaking different languages among themselves.

"Mike did some work on it," Al replied. "Not much, as I recall, just a small design suggestion."

"I have been thinking," the engineer continued. "The engines on these ships might be capable of going much faster than anyone has yet anticipated. We shall not realize, possibly, how powerful they actually are until we are in space. We may exceed fifty per cent of the speed of light. I have been considering this, doing some calculations."

"Everybody's been doing calculations," Menachem said, "and everybody's coming to the same conclusion. Frankly, I don't know if it's because they really believe it to be the case, or because they're hoping they might be able to return to an earth that hasn't changed that much, that they'll be able to get back sooner." The big Israeli pulled at his red handlebar moustache thoughtfully. "Seems to me people should be satisfied if they get picked to go. We're better off than those poor wonderful bastards that worked on the probes, or the plans for the probes, spending their whole lives on something when they might not live to see the results."

Menachem, as usual, had been too blunt. No one among the scientists wanted to think about not being chosen to go. There was room for at most three hundred people per ship; room had to be allowed for an expanding population as little more than two thousand people could get along comfortably in the quarters. And not all of the nine hundred passengers would be chosen from the physicists, astrophysicists, selenologists, and engineers that dominated the lunar population. There would have to be crews for the ships, doctors, biologists, anthropologists, other specialists and perhaps a few simpler souls with a talent for mediating disputes and just getting along with people. Everyone knew that old-timers on the moon or Mars probably had a better chance than most. After all, they had at least proven they could get along in an environment different from that of Earth. But most of them would be left behind.

Choosing the specialists would not be the only problem. Every nation would want to be sure that the travelers represented a cross-section of Earth's citizens. The silliest of the demands would probably be rejected. It would be almost impossible to get an exact representation of all nations. The committee which would make the selection, moreover, was comprised of a fairly sensible group of scientists, psychologists, and others, with a sprinkling of politicians who could be outvoted and some literary and artistic people, who would select a small group of poets, writers, actors, and artists. Someone, Al could not remember who, had pointed out that this group would provide needed entertainment and cultural activity during the flight, as well as recording a different perspective on the journey and perhaps creating new artistic forms. There would be ample time to explore the tapes and microfiche books during the trip, and the voyagers might well need new pursuits created by those on board. The artists would also be able to take on technical tasks; most of them, because of the limitations on the number of people chosen, would be people who had some knowledge of scientific disciplines.

Given all this, Al thought acidly, it probably meant that both Menachem and Ahmed had a better chance of going on the trip than he himself did. And if they were looking for as many representatives of each racial group as possible, Tom Abijah had the best chance of all. Al found himself pondering how unfair all of this was, then forced himself to ignore the feeling. Ultimately, they would pick the best, they had to for anything this important. And anyone here on the moon was the cream of the crop. *If I don't measure up, it's just too damned bad.*

"What are you glaring at, *chéri*?" Simone murmured. Ahmed and Menachem, seeing that Al had dropped out of the conversation, had switched back to Arabic.

"I'm feeling ashamed of some idle thoughts."

"You and these two, you are all alike." Menachem glanced at Simone, lifted one bushy eyebrow, then turned back to Ahmed. "Whenever you are together, one of you always slips into a private world. I know it does not bother you, but I await the day when you three will be together and one of you does not lose himself in a reverie."

"We're just moody sons of bitches," Menachem said. "You go ahead and ponder if you feel like it, Al." The big man stood up. "I've been doing too much pondering myself, I'm overdue for a workout and a turn in the centrifuge. You know, I was thirty pounds heavier before I came here. I don't know how the hell I carried all that excess blubber around."

"And even now," Ahmed said, smiling, "if you were to return, you would most likely be crushed under your own weight."

Menachem tried to take a friendly poke at the smaller man. He bobbed a few feet off the floor, nearly knocking over the table with his leg.

Al's room was near the end of one of the underground corridors in a residential area. That section of the lunar city, newly built when Al had first arrived here years ago, had once been open to the rest of the complex, but the privacy of the residents had been disturbed by lost and confused tourists wandering into the area. Now, in addition to the standard locks on room doors, there was a door at the entrance to the section with a sign saying *RESIDENTS ONLY* in several languages. Eventually, Al supposed, that doorway would also be equipped with a lock, which could only be opened when a person's thumbprint had been checked against those of people authorized to enter.

At the end of this hallway, just a few feet beyond Al's room, there was a small sitting room with a large screen. The screen, with the aid of a camera on the surface, provided a view of the lunar plain and the steadily shining stars beyond.

Al had spent several evenings in the sitting room, or what passed for evenings inside the city which operated on a twenty-four hour cycle, oblivious to the two-week days and nights of the moon. He had gazed at those unwinking stars and told himself, *I was meant to go there. Everything in my life has conspired to put me aboard one of those ships that hover around the moon, waiting to grow up and be loosed from their mother's bonds. I must go.*

Al was almost convinced that if he could observe the star ship engines in space, he might somehow find the elusive clues that would lead to the development of a star drive. If he could observe how certain materials behaved in space, if he could see what kinds of conditions must be considered firsthand—he had been approaching the problem by studying the behavior of space near certain types of dense materials. Chances were he could learn more by studying a neutron star or black hole at close range, at least as close as it was possible to get safely, than from years of work on Luna. One of the purposes of the journey was to work on a star drive, and it might be safer to carry out certain experiments in space rather than near inhabited worlds in the solar system.

Al's rooms, like all living quarters on the moon, were small, making as efficient a use of space as possible.

"Rooms" was actually too spacious a term; there were only two, and one of them was a closet-like bathroom with a plastic cocoon for a shower which he shared with the people next door. His living quarters, which he shared with Simone, consisted of a room with two small beds that were folded into the wall when not in use, two desk tops which could also be retracted, two folding chairs, two inflatable chairs, and a small table which stood in one corner with a metallic sculpture on it. The sculpture was a lunar scene taken from a novel by H. G. Wells; it depicted the Grand Lunar, head of an imaginary civilization of Selenites, on his throne. The Grand Lunar was surrounded by his over-specialized subjects, each holding the tools of his trade. A friend of Simone's, Liu Ching, had created the sculpture. Liu Ching did not care, however, to have this fact generally known. The Chinese scientists frowned on the frivolous use of recreational time and Liu Ching had thought, not without reason, that they might regard this particular piece as a commentary on what they were doing here. The Chinese woman, like Al and Simone, had grown attached to the moon and hoped to be chosen for the exploratory space flight.

Liu Ching, like many of the Chinese specialists, walked a thin line. She could not afford to be rigid and dogmatic; those selecting the people who would go to the stars were not likely to select such personalities. Yet she could not alienate her more conservative colleagues here. She regularly attended self-criticism sessions and couched her discussions of her specialty, astrophysics, in careful language, aided by quotations from Mao where appropriate. She had voluntarily returned to China two years ago to work on a rural commune. According to what she had told Al and Simone later, that had been a boring time spent mostly in servicing the machines which did most of the farming.

Few people, in China or anywhere else, were engaged in agriculture now. This fact, combined with the movement of many Chinese to urban areas, the availability of more goods and services, and the freer exchange of ideas with other nations, had loosened Chinese attitudes considerably. That land now had its revisionists, dissenters, and skeptics, most of whom chose to remain in China, suffering only occasionally under forced "re-education." Practices such as self-criticism sessions were regarded as customs more than anything else; the quoting of Mao was ritualistic. Yet the Chinese still retained some Puritan attitudes, a willingness to work hard, a concern for their people as a whole, and a general seriousness of purpose. Those here on Luna, although generally more liberal than their compatriots on Earth, often kept to themselves and, during their time off, often helped to do some of the more tedious but necessary tasks here, not wanting to appear élitist or idle. As a result, the lunar cuisine, with the Chinese aiding the kitchen machines, had taken on a distinctly Chinese flavor.

Al knew that there were certain things one had to know if one was to get along in the international scientific community on the moon. One was that not everyone had to live in the same way, easy enough to accept as an abstract idea unless one was a fanatic; more difficult to accept when a person had to live with a widely varying group of people from day to day. Another was that as far as scientific work was concerned, everyone's goals were pretty similar in spite of societal differences. This might produce a schism in the minds of some who came from more rigid societies, but humanity after all had long practice in devising different mental compartments in which to hold often contradictory ideas. As it turned out, those on the moon were more often in agreement than not. Al often thought that Luna, and those who went into space, would soon have a culture of their own quite different from any on Earth. How Earth, which regarded each national group in space as simply an extension of various national policies, would accept this, Al did not know. But he was sure that anyone or any group which could not successfully and peacefully deal with diversity was probably doomed.

Al's room was at present divided in half by a retractable wall. Since each of the rooms in the living quarters housed

two people, such a wall insured privacy when needed.
Liu Ching had once commented that hardly any of the
Chinese used this wall because it was assumed that anyone would do his best to get along with a roommate.
Those who did not were considered self-indulgent or
egotistical. She had smiled when Al recounted tales of
some who, without the wall, could not have stood the
sight of their roommates for long periods of time. Most
of these problems were solved by a change of rooms.

Al sat at his desk top, reading a paper on the space
ship engines that Ahmed had recommended to him
earlier. On the other side of the wall, the voices of Simone
and Liu Ching murmured in Chinese, providing a sooth-
ing background noise. There was no computer outlet in
Al's room; when he needed print-outs, he had to use
the one located next to the sitting room. He completed
his reading and deposited the paper in a recycling slot
just above the desk top. Then he pushed the desk top
into the wall and got up. He grasped the dividing wall
at the end nearer the door and began to push it toward
the back of the room.

"At last!" Simone said.

"What were you reading?" Liu Ching asked.

"A paper by one of Ahmed's colleagues on some details
of the space ship engine designs. I thought it might get
me going on some thoughts about a space drive, and
there is one interesting detail. . . . "

"Ah!" Simone interrupted as she turned back to the
Chinese woman. "*Une fois lancé sur le sujet . . .* we shall
be sitting here all night listening to a discourse."

"You're not being fair," he said, leaning over the back
of Simone's chair. "I never talk about my work for more
than four hours at a time."

"I would like to discuss it," Liu Ching said, "but I
cannot stay." She stood up and straightened her baggy
gray shirt and trousers. Al had no notion of what the
Chinese woman's figure was like; her compatriots rarely
wore the more revealing t-shirts and shorts worn by most
here. But her face was lovely enough to cause frequent
glances. Liu Ching's eyes were large, almost black onyx-

like gems, and her nose was small and perfectly straight. Her skin was ivory, burnished with a golden hue, her mouth full and sensual, and her hands long and slender. Her thick dark hair, like Simone's and almost everyone's on the moon, was cropped close to her head; long hair was bothersome here and could be dangerous in space.

"I must go to a political education session," Liu Ching continued. "We are truly fortunate in having the presence of Dr. Cheng, who arrived from Shanghai only a week ago. If his scientific training were the equal of his political correctness, he would be an even more remarkable man." She glanced at Al and her eye twitched in what looked suspiciously like a wink. Simone guffawed. "So I must go. I cannot be late, I would not wish anyone to conclude that I assign these sessions less than their proper place." She smiled and stepped into the hallway as the door slid open. "I hope to see you again soon."

The door slid shut. "Can't we fix the divider?" Simone asked, gesturing at the back wall. The top part of the retractable wall still protruded into the room.

"Nope. Shoddy construction, that's what it is. I'll have to get someone to make repairs." He sat down in the inflatable chair that Liu Ching had vacated and promptly sagged into it. "And this chair needs some air."

Simone got up and sat on his lap, twining her arms around his neck. "I should be nervous," she said. "I have my interview tomorrow."

"It's just a formality."

"Sean Carmody said that if the interview is short, it means that they have already decided against you."

"And Juana Delgado told me that if it's very long, they haven't yet made up their minds. I don't imagine the length of the interview has anything to do with it." The interview, after all, would only confirm whatever impressions the interviewers already had of a person.

Those who had volunteered for the long space flight had given up most of their privacy during the past three years. All of their medical records had been handed over to the committees making the selection and all of them had been subjected to both physiological and psychological tests. The work they had done in their chosen fields was being surveyed and their minds had been probed by machines designed to translate every subconscious urge. Even their personal lives were being dissected. Many of the applicants had been weeded out early; those who were adventure-seekers, unstable, those who were too weak physically or who had special problems of one sort or another.

Al had survived the early weeding-out process, as had about ten thousand others. There was no telling when the final determination would be made and announced. Although aided by computers, the selection was bound to be a complicated procedure. The ship would be finished and ready for some testing in another five years, but the selections would be made earlier than that. Al had heard rumors that the decisions would be announced sooner rather than later, to allow enough time to train and prepare those who would go. Two people would be chosen for each available place, in case something happened to one of them. Both would undergo training, but the alternate would be only an understudy. Al wondered which would be worse; not being chosen at all, or being an alternate, forced to go through the training process perhaps hoping that some disaster would befall the chosen crew member, or that the selected one would not do as well in training.

Al had gone to his own interview two weeks earlier. It had lasted for about two hours, the average length of time. He could barely remember what the five interviewers were like; at the time he had wondered whether the interviewers had any personal biases that might eliminate him from consideration. It had been a foolish thought. The entire interview had been monitored by small devices humming softly on the desk in front of him, recording various physical reactions. The interview itself had been recorded on tape. Those not at the interview would be able to view it; any personal prejudices on the part of the interviewers would become evident.

He had felt off balance almost from the beginning. He

could not remember who said it:

"Albert Swenson?"

"Yes?"

"Part of the Swenson clone," another had muttered.

Yep, Al had wanted to holler, *just another chip off the old goddamn block.* He had restrained himself. They had not pursued the matter of his birth, but they did not really need to do so. They would have access to any information about him that they wanted, including the files of Emma Valois.

"I had better rest," Simone said as she eased herself off his lap. "I want to look well tomorrow."

"Simone," he said as he leaned forward and took her by the hips, "what if you're chosen and I'm not?"

She released his hands and moved away from him. "Why do you ask me this now, Al? You never have before. You are being foolish. We are lovers, they would pick both of us or neither of us, I think."

"We assume that because we don't want to think about the alternatives. I don't think the committees will let romantic sentiment prevent them from picking the best crew available."

"I thought we had agreed not to talk about it until it was a real problem. We gain nothing by. . . ."

"I know, I know." He wanted to let the matter drop, but was afraid to let go. As if sensing that, Simone moved to his side and rested a hand on his shoulder.

"Consider something else, Al," she said softly. "I am no longer a young woman. Bearing children would be risky at my age. The journey will be long and it will be expected that some will bear children in case others should die. There will be many options for the travelers, they may have to settle a new world if something should go wrong, or live on the ship for longer than expected. They will have to be prepared for almost anything. Every older woman applying for the journey knows that the cards are stacked against her. It may not be fair but that is how it is. Each older woman closes off certain alternatives. It is the same with older men who are not as strong and vigorous as younger ones."

"No, Simone, that's not a problem, not now. There'll be plenty of equipment along, ectogenetic chambers, trained biologists. There'll be too much work to do for women to be limited by nine months of pregnancy. It wouldn't matter if you were sixty."

"But what if something goes wrong? I'm sure the committees involved are thinking of that. Natural processes must be relied upon if all else fails."

"I think you're inventing difficulties."

"Is it any more ridiculous than you thinking that I may have a better chance of going because of my race? You conveniently forget that there are many more of my race to choose from. And I am French by nationality and culture, so I must compete with that group as well." She had moved away from him again, shuffling lightly over the floor. She pulled off her shirt and he watched it drift slowly downward. "You brought up the problem, tell me." She pulled off her shorts, pulled her bed out of the wall, and lay down, bouncing slightly. "What will you do if you are chosen and I am rejected?"

"I don't know," he lied.

"Certainly you do and so do I. And if you told me you wanted to stay, I should refuse to have anything more to do with you. And you know what I would do." She folded her arms under her head. "I left a husband and child to come here. Dinh was a good husband and a fine man but his work was elsewhere. I am sometimes sad that it had to be so, but I have never regretted my decision, not even when my son cried and asked me not to go. There are others who can care for him and I know he will understand when he is grown. So you know what I would do, Albert, and you would do the same. We need not discuss it further."

He had known it before she spoke. He looked away from Simone, down at his hands, curled loosely around the edges of his shorts. He had known it already and knew that she was right about his feelings. But he could not help thinking that the words should have been left unsaid, that he should never have asked the question. Something between them had died with the words, only an illusion, perhaps, something that people might fool themselves into believing in order to remove some of the harsher edges from their lives, something that made the world softer and more pleasant.

He looked back at Simone. She had turned on her side, her back to him. He was being foolish. Did it really mean that they loved each other less? Only if he believed that a person should make the loved one the most important thing in life, sacrificing everything else if necessary. A romantic ideal, but one which in life more often produced resentment and bitterness than undying love. He knew perfectly well that if Simone chose not to go and stayed with him, she would in time see him as a stone around her neck; whenever there were problems, there would be the inevitable if unspoken accusation: *Remember what I gave up for you.* And if he chose to stay, he knew what he would be thinking: *You cannot be as interesting, as fascinating to me as new worlds and new suns.* He was fortunate that Simone had enough sense to realize this, that the situation he envisioned would never come about.

But he also knew that a world without Simone would be a darker and sadder place for him. He might in time adjust to it, but he would not forget her. He was, he thought, altogether too much like his father. Perversely, he hoped that the world would be equally dark for Simone without him. That had been the real question, not the one he had spoken.

He got up and moved across the room. "Simone?" he whispered. He sat down next to her and put his arm around her hips. He would take each day as it came, knowing that there might not be many of them left to spend with her, and hope that there might be more. "Simone?"

She was already asleep.

Al had passed one of the incomplete starships on his way to the Lagrange space colony. The dark metal globe which comprised most of its body, which would contain the frozen deuterium that would power the vessel, seemed to mirror the hopes and fears of those who had planned the voyage. The tiny pinpricks of reflected starlight on the globe's surface were isolated points adrift in a vast, black expanse. The ship's living quarters, still mostly a latticework of girders, seemed almost an afterthought, a cork on a round bottle.

It had been more practical, he knew, to build the ships in an orbit around the Moon rather than nearer to Earth. Metals mined on Luna and parts manufactured by the moon's growing industries could be catapulted to the construction crews at little cost. The moon, once primarily a scientific outpost, was becoming an industrial center; its residents were paying back the investment Earth had made in them, with interest. Although most of the workers building the ships still lived on Earth when not working, a few of them had moved their families to the moon. More underground dwellings were being hollowed out beneath the lunar surface, and Al could imagine a time when Luna would be honeycombed with mazes containing thousands of tunnels.

His personal desires had crystallized when he saw the partially built ship. He had to be on board when they left. He was convinced that whatever he might do if he stayed behind would not be anywhere near what he might accomplish on the journey.

Paul's dream. Once this had weighed heavily on him when he was much younger; why had he, among all the clones, elected to carry out his father's dreams so overtly? He had not attained the stature of Paul Swenson's name in astrophysics and this had made him depressed for a while. After his first two years on the moon, he had toyed with the idea of giving up research altogether, or perhaps going back to Earth to teach and write, hoping to find someone in his classes with a mind capable of fulfilling Paul's dream, lifting it from Al's shoulders. His common sense had made him remain on the moon. Probably even Paul, if he had been born fifty years later, could have done no more than Al himself.

The ship he had seen and now recollected had, oddly enough, at least to his way of thinking, been named the *Nikita S. Khrushchev.* Even the naming of the vessel had been the cause of some acrimonious debating. The problem was finally resolved when it was decided to name the ships after world leaders who had been in power during the earliest days of space flight. The pioneers who had died in space and the people whose scientific work had enabled humanity to leave the earth already had half of the lunar installations, craters, mountain peaks, and assorted space stations named after them, so their names had not been considered. The suggestion that the ships be named after twentieth century leaders who had first placed a high priority on space travel had been made, Al was sure, almost sarcastically. But the suggestion had been taken seriously and the ships had been named, in a compromise that fully satisfied few but at least enabled the debators to put their time to more constructive uses. The other two ships had been named the *John F. Kennedy* and the *Mao Tse-Tung*.

Al, whose knowledge of history was shaky, was not sure if Mao had much to do with space flight. But the Chinese had made it into space eventually and since they still, in a more or less ritual fashion, attributed much of their success to him and since he had been a contemporary of the other two, Al supposed that his name had as much right to be on a ship as anyone else's. At any rate, one could not insult the Chinese.

The French, the Brazilians, the Japanese and a few other nations had been annoyed by all this but were soothed by having various parts of the ships named after their own twentieth-century leaders. The passengers would be wending their way to the Charles de Gaulle Observatory or the Mobutu Sese Seko Engineering Compartment, but would no doubt come up with their own names for these places in time. Al found himself wondering why the ships and their very names had to be symbols of humanity's bickering, the kind of bickering that would have to be absent if the ships were to complete successful missions. Why couldn't they have been named after constellations or figures from myth, something more in keeping with the awesomeness of the undertaking? But there would have been arguments over that too; which constellations, which mythologies?

Al waited for Ahmed Maheib to finish dressing. The two men had exercised earlier while wearing weighted suits; after that workout, the simulated gravity of Lagrange, half that of Earth, seemed bearable. "Just think of it, no politicians," Ahmed murmured as if paralleling Al's thoughts. "No politicians on board. They would have little power, no chance to seize it or to run for reelection or to collect their rewards for years of service. It might almost be worth the journey for that alone." The Arab smiled as he tucked his cranberry-colored pullover into the waistband of his black slacks. "Perhaps some day we might let the synthesists and speculators run things, but then I am being too optimistic."

"Unfortunately, the ships will probably grow their own politicians in time," Al replied. "Wait and see." He stood up and smoothed down his short brown hair.

"I shall not be going," Ahmed said fatalistically. "I may settle down with Jane and lead the life of an English country gentleman. I have made great progress with her mother, Lady Gardiner. At our last meeting, she actually greeted me with courtesy. You and Simone must come with us on our next trip. I would marry Jane for her estate alone, even if she resembled her mother." Ahmed ran a comb through his unruly black hair. "Which reminds me, we were supposed to meet our two loves in one of the lounges."

The two men left the locker room and walked along the passageway leading to the lounge. The Lagrange space colony was a cylinder almost four miles long and one mile in diameter. It was located at the L5 libration point, a location where the gravitational forces of the Earth and Moon cancelled each other out. Lagrange, at L5, was on the moon's orbital path but situated 240,000 miles behind the moon; it would remain fixed in its relative position between Earth and Luna. A somewhat more spacious colony, Descartes, had been built at the L4 libration point 240,000 miles ahead of the moon. The colonies had been made primarily of materials mined on the moon and transported to the libration points. Al had been on Descartes before, spending a day or two adjusting to its three-fourths of Earth gravity before returning home.

Al had not been fooled by Ahmed's comments about settling down with Jane. Both Ahmed and Jane had put in their applications for the interstellar flight. Ahmed too had watched the orbiting ship with longing and Al was sure that, given the choice, his friend would not settle for an English estate.

Ahmed, although primarily an engineer, also had a lively interest in astrophysicists. He had accompanied Al and other astrophysics to Lagrange to participate in a series of seminars and discussions, the first of which had been held the day before. Since two of the most well-known people in the field, Herbert Mallory and Irina Rostova, were living in Lagrange and could not travel without difficulty because of their physical ailments, the gathering was being held here. Al supposed that the meetings could have been held over a holovision link-up, but the change of scenery would probably be beneficial to the lunar scientists.

He thought of Rostova, whom he had met at the first meeting. Even with her parchmentlike skin, crippled arthritic limbs, and clouded eyes, she was able to make everyone in the room almost tongue-tied. Her dark eyes, however clouded, would burn when she made a point or attacked an erroneous assumption. *The woman must be*, he had thought, *at least one hundred.*

Mallory, in contrast, had been meek, almost obsequious. Dmitri Grol, who had met both people before, had told Al what to expect. "Mallory," he had said, "is a wild speculator without a brain in his head who is unfortunately correct much of the time. Rostova hasn't an idea to speak of, but she'll get rid of a lot of deadwood in everyone's thinking, as you say, cut through the crap." The two old scientists had decided to live together when they came to Lagrange. Although Rostova had been as hard on Mallory as on anyone else at the first meeting, Al had noticed that she tempered her criticisms of the old man with a gentle hand on his arm, which Mallory would reward with an adoring smile. The unlikely pair seemed to get along and, in spite of their "retirement," were still contributing papers to the field. Al imagined that the two were still intellectually active because neither of them, with their particular approaches to astrophysics, felt the need to defend old theories or to rest on past achievements. The anti-aging serum, unable to heal their bodies, had at least arrested their aging somewhat and kept their minds clear. They had, unaccountably to Al, refused any other therapy. "They're from another age," Dmitri had said. "They believe, I think, that it's time for them to die."

He and Ahmed entered the lounge, a brightly lit, pale green room with round clear plastic tables and inflatable chairs in dark green and blue. Several sturdy individuals in tight overalls, probably workers helping to build a new cylindrical colony, Pascal, next to Lagrange, were enjoying a liquid lunch at the bar.

Simone and Jane were at the other end of the room, seated next to a window panel. The window overlooked a curving, concave landscape of forests and planted fields. The colony was run by solar power; a large aluminum mirror outside Lagrange captured the solar energy. Parabolic mirrors at both ends of the cylinder provided sunlight for the fields outside and could be closed during the "night." The colony, with its fields and small lakes created by combining liquid hydrogen from Earth with oxygen from lunar oxides, would soon be self-sufficient.

Simone smiled at Al as he seated himself next to her. "You look tired," he said.

"I am tired. Jane and I have been lifting weights. I shall awaken during our discussions this evening, of that I am sure. The voice of Irina Rostova will be a splash of cold water."

Ahmed was whispering something in Jane's ear. The English woman bobbed slightly in her chair as she laughed. "You are wicked, Ahmed," she said. Jane Gardiner was a pale, slender young woman with gray eyes and a mouth and nose that were a shade too large. Her fine brown hair, unusually long, almost to her shoulders, seemed to float loosely around her head. She was gazing at Ahmed with a frankly sexual look.

Jane was still in her early twenties, having finished most of her studies at an unusually early age. She had lived on the moon for two years. The first of those years had been a disappointment to those who had expected great things of her. She had gained some notoriety, even in the fairly relativistic lunar settlement, taking and abandoning lovers in rapid succession, restless, perhaps, after years of concentrated study. But at last she had grown calmer and Al, working with her in recent months, had come to respect her mind.

Jane leaned over and rumpled Ahmed's hair. "When we get married, you must learn to ride," she said to him. "You're the worst rider I've ever seen. I always thought of Arabs as fine horsemen."

"I never saw a horse until we visited your mother."

"Well, you'll have plenty of time to learn, I suppose," Jane said. Al, looking up, could tell that the young woman did not believe a word of that statement. Jane, unlike most of the others, fully expected to be chosen for the expedition. *And why not?* Al thought to himself. *She's had everything else she ever wanted.*

"I was telling Al earlier," Ahmed said, "that he and Simone should come with us to see your estate."

"He calls it an estate," Jane said. "One house in London, a drafty old stone house in the country, and a cottage in Scotland that's likely to fall around our ears. Mother's never recovered from the confiscation of our lands, all we have now are the grounds around the houses. Of course I know the land was needed for agriculture, but to Mother it was all one huge conspiracy, giving female peers the same rights of inheritance as males and then leaving them nothing to inherit except a title."

"You are exaggerating," Ahmed replied. "To me, it seemed a spacious estate."

"What did you two do this morning?" Jane asked. Not waiting for an answer, she plunged on. "I spent a wonderfully dreary time with an old cousin who unfortunately happens to be residing here. It was almost a relief

to lift weights afterward. Old Edgar looked better than
he has any right to expect at his age." Jane paused for
breath. "He's convinced himself that his grandson will
be chosen for the stellar expedition, but then they would
hardly pick two people from the same family, now would
they?"

Al restrained himself from commenting. He had met,
briefly, the grandson of Jane's cousin, a noted physicist
named Lord Anthony Hartford. Privately, he considered
Lord Anthony's chances better than Jane's.

"You're lucky you didn't come with me, Simone,"
Jane went on. "I had to listen to a recounting of Tony's
accomplishments plus a depiction, in detail, of Edgar's
new therapy. I tried to engage Edgar in some sort of theoretical discussion, but of course he wasn't interested. The
whole conversation was about Tony and this new therapy."

"For the love of God, Jane," Simone said wearily. "I
cannot understand how you can be so concise in your
papers and so verbose in your discussions."

"I'm so foolish," Jane continued. "I didn't even tell
any of you what happened to Edgar, I suppose it's history
of a sort, everyone will know soon. He was given some
new medical treatment, they've been working on him for
months. He looks at least fifteen years younger and his
arthritis isn't nearly as bad. It's your sister that's responsible, Al, the doctor or whatever she is."

Al was immediately attentive. "Kira? Is she here?"

"She's been here for a while." Jane shrugged. "Lord,
I would have told you straightway, but I thought you
knew."

Kira had grown even thinner.

That was the first thing Al noticed as he entered her
quarters. She was sitting in front of a desk top in the corner. She stood up quickly, almost too quickly. He moved
across the room and took her hands.

She actually looked better at thirty-six than she had
when she was younger. Her face was more angular and
the green eyes seemed much larger. Her long hair, piled
loosely on her head, had not yet started to gray. But there

were dark shadows under her eyes and an air of intensity about her, as if some obsession was burning inside, threatening to consume her.

She looks like Jim, he thought suddenly, at least as Jim had looked when he last saw him, six years before. Jim had disappeared after that with his friend Carole Elashvili into some unknown corner of the earth. Al had not heard from him again until a novel was published three years after that. The notes at the end of the micro-fiche copy said only that the author lived in Caracas. Al had assumed that it was Jim who had sent him the book, although there was no letter enclosed. When he tried to contact his brother, he was no longer in Venezuela; Jim had disappeared once again.

The novel had at first irritated Al, then began to disturb him. Its central character had been obsessed by some-thing also, moving through a fantasy world lined with mirrors and fractured pieces of glass. The book had done relatively well.

Looking at his sister, Al remembered the novel and felt a trickle of fear. *Come on,* he told himself. He must look the same way to Kira as she did to him. He too was thin-ner, having lost some of his body weight in the lower lunar gravity in spite of exercising; and he too had his own obsession. *We need each other now,* he thought, *all of us.* They had all retreated. Their respect for each other's privacy had grown to such an extent that they hesitated even to talk to each other on the phone. *We should care more,* he thought, *not be so afraid of each other's feelings and so worried about interfering with each other that we scarcely talk at all.* Of course, they lived in different places, they could hardly get together very often. And it was impossible to keep up with each other's fields; they were all more specialized. *Or maybe,* he told him-self, *we just haven't made time for that.*

"Kira," he managed to say, somewhat clumsily, "Jane Gardiner told me you were here, working with her cousin. On him, I should say. How are Hidey and Rina?"

"Rina's fine. I had to leave her with some people down the street, they take care of quite a number of kids, some of whom just need time away from their parents. But I'm afraid she may be forgetting who I am. At that age, a person's memory isn't exactly long." She released his hands and sat down again. "At least that way, Hidey can see her every day, it's a short walk so it doesn't tire him. He's still a little weak. That coronary didn't help him much."

"A coronary's not that serious," Al said, settling into a chair across from her.

"Not by itself, perhaps. The pacemaker's working beautifully and the new artery helps. But he's tired, Al, he's worn out. His lungs aren't in good shape, he needs an oxygen machine part of the time. He has to rest, but he hates that, he hates having to eat regular meals, taking mild exercise, having to go to bed on a regular schedule. He wants to keep working. He can keep up with everything using the computer and he's even held some seminars over the holo. But he's an old man, he abused his body for so many years and it finally caught up with him."

Kira sighed, and looked even more tired. She had been working hard for the past few years, even taking three years off to get a medical degree, apparently feeling she needed it for her work. She had her hands full. When Al had last visited her, she was working at the university, teaching, doing her research, working four evenings a week helping to administer some of the paramedical teams operating in the community. He had suggested she was spreading herself too thin. She had retorted: "What good is it for us to do our research, finding new things, if we can't get them to the people who need them?" She was functioning as a liaison between the researchers and the medics, giving the medics information that they might not otherwise have until later, when it might be too late for some of the patients.

She smiled suddenly, as if trying to shake off some of her worries. "Hidey was kind of mad when I decided Rina should stay with the Reedys. He didn't see why he couldn't look after her, especially since she's at the university child center for most of the day. But she needs to live with other children for a while. She has no social sense at all." Kira shrugged. "You know what kids her age are like, but she was really starting to think the world revolved around her. With Hidey home a lot of the time, she thought he had nothing better to do than cater to her whims. Well, at least the Reedys will give her enough attention when she needs it and maybe she'll learn, with other kids around all the time, that she can't have everything her own way. Hidey, of course, is convinced the Reedys might sit on her too hard, you know, repress her curiosity. She is awfully inquisitive. But I think she'll come through it. She hasn't asked to live at home again and the last time I talked to her, she seemed as curious as ever."

"I'm curious. You haven't said a word about why you're here."

She seemed to tense slightly, and Al realized that whatever she might say would be in some sense a mask, designed to hide from him the real importance of what she was doing. She would tell him almost everything but not the purpose, not what had burned her into the thin, intense woman she had become. *And that's the real reason we don't talk to each other*, Al thought. *We're afraid we might see too much, read each other's minds.*

"You must know some of it already," she replied. "I've been working on Lord Edgar Hartford. Well, actually two doctors and two technicians have been doing most of it, I've just been supervising. We've been using clonal cell injections, the project Hidey really started. We were fairly successful with two subjects at the university, but Lord Hartford seemed ideal for a crucial test. He's very old, he has many chronic ailments which are related to the aging process. We thought if we could help him, it might be a truly demanding test of the process."

"How long have you been here, working on this?"

"Almost four months. We've been working on it longer than that, though, the others came to Lagrange eight months ago. We had to clone various cells and prepare the injections of serum. We've refined that process; we don't clone a fetus of the subject, only the various organs, brain cells, and so on. We prepared Lord Hartford with a long series of injections, anti-aging shots, cleared out the cross-linked protein, then injected the prepared serum, replacing the old cells with new ones. So far Lord Hartford's doing pretty well, he looks years younger and he's feeling better. He's a fine historian and he knows something about the sciences, so he's promised to write about the experience. Now what else can I tell you? Do you want to hear all the details?"

"Later, maybe. You should have told me you were here. I probably could have got some time off to visit."

"I was too busy. We wouldn't have had much time to talk anyway. Is Simone with you?"

"Yeah, I would have brought her along, but she was feeling tired. I figured she should rest."

Kira took a deep breath, as if trying to decide whether or not to say more. Then she proceeded. "I'll get a chance to see you again later anyway. If everything goes as I expect it to, I'll be on the moon in a couple of months, sometime in January."

"What for?"

"Some more work." She shut her mouth tightly and he knew she would tell him no more.

"Why?" He would pursue the matter anyway, even knowing that he was unlikely to hear any more. "As far as I know, the biologists on Luna haven't done any more than what's going on below. Considerably less, I should imagine. Most of them are specialists in space medicine."

"I may have another subject there."

Al had temporarily forgotten about the older people on the moon. There were, of course, a fair number of them. Functioning in lunar gravity was easier than living on Earth, and there was growing evidence that Moon-dwellers had longer life spans. Kira would find plenty of subjects there.

"I've said enough," she went on. "Why don't you tell me what you've been doing?"

He looked at his sister and felt a flicker of resentment. Kira was supervising an important project, more important even than she was letting him know. He was familiar enough with the biological sciences to realize that. She was the *de facto* head of her department at the university; even though a man named Ramsey was officially chairman, he merely took care of administrative matters that Kira and Hidey could not handle. She had her M.D. and had earned her doctorate long ago. She had advanced rapidly through the university's academic structure. She had, he thought for a moment, gone farther than he had.

He forced himself to ignore that feeling. *What do you want?* he thought ruefully. It was difficult to advance to so-called eminent positions on Luna, in spite of the fact that there were so few people there in comparison with Earth. Everyone there, including the paramedics, food processors, maintenance people, technicians, and workers responsible for constructing and maintaining the living complexes, was one of the best Earth could send. There was little room for personal advancement in an environment that had to stress cooperation if anything was to be done. His own doctorate, compared to Kira's, Ed's, or Mike's, had been an informal affair, based on his work on Luna plus an examination given there, but a lunar degree bearing the official stamp of Goddard University or the Tsiolkovsky Institute was the equal of any on Earth and probably better.

He shrugged off his personal concerns. He began to tell her about the work they were doing in gravitational collapse, the bodies they had observed, the tentative conclusions they had drawn, and was soon lost in his recital.

After leaving Kira's room, Al headed for the nearby cafeteria. It was getting close to suppertime, as his stomach, with its rumblings, reminded him. He would call Simone from the dining area and ask her to join him there.

When he entered the cafeteria, he noticed Dmitri Grol talking excitedly to some people just inside the door. The short blond man spotted him right away and grabbed his arm, almost making Al stumble backward.

"You have heard? You are still on the list?"

"No. What do you mean?"

Dmitri lowered his voice, looking almost conspiratorial.

"You do not know. They have narrowed down the list for the star flight crews. It is down to five thousand now. They have not announced the list yet, they want to give people time to find out if they are on it." The Russian tugged at his short goatee. "No one expected it this soon. It is said they will announce the final choices and the alternates before long."

"So soon," Al said, almost stunned. "They just finished the interviews two months ago."

"They want to start training people, give them a chance to adjust to the idea, before they go."

Al hesitated. He was almost afraid to go over to the computer link-up in the corner of the cafeteria and find out the decision. "You look happy," he said to Dmitri, trying to gain a few seconds to think. "I don't have to ask you. . . ."

"Only because I am both a selenologist and an engineer, as well as being an experienced administrator," the Russian replied, a smile spreading across his broad face. "If I had not dabbled in different fields, I doubt they would have considered my feeble mind." Dmitri was being too modest. He had a dogged and persistent mind, combined with an attitude that one could master anything in time. He had done some first-rate work and was now "dabbling" in astrophysics, using some vacation time to come along for the seminars. A slow but deep thinker, Dmitri often caught things quicker minds overlooked.

"You'll be on board eventually," Al said confidently. "I'll make you a bet."

Dmitri responded by taking Al by the shoulders and gently propelling him toward the computer. "Go, my friend, and see if we may be shipmates."

Al walked over to the computer and slowly began to punch out his number and private code. *Don't get upset*, he told himself, trying to prepare for a possible disappointment. *Even if you're on this list, you're still a long way from boarding.* A red light on the small flat console began to flash. He spoke his name aloud, then made his request.

The computer console hummed for a fraction of a second as it noted his face, fingerprints, and voice pattern, a precaution in case anyone not authorized by him was retrieving the information. Privacy violations were severely punished in theory, often by depriving the offender of access to computers for an extended period except for necessary transactions. Such a law had been the only way people in much of the world could accept the accumulation of vast amounts of data about themselves. In fact, it was often difficult to catch some of the cleverest violators unless one was willing to spend days poring over computer records or hired a service to do it, an expensive proposition. The smartest criminals, with the aid of accomplices inside police offices or other agencies authorized to get certain information, could gain access. Even if a violator was caught, the case could be tied up in the courts for months.

The screen in front of him lit up as words began to appear, one letter after another. He took a deep breath.

SWENSON, ALBERT.
ACCEPTED FOR PRELIMINARY LIST
PROJECT STAR FLIGHT.

He sighed. Only one more hurdle to go. *They have to take me, they can't let me come this far without taking me.* He almost laughed. *Sure they could.* The entire procedure of selecting the interstellar travelers, with its forms, delays, interviews, invasions of privacy, and committee members who had occasionally popped up unexpectedly to talk informally with applicants, might itself be a test.

He turned and waved at Dmitri, smiling as he did so. "Come to my room later," the Russian shouted to him. "Rita Morales and I will be having a party then for the elect."

Al nodded as Dmitri left the cafeteria. He had a feeling that the seminar scheduled for that evening would be held in a distracting atmosphere. Hopefully, those who had been chosen and those who had been rejected would settle down enough so that the meetings would not be a total waste of time.

He hesitated in front of the computer console for a moment. What about Simone? He had to find out.

Simone had given him her code and had authorized him to use it. He had reciprocated. He had never used hers and knew she had never requested information about him. Exchanging codes had become the true test of love and friendship for many people. If hard feelings developed, it was easy to withdraw such authorization simply by notifying the computer or, in a few cases, changing one's code as well.

Al had never given his code to anyone but his family and Simone, although he knew people who trusted a fair number of friends with theirs. The Chinese, of course, often took pride in giving theirs to almost everyone, at least on the moon. They had nothing to hide, it seemed, at least from their own people, and would have been under great suspicion if they did not make their codes readily available, particularly to eminent officials. The Russians were discouraged from giving theirs to anyone who was not Russian; Americans, as in everything else, varied in their attitudes. The Japanese were somewhat more circumspect. One couple on Luna, the Fukudas, both medical technicians, had been married for fifteen years and had never exchanged codes.

He punched out Simone's code, then identified himself and made his request. She would not mind this time, not on something as important as this. He had a feeling that, if she knew about the list, she had already found out his own status.

The computer hummed. He tried to prepare himself for either possible answer but he could not keep from hoping. His stomach knotted. Letters appeared on the screen. He scanned them quickly, completely unprepared and bewildered by what he saw.

TRAN, SIMONE. COMMITTEE UNDECIDED.
CASE TO BE APPEALED.
FINAL DISPOSITION WITHIN ONE MONTH.
PROJECT STAR FLIGHT.

"Precisely because the existence of identical twins breaks and seems to challenge the great law of the biological uniqueness of the person, it accentuates that uniqueness and calls attention to it."

—Jean Rostand
HUMANLY POSSIBLE

". . . it is clear that genetic engineering will produce radical alterations in a very few centuries at most. Changes will not be gradual, but explosive; we are on the verge of a sharp discontinuity in history."

—R. C. W. Ettinger
MAN INTO SUPERMAN

"Nature which governs the whole will soon change all things which thou seest, and out of their substance will make other things, and again other things from the substance of them, in order that the world may be ever new . . ."

—Marcus Aurelius
MEDITATIONS

"I shall endeavor to drive from him the swarming and
    fierce things, those flies,
which feed upon the bodies of men who have perished;
and although he lie here until a year has gone to ful-
    fillment,
still his body shall be as it was, or firmer than ever."

—Homer
THE ILIAD

7. Interface: 2037

HIS sister's call had brought Ed Swenson to the moon. He had sensed an undertone of urgency in her voice, an urgency that seemed somehow out of place with her stated reason for wanting him there. A family reunion, nothing more. She was working on a project, Al was there, Mike said he would come. Why didn't he and Sheila join them?

Ed had been hesitant at first, but he was on his sabbatical and could do worse than spending time with the mathematicians on Luna while he visited. The M.I.T. orchestra would have to do without his violin and Sheila's clarinet for a while. Sheila, a researcher in cybernetics, was overdue for a vacation anyway and could come with him.

There had been one small problem; his son Isaac. Ed had assumed they would leave the boy on Earth, but that had prompted a brief argument with Sheila. She had wanted Isaac to come with them.

Ed certainly could not blame her for that. Sheila, he knew, had always been closer to their son than he had. She, in fact, had been the one who decided to bear a child. But he must have wanted the boy too or he would never have cooperated with her and would not have married her after Isaac's birth.

He had been the typical expectant father and had not minded the role at all. He helped Sheila with her exercises during her pregnancy and accompanied her to the geneticist, who had assured them the child would be healthy. He aided the paramedic and nurse during the delivery,

274

rubbing Sheila's back, encouraging her, almost sensing her pain himself. He remembered his first sight of his son; the head emerging from Sheila's body, the tiny infant covered with membrane, the first cry. He felt only relief and exhaustion at first until Isaac, washed and weighed, was placed in his arms. As he handed the baby to Sheila, he was suddenly astonished: *our child*. Such things happened all the time but it seemed a miracle to him then.

He grew to love the boy and enjoyed watching him grow, learn, and change. But he often felt awkward around Isaac, uncertain about how to treat him or talk to him. Isaac also seemed restrained; he had become a contented but serious child. He displayed an early love of music, not surprising in a child growing up in a musical family. At the age of four, he was already taking music lessons and learning to play his own tiny violin. But music was not a hobby or casual interest for Isaac, who participated almost incessantly in his spare time. At six, he had decided to live with his teacher and other music students for four days a week. Although he came home every weekend and often for an hour or so after school, his decision had upset Sheila. Ed knew she had never fully reconciled herself to it.

Ed had at last agreed that Isaac should come with them to Luna, persuaded by the fact that the boy himself wanted to go. Isaac could do his schoolwork with the computers there as well as on Earth and would get a chance to meet different children. Sheila could spend more time with him. *And I*, Ed thought, *can try to get over my awkwardness around my own son*.

When they first entered their lunar hotel room, Isaac had been fascinated, exploring every corner. He now sat quietly in a chair while Sheila and Ed unpacked the few things they had brought. It was expensive to bring too much. Isaac had brought only his violin and some clothing.

The boy was watching Ed solemnly with his green eyes. Already, he looked remarkably like his father. *Not surprising*, Ed thought, smiling at Sheila as she put away some clothes. Sheila also looked like Ed, with almost the same green eyes, complexion, and facial features. Her short hair was brown as well, but with more reddish and gold highlights, which she had passed on to her son.

Ed sometimes wondered about her resemblance to him, or, more accurately, to his sister Kira, but he never speculated about it for long. It hardly mattered. He had, however, been startled by it when he first met Sheila Sonnefeld. A friend, Eric Bartlett, had introduced them at an orchestra rehearsal. "Meet the other Swenson clone," Eric had said jokingly and except for her medium height, Sheila might almost have been one. He had loved her almost on sight, but because of the liveliness he had seen in her face, he was sure, not its resemblance to his own.

Temperamentally she was unlike him, more impulsive, more involved with other people. She had helped him conquer some of his shyness and brought some life into his quiet world. At times he wished their son was more like her.

He glanced at Isaac while putting away some underwear. "Maybe tomorrow you can go flying," he said to the boy. "You can go over to the recreation center and get some wings to try out. That's one of the advantages of lunar gravity, being able to fly around." Ed paused, feeling as though he was patronizing the child. "Or you can go outside if you want, see the surface with a guide." He closed the drawer in front of him and looked around their quarters. There was not an abundance of room, only two small sets of drawers set into the wall and one tiny closet. A computer console stood in the corner; Ed had insisted on a room with one. There was a round plastic table and some chairs, and the beds were pulled out from the walls. The bathroom, used by all the people in the six rooms nearest theirs, was down the hall with regulations concerning water use posted on the door in various languages. Each person had a certain allotment free, included in the room charge; a computer in the bathroom recorded every one's fingerprints each time he entered the shower. Using more water was expensive. There was a small room next to the bathroom where children of guests could sleep; Isaac, if he wanted to, would probably sleep there when he made friends.

"Will you come with me, Ed?" Isaac asked quietly.

"Of course I will, at least if you want me to."

"I wish you would."

Ed, feeling relieved, smiled. "Then I will."

"Let's go flying now."

Ed sighed. "You'd better ask your mother about that."

"I didn't ask Sheila, I asked you."

"I think," Ed said after a pause, "that you're probably tired after your trip and you'll be even more tired after we have supper with your aunt and uncle tonight. You should probably take a nap."

"Sheila!" the boy said in hurt tones.

"Ed's right," she responded. "You sound like you're getting cranky."

"But I don't *feel* tired."

"I do," Sheila said. "I'm going to take a nap myself. If you're not tired, you can sit at the console and do some lessons."

"I'll take the nap," Isaac muttered, climbing into one of the beds.

"We'll go flying tomorrow, I promise," Ed said to his son. He was rewarded with a smile.

As the passenger ship approached the moon, Mike Swenson watched the face of Lilo Helziger. Lilo was copper and gold, her red hair twisted tightly on her head, her golden skin gleaming. It had taken her a lot of time and patience to get that skin; hours of timing her exposure to the California sunshine, trying to tread the thin line between paleness and leathery overexposure. She had succeeded, and Mike found himself hoping that the sun-lamps used on Luna would enable her to keep her skin tone. Otherwise, he was sure she would leave quickly and head back home to restore it.

Mike looked away from her and watched the screen at the front of the vehicle. Cameras recorded the approach of the ship for the benefit of the passengers. He saw the moon growing larger; they would be landing in an hour. It was an awesome sight with its craggy mountains, deep craters, and black shadows.

He knew better than to awaken Lilo for this vision. She had quickly grown bored with the trip, although she had found the space station where they had stopped for a while amusing. She would probably find the moon equally amusing; for how long, he was not sure.

Lilo murmured something in her sleep, twisting her slender body slightly. She was a striking sight in her glittery blue and silver outfit, modeled on the tight overalls worn by space workers. Mike could see some of the other passengers sneaking glances at her. Even now, he found it hard to believe that they were married, had been married for almost two months.

Lilo Helziger had been trained to do absolutely nothing. Her parents, confronted by strict and confiscatory inheritance laws, had nevertheless managed to find a few loopholes giving their daughter part of their considerable wealth. Lilo was not wealthy; it was almost impossible for anyone to be that. But she was comfortably well off and was taking full advantage of the fact that she would never have to work again. She had been an actress for a while, acquiring more publicity than roles, before getting tired of the discipline. Her education, what little there was of it, consisted of short terms at various schools in which she had learned the art of faking her way through conversations on almost any topic. She was presently trying to remedy that lack of knowledge using their home computer. But he did not take these efforts very seriously.

He had met her a year ago, right after she quit her acting career. He had been a novelty, he knew, a physicist, prime developer of the experimental matter replicator which, when perfected, would change the world, making her own world of wealth and privilege, what little there was left of it, obsolete. He was one of the Swenson clones besides. There were still some newsfax people who did stories on the Swensons now and then, and a particularly embarrassing one had appeared on their thirtieth birthday lauding their various intellectual achievements. Lilo, Mike knew, had read that article when she was a girl, and it had made quite an impression. In marrying him, she had consummated a childhood infatuation. It was what he was, rather than the person he was underneath, that held her.

It had been her idea to get married, but he had gone along with it. They had done it quietly, although Lilo made sure that the event received maximum publicity afterward. Ed had been polite in his congratulations. Kira and Al, calling from the moon, had been horrified and did a bad job of hiding it. Jim, of course, had not been heard from.

Why had he married her? Her sexual attraction for him had been strong and still was. She was young, not even twenty, and her youthfulness had attracted him as well. Oddly enough, he considered it a good match. Lilo did not bother him when he was working or reading, being absorbed in herself anyway, and he had to admit that being her husband gave him a peculiar sort of status. Their marriage, apart from bed, was more appearance than anything else, role-playing, but it was pleasant enough.

In a rational mood, he could plot its course. Lilo would enjoy the present state of affairs for a time, she liked charming his friends and colleagues and pretending an interest in their work. She was inventive sexually and helped him relax when he was tired. She had even taken a job at his research facility's child care center, surprising everyone when she was put in charge of its recreational activities. But eventually she would get tired of that. She might want to travel more, have a child, or do any number of foolish things. She would become bored and leave him.

That was how it would go, but he was enjoying it now and by the time she was bored, he would be too. Lilo was not, apart from her public image and her beauty, a very interesting person. *And it was,* he thought darkly, *a change from Sita.*

He felt himself growing disturbed just thinking about his first wife. He would never become that involved with another person again, mired down in a constant struggle, needing to compromise, work things out, talk them over.

And where had he gotten with all of it? Sita had just gone back to India in the end, leaving him depressed and unable to do his best work for months. Sometimes, when he was tired, Mike found himself almost wishing that Sita was with him, wanting to discuss something with her, try out some ideas. Those had been the best times for them. Lilo was not much good at kicking ideas around, but she went her way and let him go his.

He recalled a conversation with Ella Tollen, an acquaintance of Lilo's, at a party. "I'm not at all interested in a person's inner life," Ella had said in her flat monotone. "We're all the same underneath, we have the same messy feelings and emotions. The surface is the only thing that varies and that's really all I care about, it's the only thing that's at all original or creative."

Well, he was satisfied, most of the time. If there were times he saw an unfamiliar expression on Lilo's face, times when she looked frustrated or unhappy, times when he suspected that she was withholding something important from him . . . he could ignore that. It was their surfaces, their external images, that had brought them together.

Lilo opened her large blue eyes suddenly and stared vacantly at him until a look of comprehension passed over her face. She glanced up at the screen and gasped. "My God," she said, looking at the lunar image. "Mike, look at that. I didn't think. . . . " She sank back into her seat and continued to gaze at the image.

Mike smiled tolerantly. Lilo's education had been so sparse that she, upon landing at the space station, had been under the impression that it was the ship that would take them to the moon. He had explained to her that an object of that size would encounter difficulties in landing on any large body. God only knew what she was thinking now. He hoped she would find enough to do to keep her from getting bored.

"Are you feeling all right?" Kira said to the image of Hidey on the phone screen. She waited, and the image at last nodded.

"Well enough. I've been getting to bed early, I've been eating three meals a day, I do exercises every morning." Hidey glanced at the ashtray next to his chair. He winced and she knew he was regretting that he had not moved it out of sight of the screen. "And I've cut down my smoking. Just a couple with my morning coffee and one after dinner."

"But you promised you'd quit altogether," she said, forgetting about the three-second delay and missing part of his next sentence.

". . . Rina every afternoon, she had supper here last night." He paused. "I am cutting down, Kira. Look, if I haven't quit by the time you get back, I'll go for conditioning, I promise. That ought to convince you. I don't like having my will bent by a bunch of psycho-technicians, but I'll do it for you."

She had heard that before. Hidey had gone once already, after the coronary. The conditioning had lasted six months. "You could at least smoke the tobacco substitutes." But she knew the answer to that too. They might taste the same, but they did not feel the same. He missed the nicotine.

For a person with his training and aptitudes, Hidey certainly seemed to have a streak of perversity. He had worked to extend life and health, yet he insisted on putting his own in jeopardy. Jim's theory, explained to her during his last visit, was that Hidey was unconsciously punishing himself for defying the inevitability of death. She preferred to believe that her husband had acquired a bad and not easily broken habit.

"Tell me how Rina is," she went on.

"Fine," he said three seconds later. "She's growing fast, we went and bought some new overalls and shoes last week. She got into a fight with a little boy who kept picking on the younger children and I don't think he'll be doing it again. She wants to cross-breed some peas in the spring and I'll help her on that. It all started when she asked me why she has black hair and brown eyes instead of green eyes and brown hair, like you."

Kira smiled. "I miss her."

"You should call her more often," he said as she spoke.

"I've been busy, but that's no excuse. I'll call her tonight."

"She really missed you this past Christmas, I guess you know. You won't recognize her when you get back. Come to think of it, you won't recognize the neighborhood. Most of the houses further up are finally gone. They'll be farming the land in the spring. I figure we'll probably have to move in two or three years."

I should go home, she thought suddenly, in a panic. *What am I doing up here, on a fool's mission?* She looked at Hidey's hair, now almost completely gray, the lines around his eyes, the looseness of his skin. *I could be down there, helping Hidey, making him well.*

But that, after all, was part of the reason she was here.

She leaned forward. "I miss you, Hidey, more than I can stand sometimes, more than I miss Rina, I think." She reached out with her hand to the screen.

Simone had only been back from Earth for a day. Al had tried his best to make her first day back a good one. He had taken her out on the surface for a walk, then treated her, along with his recently arrived brother Mike and his wife, Lilo, to a fairly expensive dinner at one of the hotels. He had not asked her where she had gone. He could guess; to see her son. Simone was trying to mend some of the bridges she had burnt behind her, in case she might need them again.

She had been quiet most of the day, even during dinner. She was courteous to Lilo and the two seemed to get along. Even Al had found himself liking the young woman in spite of himself. As soon as he and Simone had returned to their room, however, she had lapsed into silence. She sat now in one of the chairs, staring ahead of her, apparently unwilling to read, or call some friends, or do any of the things she usually did.

"What is it?" he said finally, not really expecting an answer.

"Can you not guess?"

"Why don't you let me help you? I haven't brought it up before, I figured you would. But I can't just sit by and watch you like this. At least talk to me, let it out." He drew his chair nearer to her and grasped her hand.

"You know what it is I must get used to, Al. Give me time. I shall adjust."

"You think you won't be going on one of the starships, but you may be wrong. I don't think you should jump to conclusions before they issue the final list."

"Al, you are being the fool. I do not have to wait until then. They were undecided about me, for what reason I do not know. They finally put me on the preliminary list, but do you honestly believe that anyone will be going about whom they have such doubts?"

"If they didn't think you should go at all, they wouldn't have bothered to put you on the preliminary list."

"Perhaps they do not want someone who has left a child."

"That's ridiculous. June Eaglefeather is on the list and has a good chance, and she left three children. They do consider individual circumstances, you know."

"June Eaglefeather is one of our best selenologists as well as being one of the few native Americans to apply."

He released her hand. "Damn it, Simone, this is stupid. Everybody on the ships, when you come right down to it, will be leaving a family and friends behind." down to it, will be leaving someone behind." He stopped, realizing that this was probably the wrong thing to say.

"I do not want to discuss it. She looked away from him.

"Well, I do. I think there might be a chance, I don't know, but I'm willing to try. I think maybe I can get you on the final list."

He might be sticking his neck out, maybe even risking his own chance by saying this. Interceding for Simone might be taken as evidence that he did not trust the committee, or that his personal attachments were too strong to allow him to go on the journey. On the other hand, not trying to help someone he loved might work against him.

He had already received a note from a group of astrophysicists on the committee telling him that in all likelihood he would be on that final list. He had been elated, knowing that if the group of specialists had made such a recommendation, his chances with the whole committee were excellent. He had not hidden it from Simone, he could not have anyway. She would have noticed the difference in him. The worry had been lifted from him, his life's work would not be cut off.

But he might have to leave the woman he loved. The reasonable decisions they had made earlier about such an eventuality faded in his mind. He wanted to help her but did not know what to do. He would have to leave it up to her, and do what she asked.

"You are mad," she said fiercely.

"No, I'm not. I can suggest that I need you with me. I'll be careful."

"They will only ignore you and make sure that you do not go. I will not have you risk your chance for me. I do not know if I would have risked mine for you."

Al tried to ignore that painful admission. "You don't understand," he said. "I'll say I need you as a partner in my work. It's true. How often have we exchanged ideas, how often have you pointed out something to me that started me thinking differently?"

"No. I shall not have you intercede for me. If I am meant to go, I will go, but I think I am not meant to leave with you." She gazed past him and he found it unusually difficult to read the expression in her dark eyes.

"You've been talking to Ahmed too much," Al mumbled. Ahmed's fatalism about almost anything sometimes went against all reason. The man was capable of exerting enormous energy in constructing a prototype of an improved lunar surface vehicle, for example, but when the time came to test it, Ahmed would mumble something about how the model was meant to fail or meant to succeed. It was a common enough attitude among the Arab scientists and technicians. It did not keep them from doing a fine job and it was comforting when they failed at a given task. Even those who were not Arabs fell into a fatalistic mood often enough, and it was a strangely contagious attitude among the members of the closely knit and cooperative lunar community. Even Al had succumbed to it at times.

Ahmed was on the preliminary list too. His fatalism did not prevent him from hoping. Now Simone, used to creating her own destiny, had succumbed to it. Al sighed. It was probably much simpler than that. Simone had never asked a favor in her life and found it easier than most to live with the consequences of her actions. She would not be obligated to anyone.

"There is nothing you can do," Simone said in a flat voice.

What she meant, of course, was that there was nothing he *should* do.

Ed stopped at the end of the corridor and looked down at his son Isaac. The boy stared straight ahead at the heavy metal doors in front of them. The child wore his usual expression, one of somber curiosity. At times, Ed still felt almost intimidated by his seemingly rational son, at least until Isaac would, with a gesture or a few words, remind Ed that he was only a small child after all.

Al, on his way to a laboratory nearby, had accompanied them and so had Lilo, Mike's wife. Al was being very quiet. He seemed lost in thought and murmured only perfunctory responses to Lilo's attempts at conversation. *He's worried*, Ed thought, *something to do with Simone*. Ed had sensed that without even asking what the problem was, knowing that Al would discuss his situation when he was ready to do so and not before.

Lilo, standing next to Al, seemed to shine. Her red hair glittered under the harsh lighting of the corridor and her silvery gray tunic contrasted with Al's dull gray shirt and shorts.

Lilo had got along beautifully with Isaac from the time they first met. It was easy to understand why. She had listened, apparently fascinated, to the boy's recitation of what he had discovered on the moon, interrupting him only to ask questions. Isaac had quickly assumed the role of teacher and Lilo the role of a student. The young woman was obviously more at ease questioning the child rather than another adult, who might have found her lack of education appalling.

The words on the metal doors were in Russian. Ed put a hand on Isaac's shoulder. "This is the morgue," he explained. "When people die here, it's easiest just to freeze them up here as soon after death as possible. Burial on the surface is more difficult, so people are brought here, or to other places like it, instead. Sometimes they're sent back to Earth if their relatives want that and can afford it, but a lot of them prefer to stay here and say so in their wills. That's because they've come to think the moon is their real home."

"Why do they die?" Isaac asked.

"For the same reasons people on Earth do," Ed replied. "They become sick, or an accident happens, or they're very old. You can live longer up here, because lunar gravity is easier on your system and your environment is under more control, but sooner or later you die."

"Do you have to be so morbid?" Lilo said.

"It's a fact. It's part of the life cycle, after all."

"And something we could well do without," Lilo muttered.

"Kira says people don't have to die," Isaac said.

"Maybe they won't in the future, at least not as soon," Ed responded. "Your aunt is working on ways to make people live longer. Look at your uncle Hidey. Fifty years ago, people would have thought of him as extremely old and he might not have been alive today. But he has years ahead of him, if he takes care of himself. By the time you're his age, you might look no older than me."

"He shouldn't smoke," Isaac said.

"Well," Lilo said, moving closer to the boy, "he has a bad habit. Lots of people do. I notice you like to eat a lot of candy."

"Sometimes," the boy said.

"Even when you know it's bad for your teeth. Someday you'll have to have new ones put in at the rate you're going, and that's damned painful."

"I know."

"And don't you sometimes eat too much and get sick?" Isaac glared. "I guess," he conceded.

"Make a trade with your uncle," Lilo went on. "If you stop eating candy, maybe he'll stop his smoking."

"Why did we come here?" Isaac asked Ed, apparently wanting to change the subject.

"Because your grandfather's inside this room. When he died, some Russian friends brought him here. They put him into a cryonic cylinder." His voice shook slightly at the last words. For a moment, Ed felt almost as he had when Paul had died. His stomach contracted slightly, then loosened. It had been a long time, more than twenty years.

"Why didn't you bring him back to Earth?" Isaac said.

"I think he would have rather stayed here. He spent his whole life studying the stars, and we thought he would have wanted it this way."

"Can we go inside?"

"Not today. I have to get permission for that. But I thought you should see where your grandfather is. He was a fine person." Ed suddenly felt adrift and alone, wondering what his life would have been like if Paul had lived, remembering all the times he had wanted to talk with him and could not.

"I've been inside," Al said to Isaac, breaking his mono-syllabic near-silence at last. "You can't see your grandfather, except for the outline of his head. He's standing upright in the cylinder, but he's covered except for his face."

"Why'd you go inside?" the boy asked.

"I wanted to see him when I first came here to study, so I did. I saw him again about a month ago to tell him I might be going on the interstellar expedition. He would have wanted to go himself."

"But he couldn't hear you," Isaac said scornfully. Ed winced.

"I know that," Al said patiently. "But it made me feel

a little better. You'll understand someday."

Ed glanced at Isaac, who was already growing restive. He could not really expect the boy to understand. It was only a doorway to him, and behind it rested a man the boy had never known, a distant relation as far as he was concerned. Isaac did not understand death. He had never known anyone who had died, not even a pet animal, and he probably could not see that the concept had anything to do with him. Ed could recall, dimly, his own feelings on the subject as a boy. People simply disappeared, as if they had gone on a journey, never to return. But that was before Paul had died, and Jon Aschenbach, years afterward, and Ed's close friend Mel Gladstein in Boston, a victim of a fanatic's attack on an underwater suburb of the large city. They had all disappeared.

Carole was gone, and he could only blame himself. That was what he believed when he was completely conscious, so consequently he tried to remain as unconscious as possible, most of the time.

Jim Swenson wandered along the beach adjacent to his hotel, watching his bare feet make impressions in the sand, heel first, toes curling. Behind him, the reddish-brown ocean waters erased the prints already made. He ignored the signs of warning posted at intervals on the beach, careless of his own welfare. Several people were lying on towels on the sand, brown lizards exposing their bodies to the ultraviolet light. No one swam, or even chanced wading near the waterline on the wet surface under Jim's feet. It was not safe to get too close to Florida's waters. Jim did not care.

He chewed the pasty substance in his mouth and at last felt an almost painful clarity and energy flood his mind. No, he did not want that; he waited to blur his feelings, not sharpen them. *They might be calling me now, they might have my ticket ready.* He turned around. He was suddenly repelled by the sight of the small, worn old hotel two hundred feet down the beach. Not yet, he did not want to go back there just yet. He could always take a later flight anyway. He spat out the paste and watched it drift on the water. Then he began to walk toward a nude woman lying on the sand.

She lay with her eyes closed. Her brown hair was sun-streaked and crushed under her head. As he came closer, he saw the uneven ends of her hair, probably dried out and broken from too much exposure to the sun. Her skin was dark brown; her muscular body gleamed with oil and sweat. He stood over her for a moment, then, as he started to walk away, she opened her eyes and looked at him.

"What's your problem."

"I thought you looked like somebody I knew," Jim lied.

"Sure I do. I think you just want somebody to talk to. You look kind of sad. You can sit down if you want." The woman motioned with her hand.

He sat down. At close range, the woman looked somewhat younger than he had thought, no more than twenty or so. Her brown eyes glanced at him, then closed again.

"Could you move over a little? You're blocking the sun." He moved over to his left until he no longer cast a shadow on her. "You must not have been here long. You're kind of pale. My name's Marlena."

"I'm Jim. Are you visiting too, or do you live here?"

"I'm a resident. I work over at the spaceport air traffic control. They give us a lot of time off so we don't get crazy. I work on my tan a lot, I don't like doing anything that takes effort. I get enough tension on my job." She brushed away a stray lock of hair from her forehead and he saw a thin white scar near her hairline. An electronic implant. Air traffic controllers, like many other technicians, had to become part of the computers that aided them in their tasks.

"What's it like, having an implant in your head?" he asked, suddenly curious.

"A lot of people ask that. You don't even notice it most of the time. The implant's only activated when you're working. But I'll tell you something, Jim." Marlena turned over on her stomach and propped herself up on her elbows. "There's nothing else like being tied into a big machine like that, seeing everything it sees, being part of a tremendous mind. I can't describe it. Actually, the computer mind does most of the work; we just have to be there to override or take over in case of an emergency. But it's exciting, I'll tell you. Everything else seems kind of boring afterwards."

He shuddered. "Don't you have to have a lot of training?"

"Oh, sure. I've been training ever since I was fifteen, and I only started working this year. You have to learn how to be aware of a lot of different things at once, plus training your body so that your physical reactions don't affect you on the job. We slow down our physical processes to the minimum when we're tied in, but we have to be ready to act instantly if something goes wrong. It can be a strain, I'll tell you." She sprayed some oil into her hand and rubbed it on her nose. "Jesus, I should shut up a minute and let you say something. What are you doing here?"

"Waiting for an opening on a moon flight." Remembering his purpose in being here suddenly made him depressed again.

"You going to work up there?"

"No, just visiting." He grew silent and Marlena folded her arms and lowered her head. *They'll all be surprised to see me*, Jim thought, *Hidey was shocked when I called him up.* He had told Hidey nothing about Carole or his plans after discovering that all the others were on the moon. He had not even known, until he arrived in Florida, that he would attempt to join them. It had been an impulse. He had nothing else to do, and he could hope that the alien environment might heal him somehow. Perhaps he could find something there that had eluded him throughout all his travels on Earth. For him, the trip would be a pilgrimage.

Or maybe he was simply trying to escape the punishment he kept meting out to himself in his sober moments. Carole was gone and he was to blame. His mind's pain was at once so sharp that tears sprang to his eyes. *If this was physical pain, I could not bear it, I would be dead by now. But the mind, that traitorous torturer, the mind can suffer anything, for any length of time, over and over again.*

"What do you do?" Marlena said, raising her head slightly

He closed his eyes and waited for his pain to pass. "Nothing," he answered at last. He opened his eyes again. "I wander a lot. I was living about a mile outside a village in Bhutan for a while. It was the most peaceful place I'd ever known. I felt calm for the first time in my life but, believe it or not, I couldn't write there. I could hardly write at all, except for some poems, they'll be published soon."

"You're a writer?"

He nodded.

"Maybe you didn't have much there to write about. Maybe you needed some feedback or something, like I need when I'm working."

"I don't know. There were the Himalayas, and the villagers. I guess others have done better writing about them."

"Did you live there alone?"

"The woman I loved was with me, but she died." His voice shook as he said it. He looked down at the sand, then back at Marlena, who was now sitting on her towel, legs folded in front of her.

"Jesus," she muttered. "I'm sorry."

"It was my fault," Jim heard himself saying. "I shouldn't have brought her there in the first place. She didn't belong there. She came because I wanted her to."

Marlena looked puzzled. "I don't know why you're saying that. If she went with you, she must have wanted to go there too. Otherwise she would have talked you out of it or refused to go along. It was her choice too, wasn't it?"

"You don't understand," he replied. He clutched a handful of sand and watched the grains trickle out between his fingers. "Carole followed me, she never gave any thought to herself. I knew that, and I never even encouraged her to be different. I never even asked what she thought, I just let her follow me. It was easy. At least I knew she cared about me."

He looked at Marlena and felt almost gratified when he saw the expression of puzzled disapproval on her face. "That's sick," she said softly. "You ought to see a doctor or something."

He ran down the mountain road toward the village. He had to find help there, he had to find somebody. He would go to the group of Japanese mountain climbers there, a vacationing doctor was with them. He would know what to do. He ran, straining his lungs in the high altitude, gasping for breath.

"I never thought she would die," Jim went on. "I didn't think anything would go wrong. We were going to have our first child. Once she got over feeling nauseous in the morning, she was fine. I should have taken her away as soon as I knew."

"Yes, you should have," Marlena said harshly. He waited for her accusations passively, almost wanting to hear them. "Who ever heard of somebody dying in childbirth? This isn't the Middle Ages, you know. What the hell do you think paramedics and artificial wombs are for?"

He was holding Carole in his arms. Behind him, he could hear the doctor and two villagers murmuring over the body of his stillborn son. At last she opened her eyes and looked up at him. Her face had grown extremely pale and her dark hair hung heavily over his arm. The red stain on the front of her tunic grew larger in spite of the injection the doctor had given her.

"Jim," she whispered. He leaned closer. "Can we leave now? I want to go home, I miss it. Is it all right?"

"Sure," he replied, not trying to hide the tears that ran from his eyes. "As soon as you're well." He felt a hand on his shoulder.

"I shall go to the village and radio for a plane," the doctor said. Jim glanced at the man and saw the look of hopelessness on his face. At that moment, Carole sighed. He continued to hold her, brushing the hair back from her face, before he realized she was gone.

Marlena was folding her towel. She stood up suddenly and pulled a shift over her nude body. "I don't understand people like you," she said as she picked up her towel. "You think everything is better somewhere else." He became aware again of the implant in her head and thought of it correlating data, coding his experiences and filing them away. "You ought to get some help." She walked away, weaving a path among the other sunbathers farther up on the beach, and was soon a speck near the rows of hotels and apartment buildings.

He traced a figure in the sand, then erased it with a violent sweep. *The Himalayas had mocked him with their majesty, towering around him as he walked with the village procession to the place where they would build a small pyre and burn the bodies of Carole and his son. Some of the people wailed, granting that courtesy to the outsider they had hardly known. A mist shrouded the village behind them as they wound their way along the dirt path. He would keep his promise to Carole in the only way he could, by taking her ashes with him when he left and burying them near the Michigan town where she had grown up.*

Jim got to his feet and began to walk back to his hotel. As he passed a group of nude sunbathers, the smell of lotion and sweat mingled with the salt of the sea and the odor of the dead, decaying fish at the water's edge. This part of Florida was still a cesspool after all this time, the home of the old and a vacation spot for those who could not afford to go elsewhere. Only the areas around the spaceport, and the cities and towns which housed the workers who built and serviced the aircraft and space shuttles, showed any vitality at all. But it was a machine-like vitality unfamiliar to Jim, filled with calm, orderly sorts who satisfied themselves by working with their hands, conservative engineers, or technicians with implants. Many of the younger people did not seem that different from some of the villagers he had known in Bhutan. The technicians too were in harmony with their environment and seemed to have a sense of their own place in the world. It was the Florida of decaying hotels and sun-following transients that Jim preferred.

Once he had sat in a hotel bar in Bali, speaking to a young Balinese man who had studied in North America. "You wanderers puzzle me," the man had said. "You come to a place and marvel at the serenity of its inhabitants, forgetting that you see the face of a stoicism needed to endure an always present and often unpredictable natural order. You arrive at another place and find healthy people and forget about all those who died as children or were weeded out along the way by natural selection. You delight in the interesting beliefs and customs you find and do not understand the role ignorance and fear play in their perpetuation. We do not want to lose our culture and our roots, but we do not want to exist only as living museums for you to gape at. The past does not work. Cultures change and evolve. We want and need the machines and the knowledge you are so ready to reject. We should at least be given a choice between the old ways and other ways, and be allowed to contribute what is good and valuable in our culture to yours."

Jim passed a group of brown children and heard their cries as they chased after a large red beach ball. He had wanted to apologize to Carole. He had tried as her body burned on the pyre and he had tried again while he watched the urn of ashes being lowered into her shallow grave. He had not found the words.

If it was true that Carole chose to follow him, it was also true that he had never questioned the wisdom of that course. He had been satisfied because his needs had been fulfilled and had never thought about what Carole's might have been. For a moment he hated the technological world around him with an intensity that made his knees tremble and bathed his face in sweat. The technology that seemed to surround him on all sides, he thought perversely, had made what would have been in former times an almost normal occurrence, something unavoidable, an incident that need never have happened. His decisions had become the agents of Carole's death, and not nature or the world.

At this thought he felt shame and a hatred of himself that made him long to trade his life for Carole's. Would it have mattered to Carole which of the two worlds she had lived in? She would still be gone. But at least in this one, she could still have been at his side, possibly with his son as well, that poor, dead, flesh of potentialities that would never be realized. He did not know how he would ever come to live with that fact. But he felt he deserved the punishment with which his regrets would chastise him.

Mike sat in the hotel dining room, feeling apprehensive and trying to ignore that feeling. Across the table, his nephew Isaac, dressed in a dark blue t-shirt and shorts, was fidgeting restlessly. Al sat on his left, a silent gray presence. Lilo, overdressed as usual in a shiny green gown, was on his right, talking to Ed. Their words seemed to float around him, providing background noise for his thoughts.

". . . wanted to have the experience," Ed was saying. "Sheila doesn't regret that at all, but she says the next one, if we have another, goes into the ectogenetic chamber."

Oddly enough, Lilo had not yet been bored. She was always off on some expedition, learning how to fly, exploring the lunar surface, talking to a group of actors making a film. Mike found all this activity almost as disturbing as her boredom might have been. He was beginning to realize that Lilo was changing, that she was not the same person with whom he had come here originally. He might have to make adjustments in his expectations. He almost sighed with exasperation. *Well, if I have to, I will.* It would be too time-consuming to go through another ruined marriage. Lilo was still young and she had the right, after all, to discover her own interests and pursuits.

She looked toward him and smiled suddenly. He smiled back and took her hand. *I don't want to lose you*, he found himself thinking, startled by the intensity of that desire. He held her hand more tightly, then released it.

"You're late," Ed was saying. Mike looked up and saw Sheila standing at Ed's side. "Did you get the permission?"

"He isn't there," Sheila Sonnefeld replied, seating herself next to Ed. "Your father isn't there. An attendant told me it was only a temporary move, maintenance or some such thing, but I got the feeling he didn't really know why. He's in a chamber near the medical research center." She tugged at her white shirt, then rested her elbows on the table.

"You'd think," Mike said, "that they could let Paul rest in peace."

"I don't know why they would move him," Al said, speaking at last. "Maintenance is no reason for moving someone. In fact it's risky, considering the equipment needed to maintain the body in its frozen state."

"I don't see what difference it makes if a person's already dead," Lilo blurted out, then looked around at the others as if embarrassed. She was talking about Paul, after all.

"Some people are donors," Al said. "They left instructions in their wills that parts of their bodies could be used for emergency organ transplants. So far they haven't been needed, but you never know, so their bodies have to be maintained. Kira could tell you more about it if she were here."

"She's been working too hard," Ed said. "I've hardly seen her at all since arriving. I don't like to call on her when she's not busy because I know she'd be better off resting. I have to force her to come to dinner and eat once in a while. Jim's awfully late, isn't he."

"I hope he gets here soon," Al replied. "I'm kind of nervous, I don't know what to expect. I wonder what he's been doing these past few years."

Mike glanced around the small dining room. Most of the people here were tourists or visiting scientists. The room was simple in design, containing only round tables, plastic booths next to the walls and a small bar in the back. At the tables next to them, three middle-aged couples were sampling the plain lunar cuisine. The lunar communities produced most of their own food, growing it in hydroponic vats and synthesizing the rest from soybeans and protein compounds. It was usually cooked in a simple Chinese manner, making it taste better than it otherwise would, and none of it was wasted. Mike had learned from Al that certain dishes on the menu were nothing more than leftovers from the previous day, sterilized and served again. The beverages, alcoholic and non-alcoholic, were equally nondescript; they and the drinking water here were largely recycled urine. Some food was imported from Earth, and the cost of transporting it was reflected in the high prices next to such dishes on the menu. Across the room, Mike noticed two bearded men eating what looked like an imported meal of fish and wine. It could be a synthetic meal, but somehow he doubted it. The two were consuming it with too much obvious enjoyment.

A man walked through the entrance behind the two diners and stood for a moment surveying the room. He was a tall bony fellow, with a closely trimmed beard flecked with gray hairs. His yellow shirt was rumpled and part of it dangled over the loose brown slacks which hung on his hips. He was slumped over as if carrying a heavy weight; the deep shadows under his eyes seemed almost cavernous. The man's green eyes met Mike's.

It's Jim. Mike tried to rise and found that his knees had locked. He was becoming nervous. *What do I have to say to this man, this wasted creature?* Jim began to walk toward their table and Mike felt a momentary wave of panic. *I shouldn't have come here, I knew it was a mistake.* He wanted no part of this misbegotten reunion, these parts of himself.

He suddenly hated them all, hated them for being his relations. He found himself slipping into the role of sibling again, having to spend time with people who had nothing in common with him except genes. Every meeting and conversation with them threatened his sense of identity, every family gathering erased years of effort and made him an awkward boy again, part of them yet alienated from them. He would rather be with his colleagues, those men and women who knew only the side of him he chose to reveal, whose bonds with him were based on friendship, mutual respect, and shared ideas and goals, not this herd of strangers who remembered the boy of eight or eighteen that he thought he had escaped forever. Now they would sink their tendrils into him again, and Lilo as well. He should never have brought her here, exposing her to the strands of the family web. Her parents, thank God, had been dead when he met her and she had no brothers or sisters, a fact he had regarded as fortunate. Now she would latch on to the others to replace her lost family, and he would never be rid of them. They would infect his life again. *That's a family for you, absent when you need them, ever-present when you don't want them around.*

Mike felt a flush of guilt at his angry thoughts. *Yes, they can make you feel that too. Why is it that you can choose not to see a friend or acquaintance for a while and never feel that kind of guilt, that self-accusation?* They made him hate himself. They made him hate what he was. He would get through it somehow, and then never see them again, these reflections that made claims on him which acquaintances would never make, demanding love because of a shared genetic strain.

Now he had to meet this stranger he had not seen for years and show him a depth of feeling he would not show even to his closest friends.

Jim sat down between Al and Isaac. Al reached over and flung an arm over his brother's shoulders. He began to talk to Jim and the words he murmured became an indistinct blur to Mike. Jim's eyes, gazing past Al, met his again and Mike knew that Jim was thinking the same thing he had thought moments before. *We're all trapped.*

Ed was speaking now, gesturing to Lilo, Sheila, and Isaac, introducing them. A look of pain passed over Jim's face as he looked at his nephew.

Jim was old. For some reason, this was terrifying to Mike. His face reflected years of suffering, his hair had become spotted with gray. He looked at Al and Ed more closely. Yes, there were almost invisible gray hairs on their heads. They too were thinner, almost alike with their clean-shaven faces and closely cropped hair. Ed had a small roll of fat around his middle, the legacy of too little exercise. Al was almost as pale as Jim, with his years on the moon and only ultraviolet lamps for sunlight.

Mike pulled at his moustache nervously. *I don't look like any of them, I can't.* His body was firm from regular workouts and any gray hairs he possessed were hidden in his sun-streaked hair. His skin was a healthy bronze tone and if he sometimes heightened its color artificially, what of it? But looking at his brothers made him more conscious of his age, of the passage of time, of the increasing effort it would take to maintain his appearance. He caught a glimpse of the blue-veined network on Jim's bony arms and thought, *I'm getting old, we're all aging.*

There was a pause in the conversation and Mike heard himself filling it with inconsequential phrases and questions. He was beginning to grow calmer now. He reached across the table and clasped his brother's hand while thinking, *never again, I won't let any of them do this to me again.*

"Oh, Jim," Kira said, and felt the tears trickling down her face. She gestured with her hands and at last felt a handkerchief pressed into her palm. She wiped her eyes and saw her brother reseating himself next to the computer console.

"It really put the finishing touches on the evening," Jim said. "It was bad enough before, but telling them about Carole really finished it. Everybody sat around, and Mike's wife, whatever her name is. . . . "

"Lilo."

"Lilo tried to make conversation, but she and Isaac pretty much had to take care of it themselves. I shouldn't have come." His voice trembled. "None of us should have. I know Mike doesn't want to be here."

She found herself remembering a moment years ago,

Jim's face, his voice: *You could help me, Kira, I know you could. Maybe we could do some traveling. . . .*

How could she help him now? She had turned him away when she might have made a difference and would have to live with that.

"We shouldn't be here," she said angrily. Jim looked up in surprise. "I shouldn't be here. I must be mad." She rubbed at her eyes. Everything was becoming blurred now, she was tired and would need all her strength for the next few days. She could not afford to listen to these interfamily discords, not now. She could not sit with Jim and mourn for Carole. "I'm tired," she murmured, trying to explain her outburst.

"I'll go," she heard him say sadly.

"Go to the observatory tomorrow," she said quickly. "Go on the tour. Go see the stars shining steadily instead of winking, it's a sight you won't forget. And please stay for a while. Things'll be different. We all feel a little awkward, we have to get acquainted again."

"We're almost too well acquainted as it is."

"Go on the goddamn tour." Kira rubbed her forehead. "It'll be worth it. It takes you out of yourself, seeing those thousands of constellations, millions of miles away, shining for millions of years."

She watched her brother move toward the doorway. She grew afraid. She would be alone again, and would have to consider what it was she was doing as she struggled to sleep.

Liu Ching was sitting in Simone's chair when Al entered his room. "She's gone, isn't she?" he heard himself say. "She's not coming back."

"She is still here, Al. She wishes only to stay with some friends for a while. Soon she will accept it, and come back to you."

"So they finally told her she wouldn't be going." He sat down, watching the Chinese woman. Liu Ching sat with her legs folded in front of her and her black eyes almost devoid of any expression. "I tried. I asked them to let us go together. Simone didn't know. Well, maybe I won't be leaving either."

"You will leave and so will I. It is almost certain, Al." Liu Ching smoothed down her brown shirt. "But do not think time will stand still here. We shall go out on those clunking dinosaurs of ships and we may find, by the time we reach our destination, that those back here have caught up with us, have found back here what we went out to discover. They may be waiting for us there. We may become the ones who are left behind."

He listened to her quiet, steady speech and rememberd Simone's musical voice, the restless hands which fluttered as she spoke. He wondered if Liu Ching would also be leaving someone behind. He had seen her several times with a young Chinese technician in the dining hall. Simone had told him the two were thinking of marriage.

As if answering his unspoken question, Liu Ching stood up and came over to him. She placed her small hands on his shoulders. "Simone asked me to stay with you for a few days. She thought you might wish to have a companion. To be honest, I would prefer to stay here, for my own reasons, but I shall leave if you want."

"Stay," he said. He looked up at her perfectly proportioned face and thought of Simone's crooked smile and slightly flattened nose. He had occasionally entertained thoughts of how Liu Ching might be in bed, but now he felt nothing other than a desire for a confidant. "You can stay," he repeated. Almost against his will, he pulled her to him and felt her arms move around his neck in response. *Simone*, he thought.

Liu Ching was loosening his shirt. "I can't," he whispered. But his body was responding on its own, his hands were unbuttoning her shirt. At last he drew her over to his bed.

He was at peace at last, hovering over the lunar surface, his body separated from him. Wedged under the wreckage of the surface vehicle, he saw it move slightly and seemed to feel his broken leg, his crushed ribs, but from a distance: he pulled one string and breathed, he pulled another and his hand clutched a nearby rock.

He had felt panic at first and had struggled against his death. He had watched the vehicle crash into a mountainside that should not have been where it was, then felt it lurch toward the ground. He had listened to the cries of three children in the back, each cry a crystalline note threatening to shatter the clear helmet that surrounded his head. In front of him, two young men, who had disregarded the suggestion that they don space suits at the beginning of the trip, began to scream as the vehicle smashed into the small crater ahead of them. The moonbus had spun around him and at last he had found himself under it, half of his body protruding from a broken window. He fought then, struggling for life, searching for rips in his suit with his free right hand, waiting for a rescue team to arrive.

He was now dimly aware of the fact that air was leaking from his suit, but the thought did not disturb him. He saw Sonia in front of him, pitching a baseball to him as he swung his bat. He was eight again, playing with his sister on their grandfather's farm in Minnesota. The clarity of the blue sky above him, the green grass beneath his feet, the odor of sweat and dung emanating from the cows in the nearby pasture was almost too sharp for him to bear. He swung the bat and connected with the ball, watched it arc over the field in front of him as Sonia squealed.

He stood in the Chicago night and waited for the policemen to attack. He watched one policeman, no more than twenty feet away, tapping his club lightly against his hand, and suddenly realized that the man would kill him if he could, would in fact take pleasure in injuring him or those around him. Perhaps the man had children of his own, perhaps he prayed every Sunday and was respected by his neighbors, but he would attack and beat him because he stood with the crowd, because he was young, because he wore a blue and white button with the name of a man who seemed to threaten everything the policeman believed, because he and those with him symbolized disorder.

He turned on the bed and reached for Julia, drawing her to him, searching her face for a response. He entered her and saw her close her eyes, groan, then open them again. They seemed lifeless, dark mud-eyes staring at him while her body writhed under him and her hands clutched at his back.

He saw the frothy substance of the Crab Nebula before him, and around it the black nothingness of space. He turned for a moment from the telescope's eyepiece and saw his wife below him, making her notations. The observatory's light had transformed her hair to gold, and for a moment his perceptions centered on her. She glanced up at him and smiled. He smiled back and calmly returned to his observations.

He was at peace. He lay under the wreckage and almost smiled, felt the strings attached to his face turn up the corners of his mouth. Darkness covered him now, and ahead of him he saw only a deep tunnel leading to blackness. He was not fearful of oblivion but, for a second, felt a small regret. He had not wanted to leave so soon. He thought of his children: Mike, almost too practical and sensible for his age; Jim, ruled by the extremes of adolescent emotion; Al, drawn by the brightness of the stars and the blackness of space, as he had been; Kira, whose love of life and desire to penetrate nature's secrets might lead her to question what once were unalterable facts; Ed, lonely and shy, drawn to a clearer, purer realm of ideas. He hoped they would not waste too much time in tears. He moved into the tunnel, leaving the broken body and its loosened strings behind.

He had been sleeping.

As he awoke, he felt pain in his ribs and legs, then a tingling along all his limbs. His breathing was shallow and he fought for each bit of air, taking it in slowly and then expelling it. He struggled, feeling as though a weight on his chest would crush him. He groaned and felt his head move.

"Paul?" A voice was questioning him. *Eviane watched him, tilting her head to one side. Who was she? Sonia reached for his hand.* He was supposed to know her, he was sure. Wife? Relative? He did not know.

He became aware of the fact that he was lying down, that liquid was seeping into his arm. He tried to move but could not. He forced an eye open and saw a glaring whiteness. He closed it quickly.

"Paul?" And then another voice: "Dr. Swenson?" He opened both eyes and squinted. Some people were standing by his bed, clad in white coats. He tried to focus on them. One moved closer to him; a brown-haired woman, slender high-cheeked face, large green eyes. *He lay under the craft, pressed against the dead ground, hopelessly waiting.* He watched the woman and suddenly felt spasms of bewilderment and fear.

Her lips moved. "Paul?" The word had some kind of significance and he knew he must concentrate on it. *Paul.* A name. Perhaps his name. *Paul.* Yes, he had been called that. He closed his eyes again and waited.

"It's Kira, Paul. I'm here. Rest if you need to, I'll be here."

Kira. Who was Kira? He concentrated, trying to summon up an image. *A child sat on his lap as he spoke of a farm in Minnesota and the white-haired woman who baked apple pies.* Kira. She was a child, then. But this woman was also Kira.

He was suddenly tired. The room around him seemed to recede. He drifted into a gray world spotted with scarlet stabs of pain. Dimly, he perceived a dark and empty terror circling him, waiting to seize him when he emerged once again into consciousness.

"He's awake again," Juan Colòn said. "He's very weak, but I think he'll be all right. He seems to have a strong will to live, even in this state."

"I know," Kira said wearily. She rubbed at a dark spot on the clear table top in front of her. "I went in before. I don't know if he was fully conscious the first time. I waited. When he became conscious again, I talked to him, but I don't know how much he understood." She stared at some of the print-outs on the table, then looked up at Juan. "I don't know what we've done," she said to the young surgeon. "After all the plans, all the work, I don't know what we've done."

"We all feel that way," Juan replied. He closed the door to the conference room and sat down beside her. "May I speak frankly to you? At first, I was concerned only with the surgery, with the injections, replacing his damaged kidney with our cloned one, all of that. But then, when the medical computer revealed activity in the brain . . . I became terrified. I began to pray. Can you believe that? I prayed that I had not committed a sin. Yet this is little different from operating on critically ill patients frozen for an hour or a day, and I have brought them back from that state before." The young man pressed his hands together as if praying now. "I found myself wondering where this man's soul had been for twenty years, if he were now a soulless being. I had to tell myself that this was idiocy, an hour or a year makes no difference to God."

"My problem isn't theological," Kira said. She looked at Juan's dark, expressive eyes and slender hands. It was not hard for her to imagine him as a priest; in a former time, he probably would have been one. "He's my father. I saw him look at me and he didn't know me, Juan, I know he didn't. I tried to explain who I was, and told him he'd been sick for a long time or words to that effect, but he didn't know me or didn't understand. I don't even know if he realized who he is, or where he is, or. . . ."

"You can't expect that he would know, Kira. You know what would probably happen to a brain cryonically suspended for all that time. Memories are gone, whole tracks are erased by random noise or whatever, and even if his mind is still fairly well integrated, it will take time for it to heal. Some memories may return when he's had a chance to read, talk to people, undergone some therapy. He's had broken limbs repaired, a damaged kidney replaced, injections of serum from your cloned cells, all of that. It would take time for a normal patient to recover from that, and this isn't a normal situation. I think you may be too close to all of this."

"I was too close from the start," she said. Juan gestured as if to take her hand, then seemed to reconsider.

"I'll leave you alone, if you want," he said finally. "Do you want me to get you some coffee or anything else?"

"No, thanks. I guess I do want to do some thinking for a while."

Juan got up and left the room, closing the door behind him.

Paul isn't dead now, she heard her mind say. The thought was shocking, almost as startling as the news of his death had been more than twenty years before. Perhaps he remembered enough of the past, or would recover enough of his memories in time to retain his identity. Perhaps he did not remember and never could, in which case he had been reincarnated, born into a new life, or was a different being altogether. In either case, she had wrestled with Death and brought him at least to a temporary standstill, shoulders on the mat, and might have defeated him.

Kira began to shiver. How would people react to the news? Death had been a given, assumed in every structure of society, a part of the unconscious of every person now alive. There had been a peculiar consolation in the knowledge for many. No matter what one did, or failed to do, there was the ever-present certainty that everyone, high or low, famous or forgotten, would have the same end, that they would all become equal in the grave. For those who believed in a life beyond this one, there was a comfort in knowing that justice, rarely present during this existence, would be meted out in the hereafter.

Jim had once remarked to her: "There's a consolation in knowing that eventually you'll die, that you don't even have to do anything about it and eventually you'll go. You don't even have to make a decision about it. Even if you try, it'll catch up with you sooner or later and at last you'll be out of it, oblivious, unconcerned, nonexistent, and at peace. And no one really mourns *you*, if you think about it. They only mourn the place you once had in their own lives, a place that you once filled, if you die in the normal course of things." It had been easy for her brother to say that before experiencing the death of those close to him.

But what would people do when they heard about Paul? How would they react if they came to believe that they could choose to live on? It would be terrifying. Even fearful people, or those who felt as Jim did, might choose to go on, no matter how unhappy they were, rather than deciding to die "in the normal course of things," which would itself become a form of suicide. People would have another choice to make, a fundamental one, on top of all the choices available to them now. It was easier not to have choices. It was easier to follow a pre-ordained path; no matter how difficult, it was easier to travel on such a road, laid down by others, than to decide what one wanted. Better not to live with the consequences of freely chosen actions; one could not blame one's failings on anyone else.

Kira knew, however, that such thoughts were a useless luxury. She, after all, had been given alternatives that others, even now, did not have. Paul had once told her that she, and others equally fortunate, had a responsibility to help provide others with the same choices they had, and maybe other choices as well. She had given Paul another chance at life, something no human being had ever had before.

She would have even more work ahead of her, apart from what she was already doing. She could not abandon the responsibility for what she had accomplished with her father; Paul had not abandoned her and her brothers. He had hoped that his children would achieve something with their lives; now she had to hope that Paul's second life might be an example to others.

She must try to make sure that everyone had a chance at what might be immortality, not just a select or wealthy few. She and others would have to make the choice available. A society of people hoarding their money, fearful of physical danger, living only for the times they would be renewed biologically, might be worse than not having the choice at all. Or they might grow careless and reckless, unconcerned with danger in a world where death had no lasting significance. They might become thoughtless, unconcerned with the feelings of others; in the crucible of eternity, the effects of cruel acts or damaged emotions might fade in time. People might become procrastinators, forever putting off today what could be accomplished in an almost endless tomorrow. Perhaps most of them, after absorbing the shock of the new discovery and its implications, would not change but would only continue in an endless repetition of what they had previously done.

Humanity would have to alter its most basic preconception, the knowledge that time would catch up to everyone. That knowledge had reduced some to despair, others to expending tremendous amounts of energy on great achievements, and still others to lives of pointless pleasure. It had led many to seek fulfillment and a kind of immortality through their descendants, postponing or rejecting their own development for the sake of future generations.

For herself, Kira could envision years of meetings, of battles, of communications on the subject, of administrative work to grant this alternative to everybody, of helping to formulate goals. Even if the choice were rejected at first, simply knowing it was there would in time bring people around to accepting it, then moving to implement it in accordance with their goals. The moratorium on research had died, not because people thirsted for new knowledge and techniques, but simply because they lost a few of their fears while at the same time realizing that they could benefit from the new discoveries personally. *Human selfishness*, she thought again, somewhat cynically, *will accomplish what years of well-reasoned philosophical and practical arguments could never do.*

She shook her head. *I need some coffee, maybe a drink*, she thought aimlessly. She was almost losing sight of her dream in these ruminations. She would have to bring it into focus again, especially now. She must try to communicate it to others, hoping that they might come to see what she saw.

She saw another humanity on Earth, freed from the

determinants of genetic disabilities, of aging bodies, of unbalanced minds, and of death. She saw them freed from the tyranny of time and the roulette of reproduction, able to deliberate, to consider, to enjoy each moment. She saw a people freed from the necessity to change everything around them because they could instead change themselves.

People might at last walk a peaceful path, themselves whole in body and mind, able to turn from the problems that had always beset human beings to the more important ones of purpose and discovery. They might even learn to treasure the Earth, that poor mother planet they had so abused, because they would themselves have to spend almost infinite amounts of time on her. Some would venture off the Earth and in confronting other life forms confront their own hidden desires.

She saw a world that might finally achieve the Marxist dream of the withering away of the state, the libertarian dream of freedom for each person, the human dream of lives that would not be wasted, thrown away by a profligate and domineering nature. It would not be a utopia, of that she was sure. There would be new problems, perhaps more threatening than the old. There would be terror for a person in the realization that only his own lack of perseverance could keep him from his goals. Failure, in such a world, might be too great a burden to bear, far worse than now, when there was always something outside oneself to blame. But there would be a new pattern for human existence, enough time, hopefully, for anyone to succeed, a chance for everyone to explore all possible alternatives, unlimited by time.

I don't know if I can show all of this to others, Kira thought glumly, *but I'll have to try.* She knew that she could not impose her vision on other minds and did not want to do so. But she hoped that people would see the possibilities and alternatives, that they would welcome what would surely be humanity's greatest adventure.

She got up to leave the room. She had another meeting with her medical team that afternoon, or what passed for afternoon by consensus of the lunar inhabitants. She shuffled across the floor. She had adjusted somewhat to the lunar environment and no doubt would feel comfortable here in time. But she still felt a dislocation, a longing for some fresh air, the sounds of birds and crickets, the smells of flowers, trees, and people that were absent in the purified, slightly stale air of the underground settlement. She had the feeling that, on the moon, it was taking her longer to do things; no rising and setting sun, no seasonal weather changes marked the passing of the hours and days. Even her body, under less physical stress here, requiring fewer calories, gave her the wrong cues; only the clocks in almost every room told her when to eat or sleep. She should try to take a nap before the meeting. She needed to rest.

As she opened the sliding door to leave the conference room, more personal concerns moved to her mind's center stage. She would return to Earth, she would repair Hidey's aging body, she would restore her husband. It occurred to her that her actions would forever alter their relationship. She had assumed when they married that their relationship would ultimately be cut short by his aging, and he had known it too. They had both been willing to proceed on that assumption. But she did not know what would happen now. Could any relationship survive over another fifty years, or one hundred, or more? How would they be changed?

She felt a little guilty. Here she was, preparing to aid the man she loved, willing to do that even before beginning the work that would help her share her dream with everyone else. She wondered what she would do if, by chance, she had to choose between the two, assign priorities. She was, perhaps sadly, as selfish as anyone else.

Jim sat, watching the older man in his bed, trying to understand that he was with his father again, after accepting his death and living with it for twenty years. *But this man isn't Paul.* He told himself that once again, and wondered if it was a fact or if he was only telling himself that so that he could at least deal with the situation.

The man called Paul Swenson was still being fed intravenously; a tube trailed from his left arm. But he seemed fairly alert and chances were the tube would be removed some time that day. A network of electrodes and wires covered his head and body, most of them hidden under the sheets; they were attached to the medical computer, a metal and plastic rectangular box five feet high which stood next to Paul's left arm. The computer, in addition to monitoring Paul's bodily functions, had interrupted their conversation once to administer medication, speaking in a monotonous, metallic voice which Jim found irritating.

The older man looked over and smiled tentatively. Jim in turn tried to continue their conversation. "I became interested in writing," he went on. "I've published two novels and one book of short stories. I'll have a volume of poetry, *HIMALAYAN HYMNS*, out this year, which I'm kind of proud of. One publisher is doing it in a paperbound edition for collectors, and there'll be the normal fiche edition plus a royalty payment if anyone gets it through computer print-out, but you'd be surprised how hard it is sometimes to get royalties from the computer people. Usually you have to get your own print-out proving how many people ordered it and send it to them with a threatening note." Jim began to feel that somehow this aspect of literature would not be of interest to Paul. "Well, you know what I mean," he concluded lamely. "You probably had to go through the same thing with your own books."

The man named Paul looked puzzled for a moment. "I remember something like that," he said at last. "Yes, I remember something like that. I think I wrote books once." The man gestured with his hands, as if reaching for something. Then his face seemed to crumble, sagging into a passive agony. "I don't know. I see some images, a few pictures, but there's so much I just can't get hold of." He turned away.

Jim sat, his knees locked against the chair. *Paul's still dead.* He did not want to be in this room with this man who sought feebly to imitate Paul's gestures and appropriate his memories. Yet something in the man tugged at him, and Jim sensed the other's pain.

"I'm sorry," Paul said, as if understanding that he had failed in some way. "I can recall some things. I see a park, at one end there's a stone wall, and beneath. . . . " Paul moved his head slightly, as if shaking it. "There's so much I just can't get hold of. Tell me more about everything, it helps."

"You once got mad at my friends Olive and Joey. Do you remember that?"

Paul looked blank. "I don't know. I seem to recall something. I can't be sure." He sighed. "Help me. There's so much I have to find."

Goddamn you, Kira, Jim thought angrily. *What does he do now? He can't even remember his own life.* He noticed that Paul was beginning to seem a bit tired.

Jim stood up. "I'd better let you rest," he said. "You've been pretty busy, talking to all of us. I'll come back later." He felt as if he were smothering, trapped in this pale green room with a stranger. "I'll be back," he repeated. He forced himself to lean over and kiss the stranger on the brow.

He found himself in the outside hallway. Kira was walking toward him, bouncing slightly with each step. He moved toward her and took her by the arm, almost losing his balance. "I don't think he remembers us," he said quickly. "He only remembers bits and pieces at most, incidents from our childhood or something."

"Jim—" she started to say.

He pulled her into the nearby lounge and settled onto a green benchlike sofa. She sat down next to him. In one corner, a middle-aged Chinese man was talking to three friends. At one of the small square tables, a dark Indian woman, gold ring glittering in her nose, played cards with a slender African man, both of them clothed in the white pajamas all patients wore.

"Jim," Kira said again, "I don't know what you expected. You know perfectly well that people forget things even during a normal lifetime. Besides, he hasn't even seen us since we were sixteen, if he had only been away for twenty years, he would naturally have some questions about us and what we were doing."

"That's not what I mean," he replied. "I don't know who's in that room, Kira, but it isn't Paul Swenson. He's not the same person."

"Are you the same person after twenty years? Are you the person he knew before? Think about that. Anyone would be different after so long a time. You're different too. And add the fact that for all practical purposes, the man in there is only about thirty years older than we are now and he was once almost fifty years older. That makes a difference too."

"Come on," he said harshly. "You're taking advantage of my ignorance now. Tell me what you think about him, you're the one who knows about biology and what effects freezing might have on the brain. Combine that with the fact that Paul's brain was probably deprived of oxygen for a while before the rescue team found him and that he was technically dead." He almost spat out the last word.

Kira seemed to shrink slightly. She fussed with her hair for a moment, tucking a few long loose strands back into the twist on the back of her head. "The effects of oxygen deprivation on the brain are not as drastic as we once thought in the past. As for the effect of cryonic interment, we don't really know. Tracks may have been erased. We don't know if the memory can be recovered, but we do know that Paul remembers a bit more than he did at first. For God's sake, Jim."

"Maybe you didn't bring back Paul at all, Kira. Think about that."

"And maybe you just don't want to think that a person could be restored, or resurrected if you want to put it that way. I don't think you do. I don't think you can deal with it." She stared at him until he was forced to look away.

"Maybe I can't," he admitted. "You think you've done something wonderful, you and your team. You putter around with the human body, trying to fix things up, thinking you know what's best for everyone. Do you know what you've done? Do you know how much more horrible it'll be now when someone dies, while you're waiting to start fixing everybody up? Do you have any idea? You could accept death before; it was natural and inevitable. But now every time somebody goes, everyone will know it didn't have to be that way. Those goddamn cryonics people will really make money now. No one's going to take a chance any more." He paused, trying to collect his thoughts. He had lost track of what he was trying to say. His thoughts seemed to knot together, until they centered on one figure: Carole, ashes buried in the Michigan earth, her substance and that of their child, lost forever. If he had put her in a tank, if he had been closer to the cryonic facilities in Shanghai or Calcutta, filled with the bodies of those he had once considered deluded optimists . . . yes, he could have buried her that way, and maybe lived to see her rise again, her brown eyes welcoming his presence, accusing him fiercely, or gazing past him in forgetfulness, but alive, her death a dimly recalled or faintly painful incident. He leaned over in his seat and clutched his knees, feeling tears sting his eyes, unable to stop them and not caring who witnessed his grief.

"Do you know what you've done?" he said to his sister. "Don't even think about the world, that faceless mass you use as a rationalization for your arrogance. Just take a minute and think about what you've done to me. I could have brought her back. I didn't know. I could have brought Carole back." He hunched over his knees. "Oh God, how can I live with it now."

"Jim, stop it, Jim, don't do this." He forced himself to sit up. The Indian woman was rising from her table, the African man was staring at him curiously. Kira motioned to them and they went back to their card game. "Do you think this hasn't happened before? Think of the people who had loved ones die of diabetes before insulin was discovered, or of those who died of cancer, millions, before they could be helped. You can't bring them back, you probably couldn't have saved Carole anyway. But it doesn't have to happen again, *that's* the important thing. We can't do anything about the past. We can only learn from it and go on, all of us."

"Fine words, Kira. You don't have to live with something like this."

She clutched at his arm. He winced as he felt her fingers dig into his muscles. "Stop it. I don't really know what I've done for Paul yet, what this may do to him. I have a lot of work ahead, and I may have to stand by and watch Hidey die of something that in a few years I could prevent. I don't know how long he can last, I don't know how long his heart will hold out. I don't know if he can be frozen and then revived after death, it may not work for everyone, depending on circumstances. It would take me at least a year or two to set up things so that I could replace his heart, even knowing what I know now. And I may have to decide that it's more important to help other people, to present this alternative to them." She released his arm. "I may even be forced to prevent helping him if another moratorium goes into effect for a while, and that may be the immediate reaction. Those in power may not be so willing to let people have the means for creating their own lives, not even now. It'll take time to convince them and a lot of pressure from their own citizens. I've lived with the fact that Hidey would die before I did for years, I married him knowing that, and now that I know how to prevent it, I may have to go back to that assumption."

She sat silently for a few seconds, brushing back some hair from her forehead, then rubbing her hand on her gray trouser leg. "We go on, damn it. We learn and we go on. Hidey would want me to do that, and Carole would probably feel the same way if she knew. She loved you, Jim. I don't think she'd want you to wallow in regrets now. You have to learn, and then you have to try to make sure that no one else suffers in that way if you can help it. That's all we can do. Billions of people died for us in the past and all they could hope for was that their descendants would find something better, so don't let them down."

He looked at his sister. She meant every word of it,

he knew that. He felt himself nodding.

"Just think about it at least, Jim. You may be the most important of us now, you can write for people, show them how they might realize their dreams. The rest of us don't have much experience with that." She took his hand, gently this time. "I'll be taking Paul home when he's able to make the trip, when he's well enough. He may need you then, I think both of you may need each other. He might need familiar surroundings before he remembers certain things and you might be able to help."

"I'll see."

She released his hand. "Just think about it."

He found himself nodding again. He had, after all, no place else to go.

The restaurant was filled with celebrants, whose excessive joviality threatened to drive out the scattered groups of tourists. Five asteroid miners, sitting in one corner, seemed oblivious to the merrymaking around them. The miners, three rough-looking, pale men and two gruffly attractive, bony women, were most intent on finishing the contents of the bottles standing on their table. Looking at them, Al imagined that they had been looking forward to this evening of relaxation for some time, after months in space. They certainly had money to spend. Their difficult and lonely work, which brought needed materials to refining plants on Mars and the moon, was well rewarded.

Al spotted Menachem and Ahmed, arms over each other's shoulders, weaving toward him across the room. The big Israeli waved.

"Al," Ahmed yelled. Al motioned to his two friends. Ahmed managed to squeeze past three Russian men near Al; Menachem, after a moment's uncertainty, simply charged through, apologizing as he did so. The Russians, intent on their own celebrating, did not seem to mind.

Al greeted the two, throwing his arms over their shoulders. "We made it after all," Menachem said. "You can't escape us so easily, Swenson. I'll bet we all get stationed on the same ship, too, and if we don't, you'll get an earful on ship-to-ship communications."

"They've picked everybody, then," Al said. "I wasn't sure if they had."

"Everybody except the artistic people and the exobiologists, at least that is what I was told," Ahmed replied. The three moved closer to a nearby wall and leaned against it. Menachem rummaged around in one of his overall pockets and pulled out a pint of amber liquid.

"This scotch cost me a fortune," he said to Al, "but you're welcome to a swig. You'd better enjoy it while you can, there probably won't be any where we're going."

Al took a sip, swallowed, then sipped again. He handed the bottle back while scanning the room once again. He was being foolish, hoping that Simone would show up here. It would be too painful for her. He assumed that she was still on Luna, but he was not sure, and he had too much respect for her privacy to find out, even though with her code it would have been easy. She would appear, or contact him, when she was ready. He would just have to wait.

He turned to Ahmed. "What about Jane? Did she make it?" He regretted the question almost immediately. He should have waited for Ahmed to volunteer the information.

Ahmed, however, did not seem perturbed. "No, but then I knew she would not. She was not ready for it. She accepted the news far better than I would have, and she is making plans to work on Mars next year. I imagine I shall see a lot of her there when we're going through our training." The young Arab sighed. His dark brown eyes reflected sadness and resignation. "It was not meant to be. I met an old friend today, Bader Hassan. She is vacationing here. I almost married her years ago, and today I find that she will be going with us, with the anthropologists. Perhaps, when the memory of my dear Jane fades in my mind, my love for Bader will flower once again during our expedition. Perhaps my old impulse was the correct one."

Menachem took a drink from his bottle. "Remember when we were at school in Beirut, Ahmed?" he said, trying to cheer his friend. "We used to tell everybody we might someday be going on a journey like this one, and they would smile and tolerate our insanity." He chuckled. "I hope they've all heard the news."

Someone pulled at Al's sleeve. He turned and faced a tall brunette woman. "Albert Swenson?" she said to him in heavily accented English.

"Yes."

"I am Gudrun Permaneder. If you are able, Simone Tran wishes to speak with you."

"Where is she?"

"Outside of this room. I will show you. These several days she has been with me."

Al excused himself. "I'll try to save you some scotch," Menachem said, "but I don't know how successful I'll be."

"I'll buy the next round," Al replied. He followed Gudrun Permaneder through the crowded room. As he passed the miners, he noticed that their bottles were almost empty. One of the women caught his eye and motioned to him with her hand. He smiled and shook his head. She shrugged and, turning away, gestured to a tall blond fellow nearby.

Al pressed past a group of Chinese by the door. They were celebrating quietly, sipping sweet wine from shot glasses. They had abandoned their simple costumes for the night; the men were dressed in silken blue tunics, the women in tight flowered gowns. Behind him, someone began to laugh uproariously and he could hear fragments of a German folk song. He almost stumbled over the feet of a multi-national group seated on the floor outside the restaurant, excused himself, then followed Gudrun Permaneder down the hallway.

Gudrun gestured toward an open doorway, then disappeared down the corridor. Al walked inside.

Simone sat alone in the small room, feet tucked under her. She held out her hands to him. He took them and sat next to her on the small beige sofa.

"I wanted to see you, Al, to congratulate you," she said quietly. "I just could not bring myself to go into the restaurant. I hope you understand."

"Of course I do."

"I was a bit foolish, I know," she went on. "We can still have time together before you go, and I can continue my work here. In the course of time, we might have parted anyway. I shall eventually become reconciled to this, as Dinh grew to accept my leaving him. It only takes time."

"I don't want to leave you," he said softly as he put his arms around her. She rested her head against him.

"Stay with Liu Ching for a while," Simone said. "She, too, is leaving someone behind. It will make things easier for you both, and for me as well. We must both make our plans now. Then, when we do part, it will be as friends who may meet again after your return." She smiled briefly. "You know that I would have done exactly what you are doing if it had come to that, so you must never feel guilt or regret that you have left me. Liu Ching will be a good friend to you, whether or not you part on the voyage."

Al was silent. Why was it that doing the sensible thing, being rational about this situation, should be so painful? He felt dangerously close to tears. Simone had always been more sensible, more controlled. He had never seen her cry, not ever, but she had consoled his tearfulness more than once. He had to restrain himself this time. He could not help feeling that if he gave vent to his feelings now, he would see Simone's tears for the first time.

Even though he knew he would regret such an action forever, he wanted to make the grand and irrational gesture, declaim to her that there was nothing in the heavens for him without her, that he would turn the opportunity down, that if he left he would be carrying to the stars a void within himself as black and empty as the space between suns. That, the irrational gesture, was somehow more emotionally fulfilling, more aesthetically satisfying than the reasonable path Simone wished him to choose.

Strangely enough, he found himself thinking of his brother Jim at this point. He felt almost as if he at last

understood his brother's tormented and irrational life.
It had somehow satisfied Jim, that tortuous and erratic
path, that life made up of a rejection of the orderly, the
reasoned, the scientific. Jim's life had a compelling, almost
insane beauty about it that his own seemed to lack. Its
very self-destructiveness was somehow more intense than
an orderly life; its suffering weaved a pattern that could
draw one on, forcing one to confront human desires,
emotions, and finally death. Al felt he could be drawn into
such an intensity of experience if he followed his own
desires at this point.

He began to wonder if he had in fact been like Jim
all along, pursuing his studies because of an underlying
irrationality, drawn on by the awesome and terrible
beauty of suns; the inexorable development of galaxies;
the dazzling thought of supernovae, dying suns screaming out to the universe in one last expenditure of energy,
burning out all life on the planets near them; the face
of death in black holes, those singularly terrifying collapsed stars where time and space had run out.

He would have to leave Simone if he was to continue
along the route he had chosen for himself. Perhaps this
rational path was really the irrational one, calling upon
him as it did to reject her love and friendship for a voyage
of indeterminate length with an unknown destination. He
looked into her dark eyes and wondered what it would
be like, how he would feel when he at last looked at
them for what might be the last time.

"There is a story going around, many rumors," she
said as he watched her. "The story concerns your father.
It is said that he rests in the hospital after being dead for
many years, that he has been there for several days and
more. Some have seen him there, or his room. No one
has verified it officially, no one has denied it. I imagine
the rumors have reached Earth by now."

"It's true," he said. He remembered the man he had
seen lying in the bed, that frail, uncertain person called
Paul Swenson. "The announcement will be made as soon
as he's better."

"Perhaps I shall see him with you some day. The story

made me happy somehow. I became certain we would meet again. I may be deluding myself, but it helped to hear it." She patted him on the cheek. "You will not escape me so easily, *mon ami*. You will find me here when you return."

"I hope so."

"We shall have a celebration for you, I and my grand-children."

He held her more closely.

"He seems better," Lilo said to Mike as they walked along the hospital hallway. "He was more talkative, and he looks a little younger and healthier too."

"I'm not surprised," Mike muttered. "The treatments should rejuvenate him to some extent." As they passed the hospital cafeteria, he stopped. "Let's get a cup of coffee."

Lilo nodded and they entered the room. Mike walked over to the console on the wall, punched two buttons, took out the coffee, and handed a cup to Lilo. He preferred not to think about the lonely resurrected man he had just seen. The entire notion had been a mad one, and he could not understand why Kira, whom he had thought of as sensible, had sought to actualize her idea. *How am I supposed to treat this man?* It was not Paul he had visited, but an aged child. He tried not to remember that once he and the others had been a mad idea of Paul's and Hidey's.

They sat down at a table near the door. The cafeteria was practically empty, for good reason, Mike discovered, when he tasted the coffee. Kira had mentioned to him that most of the medical personnel ate elsewhere when they could, though the food was not much better anywhere on the moon.

Lilo made a face as she sipped her coffee. "God, this is terrible. I haven't had a decent meal since we got to this rockpile." Her tan had faded and she looked more subdued today, wearing a brown shirt and slacks which matched his. Her hair was pulled back tightly in a bun. "Well, I guess there are some compensations. I could have sat with that observatory telescope forever. You can see everything with it. I could see Mars close up, with dust storms and everything."

"Lilo," Mike said, "forgive me for saying this, but I don't understand something. You still don't seem to realize what's happened to Paul, what Kira's done. You've been treating it almost as an everyday occurrence."

"How do you want me to act? I don't know what he was like before. I don't see him the same way you do." She looked down at the table, then back to him. "I know you think I'm kind of dumb about a lot of things, you've never said so, but I can tell from the way you treat me. You may think this is strange, but I always knew something like this would happen. I could tell from the little I knew, a long time ago I figured they would thaw out one of the long-term freeze cases, I figured they could do it as soon as I knew they sometimes froze people temporarily for different kinds of operations. I knew it was just a matter of time and finding the right person."

"Well. . . . " he started to say.

"Please don't interrupt me, just this once. The people I knew, sometimes they'd talk about something like this happening. It isn't really any stranger than that replicator thing you've been working on, or whatever it is. I guess I just grew up knowing inside that the world *would* be different, that things would change, that maybe, if we put our minds to it, we could have almost everything we wanted someday. Maybe I would have been smarter if my father hadn't died when I was little. He used to tell me how things might be. He wasn't so bright either in certain ways, but he had an instinct, he could tell how things might change. That's how he made his money." She shrugged. "So I'm not really surprised. You may not realize it, but I listen to people and I learn. I learned from your friends, even if you think it's just an act. I always liked people who were doing different things, and I would listen to them so I could learn and maybe figure out what I'd like to do someday. A lot of times they'd patronize me, sort of, think I was funny for asking simple questions, but I found out what I wanted to know, so I didn't care."

"Well, did you find out what you wanted to do?" Mike asked, trying to repress the bite in his voice.

"No." She glared at him as he snorted. "But I will. Even if it takes me a long time. I like working with children but I don't know if that's what I really want. When we get back home, I can study. The computer's always there. I can tune in lectures and enroll in some courses."

"That ought to keep you occupied for a couple of months."

"Goddamn it, Mike," she almost whispered in a tone of voice he had not heard before, a steady determined tone. "I wish just once you'd treat me as a person or take me seriously instead of thinking I'm an amusing child or something. You're a bully sometimes, you know that? You keep away from people, you don't open up to them, or you like to dictate to them, have them dependent on you in some way without giving them anything back. Maybe that's why you married me, I don't know. I wish you would open up to me, be what I know you are. I know why I married you. Part of it was that I had this infatuation with you, I'll admit that, but part of it was that I really loved and admired you and I could see what you really were underneath that cold surface. I wish you would let me see that more often. I wish I could feel that I was more important to you, and that you wanted to help me in whatever I decided to do, that I wasn't just a pretty toy."

Mike stared into his coffee. He felt vaguely threatened by her words, and afraid of her. This had not been part of the bargain, these entangled emotions and ambitions. He could feel himself drawing back from her.

Yet he knew he did not want to lose her. He knew that he was perhaps more dependent on Lilo than she realized. He valued her interest in his work, her curiosity, and her affection. He would have to learn to value her new-found assertiveness, too, if he were not to lose her.

He reached across the table and took her hand. "Give

me some time," he said at last. "I can't change overnight, you know, but I can try." He was forcing his words
out. "I really do love you, Lilo. Maybe I haven't been
fair to you. Just give me a chance."

She smiled. "Maybe some of it's my fault too, Mike.
There were times I figured I didn't have to do much, that
it was enough to be with interesting and creative people,
but I guess I'm starting to realize I want something of
my own. It probably won't be anything really tremendous,
like what you and the other clones are doing, but at least
it'll be mine."

"Well, you just find it and do it then, whatever it is."

She nodded and held his hand more tightly. In a way,
he was almost relieved to hear what Lilo had said. He
had not honestly respected the narcissistic girl he thought
he had married; she had been just an amusement. He
should have seen the clues when he first arrived here.
Kira and Al, those two who had been so startled by their
marriage, had got along well with Lilo after meeting
her. He should have realized they would not have felt
that way about the person he once thought Lilo was.
What he had taken for a lack of discipline or a short
attention span had been simply a young person's desire
to explore different things and find her own goals.

He could almost flatter himself now with the thought
that somehow, unconsciously, he might have sensed this
in Lilo or he would not have married her.

"We'll go home," he said, "and you think about what
you want to do, and maybe you can visit Kira and Hidey
for a while. You could probably help Paul too. You
seem to be the only one of us that could just accept it
right away."

"I think I'd like to do that."

"I wanted you to meet your grandson," Ed said.

Paul's bed had been cranked up and he sat there,
nodding politely at Ed's statement. For a moment, Ed was
afraid of what Paul might say to Isaac. The older Swenson
was still trying to recover his memory and catching up
on their activities over the past twenty years. He was

also, with the aid of the medical computer next to him, catching up on world affairs and scientific developments. The computer, which was still monitoring Paul's bodily functions, could also provide print-outs on various topics, linked as it was to the central computer bank on the moon. A hypnotherapist was helping him recover his memories; Ed did not know how well that effort was going.

Paul did look healthier. There were traces of brown in his gray hair and his gaunt face was beginning to look rounder. The intravenous feeding tube had been removed and he was taking mild exercise, walking through the hospital corridors and having short sessions in the nearby gymnasium. One of the technicians was instructing Paul in simple biofeedback techniques so that he could eventually monitor his own functions. At the time of his death, such techniques had been in more primitive stages, used primarily by athletes, the chronically ill, and those who spent a lot of time in space.

Isaac too seemed a little uneasy at this meeting. The boy stepped forward and took Paul's hand. "Hello," Isaac said, glancing at Sheila for an instant, then turning back to his grandfather.

Paul was staring past the child. "Ed," he said quietly, and Ed could not tell if his father was addressing him or Isaac. "So much time," Paul murmured, and Ed realized suddenly how much he must have resembled Isaac as a child. Paul must feel as estranged from them as they did from him. It was not the unknown adults who gathered uncomfortably around his bed who would evoke his feelings. It was Isaac, who mirrored what they once had been.

"You don't look like a grandfather," the boy said. "You look older than grandfathers I've seen."

Ed could see Sheila wince slightly at Isaac's frankness. Fear flickered for an instant on Paul's face, then faded "I've been told," he said, "that people don't age as rapidly as they did when I . . . you see, I had to be an old person before I could get anti-aging injections, but apparently that isn't true now."

"Did you really die?" Isaac asked.

"Yes, I did, at least technically."

"What was it like?"

Paul shook his head. His bewildered eyes settled on Ed. "I could accept it. That happens, you become. . . ." He grew silent. Ed sensed a feeling of loss in his father, and wondered what he had experienced. He suddenly understood Paul's dilemma. He might regain all his memories in time, only to find himself dislocated and removed by years from all he had known and loved; or he might recover so little of his identity that he would be, in effect, another person, as innocent as a child.

"Tell me about your interests," Paul said to Isaac, "what you like to do."

"I play the violin, so I practice most of the time. I'm going to audition for Julius Riggs this summer and if I'm good enough, I'll be able to go to his school in London next year and study with him."

"Aren't you very young to go so far away from home?"

"He has the legal right to make his own decisions," Sheila said sadly, "plus one advantage over adults. He can come home any time he wants and just be a kid again." She gazed hopefully at her son, who was ignoring the remark.

"Sheila's old-fashioned," Ed said gently, trying to reassure his wife with a smile. "She comes from a very close-knit family." He paused, realizing how shocking this attitude toward children must seem to Paul. As his father watched Isaac, Ed recalled an adolescent boy, years before, who had desperately wanted Paul to give up his trip to the moon.

He remembered again the pain he had felt when first learning of Paul's death. He had not known how he would deal with it, how he would go on. But he had found his way. He thought about what Paul must have felt when he discovered that the world had got along perfectly well in his absence. In spite of what his rationality must have told him, Paul must have found it a slightly demoralizing realization.

Well, none of that mattered. Paul had become something new in the world, as the clones had been years before. They had been conscious all their lives of their responsibility, trying to prove to others that they were, after all, human beings, yet having to accept the fact that they were different in certain ways as well. But there had been some privilege attached to their position. They had been given the advantage of a sound heritage and an environment that was more carefully planned than it might have been if they had been normal children. Even Paul's resurrection was part of that privilege; Kira had restored him with the aid of organs cloned from her own body. He had been, for that reason, the ideal subject. Now they would have to extend their privileges to others.

"I'm looking forward to going home," Paul said suddenly.

"Do you remember it?" Ed asked.

"I think so. I seem to recall the house, but my memories probably won't match the reality exactly. They never really do anyway, do they?"

"Mine never do," Ed answered. "I used to remember the house as bigger than it was. And Hidey's always changing something, painting a room or getting a new piece of furniture."

"Hidey." Paul smiled and Ed knew that he was remembering a few things at least. "That may be a little weird at first, getting used to Hidey being my son-in-law." Paul shook his head. "Especially since he must be twenty years older than I am now." Ed noticed a glint of apprehension in his father's eyes.

"Don't worry." Impulsively, he reached for Paul's hand. "He hasn't changed all that much, I guess he's a little more gray. He's still pretty lively and he still smokes too much."

"And Jon Aschenbach. I remember Jon too, I think. How is he?"

So Kira had not told him yet. Ed sighed and braced himself. "He died seven years ago," he managed to say. "It was unusual, a cerebral hemorrage. His body's in the university cryotorium. . . . " Ed stopped, suddenly jolted by the thought. He saw that Paul had been jolted too.

"Well, then, maybe we can't consider him dead," Paul said softly. "Strange, isn't it? I would have thought a clergyman would have had more faith in the hereafter."

"I think he wanted to donate his organs to patients," Ed said. "But they hardly ever take them from the dead, what with mechanical replacements and being able to keep people alive until they can clone new organs." Ed began to feel that his conversation was aimless. "My God," he said, and heard his father echo the words. "Everything's. . . . "

". . . changing," Paul finished. The words seemed completely inadequate.

They sat in silence for a few minutes while Isaac peered at the medical computer. Paul would be going home, to a friend once his contemporary, now twenty years older, to a granddaughter who could never have existed without a variety of medical techniques, to children who were suddenly older, to a dead friend who might even live again. And that was only Paul's one life. How much else would change? How many lives would they all live?

"You played . . . I mean, you play the violin too, don't you?" Sheila said awkwardly, breaking the silence.

"I imagine," Paul replied, "that I'll need a lot of practice."

"Isaac brought his violin," Ed said, "and Sheila brought her clarinet. I might be able to borrow two violins from the musicians up here. We'll play, maybe tomorrow."

"I'd like that."

Ed leaned over and kissed his father on the forehead. *Paul's back.* He felt himself trembling slightly and repressed some tears. He could not speak, but then, there was little more to say.

Jim had said his goodbyes, or, more accurately, farewells. He would see them all again, probably sooner than he expected.

He sat in a waiting room. He would be leaving the

Descartes space colony in an hour on the next Earth shuttle. At least that was when the shuttle was scheduled to leave. It would no doubt be late, what with delays and the problem of the very few phobic travelers who still insisted on donning space suits before the trip, so distrustful were they of the craft.

Jim had been on Descartes for two days, exercising and adjusting his body to its three-quarters of Earth gravity before returning home. He still felt somewhat heavy and weary, but better than when he first arrived.

He did not care for the space colony and would be glad to see the last of it. Descartes offended him aesthetically; the hollowed-out landscape inside the cylindrical structure was to him a poor imitation of Earth's fields and forests, as bothersome to him as the trees and plants in the underground lunar settlement had been. There was no point in trying to transplant pieces of Earth which looked woefully out of place in such alien settings. Better, he thought, to cultivate the particular beauties of the tunnels under the bleak lunar surface or the space colony, creating something that would have more coherence. Better to recognize the fact that one was not on Earth, to attempt to be in tune with the new environment. Oddly enough, some of the younger people on Luna had agreed with his views.

Jim adjusted the reading screen attached to the end of one of his chair's arms, bringing it closer to his chest. He punched a button and the words of a newsfax sheet began to appear on the screen's flat surface. He scanned it quickly. There was an editorial about Paul's resuscitation, oddly void of sensationalism or panderings to fear. That seemed to be the pattern in the few print-outs Jim had seen. It was almost as if people had been expecting it and were prepared to accept it. He remembered what Mike had told him about Lilo's reaction. *But this might just be the calm before the storm*, he thought to himself. He imagined that angry protests might begin before long.

They had, all the clones, spent the last two days before Jim's departure together. They had been more at ease then, sometimes chattering about Paul, sometimes falling into an uneasy silence about him. They had talked mostly of other things. Mike had seemed more easygoing, Kira less tense but a bit depressed, suffering a letdown after her months of work. Sheila had confided in him, telling him about Isaac's plans while he sought to reassure her.

He still carried a numb pain inside him, a pain that would occasionally seize his heart or his throat when he saw something or someone that reminded him of Carole's thick dark hair or her small chubby hands. But the sorrow had subsided at least a little.

He felt something push against his leg and looked down. A young girl, no more than ten or so, was picking up a ball that had rolled near his feet. "Excuse me," she said politely. She was black, with coppery skin and short frizzy dark hair. Except for the small gold earrings in her ears and the name "Alia" embroidered on her red overalls, he might have taken her for a little boy. She scampered away with her ball.

He closed his eyes for a moment and let his mind drift. He recalled his journey to Descartes aboard the moon shuttle. The shuttle had passed the almost-completed *Nikita S. Khrushchev*, that cathedral to humanity's new gods, the product of thousands of engineers and craftspeople. The ship was a prayer to the universe, a request for its secrets, the embodiment of an enterprise based largely on faith. But the priests and priestesses of this shrine would not wait for revelations; they would actively seek them. Their chants and holy words would utilize the power of mathematics, observation, and physical laws.

Jim remembered how small and frail the *Khrushchev* had seemed from a distance. It would seem even smaller in the space between stars. Al would be on that ship, or one of its companions. For a moment, he wondered again at how his brother could face the risk and uncertainty of such a voyage.

But Al's decision was not really surprising. Jim had taken risks, foolish ones, and faced uncertainty himself, living as he had. Kira had faced it in her work with Paul as the subject, Ed when he had finally decided to live alone. Mike was facing it now, having to redefine his relationship with Lilo and with others, with no assurance that it would work out; his replicator might topple the world's economic systems, once based on scarcity and now based on the equitable distribution of technology and the solar system's resources.

We'll all have to change, Jim thought sadly. *I can't deal with any of this.* He glanced around the waiting room. Passengers sat in the bright red chairs, staring at reading screens, talking, or sipping drinks brought from the nearby bar. One small stocky woman was chewing tobacco, the only way a smoker could survive in the space colony which, like the moon, allowed no smoking. Occasionally she spat into one of the white spittoons. The little girl named Alia was seated next to a black man, presumably her father, clothed in white overalls.

He remembered his last meeting with Al. His brother had brought Simone Tran along. Jim had wondered how Al could leave her behind until he realized that there was no alternative that made any sense. *I should have let Carole go, not dragged her along like an excess piece of baggage.* Remorse seized him, the pain circled his throat again, and he lowered his head, staring for a moment at the pale blue floor until he regained his composure.

Well, Paul was alive, at least. No matter what he might think of Kira's work, of what it might do to the world, he could not reasonably wish that Paul had remained dead or should return to that state. He was alive, and Jim would grow to accept it, in fact be happy about it. He would have to try to think of the changes that would take place in a more positive way. People untimely severed from each other could be reunited; death could become a choice at the end of a rich and fulfilling life instead of an unavoidable conclusion that hovered over all from the moment of birth.

He would have to rethink everything if he were not to be only a voice of the past, an interesting irrelevancy. His entire aesthetic, all his work, had taken as its presupposition the inevitability of death, the ultimately hopeless struggle against the universe's overwhelming odds.

What would he find to write about in the world Kira envisioned? What could anyone possibly find in his work that would be at all valuable?

Kira had tried to tell him. She had told him of a people who might find time to explore both the vastness of space and the almost infinite capacities of their own minds. She had told him of a world where life would no longer be a flower blooming briefly before fading and passing away; where it might itself become an art, shaped and developed beyond anything now possible. His task might become something new; in addition to depicting, refining, and interpreting human experience within a linguistic and dramatic structure, he might also become the creator of scenarios that people could construct and experience for themselves. Such an art would be demanding, calling on every resource of the artist. It would require new structures, new rules and limitations, new purposes. He did not know if he was capable of participating in such an art.

He sensed a movement at his side and looked up. The little girl named Alia stood there, her father at her side. "Excuse me," the man said, "but are you one of the Swensons? You look a great deal like a holophoto I once saw in a story about you." The man's voice had a faint British intonation.

"I'm Jim Swenson," he replied. The question did not really bother him now. Few people were that interested in them any more, and he had been so isolated recently that he had almost forgotten how he had once felt about inquisitive people.

"I'm Andrew Alcott and this is my daughter Alia. She wanted to meet you."

"I'm a clone too," the child said. "Father told me you were the first one."

"I was one of the first," Jim responded. "I have three brothers and a sister who were cloned with me. Are you a clone of your father?" He glanced from Alia's face to Alcott's and realized his question was ridiculous. The father's face was round with small dark smiling eyes; the daughter's slender, with a turned-up nose and large hazel eyes.

"No, Alia's not my clone. She was cloned from her sister." Alcott's face grew more serious. "Years ago, my wife died in a train accident near London. I was crushed by her death, so saddened that I fear I neglected my daughter Anna, the only child I had. She died only a few months later. I had taken her on a picnic in the countryside and she somehow wandered away from me. It was days before they found her at the bottom of a small pond. She had never learned to swim."

"I'm sorry," Jim said, not knowing what else he could say.

"I petitioned to have Anna cloned. You must know what a difficult business that is, since permission is rarely granted except in the case of certain exceptional people or in unusual circumstances. I realized of course that Anna couldn't be returned to me, but I wanted the chance to be a better father to a child like her, who would be a part of my dead wife as well." He looked down at his daughter. "Alia was cloned for me. She renewed my life. As soon as she was old enough to understand, I explained to her who she was."

"What was it like, Mr. Swenson?" Alia asked. "Being one of the first, I mean."

Jim was silent for a moment, considering his reply. "In some ways it was hard, I guess," he said finally. "We were different and people were a little afraid of what we might be. But most of the time we had the same problems everybody else has. Maybe in a way we were better off. At least we had each other." He watched the girl, wanting to say something to her that might be important for her to realize. "We knew we were really wanted too," he went on. "That's important for any child. A lot of people, even now, are born almost by chance. But your father, like my own, was willing to go to some trouble to make sure that you came into the world. You don't ever have to feel guilty or unloved."

Alia nodded gravely. He could not be sure that she understood everything he had said, but maybe some of it got through or would at least remain in her memory for a time she might need it.

"Are you waiting for the shuttle to the Dallas–Fort Worth field?" Alcott asked.

"Yes," Jim replied.

"Would you join me for a drink? I believe we still have some time ahead of us."

"I'd be delighted." He got up and walked toward the bar with Alcott and Alia. A fleeting thought jostled against his mind, then fled before he could grasp it. Somehow he knew that it was important to talk to Andrew Alcott and his daughter, that they might provide a key to his difficulties.

Kira, sitting next to Al, watched as Paul, lying on one of the gymnasium mats, lifted and then lowered a barbell that would have weighed almost two hundred pounds on Earth. Behind him, several people jogged on moving platforms near the back wall while wearing weighted belts. Six children in elasticized suits, designed to help them use their muscles as much as possible, performed acrobatics in the center of the floor.

"He's doing pretty well, isn't he?" Al said.

"He was always healthy," she replied. "We may still have to take him home in a water tank, though. We'll have to do it by stages, going to Lagrange first, then to Descartes, and he may still need an exoskeleton on Earth for a while, to hold him up."

"I'll probably be home soon after you leave, we'll get some vacation time before training begins and I may bring Simone with me." He smiled, but his eyes seemed pensive. "Maybe I shouldn't be going. By the time we get back, or even before, you may be sending your redesigned immortal superhumans out into space. Maybe we'll meet them along the way."

"You'll know before you leave if that's likely. You may be leaving with most of our techniques by then. You'll change too."

"God knows what we'll come back to."

Kira looked at Paul and then back to her brother. "I don't know," she said. "You should probably talk to

Paul about it. I imagine in some way he knows more about that now than I do."

As he walked back to the hospital through the corridor, Paul felt a little tired, but stronger than he had been. He grew conscious of an emptiness in his stomach. He was hungry. He hoped that supper would taste better than the bland stuff that had passed for lunch.

He was still a bit puzzled. Even with the return of some of his lost memories, he could not feel particularly paternal toward the two people named Al and Kira who were walking with him, nor to their brothers. This was perhaps inevitable, but at least he did feel some degree of closeness to them, undoubtedly because of their basic biological similarity.

He rifled through his thoughts, turning them over in his mind. He had been told that the hypnotechnician would only aid him in his recollections; the man would not plant incidents in his mind. He was sure the technician had kept to that procedure. Yet it seemed as though his memories had been grafted on to him. There was no emotional connection with the images of people and far-off places that had settled uneasily into his mind, with the pressured, somewhat frantic individual named Paul Swenson who had existed twenty years before. He did not share these ideas with the two people who were accompanying him through the hallway, sensing that they might be hurt or disturbed by them.

The experience of death had already receded in his mind. It had become a distantly remembered event, a bit disorienting but otherwise of no great importance.

He could look forward with some anticipation. He had much ahead of him. He would have to catch up on his scientific studies. He might even be able to aid in some way the expedition going starward. If not, he would still have time to do some work, to read, maybe do some writing. It did not really make any difference what he had done during all the years of his previous existence. He could complete whatever he had left undone and then try something else. He had time enough for almost anything he wanted to do.

He walked slowly, conscious of the lighted walls of the corridor, the flexing of his calves, and the movement of his arms. There was no reason to hurry. For now, he would devote his energies to recovery.

He looked forward to the world he would see when he returned to Earth. Yet, at the same time he remembered, dimly, feelings of apprehension and despair. He forgot his feet for a moment and stumbled slightly.

The woman named Kira caught his arm. "All right?" she asked. Her face seemed to dissolve and he found himself in front of a glass surface. *His daughter was in his arms. "My little Kira," he whispered to the infant; then he once again became conscious of the reporters standing on the other side of the glass. He held Kira more closely, as if to protect her. Again he wondered if he was right, if his children would love him or hate him, how the world would treat the little girl who was now clutching a piece of his lab coat in her hand.* A hand held his arm tightly and he shook his head, startled. The image was gone, the memories again fading. The woman named Kira was guiding him down the hall.

They entered a hospital corridor. Two technicians seemed to rush past him and a nurse was hurrying into one of the rooms at his right. He saw what was almost a blur of human activity; a doctor lumbering by with a patient, an attendant darting past him with a tray, a nurse spinning around on her heel as a doctor called to her. Around him was the chatter of voices, incomplete phrases, and speedily spoken directions, people pressed by time.

He moved toward his room carefully. The interface of past and future came to rest inside his mind, a million twisted pathways behind him, an indeterminate and misty road ahead. The time of transformation was not yet past.